Unholy Craving

Sinful Natures 1

Lynn Burke

Unholy Craving

As a newly appointed youth pastor, I blindly walk by faith, stumbling without the promised light down God's chosen path.

Until a young man resurrects the sinful nature I've rejected in my strive for purity.

Isaac Van Dusen, my pastor's son.

He's troubled. Rebellious. Off limits to my lonely heart, yet gives me breath when I feel I'm drowning and in need of a savior.

Isaac's hunger for sin rivals mine, the kind that consumes.

Burns like fire and brimstone.

I'm determined to stay in a constant state of prayer, begging for delivery from temptation—all while dreaming of being on my knees for entirely different reasons.

I want to submit to the unholy craving between us and worship the young man entrusted to my spiritual care.

But acting on the lusts of the flesh ensures our fall from grace, and I can't allow him to be the second one to pay the price for my sins.

Even if it means living a lie for eternity.

Chapter 1
Malachi

I sat outside Elkins Bible Church, my hands still gripping my old truck's steering wheel. The rust bucket had gotten me and all my meager belongings from the outskirts of Frederick, Maryland to the deep woods of northern Pennsylvania without breaking down, surprisingly.

Dad's '48 Chevy truck had outlived him by six months, and while it was a piece of junk, I couldn't bear to part with the one thing we'd had together outside of church when I was younger. His garage, his baby, grease and laughter.

Inhaling deeply, I forced my hands to move—wiping my damp palms on my dress pants and turning off the key to cut the rumbling engine.

I had promised myself a new beginning, one in the small community of Elkins as the new youth pastor for a tiny group of fifteen teens. Quiet, where no angst or strife would riddle my hollowed-out heart.

Lord, help me.

That prayer lingering in my head, I opened the truck's squeaky door to the spring's cool breeze. Sunlight glinted off the side mirror, blinding me for a brief moment as the pebbled parking lot crunched beneath my dress shoes. When my vision cleared, a forty-something man stood on the church's small porch, smiling my way.

We hadn't met in person, but I recognized him from my virtual interview a few weeks earlier.

"Malachi?" he called, his light steps bringing him down the concrete stairs toward me.

"Yes." Forcing a smile, I buttoned my suit coat and closed the distance between us to shake his hand. "Pastor Van Dusen?"

"Pastor Bram. Please." He clasped his other hand atop mine and squeezed, his hazel eyes full of warmth. Unnatural peace and light shone in their depths like I begged God for on a daily basis. "And I am a blessed man, indeed. Welcome to your new home."

My new home.

The words should have replaced the emptiness inside me with the joy I had hoped and prayed for, but nothing had been able to fill me with such feelings after the love I'd lost back in high school.

Swallowing hard, I nodded. "Thank you, sir. It's great to be here."

Pastor Bram released my hand and gripped my shoulder like he might to steer a child even though we stood eye to eye at six feet, give or take a half-inch. "Come on in, and I'll show you around."

The church's entryway smelled like every other one I had entered: lemon furniture polish and the sterility of holiness.

Purity.

Other things I strove for every day in my thoughts and heart and had done a damn good job focusing on since rededicating my life to God a few years earlier.

The soles of my shoes squeaked on the immaculate tiled floor as I followed along behind my new pastor. Double glass doors opened into the sanctuary on our right. A blue carpet aisle pointed the way to the simplistic stage with two stairs leading up to an oak pulpit—

"The offices aren't much." Pastor Bram pulled my focus to where we headed. "But they do afford some privacy." He guided me back through a short hallway into a small reception area, a little gray-haired lady standing from behind a tidy desk as we entered. "Mrs. Howard, this is Malachi Foley, our new youth pastor."

Still having to force my smile in return to hers, I stepped forward and shook her hand. "Ma'am."

"Welcome, Pastor Foley."

The title, although earned and paid for by my parents, hadn't ever sounded right in my ears. Perhaps after a few years in the ministry I would accept having accomplished my parents' dream—God's will—for my life. "Malachi, please."

Mrs. Howard nodded. "I've set up everything I could think of on your desk," she said, motioning toward the door on my right, "but just let me know if you need anything else."

"I will, thank you." I dipped my head and followed Pastor Bram into his office on the left.

It was a larger space than I'd expected, but built-in shelves lined two walls, full of books I had studied in college, making it appear narrow. My own textbooks sat boxed in the apartment I'd rented not far outside the community I'd become a part of overnight.

My office, I found out moments later, was smaller than the pastor's, and it didn't feel like home either. I hoped to change that.

In time.

We made our way back to the auditorium, the carpet hushing our footfalls, the pastor's voice muted by the wood paneling along both walls as he filled me in on the history and daily workings of the church. It appeared almost identical to the one I'd grown up in. Oak pews lay on either side of the main aisle, their backs lined with racks to hold hymnals, hardback copies of the King James Bible, and tiny shelf-like holders for plastic communion cups.

The pulpit stood intimidating at the front, the dais it sat atop making it seem as though it loomed over the congregation from a place of authority. The same as the one I had accepted as a child because my parents said to. One I submitted myself to upon admitting my sins and choosing His path.

Leaving the quiet place of worship behind, we descended the stairs opposite the office wing, and the basement space opened up into a large area with tables and chairs stacked against the far wall beside a small kitchen. A few doors stood along either side— classrooms for the younger children.

I imagined the noise of potluck dinners, the scent of burnt coffee and various pasta dishes bringing back memories from my childhood, and my lips curved upward for real. Mom, as an elder's wife, would have been scurrying around in the kitchen, cheeks pink, her curly blonde hair frizzed around her ears like mine would be if I didn't keep it short.

She and Dad had led me in the path of righteousness, attempting to raise me in the best way they knew how.

I'd been the one to fail.

Thankfully, both had gone to the grave without finding out the depths of my depravity.

My smile faded, and I reminded myself of God's grace and mercy, His forgiveness of sin in order to silence the demons wanting to drag me back to a place of squalor that would damn my soul to hell.

Putting thoughts of my past behind me, I followed Pastor Bram outside and around back to the second building on the church's five-acre plot.

Elkins Bible School occupied the single-story, more modern building where I would also be teaching the high schoolers their Bible classes for the rest of the spring quarter.

My predecessor had passed suddenly, and Pastor Bram had been filling in as their teacher until our paths crossed by word of mouth.

I had needed a job, an escape from my hometown after caring for my ailing father and finishing my internship the summer before. Although only a year out of Bible college, I landed the job courtesy of my best friend in college, Zeke. Pastor Bram's nephew.

A perfect fit, I told myself. Four hours from a house I'd just sold, from a gravesite at the opposite end of my parents' corner of the cemetery, one that drew me but I refused to visit.

Brian.

My childhood friend, my first secret lover, and the one who had paid the price for our sins.

Jaw clenching in attempts to put my past back beneath the blood of the Lamb, I traversed the small Christian school's halls, wondering how the heck they managed to stay running with only fifteen kids in high school and barely double that in the younger grades.

Kindergarten through grade twelve were all in one building—which sat quiet around us since the students congregated for lunch in a cafeteria Pastor Bram didn't bother showing me.

The job hadn't come with great pay, but when did serving God in an honest and holy way ever line a man's pockets with cash?

With my parents' blessing and financial help, I'd sought a life of fortune in Nashville the day after I graduated high school, hoping my worship leading skills would get recognized and my voice would land me a record deal like Brian and I had planned to do together before God took him from me.

Rebellion, sin, had turned out to be a bigger temptation than wanting to honor God with my vocal gift, and I'd slept with every man I could in attempts to forget my first love.

It had taken the deepest reaches of depression to make me realize I wouldn't ever find contentment and peace outside of God's will for my life. I'd enrolled in Bible college at the encouragement of both my parents, but Mom didn't live to see me graduate like I'd promised her I would.

Dad had stuck around a little longer, but just barely.

They'd had me later in life, and as an only child, I'd been lavished with unconditional love. Acceptance and grace. Mercy when God hadn't shown it to Brian.

A flicker of gut-wrenching anger lit deep inside my soul, one I fought whenever thoughts of my past rose to the choking point.

I tried to swallow it down with coffee in Pastor Bram's office, courtesy of Mrs. Howard, praying for the Holy Spirit to fill me, to take the hovering despair away.

"We would love to have you join us for dinner this evening, unless you have other plans," Pastor Bram offered.

That was the last thing I felt like doing after a long day of driving and unpacking, but I didn't believe turning my new pastor down would be the right choice. "I appreciate the invitation—thank you."

"I hope you don't mind that my nephew told me about your battle with depression." No pity, no condemnation for my inability to trust God at times, showed on Pastor Bram's face.

"Zeke helped see me through my darkness," I had no issue admitting. My college roommate for all four years knew everything in my past—and he'd never once judged me.

"My son..." Pastor Bram's voice faded off as he peered out his office window to the budding trees beyond. "He's struggling, and I believe God led you here to steer him in the right path."

I met Pastor Bram's gaze as his head swung toward me, my stomach tightening again at the sudden expectation placed on my shoulders. "In the same way I did?"

"No. Rebelliousness." The pastor shifted on his chair and glanced at a five-by-seven photo on his desk facing him. "Isaac is at that age where he doesn't talk much with his mom or me. But he writes a lot of dark poetry, words that don't make sense. It's an outlet." The pastor shrugged, but the frown on his face revealed his true thoughts. He hated that his son would rather take pencil to paper than explain his feelings to his father.

Considering my own emotions had been brushed off when I was younger by my parents and our pastor in order to "trust God," I wasn't surprised the young man didn't share anything of substance with his father.

"He had a strong dislike of our last youth pastor," Pastor Bram continued when I couldn't think of a comment that would sound God-like, "and I'm praying your younger age will help forge a connection between the two of you. I'm hoping you'll take him under your wing. Be a positive influence. Show him what it means to trust God as the Bible commands."

"Of course." I didn't hesitate to agree. Touching teens' lives had become my mission. I prayed that one day seeking God's will for my life would fill the hollowness in my chest that Brian's death had left behind.

Zeke, my college buddy, had been the only one to know about my past. Oftentimes, Mom had studied the way Brian and I interacted, and I wondered if she knew about the lies I told to cover our sins. She never confronted us, never judged. It was my understanding that my parents had gone to the grave believing I'd gone on to live a holy life while in Nashville, that I'd been saving myself for a godly young woman, a wife to complete me.

But no such woman existed unless she had a dick between her thighs.

Why would God allow such desires—

I cut off the thought as always. Homosexuality was a sin, a result of the fall of mankind. God wasn't to blame for my daily temptation. While I would never consider my sexuality a blessing as a chance to reveal God's strength in me for abstaining, I placed my hope in His ability to guide me toward purity.

Daily prayer and submerging myself in the Word had kept me on His path throughout my college years.

It was time to trust Him for my first ministry too.

* * *

Pastor Bram's wife Annabelle barely reached my chest in height. I'd learned over our coffee that the tiny Korean woman had been rescued from poverty by the pastor when he'd been on a missions trip overseas twenty-some years earlier.

Dark eyes and dimples. Pretty for a woman and sweet as anything, she welcomed me into their home that night, her demure dress typical of a middle-aged pastor's wife, exactly like I'd expected.

I wore jeans and a light blue hoodie rather than the suit I'd sweated through earlier in the day while settling into my office. Not exactly pastor threads, but outside of the office and church, I didn't feel the need to play the part clothing-wise. A piece of me clung to my college ways, the comfort of jeans, worn sneakers, and T-shirts.

Ties sucked ass—

"Isaac!" Pastor Bram hollered up the stairs, his booming voice bringing my thoughts back from a path leading to darkness.

Footsteps sounded from the second floor, heavier as they approached the landing above us.

"Gird your loins," Pastor Bram quietly stated, his own face frowning with trouble. "I warned him to behave, but he's been his usual moody self since getting home from school. Perhaps it's best if I leave you to it."

I nodded, trusting his judgement.

Pastor Bram clasped my shoulder and moved toward the kitchen behind me, and I put on a casual, unintimidating smile.

Seventeen-year-old Isaac, the troubled senior in high school.

The pastor's son who wore old black Vans and jeans with enough holes to act as an air conditioner.

He'd inherited his mother's dark hair, I noted as he descended the stairs farther. His smooth jawline and pouty lips in profile made my groin tighten.

Lord, help me...

My lungs stalled out, smile fading as Isaac reached the first floor and turned to greet me.

Our gazes met and held—and I froze, unable to tear my focus off the depths of his hazel eyes similar to his dad's. Except these were pained and filled with wisdom for one so young.

He had the same pale, smooth skin of his Korean mother.

Stunningly beautiful.

A temptation to my baser instincts, the lure of sin I fought on a daily basis.

"So you're my dad's answer to prayer." He stuck out his hand, continuing to hold my stare. The huskiness in his voice, his sarcastic tone attempted to bring life to my neglected dick.

"I'm just a man like any other," I managed to choke out while clasping his hand. Fire raced across my palm and up my arm—ten times more attraction than any I'd felt for anyone in my twenty-six years.

Isaac took a quick glance down over my body before returning my steady gaze. "*Just a man,* my ass." His quiet murmur barely reached my ears, but his eyes stated a hell of a lot more—and heated me clear through to the marrow.

I yanked my hand away from his as though he'd scorched my flesh, bone-deep.

God, what trouble have you brought me into?

His unlit path hadn't guided me to a new beginning, a home of hope like I'd asked Him for.

He had led me straight into temptation.

I prayed He would deliver me from evil.

Chapter 2
Isaac

The new youth pastor was hot as fuck. Blond hair and blue eyes, my weakness when it came to men.

Figured.

And for some reason, I couldn't keep my mouth shut at a crucial time in my life. Usually, I clamped my lips tight, only sharing my real thoughts with paper and pen.

But Malachi Foley? Just the sight of his wide shoulders and the peek of a tattoo beneath his long-sleeve T-shirt while gripping my hand lit sinful lust inside me.

He ripped his hand away from mine, finally tearing his stare off my face.

Guess he'd heard my little grumble about him being way more than just a man in my gay opinion.

Elkin's Bible Church's new youth pastor…I wondered if Dad had any clue he liked guys as much as I did. I held in a snort. Dad would've never let Malachi set foot into our house if he even got a hint of such sin.

"No wife?" I asked, leaning to my left in order to glance around him into the kitchen/dining room where Mom and Dad readied dinner.

Malachi cleared his throat, smoothing down his shirt in my periphery. "No."

His answer would have swelled my dick if I hadn't jerked off while watching some porn on my cell phone a half-hour earlier.

His blue eyes coasted over my face before his lips flatlined.

Mine followed suit in mutual dislike even if the scent of dryer sheets and subtle aftershave coming off him caused the saliva glands in my mouth to erupt.

Why couldn't I be attracted to some kid in the public school, someone as gay as me?

I was stuck inside my closet though, the door locked up tight. Dad and Mom didn't know, and they wouldn't until the minute I turned eighteen and got the hell out of our hick town where rednecks talked about beating faggots to death.

Mother would be devastated when the day of my escape came. She'd prayed for a child for years, same as Sarah in the Bible.

Thus the name attached to me at birth.

But the second I earned my freedom from their legalistic ways, their beliefs in a fairytale book, I would be gone.

Three months to go...

At least I would have some delicious eye candy to fuel my fantasies until I was unleashed to make my own choices in who I wanted to date and finally fuck.

Mom called us to dinner, and I lingered enough for Malachi to turn first, leaving me to trail behind him and check out the new youth pastor's ass.

The man knew how to wear a pair of jeans. Low on his hips but snug enough to tempt a man if he hadn't worn a shirt.

That ass…

So much for not getting a hard-on.

My heels would look good wrapped around his backside. My dick would look even better buried inside it.

Fuck.

I adjusted myself and quickly slid into my chair across the table from Malachi. Head bowed, I waited for Dad to finish praying a blessing over the food, the hands that prepared it, and the typical bullshit that sounded like drivel in my ears and had since I'd learned my ABCs.

He thanked God for the newest addition to his flock, and on that we could agree—even if I disliked the gorgeous man whose blond eyelashes brushed near his cheekbones without twitching while Dad prayed.

Pious young man. Serious and pure, I didn't doubt.

The idea to fuck with him and dirty his soul rose inside me, and I considered it until Dad ended his prayer seconds later. I dug into the chicken Mom had baked, my decision to tarnish Malachi unmade.

"So you're a senior this year." Malachi didn't ask a question so I didn't bother answering. If he wanted information Dad hadn't already given him, he'd have to insert a question mark like a true Pennsylvanian did by raising their voice at the end of a sentence.

But also, I didn't willingly offer shit about myself to anyone.

Another forkful of chicken landed inside my mouth, and I chewed, checking out the blond stubble on Malachi's jawline and his slightly crooked nose. His full lower lip I wouldn't mind tasting.

"What are your plans after graduation?" he asked.

I could lie to please Mom, but I'd had a shit day thanks to a math test I bombed, and I felt like stirring up trouble. "I'm going to head to Nashville and make a name for myself in the music industry."

Malachi's eyes shuttered—blinked—as Dad, God's man, whispered, "Isaac," with his unhappy tone.

My new youth pastor stared at me, and I ignored Dad's quiet reprimand. Malachi could try to read whatever the hell he wanted to on my face, but I knew how to hide my true thoughts and feelings. I'd been doing it for ten years since I realized I wasn't normal, that I liked boys and not girls.

Dad might preach homosexuality being a sin from his pulpit, but it was no choice for me. There was no separating that part of me any more than the hazel-green color from my eyes.

I wondered if Malachi felt the same—or if he simply attempted to squash his sinful nature when it came to masculinity and dicks.

He cleared his throat, but his voice still rasped when he asked, "You sing?"

"He's amazing with a guitar and has a lovely voice," Mom answered the question for me, a smile in her tone that filled me with warmth.

"One he should be using to praise his God," Dad added his usual condemnation when pointing out my wrong choices. Especially ones pertaining to my refusal to stand on stage Sunday mornings with the worship team.

Get up before a group of people and sing praises to a God I didn't believe in? I might hide my true identity, but I was no fake like some of the others caught up in the emotional high of the Holy Spirit.

Malachi glanced between my parents, without a doubt picking up on how one supported me and the other didn't. Supposed unconditional parental love, another thing preached from the pulpit by my dad who ignored it at home.

I expected to see judgement or maybe even pity in Malachi's eyes when his attention returned to me, but understanding resided in their blue depths. The type that made me feel like he empathized with me, that our hearts somehow reached out on their own and tangibly connected.

Fuck—definitely not what I need and sure as hell not with the man across from me.

I looked away first, my knee bouncing beneath the table as I stuffed another bite of chicken into my mouth.

"So, Bram tells me you met while he was in Korea on a missions trip." Another non-question from those lips I'd probably dream about later that night, but thankfully not directed at me.

He must have noticed my discomfort and turned the conversation elsewhere…perhaps Malachi wasn't so bad after all.

While the adults talked about Dad's first trip to Korea, his and Mom's history, and the rest of the school year ahead of our newest Bible teacher and youth pastor, I worked on a new song in my head. Obscure words only I would know the meaning of, an expression of the unnamed emotions I kept bottled up inside.

Depression, most would call it, stemmed from having to feign my truth. Having to suppress the want and longing for what my body and soul craved, what science had brought to life inside me.

I thought God was real, but I didn't *believe* it. Not like my dogmatic Dad. How could I when He would allow such a cruel thing as men desiring other men? If there was no God like I'd been taught my whole life, then the lusts of my flesh wouldn't be wrong.

But until I gained my freedom to be who I wanted to be—to be who I *was*—I had to continue living a lie.

And the longer I listened to Malachi and Dad discussing God's will and His path of righteousness that would lead to riches in glory, the more I realized I needed to avoid the young man across the table from me. He knew how to talk the talk of the Christian community, even if I was sure his sexual orientation aligned with mine.

Even if the deepest parts of me wanted to wrap around his soul and take solace in someone who understood what I faced on a daily basis, he was off limits to my heart.

Chapter 3
Malachi

Troubled, his father had called him.

Trouble for *me*.

Evasive and too intelligent for his own good, Isaac had caught the attention of my sinful nature, and my curiosity craved to be sated. I'd attempted conversation with him a few times while eating dinner, but his misdirection and one-worded answers only left me hungry for more.

Pastor Bram called me His answer to prayer.

God had led me to Elkins Bible Church.

And I wouldn't fail either of them no matter the pastor's son's beauty.

Titled as rebellious, Isaac and his eyes held no glint of mischief whenever our gazes met. No hint of a smirk over our obvious attraction I would deny until I stood before the pearly gates. And no trace of disrespect in his tone, either.

More of a...passive type resistance of authority when I'd expected lashing out from how his father spoke of him.

I had no clue how to handle such an attitude. Unflappable, my mom would have called him. Sensible, my dad would have added. Both would have loved him as they had Brian even though the two seemed polar opposites.

Isaac was smart.

Too smart.

Too...*everything*.

Strong and independent compared to Brian's tender submission. A leader, not a follower, one who would tempt me into sin and end up paying for it himself—

Lord...

I forced my focus on Isaac to keep from reliving my past.

The pastor's son twisted me up inside, and not just because of his striking looks and hazel eyes that appeared greener like the forest color of his long-sleeved T-shirt. How did his brain work? What thoughts prompted his jumping knee beneath the table that mine itched to mimic? Where had he learned the self-control to hold his tongue?

Had his dad beaten him into mock submission?

I listened as the pastor shared about the flock he led, noting the pride lacing his voice. His wife, Annabelle, worshiped him with her steady focus and smile—no evidence of coerced love on her part. She'd fallen hook, line, and sinker for the man God had blessed her life with, but Isaac clearly held no such sentiment.

Their son with his shifty glances longed for freedom, same as I had at his age.

And I expected he would head for even deeper trouble in a matter of months once he graduated and stepped into the world unknown.

My stomach churned over the possibility of him facing what I had—the heartache, the misdirection—and the choices I'd made once ruined.

Sometimes children needed to set their own paths and learn their own lessons the hard way in order to find truth, and while I didn't wish my past on anyone, I knew Isaac leaving town would be the best thing.

For both of us.

All I could do was pray for his soul and trust God to protect the young man from the evil I'd encountered.

Pastor Bram sent Isaac to ready the fire pit after dinner since the spring night was perfect for sitting outdoors, but I stayed put while Annabelle cleared the table rather than trailing after the young man out to their back yard like my flesh longed to do.

"What are your initial thoughts?" Bram asked, leaning forward, arms crossed atop the white table linen.

My eyes followed the path Isaac had taken through the kitchen toward the back door.

He's hurting and lonely.

He's anxious for his freedom.

He'll be my downfall if I don't "gird my loins."

"I think he's a normal teenage boy who's going to have to find the truth of God for himself," I chose to state instead of voicing my true feelings.

With a heavy exhale, Pastor Bram sat back, lips thinning. "You've gotten a taste of his reluctance to communicate. I'm praying that your instruction will inspire him. That he'll be honest with you about what's in his heart."

I could guess at what was in the young man's heart, and it would take a hell of a lot more than being his youth pastor to get him to open up. That would require friendship.

I'd rather avoid him at all costs to save myself from temptation.

Lead me not...

What choice did I have but to trust Him, even if darkness continued to shroud the path He'd planted my feet upon?

"Maybe he'll be willing to talk to me in private," I suggested rather than taking off for my new apartment like self-preservation urged me to do.

Pastor Bram motioned toward the back door. "Feel free, Malachi. I'll be praying God gives you the words to say."

Best if he prays for God to keep my and his son's souls from burning, I thought while standing, my stomach fluttering as I smoothed my shirt down over my abs.

"We don't stay up much past nine," Pastor Bram said, also rising from his chair, "so if Isaac doesn't flee to his room until after then, feel free to linger as long as God leads. We'll remain inside, allowing the two of you some time alone."

Nodding, I left him to help his wife clean up the dinner dishes.

Lead me not into temptation...

Damn prayer was going to be on repeat until Isaac graduated, I didn't doubt.

He sat across the darkening yard, his back to the house. The fire in front of him outlined his hunched form, bulked by a sweatshirt he'd pulled on before heading outside into the cool, spring night. He didn't turn as I approached through the grass, my sneakers announcing an arrival he couldn't pretend to not hear.

"Hey." I settled into the lawn chair beside him, keeping my attention on the ring of stones and entwining yellow and red flames rising into the sky rather than the face I wanted to hold.

Caress.

Kiss.

"Hey," he grunted a reply, poking at the fire with a stick.

I rubbed my hands down my jean-covered thighs, more ill at ease and nervous than when I'd taken my senior finals at college the year before.

Isaac's manipulating of the kindling sent a burst of sparks upward.

"Think we can start over?"

He grunted but didn't verbalize a reply.

Letting out a heavy exhale, I decided to just dive right in. "So what makes you think I'm your dad's answer to his prayers?"

He leaned back, a stick resting between his spread thighs, peeks of pale skin through ripped jeans drawing my attention.

I tore my gaze off his legs before my imagination wandered.

"Because I'm a depressed, hurting soul who needs God." Isaac's reply sounded like a canned, repeated phrase rather than his own thoughts.

"Why don't you tell me about yourself in your own words?"

He wouldn't look at me but poked at the fire again. "What do you want to know?"

"What you do for fun in this podunk town. Your hobbies. Passions."

"There isn't anything fun about this town. Hobbies are nonexistent. And there's no point in having passions."

I turned toward him fully, needing to read his face since his tone suggested a wall ten feet thick sat like stone between us. "So, what would you recommend a newcomer do on lonely nights?" I hadn't meant the question to be suggestive, but Isaac tilted his head my way, lifting his eyes to meet mine.

Lust lit between us as quickly as a gasoline-soaked newspaper, tightening my groin and snagging the breath from my lungs.

Isaac's focus dropped to my mouth, and he pinched at his lower lip with well-manicured fingernails as though attempting to draw my attention to its natural pout. The brat did it on purpose—and it worked. "You tell me, Pastor Foley."

"Malachi," I rasped what I wanted him to call me—what I wanted to hear him groan while burying my cock deep inside his body, marking him with my scent, my cum—

I cleared my throat and shifted on the rickety chair before tearing my gaze off of sin personified.

"My dad wouldn't allow such blatant disrespect as to call you by your first name," Isaac stated quietly, his tone bland, but I couldn't look at him to read if his face revealed more.

"My dad wouldn't have either." I swallowed hard, expecting I needed to find common ground between us in order to connect outside of my attraction for him. "Like you, I was an only child. Prayed for. A gift."

His soft snort reached my ears—I'd never considered my life a gift either, no matter how many times my parents had assured me of their truth. It seemed another tether sprang to existence between us.

Scuffing the ground beneath my sneaker, I wondered how much would be too much to share. Isaac seemed the sort who would end up learning by living rather than hearing of someone else's mistakes, exactly as I'd told his dad.

But uncovering my sins might invite unwanted advances.

Unwanted.

Don't lie to yourself...

"So you sing?" I went for the next thing I'd learned about him over dinner that had made me want to relate with him.

"Here and there," he said with a shrug.

"The second I was old enough, my father pushed me to join the praise and worship team at our church."

I could feel Isaac's gaze as I stared into the flames.

"It was an outlet for me but not enough. I wanted more. The fame, the money." I bit the words off, clenching my jaw against heading down memory lane. It came anyway, churning my bowels and knifing renewed grief through my chest.

"What happened?" His voice hinted at actual interest, but I'd bonded with him enough for one night.

Still, I couldn't find the strength to leave.

"Long story," I said, thinking on how I'd pushed Brian into sharing my dream and had lost him for eternity. "It's one I'd rather not relive."

Isaac accepted my desire to not share, intensifying the connection I felt simmering between us.

"You remind me of someone I used to know," I admitted before giving it proper thought. Similar through the emotional response they evoked inside me at least, not by personality and definitely not looks. Brian had been a blond with eyes the color of grass in summertime, not dark like Isaac.

"Old boyfriend?"

My head whipped Isaac's way. His hint of a smirk highlighted by firelight was like a kick to my gut.

"Friend," I rasped, hating how easily Isaac got beneath my skin and made me want things I'd left behind.

"If you say so, *Malachi*."

My name on his lips... Disrespectful, according to his father, but ignored. I couldn't begin to imagine what other rules and truths the young man might set aside in order to get what his eyes suggested he wanted.

Isaac Van Dusen would be more trouble than I'd imagined.

I feared for my soul.

Chapter 4

Isaac

And Malachi thought he was there to save me from damnation.

I almost snorted again.

The hot piece of ass sitting in Dad's lawn chair had to stop lying to himself. What better way for me to help him see that than fucking with him? Even in the darkening sky, I could tell Malachi's pupils swelled at hearing me call him by name. Add in the emphasis, the hint of a groan I'd inflected in my voice, and the poor man just about came undone.

Breath audibly caught, he stared at my mouth where I'd pinched it to see how he'd react—exactly as I'd wanted. Considering my imagination, I wondered how far his own mind went.

Greedy kisses, grasping hands—his on me, mine on him...

Fuck, how I wanted to experience it rather than just sneaking porn while shut up in my room.

Naked hunger filled his eyes, and I silently thanked all things unholy he hadn't appeared so damn readable inside in front of my parents at the dinner table.

"Tell me more about your friend."

A muscle ticked in Malachi's jaw before he turned to gaze at the fire, the minutes dragging as he seemed to consider opening up to me in the way I knew he—and Dad—hoped I'd do with him.

Something he'd never accomplish in a million years.

"He died when we were seniors in high school," he finally said, and I realized I'd held my breath.

I expected a shit ton more lay behind his single shared line, but I wouldn't push for a story he didn't want uncovered any more than I did my own inner workings.

That didn't keep me from staring at him until he shifted on the chair again though.

Maybe if I made him uncomfortable enough, he'd leave me alone so I could go back to living undisturbed in my corner of the world.

But my dick had other ideas.

Malachi leaned down and picked up a small stick off the ground before I could think of other ways to make him squirm, to keep him close so I could continue living in my lust. "Your dad said you write poetry."

I narrowed my gaze, studying how the fire's light glinted off the gold highlights of his short hair as he snapped the twig in two. "What of it?" I asked, my fingers itching to run over the wavy strands.

Mine weren't ramblings like Dad always called them, but I wasn't about to admit the truth of what my journals held.

"Is that how you express your feelings?" Malachi glanced at me, keeping his focus on my eyes rather than my lips. His quick study of my face and the obvious want in his blues tightened my groin.

"With words?" Not that I needed clarity, but my notebooks, my songs, weren't something I shared with anyone, even if Malachi had attempted to do what I dreamed about with my life.

He paused before answering, seemingly lost in his past, with his focus on the firepit. "I knew a songwriter once."

"That friend of yours?"

Malachi tossed one of the sticks into the flames. "He struggled to express what was in his head, so he took pen to paper. Created magic with those words."

Again, I expected more lay behind his story, but my new youth pastor was about as open as I was.

"He planned to go to Nashville, same as me." Malachi's voice broke off abruptly, and I focused on the ground between my old Vans, allowing him the moment he obviously needed. The other stick he'd held arced through the air in my periphery to land with a burst of sparks in the fire.

An ex-boyfriend, if I had to guess from his obvious torment...maybe losing him was what had turned him toward God.

I wondered if that was why he'd taken interest in me and followed me outside.

Frowning, I poked at the fire again. Chances were, even if he did admit to wanting me, I wouldn't ever compare to the ghost that owned Malachi Foley. Same as I wouldn't ever be good enough in Dad's eyes.

What was the point of trying?

My semi I'd been dealing with all night wilted, and my scowl deepened.

"It's not a sin to have ambitions, Isaac." He finally broke the silence between us, his voice resigned as fuck. "But it's the choices you make in pursing what you want that will mold your future."

"That friend of yours never got a chance to pursue his, did he?"

A muscle ticked in his jaw as he stared unblinking at the dying flames. "No."

"Nothing's going to stop me," I stated with the same conviction Dad did while spewing his thoughts on homosexuality and sin from the pulpit.

"I hope it doesn't." He let out a heavy sigh that physically caused his body to shudder. "Every person should have a chance to fulfill their dreams—even if it's not exactly what God would have for their life."

He was hurting, no doubt about it. I wanted to reach over and wrap my arms around him, to take his bad memories away. I sat stunned at the weird desire to give him comfort.

"Do you have a cell?" His question seemed out of left field.

"Yeah." I pulled my phone from my back pocket.

"Add me as a contact," he said, and I did as he gave me his number. "Call me—anytime, Isaac. If you need an ear, need to unload...whatever and whenever, I'm available."

An offer of friendship, but the word *unload* had my mind going straight to the gutter and bringing blood and a whole lot of want back to my dick.

A smirk started as I tucked my cell away, but Malachi stood and walked off before I thought up something sarcastic to say to get under his skin.

He bypassed the back porch for the path leading around to the front of the house.

A sense of loneliness swept over me, worse than the usual kind that brought on my depression. Scowling again from the sense I'd lost something, I poked at the fire, stirring the embers to cause flying sparks.

An engine came to life out front and faded into the night, leaving me more alone than I'd ever felt.

For the next two nights in a row, I dreamed of golden hair beneath my fingertips. Biting the full bottom lip of a forbidden man I shouldn't even consider thinking about. Looking into his eyes while he buried himself so damn deep inside my body I couldn't breathe.

Waking with my dick in my hand Sunday morning, I finished myself off the same as the day before, groaning, my hips jerking with every spurt of cum splattering up over my abs.

Shit.

I heaved for breath, holding my length until it softened fully, the memory of Malachi and his scruffed jawline so deeply embedded in my memory I could see him in vivid detail every time I closed my eyes.

Dad had asked me what I'd done to send his youth pastor home Friday night without saying goodbye to them. He didn't believe my lie that we thought they'd gone to bed.

The stern look he gave me when I sat down for breakfast Sunday morning let me know he still didn't.

But when had he ever believed a word I said?

I'd been full of shit as a younger kid, always telling tales to save myself from getting Dad's belt or Mom's wooden spoon.

Stole a piece of a candy? No rod spared.

Didn't do my Bible studies for Sunday school? Belt.

Forgot to place my shoes in the mud room's bin where they belonged? Wooden spoon—and Dad's belt as a second discipline when he got home from his office.

Failure after failure, no matter how hard I tried to do right.

But they wouldn't have to put up with my bullshit for much longer.

Dad took his car to the church early like he did every Sunday while Mom and I ate bagels and cream cheese together in peaceful quietness, both of us showered and ready for a day of listening to the Word and reflection.

Apart from breakfast with Mom, Sundays sucked, and not in the way I wanted to experience for myself—giving and receiving. I wondered while staring out the passenger window as Mom drove us to church if Malachi had any actual experience with swallowing a guy's dick, or if like me, he'd only wished and wondered. If he dreamed and came over thoughts that in Dad's world would condemn us to eternal damnation.

I wanted God to be a farce, a crutch for those too weak to face the reality of death being just that—nothing. A void of darkness, same as before a person's first cognitive thought.

Then I could live my life without question, standing or falling before my own sense of morality rather than a supposed all-knowing being beyond the pearly gates of heaven where a mansion of gold awaited those faithful to His commands.

No such house awaited me and never would.

47

Chapter 5
Malachi

Pastor Bram's flock jammed into the small place of worship, close to two hundred members. Hardly a mega church like I'd been raised in, but the spirit of God seemed to fill the room before service started. Kindness greeted me with every introduction, and even though I felt the stares of the congregation while I sat on stage with our pastor, I didn't get a sense of judgement over the new, *young* youth pastor.

If they'd known my past, things would have been different.

Of a young enough age to catch the interest of the tittering high school girls, I should have preened at their obvious attention, but it was the blatant stare of darkly-lashed hazel eyes that had me shifting on my seat.

How a boy of seventeen managed to unhinge my mind so easily baffled me. No one had made me question my upbringing and my sense of right and wrong since Brian.

Isaac Van Dusen.

Thoughts and dreams of him over the weekend had filled me with an unholy craving I wished I could loathe.

I wanted inside his head. I wanted to know his thoughts, the dark words he wrote in his journal. I wanted his body beneath me, his moans and whimpers in my ears.

Damnit.

Jaw clenched, I forced my focus to remain on the pastor God had led me to labor beside, to submit to.

Just a few months...I could handle this temptation with constant prayer.

If only I felt like praying with the same urgency I felt for jerking off to fantasies about the pastor's son.

After the service, I stood at the back of the church by the doors leading out into the warm morning, shaking hands with everyone who passed by.

The hairs on my arms rose beneath my suit coat, but I didn't glance toward the group of young men hanging by the auditorium's entrance. Annabelle came through the receiving line, inviting me to have lunch with them, but I declined with a smile, thanking her all the same.

I had shit to do—not that I used those exact words.

In my periphery, I kept track of her son moving off toward a side exit. My breath eased as he disappeared outside, but my chest stung. For all the attention he'd given me during the service, I'd expected a clashing of gazes or a handshake held a few seconds too long.

I'd looked forward to it, I realized as the metal door slammed behind him and his friends, taking his energy from the building and leaving me behind.

Keeping my smile fixed in place and ignoring the drop of my stomach, I greeted those behind Annabelle, including the young woman who helped with the youth group.

She was single.

A cute brunette with big doe-like eyes.

But nothing about her tempted me like Isaac did.

"It's nice to finally meet you!" She smiled, joy lighting her face and causing her eyes to twinkle. Attraction for me or an outward manifestation of God's love, I couldn't decide. Either way, I wasn't interested. "I'm Jennifer, your partner in crime with the teens. I also teach music at the school."

"Malachi," I replied, shaking her hand.

"I'm sorry I haven't been around since you arrived," she said, glancing at the people still waiting to greet the newcomer. "I was out of town. But." She let go of my hand and grasped her purse in front of her. "I'll stop by your office tomorrow to fill you in on the upcoming retreat."

"Sounds good," I murmured with a nod, not unkindly, but zero trace of interest inflected my eyes and voice.

"Is ten okay? Neither of us have class at that time."

"I'll be in my office."

She smiled again and moved onto Pastor Bram as the next in line greeted me.

Why couldn't I be attracted to someone like her? Why couldn't the bubbly young woman hugging Annabelle after Pastor Bram with a sparkle in her dark eyes draw me in like Isaac did?

Why, God? Why allow such feelings, such want in a man's soul if it's a sin?

My throat tightened, and my feet grew restless, my legs needing to flee. I longed to hop in Dad's truck and escape to my small apartment, to soak in the quietness while praying for God to fill the emptiness in my chest.

Fifteen long as hell minutes later, I managed to do just that, sweats and a T-shirt replacing the restrictive suit I'd worn to church. A frozen tray of my favorite lasagna cooked in the microwave, and I leaned against the counter with both hands, watching the turntable slowly spin, the whine of the machine static in my ears.

All my lunch had to do was sit there and let fate have her way. Manipulating its movement, the microwave changed the cells inside to heat it through so the food could be consumed without causing illness.

I wished God would take over in such a way, to finish the work he'd started in me, but prayer wouldn't come to ask Him to remove my burden and guide me through life.

As God's children, we were called to hate the sin and love the sinner—but I couldn't find hatred for the part of me that defined who I'd been since high school.

I was as gay as the winter nights were dark. There was no denying that truth.

Anger stirred inside me whenever I thought too long on where God's mercy had been when allowing such sins to come about, but the microwave dinged, keeping me in the present.

Famished, I sat at the small table and stared at my lunch, wondering what Annabelle had served her family and what I'd missed out on by declining her invitation.

"Probably fifty times more appetizing than this shit," I muttered and immediately asked forgiveness in my head for swearing even though I loved frozen lasagna and didn't feel the curse word shit deemed the need for repentance.

My cell rang, and I left my untouched lunch behind to retrieve the phone from where I'd placed it on my dresser.

Zeke.

Grinning, I swiped to answer, true happiness coming over me for the first time in weeks. "What's up, Ezekiel?"

"Asshole." My best friend from college and newly certified Christian counselor hated his full name.

I chuckled. "What's going on?"

"How was your first day with the new flock?" he asked rather than answering.

"Good," I replied on auto pilot, settling back at the table where my steaming lunch waited. "Your uncle Bram seems pretty cool. The congregation was very welcoming."

"Any hot women?"

Of course his mind went straight to what we'd both hoped for—for my sake.

"Not a one," I answered truthfully, my smile flatlining.

"Men?"

Zeke was the only one on the face of the earth other than those I'd fucked during my wild days in Tennessee who knew what drew my attention. He'd also heard all about my daily struggles with the sin rooted deep inside me and my inability to find the female form attractive.

The hollowness inside my chest expanded over my failures, and I let out a heavy exhale, my eyes falling closed. "Isaac."

"Oh fuck."

I pinched the bridge of my nose, knowing Zeke probably did the same. "Why would He lead me to a place of temptation like this, Zeke?" My voice wavered on the edge of cracking.

"To give Him glory."

A canned response, one I'd expected from a man trained to walk the walk and talk the talk. He'd been raised in a mega church himself up near Boston.

"I'm on a path with no light," I muttered. "An unseen track I'm aimlessly stumbling down." I sat back and slouched in my chair.

"You need to give your weakness to God."

"I've offered it up hundreds of time," I snipped out, my hand fisting on the table beside my cooling food.

"Faith is the evidence of things unseen," Zeke said quietly, and I wished I could hate how easily he stated truth when I fought to even convince myself of it.

"Blindly trusting I'm doing the right thing isn't a pleasant experience," I grumbled.

"God will reveal his will for you in time—you know that."

Did I?

I longed to agree, to understand, and experience the same emotional sense those in worship had earlier that morning at church. They'd raised hands while singing praises, their inner peace and joyful countenances covet-worthy.

Except for the handful of teens who appeared bored out of their skulls, one especially I'd refused to look full in the face.

Isaac struggled like I did, but not being in a position of authority left him free to say and do what he wanted.

I swallowed hard over the confession about to pour from my lips. "He makes me feel things I haven't since Brian."

"Shit."

Zeke might be a spiritual guy who loved helping hurting souls, but swearing proved his daily struggle. Raised by reformed heathens with sailor-like mouths, my best friend often dealt with issues from his early years before finding God.

If only mine were a lot less depraved like his.

"I'm not sure how well you know him?" I asked.

"I haven't seen Isaac since he was around ten."

"He's rebellious and quietly owns his sexuality." I filled Zeke in. "Has beautiful expressive hazel eyes he doesn't bother shielding."

"Is my uncle aware?"

"If I had to guess, I'd say no." I let out another audible exhale. "Pastor Bram just said he's shut off. Quiet. Won't share anything with either of them."

"Sounds like someone I know."

"Yeah." I pushed aside my lunch, kicked my legs out straight, and thoroughly sank back in my chair, eyes closing again. "Reminds me of me." Straight down to the independent, driven spirit.

"What helped put you on the right path?" Zeke asked, even though he was well aware of every detail from that time.

"Hitting rock bottom."

"Sounds like my little cousin needs to get out on his own and live his life. Make mistakes and find God."

"He's graduating in May and turns eighteen in July." I might have looked at his school records so I could count down the days until he took off to chase his dreams like he said he planned on doing.

"So three months."

"Give or take a couple weeks, yeah."

"God placed you in Elkins for a reason, Malachi. The doors opened up for you to step into that role there—those kids need you, the school needs you. Whatever the reasons, He'll see you through. You have to trust Him in that."

I wanted to—hell, how I wanted to live the truth my parents had held close in their hearts.

"Do your thoughts ever stray?" I opened my eyes as Zeke hesitated in answering.

Zeke found women attractive—but sometimes men caught his eye too. But unlike me, he'd never gone down that road. His secret sin had only been in his mind—he'd never felt the clench of a forbidden hole grasping at his dick, sucking his length into tight heat. He'd never shot his spunk over a man's tongue, holding a masculine jaw while unloading.

My dick swelled, and grimacing, I squeezed the base in an attempt to keep from thickening fully.

"They do," Zeke finally spoke. "But when temptation to taste that sin enter my head, I get on my knees and lay them before the throne of God."

Those straying ideas used to send me to my knees for a completely different reason. One I enjoyed, that used to make me feel powerful. Sexy.

"I gotta go," I rasped, memories and new fantasies taking me past the point of no return. It'd been too long, and my balls filled with an ache I knew from experience I wouldn't be able to pray away.

"I'll lift you up in prayer," Zeke promised quietly. "Call me if you need me."

"Yeah." I hung up, needing a hell of a lot more than a friend's ear.

I tossed aside my cell and slid my sweats down to let my aching dick have some freedom. It was fully swollen, and a bead of precum welled at the slit. Thoughts of Isaac on his knees for me, lips parted and waiting to taste me pulled my balls up tight against my groin.

Groaning, powerless over my sin, I smeared the droplet around my palm and fucked up into my hand.

"Fuck," I cursed between clenched teeth, slowly jacking myself, all thoughts of God demolished from my head.

I imagined glinting hazel eyes. Nostrils widening as I pressed deep into Isaac's throat, cutting off his oxygen. Tears welling, drool smearing.

I wanted to grasp his hair, fuck into his throat, and soak in his whimpers while he jerked himself—got off over pushing me past the point of sanity.

Cum erupted up through my length, splattering my T-shirt, my wrist...a full week's worth I'd been holding back, refusing myself.

In my opinion, masturbation as a form of release to a virile man celibate for almost five years couldn't be wrong. But to thoughts of a beautiful young man who hadn't yet reached adulthood? Legal in the state of Pennsylvania, but still off limits. Never mind the fact he had a dick of his own between his thighs rather than a vagina I couldn't even think about without grimacing.

Gay.

Thoroughly.

A sinner.

Sucking oxygen, I eyed the globs of white coating my hand and soaking my shirt rather than dripping from a gaping hole I wanted to taste.

"Dammit." Ripping my shirt off overhead, I stood, my gut hard and my throat tight.

Lunch remained where I'd pushed it, untouched, and I hopped in the shower to wash myself.

My cum disappeared down the drain—if only I could cleanse my soul of sin so easily.

Chapter 6

Isaac

I sported a hard-on all through church and made sure
to avoid Malachi after the service ended. Me and two
kids from the youth group I hung out with on occasion,
Chris and Tyler, snuck out the side door and lingered
at the back of the parking lot until my mom made her
way to our car.

Dad would be home after locking up which left me with
a good half-hour to milk my balls dry while Mom
finished preparing lunch.

It took all of ten seconds from the time I locked myself
in the bathroom to come, my fist around my dick as I
imagined Malachi fondling me.

"Shit," I gasped out, the second shot more a dribble into the toilet I stood in front of. Zero evidence that way, unlike a ball of tissues—couldn't have Mom finding out I enjoyed jerking off as much as I did. She'd tell Dad, then I'd get the lecture about masturbation being a sin and that I shouldn't be touching myself while having lustful thoughts about women.

If they only knew the truth.

Huffing a snort of laughter, I tucked myself away, washed up, and went out to help Mom, feeling relieved but far from relaxed.

"So, what do you think of the new youth pastor?" she asked while setting the plates on the table. I followed along behind with the flatware, my body still tingling from the aftereffects of busting a nut.

"He's cool, I guess."

Hot as fuck. Fantasy fodder.

"Your father really likes that he's younger. I'm sure he'll connect better with the youth group."

I grunted a non-committal noise she could take however she wanted. While Mom was easier to talk to than Dad, the less I said, the better off I'd be. If Mom caught on to the truth about me, she would tell Dad.

Couldn't have that shit.

"I know you don't like to share your inner workings, Isaac," she said, softly touching my shoulder.

I placed Dad's fork and knife down without looking at her even though her affection warmed my insides.

"But I can see you're struggling. Maybe Malachi could help."

"You want me to go to him for counseling?" I didn't need to ask—I'd overheard my parents speaking about that very thing the night before.

"I'm just suggesting that you could use a friend, one who has your best interest and God's will in mind."

If Malachi's eyes indicated anything, he didn't have either of those interests in his mind. He might believe God's will was what he ought to think about, but the strong vibes between us couldn't be denied.

He wanted me under his hands.

I wanted his hands *on* me.

But he was also a godly man determined to do right. The clenched jaw and the blatant way he'd ignored me all morning during church solidified that truth in my head.

"I'll try," I lied to Mom, knowing I could never do such a thing. Malachi might want to fuck me, but his God would always come first. I didn't need to make myself vulnerable only to end up disappointed.

Best to wait to experience all my firsts once I escaped my prison bars and could stretch my wings and fly.

* * *

I had Bible class first period, and what a way to start off the day. Malachi sat at the teacher's desk when I walked in. His button-down blue dress shirt matched the color of his eyes with the sleeves rolled up to expose vein-lined forearms with a tree tattoo I'd only caught a hint of prior.

I wondered if Dad knew he'd gotten inked—but Malachi's gaze pinned me in place, stealing my breath and causing me to stumble to a stop in the open classroom door.

Someone bumped into me, pushing me forward.

"Morning," he said, turning his focus on the person behind me—but his rasped tone and the want in his short-lived gaze caused energy to buzz like a zap of lightning through my blood.

I slid into my seat to calm my racing heart and hide the instant chub I sported.

And I'd emptied my balls an hour earlier while in the shower since I would be seeing him for first period.

Rather than listen to his lecture on Paul's letter to the Corinthians, I focused on how Malachi's mouth moved. Lips shaping words, the flash of white teeth, a peek of the tip of his tongue.

Sexy...so damn hot I couldn't even begin to imagine how both would feel on me.

My mind went down the rabbit hole of so-called immorality, and I got so caught up in fantasizing about him getting on his knees for me that I didn't give two shits if someone noticed my lust for our new youth pastor.

I'd hidden my desire for the same sex for years and feared the truth coming to light...but for Malachi, for a taste of him, the chance to touch...hell, I'd do whatever it took.

No.

Ripping my focus off his mouth, I frowned at the Bible in front of me. He would never accept me or what I wanted. Malachi was a man of God by intent, and falling for him would only end in my heart getting crushed beneath his heel. The thought of making myself vulnerable to that kind of hurt churned my stomach.

I wouldn't ever give a man power over me like that. Ever. Dad had dictated my entire childhood—I wouldn't allow another man to keep me beneath his thumb.

Best to continue telling myself I didn't like Malachi. That ignoring his gorgeous blue eyes, the broad shoulders, and the tattoos on the lower half of his right arm, no matter how fucking sexy they were and no matter how hard he made me, would be for the best.

The second the bell rang, I shot out of my desk and booked it for the door, sucking in oxygen the second I escaped the feel of his gaze on my backside.

Did he want to fuck me? Did he imagine holding me down while claiming what no man had ever touched?

Fucking hell.

Frowning, I stomped into music class, nodding at Miss Jennifer when she greeted me with a cheery smile. While the rest of the students filtered in, I sat in the corner, my mind needing to vomit words, to create something to express the feelings inside me.

I pulled out my latest journal, its pages almost filled with ramblings others wouldn't be able to read or understand. Sometimes dark, sometimes more on the gray side, but all my inner emotions in random phrases.

My writings were the source of Dad and Mom's concern, the reason they wanted me to get counseling.

But I couldn't share what went through my mind. Doing so would bring me out of the closet I had padlocked ten times over.

Three months to go.

My throat tightened while I wrote down sporadic words, ones plucked from the full thoughts in my head. Evidence of my truth but not revelation.

Good thing for me Miss Jennifer's class focused on the outward expression of the Spirit of God working in our lives. Creative writing through music. Definitely a different take on chorus or band like Chris and Tyler over at the public school endured as an elective, but I enjoyed Miss Jennifer's class. It fit with my dreams.

I imagined my guitar in my hands, plucking out chords...the words in front of me stringing along as nonsensical to anyone but me.

Broken.

Wanting.

Filled up...not alone.

Worship—but not in the way Dad preached.

Communion, and not the cracker and grape juice we partook of once a month.

Underneath, all around.

Consumed by raging fire.

I hummed beneath my breath, my fingers moving on my lap as though playing my guitar.

"What are you working on?" Miss Jennifer asked from beside me, jerking me from my dream-like trance.

I cleared my throat and shut my journal. "Just jotting ideas down like you told us to."

She sat in the empty chair beside me. "Have you given any more thought to joining the praise and worship team?"

The idea tempted bile to rise up the back of my throat. I could lie to anyone's face about who I was. But to stand on stage and sing praises to a God who didn't love mankind created in his image enough to keep lusts of the flesh from entering the world?

No fucking way.

"Nah." I shrugged and glanced around the room at the other kids bowed over their own papers, attempting to create music from the words in their minds.

"You're incredibly talented."

I picked at a hangnail.

"You should be using those gifts for God."

"Maybe someday," I offered even though I would do no such thing. My music teacher was the piano player in our church's praise team, and she'd been on me to join them ever since she'd caught me singing almost ten months earlier.

Had I'd been aware anyone stood within earshot at the youth retreat the summer before, I never would have sung the tune I'd been playing in my head and practicing on my guitar for weeks on end.

She'd told me later she heard the entire song, and while she hadn't understood the lyrics, she recognized my ability to weave music outside the usual three chords of pop music. Intuitive, she'd called me. Artistic and different, both of which I already knew and hinged my dreams on.

"Are you going on the retreat this year?"

I nodded. Dad wouldn't allow me a choice even though I would be a high school graduate when the youth group drove up to Maine in a couple months like it did every summer.

But Malachi would be behind the wheel of the van, and a week-long stint in the deep woods where I wouldn't be able to escape him...

Maybe I would pretend to be sick. No fucking way could I be in a bunk room with him lying mere feet away.

No. Fucking. Way.

"I know you aren't comfortable with performing in front of people—"

She had that part wrong—I lusted for it almost as much as I did Malachi.

"—but starting out in a small group like the one heading to Maine would be a good beginning. Will you at least bring your guitar along again this year?"

I shrugged, figuring I could find some time alone to work on my songs. "I guess so."

At least at camp I could sing whatever the hell I wanted and not get chastised for them being non-Jesus songs. Anything Dad didn't recognize as praising God wasn't allowed in his house.

"I would love to send a demo of yours to my cousin."

My focus jerked toward her face. "The one in Nashville?"

"Yes." Miss Jennifer smiled, excitement in her eyes. "He's been searching for up-and-coming talent. I think he'd really like your music. It's unique, something I haven't heard on Christian radio before."

Probably because nothing about my lyrics suggested a Christian wrote it. Guess my song from last summer had been cryptic enough that she didn't have a clue.

Boy, would her cousin be disappointed in learning the truth about my ramblings.

"I'm not really ready for something like that," I finally answered, at a loss for what else to say. What aspiring musician turned down that kind of offer? But I couldn't fake who I was.

Miss Jennifer patted my shoulder. "When you are, Isaac, I'd love to sit and hear more of your work. It's groundbreaking."

She left me, and my gaze trailed after her as she went to the next kid to see what they wrote about. A great girl. If only I was a dick enough to take advantage of what she offered.

A foot in the door. Maybe make some connections...but I couldn't use my music teacher like that. She was too sweet, and I didn't expect her cousin would want an openly gay musician signing with the Christian label he worked for.

Well, openly gay once I struck out on my own.

July and my birthday couldn't come soon enough.

Chapter 7
Malachi

Ten o'clock on the nose and a knock sounded on my office door.

"Come in!"

Jennifer did as bid, smiling like always with the joy of Jesus on her face.

Guilt weighed my body heavier into my seat. Catching Isaac's gaze when he'd walked into class had thrown me for a damn loop. Took my brain off the lecture I'd planned for my first day of class with the high schoolers. I'd struggled through my first two classes before break.

And I couldn't find the ability to make myself pray and ask for help.

"How were the kids this morning?" Jennifer sat primly on the chair across from me, hands clasped lightly on her lap. A fifties-like dress covered her from neck to below her knee, but even if she'd been in a tight, low-cut blouse and short pencil skirt, she wouldn't have gotten a rise out of me.

Such a shame.

"Good," I stated and cleared my throat, straightening some papers on my desk. "They were all well behaved and listened better than I'd expected." Except for Isaac. He had stared at me, making me uncomfortable in my own damn skin. I doubted he'd heard a word I said if his eyes portrayed what went through his head.

The same thing I'd fantasized about, the craving that grew with every inhale in his skin-tingling presence.

"We've really been blessed with an awesome group of kids the past couple of years." Jennifer's voice was too damn bubbly.

I need more coffee, I told myself, *not the pastor's son.*

"Hardly any drama with the girls and no fights between the boys," Jennifer continued. "But with the Maine trip, being in close proximity for a few days without a break will bring in a bit of both. It always does."

The Maine trip to a youth hostel in the woods near Moose Head Lake would be a place to labor for the Lord with our acts of servitude. Painting. Landscaping. A chance for the kids to semi-vacation without watchful parents. An opportunity to explore in dark corners or behind trees the things they wouldn't attempt at home.

I'd been such a kid once. Me leading Brian into the darkness...

"Are you alright?"

"Hmm?" I lifted my focus to Jennifer, whose brow had furrowed. Guess I'd sat frowning at my desk too long. "Yeah." I forced a smile. "Just remembering my own youth group trips."

Her smile returned. "The singing around the campfire is always the best. S'mores. Silly ghost stories and laughter."

"Sounds like a good time."

"It is." Her smile remained as she studied me until I shifted in my seat.

"So it looks like everything is all set for June," I said, picking back up the file for the upcoming trip that my predecessor had already pretty much handled.

"I'm sending out consent forms and waivers next week," Jennifer said. "We require the parents for those kids attending to sign them."

I nodded, knowing how things had changed since I'd been in the youths' shoes. "So there are two large rooms, one for the girls and one for the guys," I repeated what I'd read in the file.

"Yes."

"Have there been any issues with kids sneaking out in the past?"

"Once," Jennifer said, her cheeks turning pink.

I raised an eyebrow, waiting for her to expand.

"Um...I was the guilty party."

My other eyebrow lifted. "You?" I couldn't believe it.

"Yes." She glanced away, her guilt obvious even though a good ten years must've passed since her graduation. "Me and my boyfriend at the time decided we didn't want to wait for marriage, and we snuck out of the rooms once everyone slept."

I stared, struck dumb. Sweet, bubbly Jennifer Sutton, godly woman who served the Lord… "You had sex," I sputtered. "Outdoors. While on a youth trip?"

She gasped, her eyes widening. "Oh my goodness, no! Just kissed. I would never!"

Kissed… *Holy hell.* I barely held in my burst of laughter. "You mean to tell me you weren't going to kiss a guy until marriage?"

"No-touch love is the best way to keep your purity until marriage."

I stared, my smile fading. What the hell did they preach at Elkin's Bible Church? No-touch love. Abstinence from…everything? Shit, I couldn't imagine being a horny teenager and not even feeling you had the right to kiss the person you crushed on.

"Does the no-touch love teachings include holding hands?" I had to ask.

"Once you're engaged, it's allowed."

What kind of church had I submitted myself to? Not that I wanted to hold a woman's hand or kiss her lips, but still. Talk about restrictive as fuck—even more so than the Bible church I'd grown up in.

"Have you heard the pastor's son sing?"

Her one-eighty question caught me off guard. "Huh?"

"Isaac. He's got an incredible voice. I'm hoping I can get him to share his gift while we're in Maine. I caught him singing while hiding away last year, and let me tell you, that boy is talented beyond words."

"His mom mentioned it, yes," I replied, remembering all too well how she'd supported his dreams while his dad didn't. A situation I'd seen before with Brian, the heartbreak of which I'd attempted to soothe.

Memories flashed in my head of me and Brian cuddled together, our voices in perfect harmony, and my promises afterward to stand by his side when the time came for us to leave for Nashville.

I cleared my throat, pushing against the past, against the similar connection I felt with Isaac.

"He's *so* good," Jennifer gushed. "I'm dying to send a demo to my cousin down in Nashville."

Pausing in shuffling papers on my deck, I glanced up at her. "Your cousin is in the music industry?"

"Elliot James."

Oh, holy hell. The blood drained from my face, leaving me feeling light-headed as fuck. "*The* Elliot James?" I managed to ask.

"One and the same." Jennifer beamed, and I wondered if she considered pride as much of a sin as breaking the no-touch love teachings.

But Elliot...

A bi-man who hid his truth. A guy who'd been interested in me as a gay virgin and not because of my talents. All it had taken was hints of his interest in signing me on with his label, and I'd gotten on my knees for him. Twice. Once to give him my mouth, and the second time to give him my ass. The second had been a first for me since Brian and I hadn't gone beyond mutual hand and blow jobs. Painful yet hot, Elliot's and my passion had burned as bright as the stars.

Naive and innocent, I'd thought it had been love, the man who would heal me from my loss of Brian.

However, Elliot had kicked me out of his fancy apartment in downtown Nashville immediately after taking my virginity like I'd done something wrong.

Talk about a damn insecurity feeder—and the beginning to my complete downfall.

"Do you know him?" Jennifer asked.

Intimately.

"No," I forced out the lie and cleared my throat again, pushing aside thoughts of my further failure, how I'd gone on to other beds and dark hallways in my rebelliousness. I'd given it up once, so why hold back? Luckily, God had protected me during those years, and physically, I'd escaped unscathed. "I know *of* him, but not him personally."

Oh, the deception...if Jennifer asked her cousin about me, would he uncover our sins? Blab the truth of my past and ruin the path I'd chosen because of my promise to Mom on her deathbed? Doing so, though, would reveal his sexual preferences too, and as a big exec in the Christian music industry, I expected he'd want to keep that shit under wraps.

"He would sign Isaac in a heartbeat," Jennifer mused.

My blood pressure rose, probably bringing color back to my face. He'd try to fuck the boy too, I didn't doubt. I'd heard through the grapevine he took advantage of other dreamers like I'd been once upon a time.

"Pastor Bram wouldn't approve of a demo," I stated with a stern voice even as my hands fisted atop my desk. The last thing I could imagine was Isaac giving up his firsts—if he hadn't already—to a man bent on stealing them with alluring, false claims.

"You don't think?"

"No."

Jennifer let out a sigh at my hard tone, even though I didn't know if I spoke the truth or not. "He's just so, so talented—gifted, I mean," she hastened to correct herself that God was the giver of Isaac's voice.

Her words made my mind whirl. Yet another thing Isaac and Brian—and *I*—had in common. Another connection that could easily sway me toward the young man when I needed to keep my distance.

"He just needs to overcome his insecurity so I can get him to help with the praise and worship team," Jennifer said with a sigh as though her thoughts on Isaac's situation, her *truth*, was the absolute answer. "He needs to let go, and let God."

My stomach twisted at Jennifer's canned words, a cliché phrase I'd heard hundreds of times in various churches. Let go of the old man, the inherent sinful nature, and let God have his way.

She obviously didn't struggle like I did to accept what had been spoon-fed to me since childhood.

I walked her out of my office a few minutes later after going over last-minute retreat plans, grabbed that coffee I needed, and headed back to the school building behind the church.

At least I wouldn't have to see Isaac in class for the rest of the day.

Chapter 8

Isaac

Miss Jennifer followed Malachi around like a lost puppy, but what single woman in her twenties wouldn't? His presence couldn't be ignored, and his vivid light eyes drew a damn soul in with an intensity that hitched breaths and pinkened countless cheeks.

But not a single female got under his skin like I could.

One suggestive glance was all it took to fluster my Bible teacher. And at Wednesday night youth group? He couldn't even look at me, no matter how silently I begged him with my sharp gaze to give me the time of day.

But I didn't want his attention.

Not really.

At least, I told myself that, considering he was too religious like my dad.

The evil part of me, hidden in the deepest reaches, wanted to soil his purity. Break down the fake-ass walls he'd put up as a front. I lusted to see him dirtied in the eyes of my dad who couldn't keep from singing his praises as if telling me how awesome Malachi was would make us friends.

And seeing Malachi smile, relaxed and at ease with Miss Jennifer, pissed me off. Unguarded, he seemed open with her when he didn't realize I was around, watching him like a fucking creepy stalker.

Perhaps the reason he'd made it a point to ignore me was because he hated me. Or maybe the attraction between us sickened him.

He wanted a godly woman, not the too-young pastor's son who dreamed of dick.

Malachi preached acceptance in Bible class on Tuesday and Wednesday. He showed mercy to one of the ninth graders who hadn't gotten their homework turned in on time. But me?

He treated me as though I didn't exist, and I hated it like the little brat I couldn't help but be.

On our second Wednesday night with the new youth pastor, I sat in our school's gymnasium with my friends Chris and Tyler. I knew I could rile the two guys up since they usually stirred trouble when pushed. While waiting for Malachi to get started with the night's lesson, I shot the shit with them and got them talking about girls.

Whispers and snickers of which ass they'd tapped, the latest party they'd been to. How much they drank, who I needed to hook up with if I wanted to get high— them. While I could care less about pussy, for the sake of making waves, I could definitely pretend I did.

"What about the Burns girl?" I asked, leaning in, my voice lowered so no one would hear with the other clamor going on around us from the metal folding chairs.

"Lindy?"

"Yeah. The blonde with the huge tits," I whispered what I'd heard them talk about the week before. "Either of you had a taste of her?"

Chris snorted, his lips curling. "Everyone's had that whore."

Unlike me, he couldn't keep his voice down. The word *whore* drew some attention—both Miss Jennifer and Malachi frowned at us as they chatted with other kids close by.

Chuckling, I elbowed Chris. "Heard she smells like day-old tuna left out in the sun."

He burst out in laughter, and Malachi's scowl deepened.

"Let's get settled," our leader stated, his voice stern as he glanced around the circle of teens and sat into the chair beside Miss Jennifer. "Quiet down and open with prayer."

"I'd rather have a handful of tits and worship a woman's pussy," I whispered so only my two buddies beside me would hear.

Chris barked out another laugh, and I bit against my own laughter wanting to burst out, my arms crossing as I slouched in my chair.

Malachi eyed the three of us, and I held his stare with a blatant one of my own. Lips pursed, he lowered his head, the rest of the group honoring his call to order.

I studied the wavy blond hair atop his downturned head while he prayed God's blessing on our gathering, wondering if the strands would feel as silky between my itching fingertips as they appeared.

He said a hearty *amen*, and I leaned toward Chris, whispering truth out of the side of my mouth, "Worshiping *ass* would be even better."

"Hell yeah," he whispered back, shifting and chuckling.

Malachi glanced at us again.

Talk about a fucking power trip. Simply acting out gained me attention in the best way—his intense blue-eyed stare. Even disapproving, his rigid looks heated my blood. Thickened my dick.

I adjusted myself while he watched, a smirk on my face.

His gaze shot away, red creeping up his neck while he quoted scripture about unconditional love and acceptance, the same lesson he'd been teaching in Bible class for two weeks.

Fuck, what a trip.

Malachi tried, oh, how he tried to ignore me while in our circle of sheep-like teens, but whatever it was between us kept him coming back for more after he watched me adjust my junk.

The next time our eyes met, I touched the tip of my tongue to my lower lip.

Sucked it into my mouth the second time he looked my way.

He shifted too, sitting forward with elbows on his knees while talking to the group about showing kindness to our peers. Revealing God's love to all mankind even if we didn't agree with their religion or lifestyle.

Awesome lessons, just not ones usually followed by the Christians I'd known in my seventeen years.

"We can love the sinner without loving the sin," he stated, drawing more than one bob of head in agreement from kids who'd had the same teaching bashed into their heads since childhood. "Didn't Jesus sit and dine with Zacchaeus? Didn't he tell those wanting to judge the woman who'd committed adultery to cast the first stone only if they were without sin?"

He listed a few other times the God of the New Testament showed love when He could have condemned souls.

But Malachi didn't come right out and state that homosexuality was a sin—or bring up any of the others actually listed in the Bible. He didn't mention fire and brimstone or burning for eternity if one gave into the sins of the flesh like Dad preached at least once a month ever since that girl in high school got pregnant out of wedlock thanks to Chris's dick.

She'd gone to live with her grandparents, gave the kid up for adoption, and never came back to Elkin's Bible Church. She'd been quietly shunned, spoken of by Dad with his deacons and elders over the phone when he didn't know I listened in. But with Chris being an elder's son, he got off with a public repentance one Sunday morning after service.

Dad was judgmental as fuck, looking down his damn nose at those who fell, and if Chris had never repented, I'd have been forced to give up one of my few friends.

And Dad would behave the same and require the same if the truth about me ever came out.

A couple months until freedom...

But in the meantime, I kept on with my snide comments, riling the non-Christian school guys up until our whispers and laughter disrupted our youth group and drew attention like I'd wanted it to.

"If you boys don't quiet down," Malachi stated, "I'm going to have to separate you."

"What are we?" I muttered under my breath to Tyler on my left. "First graders?"

"Do you have words you wish to share with the rest of the group, Isaac?" Malachi called me out.

Arms crossed, I held his gaze. "Nope."

"You sure about that?" He surprised me by pushing. "Because it seems you've got something on your mind."

Oh, the things in my head. How would the so-called pious youth pastor behave if I told his youth group exactly what I thought about him and the lust I clearly saw in his gaze every time our eyes met?

My lazy grin hardened his countenance, and he looked away, changing the subject back to the lecture I expected he believed God had given him for the night.

Chris elbowed me, chuckling. Guess I'd earned his admiration, not that I cared.

Malachi's teaching veered into the importance of honesty. The fucking liar thought he could preach to the damn choir.

My first snort earned me a glare.

The second caused Miss Jennifer to shift in her seat beside him, her glance flickering between us. Malachi had to do something, and my stomach fluttered in anticipation. I imagined him dragging me out into the hallway. Slamming me into the wall and getting all up in my face.

Anger, an exchange of heated words—hell, maybe even heated touches.

Damn.

Another adjustment of my dick drew his focus.

He wrapped up his little lesson early, and the kids meandered into the usual social groups to play board games.

I stayed put, eyeing the youth pastor. Wondering and waiting as Chris and Tyler ambled away toward the senior girls.

Malachi and Miss Jennifer spoke quietly, and he glanced my way.

Come on, pastor man. Bring whatever discipline you want. I'm game.

I raised an eyebrow. Waited.

Lips pursed, his chest rose and fell like he took a fortifying breath—and he stood, walking toward me with sure, measured steps.

Fuck yes.

He took the empty seat beside me.

So much for those thoughts of being dragged into the hallway and pushed up against the wall.

"Are you okay, Isaac?"

I sucked in a lungful of his scent—dryer sheets and subtle aftershave. Damn delicious. Made my jeans strangle my dick. "Why wouldn't I be?"

"You seem...off tonight. Troubled."

"Troubled." I huffed a sarcastic laugh. "Sounds like you've been talking to my dad."

"I'm here to help, not judge."

I met Malachi's gaze, loving how an undercurrent of energy seemed to zap back and forth between us. Sitting that close, I noticed a few freckles on his nose. The perfect arch in his thinner upper lip. The pink in his plump lower one.

Not quite pouty but lickable all the same.

"Don't."

His one word jerked my focus off his mouth. "Don't what?"

"Look at me like that," he half-hissed, glancing around to see who might be watching our discussion.

"Like what?" I pushed, my pulse thrumming, my eyes narrowing.

He turned his attention back on my face. Held my stare until I felt lightheaded with need for something...*more.*

"I think you know what," Malachi stated sternly as though unaffected by our mutual attraction, "and it has to stop."

I pinched my bottom lip between two fingers, snagging his focus, my mouth curling at the butterflies wreaking havoc on my insides. "I like this."

"This?" he asked, his voice raspy and sexy as fuck.

"Us," I whispered, leaning forward slightly into his personal space.

"There is no us," Malachi snipped. "There never will be an us, and I would appreciate it if you would behave."

"But behaving is so...*boring.*"

A muscle ticked in his jaw, and I wondered what words he wanted to spew at me but felt as God's man he couldn't. "Don't push me, Isaac."

"Or what?"

Heat flared in his eyes, the kind that sent an ache through my groin and smeared pre-cum in my boxers.

"Or I'll have a little talk to your father. Tell him why you act out."

"And why is that, *Malachi*?"

Fuck, he liked his name on my lips. His pupils swelled, and he leaned even closer, stealing my breath and stalling out my heartbeat. "To hide who you are inside."

Our gazes remained locked for a moment longer before he walked away without another word. I stared after him, processing, my held exhale leaving in a rush.

Who you are, he'd said, not what I *chose* to be, like Dad preached about my particular "sin."

My truth.

Malachi didn't believe homosexuality was a choice. Wondering what had led him to such a place solidified my thoughts on the man clear as hell in my head.

We were the same. We definitely *wanted* the same.

He'd tried to redirect my pursuit for attention, and he'd done nothing but double my craving for another verbal sparring match—and possibly more.

So, *so* much more.

Chapter 9

Malachi

Days passed. A full week, and another.

Isaac continued to test me, his vocal rebellion growing with every passing minute in his presence. I should've hated how he made me feel, the energy I fed off of, the *life* he swelled inside my chest.

He became the only person I could breathe freely around, and I didn't understand why, considering how the lust in his eyes caused my lungs to seize.

While he tempted my flesh and called to a libido left to rot where it belonged, I couldn't help the fact I came alive around him. Suppressing my desire for the young man didn't lessen the draw.

The craving for him.

Isaac was desperate for attention, same as I'd been as a kid. Pastor Bram, I came to realize within a matter of weeks, lived for his church. It was all he spoke about—his flock, his aspirations. Rarely did he mention his only son or any pride he felt in being a father.

The only time Pastor Bram talked about Isaac was when spouting off disappointments and negativity. His son had been the blessing he and Annabelle had prayed for, but the man took no joy in Isaac like my dad had done with me, especially when I'd approached him about Isaac failing Bible class.

The truth of his father, the exact opposite of my loving parents, expanded my empathy for Isaac, and I couldn't help but take it easy on him, regardless of how he got the boys in youth group going or how he shot me knowing looks that stiffened my dick to the point of pain.

I gave into the need for release and emptied my balls every day before leaving for the school or church. All in hopes that by sating my lust of the flesh, the appearance of Isaac wouldn't cause sinful imaginings since my prayers went unanswered.

But every glimpse of him, whether in the school's uniform blue slacks or ripped jeans on Wednesday nights youth group, cast my mind into depraved unholiness. Harmful thoughts, the type that God would punish me for if I didn't atone.

I couldn't talk to my pastor—hell no.

So I called the only man I could. As a Christian counselor, I knew he would give me nonjudgmental truth.

"I'm on the cusp, Zeke."

"Talk to me."

I pinched the bridge of my nose, my head tipped against the back of my couch and my eyes clenched shut. We hadn't spoken in the three weeks since I'd arrived in Elkins, but I'd reached a breaking point. "Coming here was a mistake."

"Isaac is proving too much a temptation?"

"It's a strong draw between us, ten times more than I'd felt with Brian...it can't be ignored. I feel like I'm drowning in need."

"The lusts of the flesh."

I wanted to agree with the words Zeke spoke, but I couldn't. "It's more than mere lust," I admitted, letting out a heavy sigh, my free hand falling to the couch beside me. I saw Isaac in my mind's eye. His flashing hazel orbs and the smirk I wanted to bite off his lips. The hurt I sometimes caught when he glanced at me, the connection of...loneliness I felt radiating off him.

"It's more than lust," I reiterated, sitting forward to rest my elbows on my knees.

"More how?"

"I—I don't know." I huffed an exhale, hating how my stomach churned. "I want to protect him, to keep him from experiencing the same hurt I did."

"What do you mean?" Zeke sounded relaxed, settled in for a long ass talk.

"He's a singer/songwriter." My throat tightened.

"Fuck."

"Yeah." My eyelids slid shut, my head hanging between my shoulders. "He's headed to Nashville after graduation, and the thought of what he'll face there, the temptation and evil... I can't allow that to happen."

"He needs to live his own life, Malachi. Make his own decisions, learn from his own mistakes."

"And end up in the same hole I barely managed to crawl out of?" I shot back, a spark of anger in my chest giving me something solid to hold onto.

"God pulled you from your depression."

"Did He?" I asked, truly wondering for the first time. "Because it sure as hell felt a lot like me dragging my own ass out. There was no angel's trumpet, no sense of heavenly arms wrapping my heavy heart up and carrying me to contentment. It was my decision to return to the Lord as Mom lay on her deathbed.

"Are you happy?"

Zeke's question caught me off guard, and I took time to consider what he asked.

True happiness came from the Lord and couldn't be manufactured by man, one's conscience, or another person in your life. However, I felt no such joy, no peace. I couldn't remember feeling that way since before Brian's car accident.

"No."

"I don't know what to say," Zeke murmured through my cell, and I swallowed hard. "I can only speak truth as I see it. God has a plan. He'll reveal himself in His time. You just have to trust Him until He does."

Trusting. Blind faith.

When what I longed for stood right in front of me.

"Can I pray with you?"

I didn't deny my best friend's need to offer comfort in the only way he could with being a few hours away. The words of thanks on my lips didn't resonate in my soul when he finished, nor did my vocalized appreciation when he promised to continue to pray for God to guide me.

Hanging up, I didn't feel any better than before I'd placed the call.

God still hid behind a shroud, but I began to wonder if the darkness closing over me was of my own making.

I fell to my knees, tears on my cheeks, begging forgiveness for my sinful thoughts, for my wandering mind.

No sense of calmness swept in to smother my guilt in the hour I knelt before His throne.

And no joy promised in the Bible came in the morning either.

Chapter 10

Isaac

School sucked. Church sucked. Youth group made my gut clench to the point I felt like I was going to puke every time I entered the gymnasium and found the usual circle of folding chairs.

Like a damn accountability group...

I glanced around the echoing room, arms crossed and offering glares for each and every one of the idiots around me. Behaving like a brat came easily, stemming from bottled up anger. I wanted to lash out. To barrel through anyone who stood in my way.

I needed to escape.

"Hey." Miss Jennifer's light hold on my arm drew my focus off of Malachi chatting with a few of the younger kids over near the games table.

"Hey." I gave her my full attention, an impulsive decision slamming into my brain. "I want to do that demo for your cousin."

She bit her lip, glancing across the gymnasium. "About that..."

"What?" She'd been so damn on board, pushing for so long, and now she hesitated?

"Malachi said your dad wouldn't approve."

"My dad." I clenched my jaw, catching the youth pastor's gaze across the spacious room that echoed with laughter, something I hadn't felt in too long.

"I know your father has high hopes for you, Isaac. Bible college...maybe seminary."

My dad wanted me to follow in his footsteps, but if he had any inkling of my inner workings, he would never suggest such a thing.

If anyone, Malachi would understand my urge to get away—far away—and make my own decisions. Stating my father knew best...

Heat roused inside me, and not the kind that tempted me to attack him in some dark hallway with grasping hands and searching lips.

"Whatever." I pulled free from her hold and found a chair. I slouched there, arms crossing once more, my stare on my sneakers.

Chris threw himself into the chair beside me, filling me in on his latest conquest—some college chick home for the summer already. Blow jobs, hands jobs...I barely heard a word he said with how my mind churned over the youth pastor's audacity to attempt directing my future.

Although hot as fuck, he'd landed on my shit list again.

Malachi called our little meeting to order while I wondered why the fuck I sat in a circle of teens I didn't have a goddamn thing in common with. Not one.

They wanted to worship a God I didn't truly believe in. Sing his praises while I stayed silent. Malachi's husky tenor united in perfect harmony with Miss Jennifer's as they led us in songs.

Closing my eyes, I drowned in his voice. Focused on it amidst the sea of off-tune girls and the one teenage guy in our group who thought he could sing.

I hummed a weaving harmony around Malachi's in my head, taking the alto when he stayed on tenor, seamlessly switching parts as the music led him. The beauty we created—fuck, it made me hard. Got my blood rushing full of adrenaline and a high I could ride for eternity.

He and I would blend like fucking perfection in real life —I didn't have a doubt. But I refused to sing praises in church.

And Malachi wanted to stomp on my dreams.

I attempted to squash down the brew of hope inside me, facing reality. Malachi going the Q&A route that night, drawing in the teens for conversation about God's word, their beliefs, and their convictions, made it easier. I scuffed my toes against the gymnasium floor, only half listening, just waiting for the night to be over already.

"It's just so wrong, you know?" The girl beside me stated and let out a sigh, her voice trembling enough that I paid attention.

"If there's a heartbeat," one of the boys said, "it's murder. Plain and simple."

I glanced up at the boy—one of the deacon's sons. Dogmatic as fuck, a self-righteous tenth grader who probably hadn't realized he could do more with his dick than take a piss.

"Abortion has been fought over in the courts when it has to do with God's word, not the law." That last statement from a girl too young to know her pussy from her ass caused my brow to furrow.

"So you're suggesting a woman's womb is nothing but an incubator?" I shot back, earning me her wide-eyed stare. "You think a woman shouldn't have a say over what she can and can't do with her own body?" I huffed a snort. "What happens when you get kidnapped off the street one day while walking home from school?"

"Isaac."

I ignored Malachi, my gaze plastered on the young girl. "What happens when he rapes you?"

"Isaac!" Jennifer gasped.

"And you end up pregnant," I continue, ignoring the shifting and murmurs around me. "What do you do then? Thank God for the life growing inside you fathered by a sick rapist?" I snipped, my blood pressure rising. "You don't think you should have the choice whether you raise the life or end the pregnancy before it even begins?"

One of the deacon's sons jumped in. "There's a heartbeat at—"

"I don't give a flying fuck when the heart first beats."

"Isaac!" Malachi stood in my periphery, but I kept my glare on the kid who spouted bullshit at me.

"You believe a woman should be forced to carry around a pile of cells and be thankful for nine months of hell after suffering rape? What the hell is wrong with you?"

A hand closed over my arm, yanking me to my feet. "Let's go."

I stumbled along behind Malachi out into the hallway, my dick swelling to life at the firm hold he had on my bare arm.

Skin on skin.

First contact since our handshake weeks ago.

His touch seared me, and goosebumps skittered across my neck. Took my dick to full mast in three quick breaths.

He slammed open the janitor's closet, shoved me in, and flicked on the lights. "You've been asking for it all night."

Malachi had no fucking clue what I really wanted to ask for, what had me pissed off at the world. The heat, the energy boiling up between us, took me to the edge of reason.

"The fuck is *your* problem?" I half hollered, shoving against his hard chest. Lusting for more. So much more. "You come in here all high and mighty, thinking you're God's man—"

He growled, grasped my neck, and slammed me into the wall.

Fuck yes.

Heat exploded throughout my body, and I gasped, needing him to fall over with me, to lose himself in whatever it was that boiled like lava between us.

"I see the way you look at me," I spat, glaring and ready to punch or bite his face. I couldn't decide which I desired more. I settled for grabbing his wrist as he held me in place.

"How do I look at you?" His voice quivered, his eyes half wild. Pupils blown wide.

So goddamn hot I wanted to sink my teeth into his lower lip.

"Like you'd love nothing more than to bend me over the nearest desk, pew, or chair, and fuck the brat right out of me."

A shudder rippled over him, but he didn't speak. Didn't deny what I'd bet my life was true.

I snorted, lifting my chin even higher, submitting my neck to his hand. "You think you know me. Think you can work alongside my dad to keep me bound in these chains when all I want is to breathe free? I'm going to

Nashville the day I turn eighteen, and I don't give a flying fuck—"

"No."

The fucker had balls. "I heard what you told Miss Jennifer. Who the *fuck* do you think you are to rain on my damn parade?"

"Someone who's lived it. Failed at it. *Hurt* for it." Pain filled his voice, his eyes, but I wasn't about to soften for his ass when he still held me tight against the wall.

"So?" I shot back.

Malachi closed the distance between us. Clothing separated our skin, but I could feel the hard length of him, the muscle, the bone. A body I wanted to fall to my knees and worship.

Pure agony overflowed from his blue eyes, damn near stabbing me in the heart. "I can't bear the thought of you feeling what I did. The mistakes I made..."

Oh no, he wasn't going to trail off and leave me hanging. I wanted his secrets. Needed to hear why he buried who he was deep inside, refusing to let himself live. "Tell me."

Malachi stilled, his whole body seeming to buzz with an energy that reached through my clothing to whisper against my skin, lighting every cell inside me on fire. "I can't, he whispered, but he didn't release his hold on my neck as his gaze slid down to my mouth.

I swallowed, knowing something deep rooted inside him, issues he wouldn't uncover no matter how much I begged. But he didn't have to speak them. "So show me," I rasped out, shifting so our dicks rubbed against each other, lighting fire in my veins.

"Isaac."

My heart fluttered crazily in my chest. "I want it, Malachi."

He groaned and took my mouth with bruising force. Lips, teeth, tongue—my first kiss. He sucked the oxygen from my lungs and dizzied my brain with every hungry groan escaping him.

Affirmation.

Pleasure I hadn't expected from a simple act.

Malachi owned me without speaking a word. The firmness of his lips and the hint of coffee and wintergreen on his breath as he licked at my mouth damn near brought me to the ground.

If he commanded me to get on my knees, I would willingly go.

If he'd ordered me to turn and bend over to let him fuck me without a damn drop of lube, I'd have gladly done so.

He devoured me, ate at my mouth like a man starved for salvation, a soul surrounded by a sea of hopelessness, floundering.

Lost.

In need of saving.

Same as the deepest parts of me. I wanted him to know I understood—that I needed the same thing as him.

I reached between us and grabbed hold of his length through his slacks. Malachi's dick was bigger than mine. Thicker. A shudder wracked through me as I imagined him shoving his length into my body, claiming and taking what we both craved.

"Malachi," I whimpered as his lips and teeth trailed along my jawline, his grasp on my neck tightening as he thrust into my hand's hold again and again. "Fuck..." I swallowed, his palm closed over my throat making it damn near impossible.

He shuddered and breathed hard, resting his forehead against mine, the bulk of him still holding me against the wall. "This is wrong."

The rasp in his voice caused precum to ooze from my dick, and I ground my groin against the back of my hand working him over his pants.

"Stop." He grabbed my wrist to stop me from tempting him for more. "Please, Isaac...I—I can't do this."

"We already are."

"We can't." He stepped back, his eyebrows furrowed and eyes darkened by lust yet full of guilt. Fists at his sides and his entire body trembling, he stared at me.

I gasped for breath. Hoped my neck would bruise so I'd have something to remember my first kiss by.

"I made so many wrong choices, Isaac." Malachi shook his head as though trying to rid his mind of the past. "I would do anything to keep you from the same. And this…this is definitely a mistake that would lead to something I can't be responsible for."

"I'm going to pursue my dream," I stated with a shaky voice, refusing to be commanded by yet another man who thought himself in a position of authority over me.

A muscle ticked in his jaw, but he didn't make a move to touch me again like the energy between us demanded.

I couldn't bear the idea of rejection—so I left on shaky legs. Walked around him and out of the closet without another word, without a backward glance even though my heart longed for both.

Our time together grew shorter and shorter.

But I wasn't done with Malachi Foley.

A combustion awaited us, I didn't doubt, but the timing, the when and how…

We just needed a few moments away from the church, away from a place that would remind him of his job, my age, my parentage.

Maine, I promised.

Chapter 11
Malachi

The door slammed shut behind Isaac, and I leaned my forehead against it. His flavor lingered on my lips, and I found myself licking them, hoping for another hint of cinnamon. Spicy and sweet—a damn addiction I'd gotten a taste of and feared I wouldn't ever rid my mind from its draw.

Addiction.

Of the worst sort, the sinful kind, of which action would damn us to eternal hell, same as it had done to Brian.

"I won't allow it," I whispered into the janitor closet's ear-ringing stillness. Sucking in a lungful of chemical-laced air, I fought against the throb in my dick, the tightness in my groin. "I won't lead him into temptation like I did with Brian."

An ache replaced the hollowness in my chest, and I rubbed at my shirt, hating it more than emptiness.

Speaking the truth I wanted wouldn't make it come to pass, no matter how much the Bible promised.

Just a few weeks left to the school year—and then I would only have to put up with his rebellious ass on Wednesday nights rather than every day. But if I was being honest with myself, I would miss the ebb and flow of teasing and annoyance that had led to the most heated kiss of my life.

My lips continued to tingle, my fingertips still throbbing in time with the pulse I'd felt strumming like hell beneath them when I'd held Isaac by his neck.

I didn't doubt I'd taken his first kiss. I'd caught him off guard, but he'd overcome his surprise, giving back in the same way I'd lusted for with unpracticed lips. Uninhibited, he'd been handsy and greedy for more.

Fuck, what a temptation he was.

Standing, I filled my lungs and squeezed the base of my dick rather than jerking off like I wanted to do.

Seventeen.

Pastor's son.

Male—the biggest forbidden element as far as my station was concerned.

But I told myself all I wanted to think on was saving him from himself, from heading off into the unknown as a naive young man dozens would prey on given the chance. I couldn't allow it. Wouldn't. I had to find a way to save him from the life I'd lived.

* * *

I managed a few prayers in the following weeks while counting down the days until classes let out for the summer. Begging God for strength, for His mercy—but I couldn't find it in myself to ask forgiveness for putting my hands on Isaac. Dominating him with a mere hold on his neck, fucking into his fumbling grasp on my dick.

Jerking off to the memory became my favorite pastime, and as every day passed, my guilt over doing so lessened more and more.

I grew numb to the sin of taking myself in hand and fantasizing about a teenage boy. My body's craving for him couldn't be sated.

At least I made the right decisions whenever in his presence. I ignored him and pretended the energy he brought to my existence wasn't real.

It was for the best, even though it killed me inside. Sticking to what was proper leader-wise, I shared passages of scripture that spoke of choosing a holy life, making right decisions and forgiving ourselves if we failed, trusting God's plan —his path.

All of which I didn't, couldn't, do.

Maybe if Isaac heard the words of grace and mercy enough, he'd reconsider when faced with choices that could lead to devastation.

On graduation night, I sat in the church's auditorium, clapping with pride for each and every kid who walked up in their blue robes and caps with happiness on their faces.

Alphabetically, that left Isaac last to cross the stage, but the smirk on his face wasn't one of joy—it was full of mischief, a glint of rebellion that promised he'd be gone from my life soon.

The substance his presence always brought to my chest faded as I considered him truly leaving.

I knew he wouldn't stick around Elkins.

Nashville hadn't ever been spoken of again, but he'd made his dreams clear, and his dad grumbled about Isaac stating he wanted to take a year off before heading to Bible college.

Isaac had no such intention of following in Pastor Bram's footsteps, I didn't doubt that one bit. He would choose the way he wanted, religion, his parents, and the church be damned.

And I would be left behind where I belonged, once more struggling to breathe, having nightmares about what choices he faced every day without guidance.

I just hoped the words I'd shared through the weeks would help keep him in truth. Keep his mind, body, and soul safe.

Isaac's focus flitted over the congregation as he crossed the stage, his gaze landing on me for a brief moment. I allowed him to hold me enthralled, the touch of his tongue to his lower lip tightening my groin and making me rub over my pectorals.

I want you.

Crave you.

You're my worst temptation and the air in my lungs.

I tore my focus off him and smiled at Annabelle beside me, the joy on her face making me wonder if she might choose to love her son once she and her husband learned the truth of who he was.

Not my circus, I told myself, glancing over the rest of the graduates as they tossed their caps into the air. *And definitely not my monkey.*

Chapter 12

Isaac

Almost free...almost free...

I chanted my new favorite saying in my head while watching the backs of Malachi's and Miss Jennifer's heads in the bus's front seat. We ended up hiring an actual full-sized bus and driver for our trip to Maine since so many of the teens in youth group had signed up.

Kids chatted around me, and some played road games, their laughter nothing but a buzz in my ears.

Tyler hadn't been able to make the trip—summer soccer or some such shit—so Chris ended up being my seat partner, my only friend in our group. Not that he knew a damn thing about the real me though.

Miss Jennifer leaned close to Malachi, her bright smile in profile, and he smiled at whatever she said to him.

I stewed on my plastic seat that squeaked every time I moved, the material sticking to the backs of my thighs since I'd been an idiot, and I'd worn shorts rather than jeans like I usually did.

Almost eight hours in and I'd had about enough of the noise and enough of the BO from the beefy guy beside me. The singing encouraged by Miss Jennifer who stared at Malachi with stars in her eyes made my skin crawl.

Did he even realize she had a thing for him? Did he understand that continuing to be friendly, to laugh and listen, encouraged her? His gay ass obviously had no fucking clue—or was he forcing himself into a role that was expected by good little Christians? Did he want to choose a woman so that everyone around him wouldn't know about his "sin?"

Did he want to be so-called normal in the eyes of man?

As though hearing my thoughts, he glanced over his shoulder, our gazes connecting.

Clashing with a flow of energy, of lust and longing that chubbed my dick.

We hadn't spoken a word to each other in private since that moment in the janitor's closet. Not since the day he'd blown my world to bits and gave my mind the best fuel to fantasize over.

I remembered the feel of his mouth, the hunger of his groans, and the hardness of his dick in my hand.

I wanted that dick.

In my mouth. In my ass.

I just lusted after Malachi Foley in every sense of the word, and sin and parents could go straight the fuck to hell as far as I was concerned.

And a five-day trip awaited us, one without Dad and Mom, one with an authority figure I knew how to wear down.

My A-game lay in wait.

Naughty as fuck, my mind had conjured up some good shit to break him down. I wanted him putty in my hands—and I needed his hands on me. Wrecking me. Breaking me. Putting me back together again.

Whatever it was that connected us, that made me aware every time he drew within a few feet's distance of me, it was potent. The kind of drug that swirled my head in what I expected drunkenness or being high must feel like.

His face remained passive as we stared at one another. His eyes were empty of emotion, lips void of the parted inhales of passion even as the memory stiffened my cock while sitting on a damn bus surrounded by innocence.

I pursed my lips in a slight, mocking kiss he wouldn't be able to misinterpret.

Malachi turned back around, his countenance impressively unmoved.

Fucking liar.

Smirking, I studied the back of his head.

Soon, my dear youth pastor. Soon.

"Did Tyler tell you I asked Sara out?"

I shook my head at Chris's question, glancing at the girl he spoke of on the other side of the aisle and up two rows.

Short blonde to his dark mass. Day and night. I couldn't imagine how their hooking up could be accomplished considering their height difference. Not that I wanted the visual.

"She's on the no-touch love train," I told him, casting him a sideways glance.

He stared at her like I did Malachi, but the bonehead obviously hadn't noticed my actions the way I did his.

"She's got curves for days," he said, still staring. "Those tits would fill even my hands." He held up said massive hands, turning them with his fingers spread, as though grasping her breasts.

"Great rack," I agreed without a bit of truth behind my statement.

"I'd like her on her knees," he mumbled even though the teens on the seats around us couldn't hear in the ruckus of the bus. "Holding those tits together, letting me fuck them. I'd blow my load all over her skin."

Any normal guy's dick would get a rise out of that idea, so I played along. "Can I watch?"

He chuckled and elbowed me. "Sick fuck."

"Voyeur at heart," I lied some more. "So, what's your plan?"

"Get her to take a little walk with me one night instead of singing Kumbaya around the campfire."

Fucking awesome idea, a definite way to get someone alone.

I eyed the back of Malachi's head again as Chris laid out his thoughts on how to get a taste of Sara. Eventually talk her into fucking because that was one pussy he wanted to own.

"Let me know if you need any help in making that fantasy come true," I told him, my own mind considering how to get our youth pastor all to myself again.

Somehow, someway...

Not soon enough.

We finally pulled into the youth hostel before I figured out a clear plan of how to do more than wear him down. A sprawling disjointed motel-ish building, the likes of which I'd never seen outside of Maine, sat in the downpour that had pounded the bus's roof the last few miles while driving through the woods.

A barn connected to the garage, connected to a mudroom of sorts, connected to a laundry room, connected to an old eighteenth century house, connected to an eighties "modern" home. The last was two floors, the second of which housed the large rooms all the teens would bunk in.

I followed on Malachi's heels as our host led us up the stairs I'd climbed three times before in my high school years. He sat his bag on the lower bunk beside the door like our old youth pastor always used to do—I put mine on the next bed rather than as deep into the room as I usually did, sliding my guitar case beneath.

He didn't look my way and didn't acknowledge my presence, but I saw the stiffness of his shoulders as I claimed the bed closest to where he would lay at night.

Hopefully in nothing but boxers. Naked would be even better.

"Don't worry," I murmured, walking past him and out the door. "I don't snore."

He shivered. Full on body ripple that caused excitement to swell in my veins and puff my chest.

Chuckling, I made my way downstairs, shoulders back, chin tilted up with an arrogance that Malachi himself had brought on even though I'd never lacked in the self-confidence area. While I wasn't ripped like a body builder and didn't pack bulk onto my medium frame, I didn't have an ounce of fat on my body. Lean swimmer's muscle covered my bones from countless hours swimming and mowing lawns, and I took pride in keeping them defined.

Considering how I'd caught Malachi checking me out when he didn't think anyone looked, I knew he liked what he saw. Made me want to preen like a damn peacock. Stick out my ass a bit more than usual, maybe even add a sway to my hips.

Every one of the teens drew straws, and I ended up on dinner duty, helping the older couple hosting our group to get food on the table. Spaghetti with sauce from a jar, iceberg lettuce chopped up with ranch dressing. Loaves of generic white sandwich bread with buttery spread from a tub.

Nothing like Mom's home-cooked meals, but everyone ate without complaint.

At least the church taught good manners in honoring their elders.

I had zero intentions of honoring jack shit when it came to Malachi though. I would serve like we'd gone to Maine to do. I would labor outside in the garden and flower beds that choked with weeds. I would help rebuild the rock wall falling down on the eastern section of the property closer to the Appalachian Trail.

But I would find a way to wreck him.

He had said that day in the janitor closet that we *couldn't*...that there was no *us*. Well, he didn't know the level of determination I had residing deep inside me. My desire to know him, to sin with him, would damn our souls to hell for eternity if one believed in such a thing.

Even if he was like Dad with his holier than thou shit, I didn't care. He looked too damn good in a pair of low-riding jeans and tight T-shirt to be ignored.

Especially once said shirt grew dark with sweat and smeared with mud the next day.

I stared more than I ought to while he lugged rocks around with Chris, sweat beading on his brow, dripping down his cheek. Forearms flexing, veins popping along his tree tattoo that led up to tribal ones on his upper arm I wanted to trace with my tongue. Moving rocks alongside him, Chris, and a few other guys didn't come easy while dealing with a semi all afternoon.

And too bad the showers weren't an open concept in the gym like at the public school. Two separate stalls with curtains...but I made sure to head to the bathroom at the same time Malachi did after we finished our labor of love for the day.

I hadn't gotten a peek when he'd shimmied out of his boxer briefs—beneath the towel wrapped tightly around his trim waist. But at least I'd had a few seconds to check out his ass in the cotton clinging to his backside.

My youth pastor was sex on a stick while moving into the adjoining men's bathroom, a tease of the worst proportions, and holy hell did I drool. At least on the guy's side of the second floor and bathroom, no Miss Jennifer stood around to enjoy an eyeful of his golden, tanned skin like I managed to do.

I finally got to see Malachi's tribal-like tattoo on his upper arm that ran over to his shoulder. Bare, hairless chest with pecs I wanted to bite. Nipples that would look hot as fuck with rings pierced through them.

He didn't glance my way when I followed him into the bathroom and shut the door behind us. He didn't speak. Didn't turn.

My dick tented my towel, and the second he disappeared behind his chosen stall, towel flipping up and over the wall, I stepped into the one beside him. Hung my own towel, my pulse racing.

Grinning like a fool because I'd managed to beat Chris to the bathroom who'd grumbled about getting first dibs on the shower. He'd run into Sara who'd been working in the garden all day. She'd pulled him up short in the living room area on the first floor.

I turned on the blasting water and closed my eyes as it heated, listening to the spray from both shower heads and imagining Malachi washing his gorgeous body from neck to toes. My fingertips tingled with the wish to do it for him.

I soaped up every inch of my own skin, envisioning his hands smearing the suds, cupping my balls, and stroking my aching length. Lower lip between my teeth, I gave over to the fantasy wholeheartedly until my head tipped back, and I sucked oxygen through flared nostrils while fucking my hand.

The bathroom walls did nothing to muffle noise, and I knew if I groaned too loudly, other guys out in the bunk area outside might hear.

Couldn't have that, so I half-swallowed my moans, still audible enough to the one man in the bathroom with me.

Skin slapped, an unmistakable sound to any guy.

Whimpers rose from my chest as I fucked through my fist, fantasizing Malachi's hot breath brushed over my ear, his raspy voice telling me how much he wanted to watch his cum drip from my gaping hole.

"Fuck," I whispered—and spunk shot out of me, a boatload since I hadn't jacked off in two days.

Holy hell...

I lowered my head with a groan Malachi would hear and watched my hand milk myself dry, my ass clenching at emptiness I wanted him to fill with every thrust.

The clearing of a throat to my right made me grin as the last spurt dribbled from my slit, and my lips parted to suck down oxygen.

He'd definitely heard me.

I rinsed and shut off my water, my stomach light and my head giddy. Relief, even if not in the way I would have preferred, lessened the tension that had ridden me all day. I strained my ears to listen, wondering how Malachi's body reacted and if he would care for it the same way I had.

His shower still ran, the unmistakable sounds of schlicking—hand fucking—in my ears.

Fuck, yes.

My lingering semi twitched while my mouth watered, but I'd drained myself dry and wouldn't get it up again for at least fifteen minutes or so.

Rather than dry off in my stall, I stepped out into the bathroom, hoping for a peek around Malachi's curtain. The fantasy of seeing him jerk off was potent enough that I almost reached out and moved the damn barrier between us.

A quiet gasp from his shower stall picked my pulse back up, and I swallowed hard. "Need any help?" I asked quietly, unable to keep the smirk off my face as my insides buzzed.

Malachi let out a curse—a grunt—and the slick sounds of a fist fuck ended.

Shit...holy fucking hell, he did it.

Did he watch himself empty like I had? Lips parted while panting quietly, wishing it was me who'd been the one touching him?

I hoped it was my ass, my mouth, he imagined while getting himself off. Even better, I wanted my body doing the work for him.

Cursing in my head and shaking from the adrenaline rush over what we'd done, I toweled myself dry.

His shower shut off, his towel hanging over the wall yanked from sight.

I rubbed mine against my hair, eyes on his barrier, waiting for it to move.

Head down, he slid the curtain aside. Water droplets still clung to his chest and dripped from his hair. The towel wrapped snug around his waist, but the sight of his lower abs and that sinful V and light-haired happy trail disappearing beneath cotton readied my dick for action even though I thought I'd need longer to recoup.

Enough sexual tension clung in the humid air between us that I didn't need to speak. Breathing heavily, I turned sideways, giving him the opportunity to glance my way if he wanted—and he did.

Right at my swelling dick. It jumped beneath his heated stare while I toweled at my hair again, my heart racing.

Turning, I gave him a full view.

He jerked his head away from me faster than a serpent's strike.

Lower lip between my teeth again, I dried off my sack, my dick bobbing.

He side-eyed me, so I repeated the action.

"Isaac," he croaked out my name, and I grinned.

"Yeah?" I rasped out a reply, my hands falling to my sides, the towel at my left.

Lips pursed, he shook his head—and stalked out of the bathroom, leaving me alone with my hard dick and a big ass grin on my face.

My youth pastor wanted me. Badly.

And it was only a matter of time before he gave in to what he considered temptation—what I knew would be heaven on earth.

Chapter 13
Malachi

Every time I turned around, either Jennifer or Isaac was up my butt. The thought of taking a *dick* up my ass hadn't interested me since that first time with Elliot, Jennifer's cousin.

But Isaac? He made me lust for things I never thought I would again, most of all, the chance to bottom.

There wasn't anything I didn't want with him. Hearing him jerk off in the shower beside mine lessened my willpower to say no.

Other teens had been in our bunk room when we'd wrapped towels around our waists and dropped our drawers beneath. He'd followed on my heels like he'd done all day, and it would have drawn more attention for me to tell him to shower later, after me, when there were two stalls in the guys' bathroom.

The thought of being alone with him in that small bathroom had me half-hard before I yanked the shower curtain closed behind me, and being the brat Isaac was, he didn't bother keeping quiet while jerking off.

My ears strained as I washed, catching the quiet gasp, a slight moan. I fisted myself without thought, slowly riding along with him, wishing for an alternate reality where I could lock the bathroom door and push aside his curtain.

Watch as he fucked his own hand.

Press his chest against the shower wall and grasp his chin to hold his head to the side so I could devour his mouth while I took over and fucked the ass he liked to stick out and tease me with.

Eyes clenched shut, hand working regardless of the prickling guilt in the back of my head, I soaked in every muffled noise from him, the echo of spraying water nearly drowning out the sexy as hell whimpers I could hear passing those pouty lips.

He cursed, and I bit back a groan, knowing he came.

I cleared my throat on a near cough to show my disapproval, but I couldn't help the need coursing through me.

Panting, I tilted my head back, hips meeting my downward strokes...faster. Harder.

Isaac's shower cut off, the squeak of curtain rings over metal letting me know he stood a thin plastic material away. Did he stare at my shower stall, wondering what I did? He had to hear it at least, since I damn near strangled my dick.

Fuck.

Unable to help myself, I faced the curtain, watching it through rising steam from the hot water pounding my aching shoulders. I imagined Isaac's focus on me, my tightened abs rippling as I fucked my hand, envisioning it was his tight hole squeezing the life out of my length.

A gasp flew from my parted lips as tingles raced up through my balls.

"Need any help?"

I imagined him bent over, my hands holding his cheeks apart...on his knees, mouth wide open and wanting, his mischievous eyes focused upward on my face.

Oh fuck.

My balls erupted, and I grunted my release regardless of the fact he knew what I did hidden from the world like I was.

Fucking brat. But what had I thought would happen when he followed me into the bathroom? I should have stopped it before it even started.

Jaw clenched and legs weak, I rinsed myself and shut off my shower. Quiet rang in my ears. I yanked my towel from the wall and did a half-dry, needing to get the hell out of that bathroom—far from sin incarnate.

Tucking my towel tight around my waist, I inhaled until it hurt. Threw open my curtain with my gaze on the floor, intent on escape.

My periphery showed he held his towel at his side. Dried off a bit and angled away, giving my frozen dumb ass a chance to look at his naked perfection. I took it in like Eve must have with that first juicy bite of forbidden fruit.

Isaac's dick stood upright, a good inch shorter than mine, but the girth made my asshole clench. His length pulsed beneath my stare, bumping against his tight lower belly.

He turned toward me, and I tore my focus from him, still unable to make my feet move. He dried off his balls in my periphery, and I gave him my full attention with a side-eye stare, uncaring that he knew I watched, unmoved as I was.

My hands clenched at my sides, my entire body vibrating with need—to attack him. Touch him. Kiss and bite his lips, take his dick in my hand and jerk us off together. Pick him up and order him to wrap his pale legs around my waist so my dick had access to his virgin ass.

Fuck, I wanted him to be a virgin. Mine.

"Isaac," I heard myself whisper his name like a prayer at the thought of sinking deep inside his hot body and owning the fuck out of him.

"Yeah?" He dropped his hands to his sides, not covering his nakedness or making any attempts to ward me off or tell me no.

Fuck. Fucking hell...Christ.

Swallowing hard, I stalked away on reluctant feet, yanking the bathroom door open so hard in my attempt to escape temptation I was surprised the damn thing didn't rip from its hinges.

Isaac stayed shut up in the bathroom long enough that I had time to throw clothes over my damp body and get the hell downstairs to safety.

Jennifer sat in the living area at the bottom of the steps leading up to the boys' bunk room, obvious interest in her eyes as her gaze flicked over my wet head, my scruffy jaw, and down over my T-shirt. She looked away just as quickly before reaching my groin that wouldn't have tightened beneath her wandering eyes for anything.

Jaw still set, I settled in the recliner to her right, facing the stairs.

"You must be beat," she said with a smile in her voice like always. "You guys moved a ton of rocks today."

I grunted an affirmative. Lifting boulder-sized chunks of granite all day, the largest in the various piles due to Chris and me being the only big guys in our group, had done my muscles in. But exhaustion lay far from my mind.

"The weather will be perfect for a campfire tonight."

I grunted another affirmative.

"Usually the first evening is the best, the kids riding the high of being cooped up in the bus all day. Excitement and lots of praise and worship time."

It'd rained when we arrived at the hostel the night before, the rambunctious kids trapped in the room Jennifer and I sat in. A handful of other kids scattered around the room waiting for dinner, some playing board games and two reading in their own corners.

"I was thinking..." Jennifer's voice trailed off in my consciousness as the stairs creaked, and every single brain cell I had focused on who descended.

I recognized the ripped jeans and black Vans as they appeared, and my pulse picked up as Isaac stepped into sight.

He wore a dark green shirt that always made his eyes greener than hazel. Lower arms slightly sunburned since I hadn't allowed the guys to take their shirts off while laboring outside.

Paler neck. Pouty lips. Pink cheekbones that had also gotten too much sun. Eyes focused on mine, full of heat and intent. And his damn smirk. I lusted to hold him down and fuck it right out of him until he whimpered and cried for me to let him come.

Caught by the kid's stare, all I could do was breathe, my hands grasping the recliner's worn armrests.

Isaac reached the floor, the knowing in his eyes like a punch to my gut. Our gazes glued as he ambled past, the set of his shoulders and the angle of his chin revealing a cockiness that intensified my desire to get a true taste of his sweet and spicy mouth.

I craved to have him boneless, sweat covered, and sated beneath me. Begging for me to stop because his ass had enough.

But I wanted to be wrecked by him too.

Refusing to turn my head to watch him pass into the kitchen area, I swallowed hard enough I coughed. My heart pounded in my chest, and I fought to focus on whatever Jennifer talked about. Something about two of our dating teens…she'd heard a rumor.

Her voice lowered, and I turned to face her fully, forcing myself to pay attention as the youth leader, the responsible one in charge of over a dozen teenagers.

"Sara's friend Marley told me she overheard her and Chris talking about sneaking away tonight."

That bit perked my ears up. That sounded like a damn good time if it were me and Isaac, but I frowned. "We'll need to keep an eye open."

Jennifer nodded, her gaze flitting over my face.

The light in her eyes made me uncomfortable as hell— like she imagined slinking off into the woods with me rather than sitting by the planned bonfire. She'd change her tune real quick if she knew who *I* wanted pressed up against a tree trunk.

Isaac moved around the dining area beyond Jennifer, helping our hosts prepare dinner even though he hadn't been on duty that evening. He smiled, carrying on a conversation with the elderly woman and carrying things to and from the table while Jennifer continued to chatter in my ear.

He placed napkins alongside each paper plate. Set out plasticware with precision, bending a few times to showcase his round ass in those jeans my fingers itched to rip from his body.

As though he could feel my stare, he glanced over his shoulder with hooded eyes and the damn smirk that plumped his lower lip.

Fuck.

Jaw once more clenching, I shifted my focus off him. If Isaac knew I watched him, others had to notice. None of the kids in the living room paid attention to me and Jennifer, I took note of while my gaze flitted around the spacious room.

"I think separating them would be best," Jennifer continued to speak, her countenance revealing nothing but attraction for me. Not even true concern for the two kids she discussed.

I agreed with her, deciding to stick close to Chris. The idea didn't turn me on, but knowing Isaac would be attached to him like he'd been since climbing on the bus definitely did.

At least if Isaac sat on Chris's other side, I wouldn't be faced with having him in direct line of sight. Less chance of my attention snagging on him—and getting caught by the others with sinful lust written across my face.

We started off the night with making s'mores, the kids all having to get their own sticks for roasting marshmallows. I stayed on Chris's heels as he and Isaac headed off with Sara and Marley in the direction of the woods, mere feet from the fire pit area.

The flames already reached upward into the sky as we burned old oak pallets, lighting the way toward the woods' edge.

Chris walked with Sara, leaning down to whisper in her ear. She giggled, glancing at Marley on her right.

Isaac slowed his step, bringing him alongside me. "Nice night."

I side eyed him, keeping my main focus on Chris and wondering what the hell the boys had up their sleeves.

"Kinda warm, though."

I grunted a noise he could take however he wanted.

"Gonna need another shower."

A flash of him with his head tipped back while fisting his length made me stumble over a root as we stepped into the woods.

"I think I used up most of the hot water," Isaac continued with a conversational tone, "but beating off never felt so satisfying."

"What?" I turned, giving him my full attention, sure I hadn't heard him right.

He grinned at me, half of his face lit by the fire, the other half cast in darkness from the night. "I said, the hot water beating over me never felt so satisfying."

Had I been so damn caught up in the memory of listening to him earlier in the day that I'd misheard? Shaking my head, I lifted my focus to check out the closest tree. A few branches hung low, offering perfect marshmallow sticks.

I reached up, pulling one down.

Isaac stepped in close, keeping me distracted, the clean scent of his soap and cinnamon reaching me through the pine needles and leaf litter beneath our feet. Even the waft of woodsmoke from the fire couldn't erase him from my nose.

Drool coated my mouth at the memory of his taste. Sweet and innocent. Hungry and fumbling for more.

Definitely a virgin.

"Need any help?" he asked too damn close to my ear.

I scuttled sideways, focusing on stripping the smaller twigs off the branch I'd ripped from the tree rather than how he made my groin ache. "I'm good."

"I'll bet you are," he murmured, heading back the way we'd come, swaying his ass enough that I knew he did so on purpose.

Damn brat.

Scowling, I stalked after him, realizing we needed to have a talk. But how and where? Getting him alone for such a chat would put me in a seriously compromised situation where I wouldn't be able to choose right. My flesh would rule, I had no doubt.

I should've been in a constant state of prayer while approaching the small table that held the marshmallows, chocolate pieces, and graham crackers. I should've been begging for His strength as I shoved my marshmallow-tipped stick close to the fire.

Heat singed my face as I stared at the flickering flames rather than acknowledging the too-young man a seat away from me doing the same.

I glanced at Chris's chair and found it empty.

Damnit.

I turned to scan the back yard, my gaze landing on and dismissing every kid in sight—including Marley who sat with a few other girls.

Jennifer hovered around the table, handing out s'mores supplies.

Shit.

I dropped my stick into the fire and stood.

Isaac whistled a song behind me as I stalked back toward the woods, but I didn't pay attention other than to noting he continued on with Kumbaya in perfect tune.

Quick, quiet footsteps took me back to where Isaac and I had collected our marshmallow sticks. I studied the direction I'd last seen Chris and Sara. A dozen or so strides deeper into the woods and I found them.

Lips locked, Chris's hand up Sara's shirt, her arms around his neck as he palmed her breast.

I cleared my throat, and they tore away from one another, Sara moving quicker than Chris who didn't seem to care as much about being caught. "Inside," I commanded, my tone hard. "Now."

My first true failing as a youth leader had my heart dropping into my stomach, guilt rising to fill my chest.

And since I couldn't have the other kids thinking I was a pushover, I decided on a harsh penalty for the two teens breaking the no-touch love teachings of the church.

Had it been a simple kiss, no seeking hands, I might have taken it a bit easier on them.

But I knew Chris, had been warned by Pastor Bram of the kid's reputation at the public school for chasing girls. Turned out, he'd gotten a young woman from the church pregnant a few years earlier.

At fifteen.

I sat them down in the living room and preached at them as the pastor would do—and made a few phone calls that ended their quasi-missions trip to Maine.

Chapter 14
Isaac

I whistled as loud as I could, the way I'd promised to do for Chris if he and Sara didn't make it back before Malachi noticed their absence. At least I'd managed to distract our youth leader, allowing the two to sneak off for a little bit of time.

My whistle to alert Chris didn't work.

Malachi stormed toward to the hostel a few minutes later, Chris and Sara on his heels, the little blonde's head hung in shame. Chris glanced my way, his lips in a tight line, and shook his head.

Fucking busted.

I wondered if he would rat me out for my part in helping him get her alone for the time they had. Lucky fuck had at least ten minutes with her. I hoped he'd at least gotten a handful of tits.

My first marshmallow burned, but I toasted two more perfectly and scarfed them both down before Malachi returned.

Chris and Sara didn't.

He spoke a little while with Jennifer off to the side before she headed toward the hostel.

Malachi called the group around the fire to order and spoke a devotional like the leader always did for the nights we would be in Maine. His focus was on no-touch love. Obedience to God's word. Honoring those in authority.

Short, not sweet, and definitely unplanned—brought on by what had transpired in the woods, I didn't doubt.

I sat slouched in my chair like usual whenever someone preached, my arms crossed. Rather than staring into the fire and ignoring the words spoken, I gave Malachi my full attention. Stare unwavering.

Silently begging him to look at me, to question his own stance on what he taught.

Think on how he'd kissed me.

Licked at my mouth.

Jerked off in the shower and stared at my stiff dick that afternoon like he'd wanted to touch. Taste. Take.

He didn't appear to remember jack shit and ignored my presence a seat away which annoyed the fuck out of me.

Jennifer never returned to the fire, so I didn't get asked to pull out my guitar from its case leaning against the back of my chair. I sure as fuck didn't offer.

When all the guys went upstairs later that night, Chris lay on his bunk, facing the wall.

I stripped down to my boxers, my attention on Malachi rather than my friend who didn't roll over to acknowledge any of us.

Keeping his back to me like he'd done prior to showering, Malachi pulled off his shirt, giving my drool factory something to get excited about. Rippling muscle beneath golden tan skin across his wide shoulders. Full-sleeved tattoos.

He pushed his jean shorts down, allowing me a nice view of his ass encased in blue boxer briefs that time—he flicked the lights off, leaving us in darkness, the memory of him etched in my mind.

I slid onto my bed, too hot to climb inside the sleeping bag.

Guys shifted around us getting comfortable, same as the night before, but most stayed quiet after the long day of laboring for our hosts. I stared at the empty bunk overhead, listening to Malachi breathe beside me, mere feet away.

Snores and heaving exhales eventually filled the room, and still I lay wide awake, my skin buzzing with awareness.

Turning my head, I could barely make out the image of Malachi from the room's lone window beyond him, an old curtain allowing in a sliver of moonlight.

Eyes open, he too stared overhead. Pecs prominent, hands clasped on his stomach. The bulge beneath his torso caused my fingertips to itch. I shifted on my cot-like mattress, my dick's growing discomfort making it difficult to get comfortable.

Malachi turned his head toward me, but his face lay in shadow. "Go to sleep, Isaac," he whispered, my groin tightening at hearing him say my name.

"Can't," I whispered back.

He didn't move, didn't speak, and I wondered how clearly he could see my face, my eyes in the darkness. Did he look at the outline of my body? I slid my hand down over my stomach to rearrange my own bulge, even though it wasn't restricted by tight briefs. Good thing, boxers.

Malachi's breath caught, and I smirked, giving myself an extra squeeze, enough that my hips lifted.

"Isaac," he warned, his own lower half moving on his mattress.

"Hmm?"

"Go to sleep."

I released my dick and let out a heavy exhale, facing away from him so he could check out my ass all he wanted.

No whispered curse rose like I'd hoped to hear, but I caught the rustle of material, like he adjusted the ache I'd caused.

At least, that was what I hoped for. Pretty sure I still smirked when I drifted off fuck knew how much later.

The next morning while we ate breakfast, Chris's and Sara's dads showed up together at the hostel's front door.

My jaw stopped working to chew the Raisin Bran we'd been offered for breakfast in those single-serve boxes I needed four of to fill my stomach.

Chris hadn't looked at me that morning and hadn't spoken a word to me, even when I'd whispered his name while we'd been getting dressed for the day. He'd merely shaken his head and disappeared into the bathroom.

He didn't come down for breakfast, and I realized when his dad walked in that Malachi had taken consequences to the extreme.

He'd sent the two to bed early the night before, not allowing them further interaction with the group. He'd called their dads to come pick them up. Didn't allow either Chris or Sara to come to breakfast, I noted, glancing around the girls' table to find her absent too.

Malachi motioned the two men into the living room and around the corner.

The rest of us in the kitchen/dining area remained quiet while eating, everyone glancing around and wondering what was going on even though it was obvious. The sound of plastic spoons on plastic bowls and chewing were the only silence breakers.

Jennifer sat at the end of the table, seemingly caught up in her own cereal.

Murmured voices reached us, but even with me being the closest to the three men, I couldn't make out what they said.

Minutes later, Chris and Sara followed their dads out the hostel's front door, their bags in hand. Feet shuffling, their heads downcast.

No one questioned why they would leave without looking our way or saying goodbye. No one's voice rose in inquiry about what had happened that was so terrible Malachi would send them home.

But rumors abounded throughout the day as we got to work. Malachi's thin-lipped scowl and silence reminded me so much of my own dad when disappointed that my stomach cramped.

Could have been the Raisin Bran, but my guts churned at how he'd handled the situation. It wasn't like he'd caught them fucking. I doubted Chris would have talked Sara into letting him have her virginity out in the woods, a mere ten minutes into their first time alone.

For a simple kiss? Maybe not so simple?

Had she gone down on him or had he buried his face between her thighs?

Who the hell knew—all sorts of whispered ideas rose from the other teens whenever Malachi and Miss Jennifer weren't in close proximity.

Eventually, my anger, my disgust over how he'd done exactly as my dad would have rose to the point that I couldn't look at him. I avoided him when we finished the rock wall and went down to the lake to cool off with a swim, one of the things I usually enjoyed the most seeing as how I'd spent lots of time at my family's cottage on Lake Wallenpaupack.

I sat with my journal in hand, scribbling nonsensical pissiness while the other kids splashed and laughed, Chris and Sara seemingly forgotten.

Even the sight of sun-kissed skin and tattoos down our youth pastor's right arm couldn't hold me enthralled.

Malachi Foley was a judgmental asshole, a fucking liar of the worst sort.

And I was so over him.

Chapter 15
Malachi

Isaac ignored me the next couple of days, making the hours longer and the evenings even more brutal. I'd planned nightly devotionals, but the interest he'd shown with his hazel-eyed stare the first night I spoke around the campfire had vanished, and it bothered the shit out of me.

And then...then he played his guitar at Jennifer's insistence while the ring of kids around him sang. Lips pursed, he plucked notes, strummed like a goddamn pro, drawing me deeper into his grasp. Giving me breath. Desire beyond the physical.

My heart ached to join him, to hear his talent, knowing his dreams would take him far away—which was best, for me at least.

Him, I doubted, but more out of fear due to his flirting nature that had completely cut off toward me during those days of laboring in the sun for the glory of God.

I hated how he wouldn't acknowledge me when I should have rejoiced that he'd appeared to have gotten over his pursuit of what could never be.

I loved that he slept beside me. Cursed that I couldn't reach out and touch, to span the short distance separating our bunks.

My gut hardened over the decision to send Chris and Sara home, and I didn't doubt Isaac's anger stemmed from taking his one friend from him, but it'd been necessary—as a warning to myself, not just the teens.

Isaac had too much talent and was too beautiful to end up six feet under in an early grave like Brian. Spewing the shit of my past and the reasons I denied us would have opened his eyes, but I also would have ousted my biggest sin, the part of me that would keep me from serving God in the future like I'd promised my mom.

Isaac sulked in his passive aggressive way, but I wouldn't relent in my silence or refusal to give him attention outside of sharing God's Word with him in a group setting.

Like a petulant child with his candy taken away, he pouted, dragging his feet about helping around the hostel or taking his part in whatever chores he'd been assigned.

And that lower lip tempted me to the point of pain. I woke every morning with a raging hard on. Jacked off in the shower soon after crawling out of bed and a second time once the day's work finished.

Yet still I ached, my heart and mind just as much as my body.

With guilt, with concern for his withdrawal from the rest of the group. While the rest of us swam in the lake, he sat off alone. While we all sprawled around the campfire and shared ghost stories and memories of past retreats, he picked at his fingernails or imaginary lint off his jeans. At least he continued to play his guitar for our time of worship, and every night, I tried not to stare while soaking his talent—his gift—in.

With proper guidance, he could make it big in Nashville. Half Korean, his beauty would catch attention. Add in his broody nature, that "it" factor agents and record labels looked for, and I didn't doubt his successful future.

And I hadn't even heard him sing. But I could imagine how he'd sound, considering the natural husk to his voice and how well he'd whistled that first night I'd sent Chris and Sara home.

But how to point Isaac in the correct direction? How could I encourage him on the right path if he wouldn't even acknowledge me or the words of my nightly teachings?

Our final night in Maine we went out beneath starlit skies, crickets and night insects' calls rising enough to be heard over the fire I helped our host create. I ended up beside Isaac somehow—not my doing—for the devotional.

The scent of cinnamon clung to him and filled my nose.

Clearing my throat, I glanced around our circle of kids, smiling. Jennifer beamed at me from a few seats away on my right.

"Tonight we're going to talk about showing others grace and mercy."

"Like you did Chris?" Isaac muttered under his breath, his first words to me in days.

I ignored him, hoping others hadn't heard while opening my Bible on my lap to the passage I'd bookmarked earlier in the book of Micah. Guilt and anger mingled together in my head, and I fought them off before beginning the evening's message.

I read a highlighted verse in chapter seven which spoke of God pardoning sin and forgiving transgressions. How His anger didn't last, but His mercy did.

Isaac let out a quiet snort, and I paused, considering calling him out for his disrespectful behavior.

But I chose mercy, understanding he was pissed off over his only friend being sent home.

I kept my Bible open but lifted my gaze to the faces turned my way, the apt focus I knew I would only have for a few moments before attention spans ended and the shifting began.

Feelings of incompetence rose as I preached the Word to a bunch of impressionable kids. Ones, I hoped still had yet to make life-changing choices like I'd done.

My stomach twisted as flashes of my memory, my past sins, filled my head, and I ended the devotional sooner than planned, looking to Jennifer to start our time of singing.

"Isaac?" she asked, leaning forward to catch sight of him on my other side. "Would you play for us again tonight?"

He didn't answer, and I forced my focus on his face.

More imaginary lint disappeared off his jeans, and I glanced at the back of his chair. No guitar propped against it as it had been in the previous couple of nights. "Isaac."

"What?" He snipped, glaring at me when he lifted his head.

Our gazes clashed, heat and energy rippling between us that I feared others would notice.

"Jennifer asked if you would play for our singing tonight," I stated, keeping my tone conversational when I wanted to throttle the brat. Kiss his mouth. Bite his nipples. Fondle his—

"Nope." He popped the P.

"Go get your guitar," I ordered quietly, fighting the desire to grab hold of his shirt and shake the shit out of him. "Now."

His eyes narrowed, but he hopped up, his folding chair toppling, and he stormed toward the hostel.

Jennifer stood to go after him, but I grasped her arm. "I'll talk to him."

I righted his overturned chair, my stomach hard, knowing as the authority figure I had to do something, say something.

Even if heading into a dark building—alone—could lead to my fall from grace.

Or maybe he didn't want me anymore with how he'd changed after I'd sent Chris and Sara home. I hoped yet hated that might be the case.

The hostel sat quiet, making my exhales loud. I stood in the entryway, the dim kitchen on my right, the living area on the opposite, and the stairs leading upward beyond the lamp's glow left on at an end table beside a couch.

Darkness shaded the top of the hallway, the way to the second floor impenetrable by a human's eye.

The path represented so much more than mere stairs in my mind, but I didn't have a choice. Prayers should have whispered in my head, ones of delivery and protection against temptation, but my thoughts sat quiet, no whispered pleas for help from an omniscient God.

Perhaps Isaac would descend—I could wait for him there, and we could talk in the light of the living room. No noise sounded from overhead, so I filled my lungs and crossed the room with sure steps, even though my heart faltered and my legs shook.

My lips pressed into a thin line as I moved up the stairs, the muffled singing voices outside letting me know the youth group continued on without us.

"Isaac?" I called out as I neared the top of the stairs.

He didn't answer, and I turned into the open room housing the guys' bunks to find him sitting on the floor between our beds, knees drawn up and head against the wall.

Even in the dim light filtering through the window, I could see he scowled at me. "What?"

"I told you to get your guitar."

"I'm not playing tonight."

I stayed put in the entryway, fighting my body's desire to go to him. But we needed to talk and not with a bed hindering my view of his face.

I rounded my bunk and hesitated at the end, less than eight feet separating us as I stood over him, hands shoving into my jeans' pockets.

"What's the problem?" I asked, expecting he needed to unload his anger on me in order for us to move forward.

"I want you." His pissy tone suggested he hated that fact.

A lack of desire filled his one eye unhidden by shadow, but his words punched like a fist to my gut, stealing my breath all the same.

"You're too young to know that," I spewed with a ragged voice rather than admitting the truth.

"I'm *legal*," he shot back, "and I know *you* want *me*."

I lifted my chin, attempting to give him the same haughty look. "I don't."

"Liar." He stood, putting us on more an even level, and I stilled all except for my dick swelling with life of its own. Every cell in my body tensed, and even though I slid my hands out of my pockets, I readied to fight rather than flee which would've have been smarter.

Three steps brought him within touching distance, and we both breathed heavily, staring through the charged air simmering between us. Hands fisted, I trembled as his focus slipped down to my mouth.

My lips tingled at the memory of his touching mine. Tongues dueling. His panted breaths against my mouth, the sweetness of cinnamon I wanted to inhale until he filled my lungs fully.

"Liar," he whispered again, moving one last step.

Mere inches separated us.

Long eyelashes blinked, the lust for sin in his eyes tightening my balls against my body.

My mind emptied of all rational thought, 3 dictating my brainwaves.

His hands touched my hips as I lowered my head to suck his exhale into my lungs. Lips hovered close, hot breath mingling.

Need. So fucking *much—*

I moved with force, taking his mouth in a bruising kiss, one hand reaching up his back to grasp his neck, the other on his ass as I shoved him, slamming his back and my forearms against the wall.

Lithe muscle pressed against me rather than melting, our fight for more one of unrestrained passion rather than submission, and that lit my skin on fire. Shoving my tongue into his mouth earned me a whimpered moan that had pre-cum leaking from my dick, but he didn't relax in my arms, didn't just let me have my way with him like Brian had always done.

His hunger for me rivaled mine for him, the kind that consumed. Burned.

Isaac fumbled at my zipper with desperate fingers, muffled curses against my mouth until he got the access he wanted. No hesitation—the kid shoved his hand beneath my boxer's waistband, going straight for my dick.

His firm grip closed around me, causing my length to jerk in his hold and my entire body to shudder.

I cursed against his mouth, his hand sheer torture, fingers soft...so fucking perfect.

More.

I released his ass to grab his dick through his shorts.

"Oh fuck." He gasped, ripping his mouth from mine to lean his head against the wall.

I stared at his hooded eyes while we both panted, my hand squeezing him hidden by darkness.

"Fuck...touch it. Touch me. Please."

My fingers didn't shake while yanking open his zipper and shoving his shorts and boxers to mid-thigh.

"Oh shit." He gulped, losing his hold on my length as I put space enough between us to push mine down as well.

My entire body a raging furnace, I came at him like a rabid dog, taking his lips again. Pressing our groins together, swallowing his whimpers as I closed my fist around our dicks.

Enough pre-cum from both of us coated my hand, the kind of slickness that created one hell of a fist fuck. He shuddered as I jerked us off, my tongue fucking his mouth in time with my hand gliding over hot, hard flesh.

My heartbeat pounded in my ears as lust overrode all my senses.

Nothing but trouble would come from our sins, but in that heated moment of passion flaring between us, I didn't care. Couldn't. Too much need had built up, and I had no strength to deny him.

Us.

We'd been on the edge of combustion since meeting. Karma, fate, temptation...whatever had brought our lonely souls together couldn't be set aside for someone else's greater good. Selfishness led—and I followed.

Chapter 16

Isaac

Over Malachi Foley, my ass.

A sense of breathlessness lightened my head, and I turned my face away from the demanding mouth I'd told myself the past couple of days I didn't want in order to fill my lungs.

My hips thrust in time with his downward tug over our lengths pressed tightly together. I'd dreamed of his hands on me, our dicks in his grasp, his hot breath on my neck. The reality of Malachi and me together shattered all my porn-fed fantasies.

Silk and steel, slick...ball tingling perfection that flooded my mouth with drool.

"Fuck. Oh fuck." I swallowed hard, the feel of his hard length against mine, heat, wetness…his firm grip foreign and knee-weakening.

"Mmm," he moaned his agreement, the rumble of his chest drawing my balls up tight.

"G-gonna come, Malachi. Fucking hell," I gasped, thrusting and trembling.

"Yes," he groaned, peering down between us. "I want to see it."

Too dark—too damn dark.

I stared like he did, trying to make out what I could hear, the schlicking noise of a pre-cum soaked hand sliding and twisting, rubbing and tugging. Panting, I fought off the brewing in my balls, the impending explosion.

Doomed.

No power.

"Give it to me, Isaac," he whispered against my ear, all rasp and sex.

At the first sense of cum erupting, I grabbed hold of Malachi's head and brought his mouth back to mine.

My teeth clanked against his, our tongues wrestling as we rutted against each other. He swallowed my grunted whimpers, pressing me tight to the wall.

My dick jerked in his fist, spurting.

Head spinning, I mentally spewed curses, trembling in Malachi's hold. My entire body shook, threatening to drop me to my knees.

"Yes," he groaned again and shuddered, wetness smearing between our groins as he milked us both with a firm grip, coaxing every last dribble from our lengths. "Christ..."

Gasping, he tilted his forehead against mine, sharing the air between our lips as my fingers stayed speared in his silky hair.

Every muscle in my body went lax, his hard mass keeping me in place.

"Fuck," he whispered harshly, giving our flagging lengths one last pull.

"Mmm," I agreed, soaking in the tingles racing over my skin, through my blood. Mind empty, I breathed in the scent of his soap and dryer sheets, my hands sliding down to hold his shoulders.

Muscles bunched beneath his T-shirt under my touch.

A shudder rippled through me as a sigh escaped, my lips curving upward over Malachi giving me another first.

So. Fucking. Good.

He stepped away, leaving me sagging against the wall, and my wet groin cooled without his touch.

"Damnit." He ran his clean hand through his hair, down over his face, the rasp of his palm against whiskers making me want to feel them on the backs of my thighs while he ate my ass.

My smile widened. "Deny you want me now."

Like a heavy fog falling down over my head, I could see the shroud of guilt blanket him, and my triumphant grin faded, a frigid chill replacing the warmth inside me.

Malachi looked away, his head lowered.

"Don't." I bit out the word—but he stalked off toward the bathroom before I could beg him to not erect a wall of regret between us.

Water ran, and I couldn't move, my entire body as spent as my limp dick still hanging out in the open. I watched the bathroom door. Waited for him to decide his thoughts and feelings on what we'd done.

Malachi returned with a handful of wet paper towels but kept his distance, his expression closed off. Hard, from what I could see from the moonlight filtering through the window.

My heart seized inside my chest.

He'd cleaned up. Zippered up. "You need to change." His husky voice twitched my dick as I glanced down.

We'd made a mess of my favorite green shirt.

I ripped it off overhead, my hand shaking as I balled it up and tossed it into my dirty laundry bag beside me.

He gave me the wet towels, and I muttered a thanks while taking them from him to clean myself. Heart like a lump of stone in my chest, I wiped up, and he rifled through my gym bag at the foot of my bed for a clean shirt.

"We shouldn't have done that," he whispered, remorse lining his voice and twisting my guts up tight, erasing the after-tingles I usually enjoyed from emptying my balls.

I tucked my dick away, wanted to argue, but what could I say that would sway him to my side?

A youth pastor jerking off the pastor's son in a hot as fuck make out session.

Even I could see the taboo in that.

It didn't make me want him any less though.

"This can't happen again, Isaac." Hardness edged his tone, and I finally lifted my gaze to his.

He tossed me a clean shirt.

His eyes promised we wouldn't, that he refused to even think on it.

Malachi voiced his desired fate for us, but I'd broken him down once. I could do it again.

While I pulled on my shirt, he bent to retrieve my guitar from beneath my bunk.

"I need a few moments alone," he muttered, handing me my case.

I wanted to assure him that we *would* happen again, that I wouldn't rest until I made it so.

Malachi could stand firm and beg his God for forgiveness each and every time we came together, but we would.

I refused to think anything contrary.

Without another word, I brushed passed him, my knees weak but my steps light rather than dragging with guilt like his probably did. I rode the high of having the best orgasm of my life, and nothing would take it from me.

I could still taste Malachi on my lips and smell a hint of dryer sheets. Curling my fingers into a fist, I attempted to hang onto the feel of his hair against my palm.

Our dicks, hot and wet, gliding together in the best fist fuck a man could have.

Warmth flushed through me from head to toes at the memory of his groans, his hot breath ghosting over my neck.

Shit, I need to calm the fuck down.

Biting back my grin, I rounded the hostel into view of the campfire and the others still singing.

Miss Jennifer's smile lit as she caught sight of me, her lips faltering to stay tilted up as she glanced behind me and found Malachi absent. Fuck, how I wanted to brag about leaving him sated up in the guys' bunks.

Instead, I sat on my chair and pulled out my guitar. Plucked a few notes, adjusting what needed to be set straight while breathing in the woodsmoke and night air, and I found the key the youth group sang in, my playing taking over the lead.

But I didn't hear a goddamn word coming from their mouths. I got lost in the strings of my guitar while reliving what Malachi and I had just shared. Hopefully, the first of many such run-ins.

We finished a minute later, and Miss Jennifer thanked me.

They sang another song while I accompanied them, but still Malachi didn't join us.

Had he dropped to his knees to pray? Cried tears of repentance for putting his hands on me? Eating at my mouth and swallowing my cries while he brought us both to orgasm?

The first not of my hand...

My lips twitched for the tenth or so time since leaving him upstairs, and I wondered if he knew that truth while Miss Jennifer's soprano praised God.

Deciding I needed to tell him that I wanted him to have *all* my firsts, I kept playing when the praise song ended and morphed it into one I'd written. A cryptic song that if the meaning wasn't known could be taken as God and church approved.

Well, it'd been written as a worship song—just not to the One my company thought worthy of.

The other kids stayed quiet in the night, Miss Jennifer allowing me to pluck a tune I'd written in the previous month that had nothing to do with God but his creation. The man of my obsession.

But they wouldn't know. The obscure words could be taken either way.

Still riding the high of release, I closed my eyes, the decision coming as easily as Malachi had pulled my orgasm from my body.

The crackle of the fire accompanied my song—my voice—rising into the night, and with my eyes closed, I sang praises to him, my muse.

The one who drew me in.

Broken and bleeding.

Needing what only he could give.

But he wasn't capitalized like a proper noun, simply a man. The one I longed to worship.

The one my soul craved.

Chapter 17
Malachi

Devastation had me sinking into my bunk, and I sat hunched over, my elbows on knees and my head in my hands.

Failure. Sin.

Of the worst possible sort.

Kissing Isaac in the janitor's closet had been bad enough, but touching his flesh? Lusting for it? Hearing and feeling him come undone in my arms, his hard, lithe body pressed against my front?

Hell.

Eyes dry, I lifted my head to heaven, peering into darkness and wondering if the Holy Spirit intervened for me like the Word promised for those who didn't have the strength to pray.

So weak to the lusts of the flesh.

"Put on the whole armor of God," I repeated what I'd preached dozens of times, the encouragement I gave the teens to help them face life's decisions. Easier said than done.

If we didn't plan to leave the next morning, I would have called Pastor Bram and told him to come get his son like I'd done with Chris and Sara's fathers. Knowing I didn't have the strength to deny us, I needed him far from my sight, my reach.

And yet my heart hurt for him. I understood his circumstances, the attraction to men, the desperate desire for attention—both of which I suffered from as well.

I craved physical touch like I required breath. Wanted words of affirmation and edification spoken out loud rather than read between the pages of a leatherbound, God-inspired, Bible.

No spirit of God filled me. No sense of peace in mentally acknowledging my sins I couldn't speak out loud and couldn't beg forgiveness for.

Longing for Isaac's nearness and feeling more alone than I ever had, I got to my feet. Hurried down the stairs and into the night.

Just damn *needing*.

I caught the sound of a guitar first.

Then a male voice, one I recognized even though I'd never heard Isaac sing.

Rounding the hostel, I pulled up short as his husky tenor swept over me.

Not a song I knew, but I stood unmoving, breath and stare ensnared, caught up in the purity of his tone. The rasp that would make anyone swoon, male or female alike.

Jennifer and the kids sat still as stone, staring at Isaac as he lifted his voice into the spark-lit night, the stars overhead baptizing his dark head.

Desire swelled in the deepest parts of my soul, beyond physical lust, beyond wanting affection. His tone swirled inside my head, descended through my body, and caught me up in a vortex I couldn't stop even if God lassoed His righteousness around my chest to hold me back.

Isaac's eyes opened, and his focus turned toward me as though he felt my stare, that mouth, those lips still moving and pouring magic from his lungs. Tempting me to believe the truth of the song he'd written.

He sang his words of brokenness and longing to *me*—not God like the others doubtless believed.

Broken.

Bleeding.

His tone rasped, ripping through my chest as our gazes held.

Wanting to fall. Worship you.

Needing you.

Without words to beg for your touch.

I stood struck dumb. Enthralled. My body responded to the lure of his voice, manipulating my desires as easily as his fingers strummed the guitar's strings.

His voice and the notes faded into the dark night too damn soon, leaving a buzz in my ears as our gazes remained locked in the sudden stillness. My entire body tingled to erase the distance between us. I craved his exhales to flood my lungs, craved to slide my lips over his skin. To lick and taste. Fill up my mind, my soul, with everything he would allow me.

Hoots, hollers, and clapping erupted, blinking me back to reality, tearing my focus off his face.

The fire burned bright yellow and gold in the night as though reaching for heaven, sparks fading up into darkness overhead.

Disappearing, their lives snuffed out.

As though they never existed, the memory of them fading with every heartbeat thumping in my ears.

"Malachi," Jennifer called, and I forced a smile and my feet forward, every inch of my body *alive*.

I took the seat I'd emptied earlier, putting me beside Isaac who still sat with his guitar in hand.

Electric waves pulsed from him, raising the hairs on my arms even though I refused to look at him. Rubbing my palms over my jean shorts, I told myself to get a hold on my thoughts, the tumbling desires lighting me up like a damn rainbow after the rain clouds dissipated.

"Will you sing another?" Jennifer asked Isaac, and the kids all piped up their request.

Isaac didn't say a word surprisingly but started playing without his usual rebellious attitude, his head bent over his guitar.

A tune I recognized emerged rather than a hidden-meaning song he'd written for me, thank God.

I let out a heavy exhale and closed my eyes, trying to focus on the words he sang about being beautifully created. Wholly accepted. Not a more popular worship hymn, not specifically mentioning God. A song that could be taken as a love ballad had it not been created by one of contemporary Christian music's most popular singers.

Some kids joined in the chorus, but most simply listened to the perfection of Isaac's voice.

Chords from the song rose inside me, and I hummed along without thought. Another verse...the chorus...my lips parted, and I joined with him, our voices entwining as we sang in the kind of pure harmony I'd only heard once before.

Pain lanced through my chest, but I couldn't stop, couldn't contain the draw to sing along with Isaac and create such utter perfection my entire body ached.

The others fell silent around us, but I kept my eyes closed, blending my voice with his. Basked in the warmth radiating inside me—and not the peace of God in the purity of worship. Adrenaline rushed through my veins, seeming to wake my soul and cause my heartbeat to drum in my chest.

Our notes wove together, tight. In unity—as though our souls entwined, never to be put asunder.

A sudden release of tension, of guilt, of remorse left me lightheaded.

Giddy.

Wanting to grin like a fool in love...

I breathed smoke-scented air easily between the lines we sang together, the oxygen a life-giving force that tingled my extremities. My lips smiled on their own, a lack of tension and stress loosening my muscles.

No desire to escape filled me. I *lived* in the moment, wanting to spread my arms wide to hold onto the sense of happiness flooding through me.

Pure joy, the kind I'd been searching for my whole life. The kind God's word promised but hadn't ever gifted.

Our song ended.

And wild applause ensued.

I opened my eyes and met Isaac's stare. His soft expression, the flush on his cheeks, and his relaxed posture brought on a craving for *more* that had me shifting in my seat.

"That was amazing!" Jennifer gushed, her grasp on my arm pulling me away from the person I wanted to lose myself in.

Reality slapped me like a hand to the face, and I blinked her into focus as my heart stuttered.

"The two of you...just wow! Seriously, the two of you sound beautiful together!"

We would be *beautiful together.*

"You need to sing a duet in church. Holy cow..." Jennifer's voice faded from my consciousness as I glanced around the ring of kids, the firelight playing on their smiling faces.

Filled with the love of God, wrapped up in emotionalism.

Isaac and I had done that for them through song—but neither of our hearts had been in the right place when singing the words meant to praise our maker.

The thought hit me like an axe to the chest, stealing my joy entirely. Sweat broke out on my brow, and thickness in my throat kept me from swallowing hard like I needed to do.

Immorality. An abomination.

My pulse raced over the truth that the wages of sin was death, and I jerked my head back toward Isaac to find him tucking his guitar away. I'd been responsible for one young man's demise.

No way in hell would I send another there to burn for all eternity.

I became the avoider, staying as far away from Isaac as possible. And my heart ached because of it, the hollowness in my chest intensifying to the point I often gasped from the pain.

The draw of him, the longing in my soul to sing, to touch, to taste, was more than I could fight in close proximity.

Once home from our retreat, moving through daily living proved easier. With school out, the only time I had to feel the energy between us that my soul craved was Sunday morning worship and Wednesday night youth group.

The first Sunday, I stayed away from him until I couldn't. He exited the church's front doors rather than sneaking out the side like usual with Chris and Tyler.

Every member of the church walked through the line, bringing him closer. My pulse thrummed, making me hyperaware of the buzz of energy swirling inside me.

"Malachi," he stated in greeting, raising the hairs on my arms beneath my suit. His eyes studied my face as I offered him a brief nod, shaking his hand and pulling it back as quickly as possible.

My entire body itched to haul him toward me, wrap him up in my arms, and take all his worries, his future hurts onto my own shoulders.

I moved my attention to the couple beyond him rather than responding to his greeting, smiling and thanking them for coming that morning.

Isaac moved off, leaving a crushing weight on my chest. I couldn't breathe and didn't have the focus or energy to disregard the shame of being an asshole.

Guilt crept in.

As his youth pastor, it was my duty to encourage, edify, and love the teenagers—including Isaac. Shunning him was unacceptable.

But I couldn't find it in me to seek him out to apologize. Doing so would only put us in a compromising situation I feared I'd fail.

Wednesday, he sat silent in his folded chair while the kids sang, their voices echoing in the gymnasium. No guitar. Arms crossed, slouched like a brat once he realized I refused to interact with him. I ignored his whispers with Chris and Tyler, his attempts to gain my attention. I ignored the urge to talk to him since I couldn't discern the Holy Spirit's guidance from my fleshly desires.

The next week passed in the same manner, my feigned disinterest obvious enough that Isaac didn't even look at me, thank God.

That Friday, I breathed a bit easier, knowing I still had forty-eight hours before having to bear his presence, his stares from the congregation again.

Pastor Bram knocked on my office door, poking his head in when I called out for him to enter. "Busy?" he asked with a smile.

I shook my head, grateful for the interruption of thoughts I couldn't keep from wandering toward his son—and the pastor's ignorance over what had transpired between us. "Come on in."

His smile faltered as he sat in the chair across my desk. "So, Isaac..."

I stilled, fighting to keep my smile in place, my eyes unshielded or burdened by guilt. I also knew better than to open my mouth, so I let him work through whatever he wanted to say to me as a few tense minutes passed.

"He's really struggling. More than usual." Pastor Bram lifted his eyes to the ceiling as though in silent prayer for his son. "I know all I can do is trust God to lead his steps, but I'm finding it difficult to even think about Isaac going off to a whole other state without guidance. No matter how much truth or scripture I give him, he's unresponsive. He'll be eighteen in a few weeks, and I can't force him to stay here at home. I'm deeply troubled for his soul."

As was I—for both of us—but I kept my thoughts to myself.

"I was wondering if you would meet with him in a non-church setting," Pastor Bram continued, glancing my way once more. "Become his friend rather than just his youth pastor if possible. Maybe he'd be willing to open up to you if you build a rapport outside these doors."

A close relationship.

If only he knew how close we'd already become, the feelings and the push and pull between us that had filled the night with gorgeous harmony when we'd been in Maine.

I cleared my throat while smoothing down my tie, knowing I didn't have a choice. My boss, my pastor, wanted me to counsel his son which meant God led me toward that path. I had to trust His light would steer my way, even though I feared it would end in my destruction.

"I can do that, yes, but I'd prefer to meet him here in my office if that's okay with you." Doing so would keep us from sinning again—I hoped. At least being on holy ground would make it easier for me to turn away from temptation.

Pastor Bram's face lit with the joy of the Lord. "Thank you."

He wouldn't be thanking me if he knew what trouble his son and I managed to get into when alone.

Chapter 18

Isaac

To top off the bullshit of my life, Dad and I got into it over Nashville.

Again.

And Mom sat silent at the dinner table Saturday night, refusing to back me up or even encourage Dad to just listen to what I had to say.

Aggravation kept me on edge, got my mind going. Only a couple weeks lay between me and my eighteenth birthday, but what held me back from leaving right away? With Dad and his focus on all things law and doing right, I expected he'd contact the police about me being a runaway or some shit.

But by the time they would catch up to me, I'd probably have turned eighteen.

Who else would attempt to stop me from seeking freedom early?

"It's too risky heading into the unknown," Dad repeated what he'd said before, but I didn't tell him I already had a plan, that I knew where I would go and what I would do. "If you need a year off from studies, stay here. Immerse yourself in God's word. Seek his will for your life before starting Bible college next fall."

I shoveled more mashed potatoes into my mouth to keep from telling him exactly what I thought about *his* plans for my life and how opposite they were from mine.

I ought to pack my bags and take off the second they fall asleep.

The idea made my blood race, but I couldn't leave without seeing Malachi again. I needed that opportunity to have him, to finish what we'd started. My body, my mind—my damn heart—demanded it, no matter how much I told myself I didn't want him, didn't like what he'd chosen to be.

I'd ridden a high from being with him in Maine, hearing his voice weave with mine—fucking magic.

But his avoidance of me began immediately after that bonfire. He wouldn't look at me as I'd laid in my bunk, staring at him until drifting off. He wouldn't talk to me after his regrets of getting us both off. The heaviness in my chest dragged my feet.

"I've set up a meeting for you and Malachi." Dad's firm tone would usually make me scowl.

I stopped chewing my steak, eyeing my dad. My stomach twisted up tight as fuck over whatever it was he had planned—or what the youth pastor might have told him.

"Since you won't share personal stuff with either of us," Dad said, motioning between him and Mom, "I thought he would be the next best choice."

Shit.

I released my held breath and finished chewing my mouthful of food. The cramp in my gut over the fear of being found out dissipated as quickly as it'd started, even though the adrenaline left me a little shaky.

Having Malachi all to myself behind closed doors? Yes, please and thank you. I didn't care where we got the chance to be alone, just that we would before I left.

"When?" I asked, trying to not show too much enthusiasm.

"Tomorrow morning before service," Dad said, his lips immediately thinning.

The disappointment lining his face no longer bothered me. Knowing what I did about myself, what I refused to share with my parents, ensured it was all I would ever be to the Bible-thumping, dogmatic ass who'd donated sperm to help give me life.

I nodded, acknowledging the meeting, and went back to eating, trying to hide the tremors in my hands.

A chance to have Malachi bend me over his desk. Fuck into my ass slow and deep, taking what I craved to gift him more than anything. I wanted him more than I did Nashville.

And the clash of that truth in my mind kept me awake long into the night, leaving me adrift, like I bobbed in an ocean with no land in sight. The clench of my guts returned as I worried over a man who'd turned my world upside down. Took first place over my dreams.

But I didn't regret it.

Malachi Foley made me feel...*things* I didn't understand. Couldn't name or even put into words. I just knew that no matter how much having him in my life had fucked shit up, I wouldn't have gone back to change the past even if I could.

At two in the morning, I grabbed my journal and spewed a bunch of gibberish even I couldn't make sense of.

Once I finished, my soul emptied, and I closed my eyes and dreamed about a reality where I got everything I wanted. A record deal. Screaming fans who accepted me exactly as I was.

And Malachi.

Beside me in my bed, loving me without hesitation. Unconditionally.

I drove to church with Dad the next morning, staring out the passenger window rather than having bagels and cream cheese with Mom. Trees whipped past as he quietly talked to me about sharing and being open with my thoughts and emotions. He encouraged me to be honest with a man who could be more than a youth pastor to me.

But after the dreams I'd floated in while sleeping, I would never be satisfied having Malachi for a mere friend. I *wanted* him to be more.

So much more.

Clamping my lips as though I agreed with Dad kept him from raising his voice at me. But I barely listened anyway since my heart raced and my thoughts filled with the "what ifs" over the meeting ahead. Damp palms, itching skin…I felt like I had hives, and nothing I did calmed my insides.

We pulled into the church's lot, pebbles crunching beneath the tires.

Malachi's old truck parked in his assigned spot, a pile of rust and mismatched quarter panels of various colors. Not the kind of vehicle I expected Dad approved of for a man in authority at a church, but I sure as hell did.

The truck sat imperfect.

Showing signs of having lived powerlessly beneath an onslaught of weather dished out on it.

Kinda sexy even.

My lips quirked as I climbed from Dad's car.

"Please be open with him," Dad stated for at least the tenth time, solidifying my desire to say absolutely jack shit to Malachi about anything personal. I wanted his dick, nothing more, since reality would never live up to my dreams, same as I would never be good enough for Dad.

I grunted a response he could take however he wanted while following him into the church's foyer.

The scent of lemon cleaner burned my nose, but I kept my lips sealed so I wouldn't taste the chemicals meant to scrub and cleanse germs from every surfaced touched by the flesh of man.

The smell offended my senses—same as Dad's bullshit spewed from the pulpit.

Breathing deep and slowly exhaling didn't ease the tension riding my shoulders and making my legs shake.

I'd jerked off twice while in the shower so Dad wouldn't see me sporting a boner, but even an hour later, my dick chubbed up at the thought of having Malachi behind closed doors. Alone. Just him and me and the connection linking our souls.

Dad knocked on his office door, and when Malachi told us to enter, he pushed it in and stepped back.

"Be open," Dad murmured as I stepped past him.

I nodded, my focus going to Malachi behind his desk. He wore a light blue dress shirt, striped tie...freshly shaven cheeks, lips in a thin line as he shuffled paperwork on his desk.

Dad closed the door behind me, and I shifted on my feet, waiting for Malachi to acknowledge me. To give me his eyes. The attention I yearned for.

The hives feeling returned, and I recognized the craving to have him putting his hands on me and showing me the kind of affection my body and mind lusted over.

"Have a seat," Malachi said, focusing on the shit atop his desk.

I forced steady breaths while sitting in the chair across from him, every cell in my body buzzing from the close proximity. Chin tilted upward, I waited. Gaze locked on him.

He closed his eyes a moment and stilled—probably praying for strength, for wisdom.

My lips twitched, hoping God didn't hear his pleadings.

A heavy exhale and Malachi lifted his head.

We stared at one another in the silence, my arm hairs raising regardless of his shuttered eyes. Trouble lined his face, like his will battled the lusts of the flesh. His fingers clasped atop some papers, knuckles white as though he fought to keep from reaching for me.

Giving us what we both wanted.

"Did your father tell you why you're here?" he asked, his tone level, almost...reluctant.

The only time he'd acted differently toward me was when he had his hands on my body.

My dick twitched as I considered ways to get those fingers ghosting over my skin and his lower lip between my teeth.

"He wants us to be friends," I stated what couldn't happen platonically.

"And you know that can never be."

Well at least the struggling man decided to shoot straight for a change, saying exactly what I'd expected.

"I disagree," I said. "I think we can be friends and a hell of a lot more if you'd pull your head out of your ass."

"Isaac."

"Ask me what I want." I sat forward, elbows on my knees, holding his gaze. "Ask me how we can move forward...because I have all sorts of ideas."

Fuck, did I ever.

Malachi cleared his throat, glancing away and back again as though hitting return on his laptop. "When do you head to Nashville?"

Sure enough, he'd started a new paragraph, poking at my insecurities enough that I sank back into my chair.

"Trying to get rid of me?" At least my voice didn't sound close to tears like my tightened chest suggested releasing.

Malachi let out another long exhale. "No." He moved his focus away again, shifting on his chair. "Yes." A soft snort accompanied a shake of his head. "Honestly, Isaac, I don't know."

I focused on the "no" answer, and warmth flooded through me with the understanding that we both bobbed in the ocean.

My threatening tears of hurt turned into ones of relief, but I choked them back. "I'm leaving in three weeks." I answered what I would do on the day I turned eighteen —no matter what.

He nodded, his attention once more returning to my face. Worry etched his brow. "Do you have any arrangements in place? A place to stay? A job?"

I might only be seventeen, but I wasn't a moron like Dad assumed. Heading out of state to chase my dreams with all my belongings in the back of my Camry was no plan.

"I have enough money saved up from mowing lawns the past four years that I won't need a full-time job for a couple months," I told Malachi what Dad didn't know, what he'd never considered asking. "But I have over a dozen applications in at retail and grocery stores. Two restaurants for a dishwasher position too."

He nodded. "And where will you sleep?"

"Until I have a job and can find a roommate, I'll be staying at the backpacker's hostel in midtown."

"It's a nice place. Clean. Safe." He grimaced like he'd said too much.

One of my eyebrows arched. "You've been there." I didn't bother raising my voice at the end to insinuate a question.

"Yes," he answered anyway, his lips immediately flatlining again.

"Want to talk about it?"

"No." He cleared his throat. "I know you don't think your parents love you—"

"Mom does. Dad doesn't."

Those blue eyes searched mine, and I didn't shield my expression like he did. Let him see what he would. We'd connected that first night by my parents' fire pit over both of us being gifts to our parents, prayed for by God. You'd think those who'd longed to hold a son of their own would treat them a little better though.

"He wants what's best for you," Malachi finally said.

"Sure as hell doesn't act like it." My chin tipped upward as I pushed away the stinging pain that always accompanied my reiteration over Dad loving his Bible, his God, more than he did me.

"He's worried for you."

"He doesn't know me."

"Have you offered him the chance?"

I held Malachi's stare for a few tense, silent moments. "Did *you* give your parents that chance?"

He tore his gaze off my face to his fingers still clenched atop his desk.

Guess not. Yet another thing he and I had in common.

I willed him to unclench his hands, round the desk, and touch me. Hold me. Allow us to offer each other what we both craved. Affection. Acceptance.

Maybe a climax or three.

"No, I never told them," he whispered rather than calling me out for turning the focus on him.

His answer was a confession as far as I was concerned, of who he was, *what* he was. But I wanted more. "Why not?"

"Because I grew up believing there was something wrong with me."

I could *feel* the connection between us, and by the way he peered at me without judgement in his eyes, I knew he did too.

No need for me to admit the truth of my insecurities, but I could steer our conversation to a different truth.

"Getting hard for another guy isn't wrong."

He swallowed, his Adam's apple bobbing. I imagined licking over it, tasting his skin.

My chub returned.

Malachi once more turned his attention to his hands like he couldn't bear to look at me. "It's a sin," he rasped.

"Yeah," I snorted, "according to a fairytale book written by a bunch of men who didn't know their assholes from their mouths—if they even existed at all."

He closed his eyes. "I believe the Word of God is true."

I sure as fuck didn't want to, but a part of me deep inside my soul feared it. If God *was*, then that meant He had allowed me to be formed with desires for the same sex. And yet He would reject me for living the life He'd supposedly blessed me with?

Talk about utter bullshit.

"So, you think we'll burn in hell for what we did." I didn't voice a question since Malachi thought the same as my dad.

"I'm sorry for my actions, Isaac. What I did was inappropriate. What happened between us was a mistake I've repented for."

I crossed my arms, my gaze narrowing as he lifted his head once more. The linking bond between us snapped back into place. "I sure as fuck haven't—and I never will. That was the hottest night of my life, and I can't stop thinking about it. Dreaming about it."

My dick agreed, swelling inside my boxers.

"I would appreciate if you wouldn't bring up what's been covered by the blood of the Lamb."

Words. All a bunch of repeated nonsense. Fucking bullshit. Having Bible terms tossed in my face only ever roused anger inside me to the point I seethed.

So much for that boner.

"The fuck, Malachi?" I scowled, hating that he'd deviated away from his straight shooting.

"He promised in the book of Ezekiel that He would cleanse us from our impurities."

I studied the man before me, looking for the peace and joy Dad's flock all sought after. "And has He given you that new heart, the new spirit He promised in the verse following that one?"

Pansy ass wouldn't even glance my way, couldn't be honest with himself.

Malachi would blindly choose his faith, his God, the words written by man that I'd been forced to memorize, over what brewed between us.

An ache spread through my chest, even as I pushed at the truth wanting to drown my heart.

"Tell me you aren't hard right now, Malachi." My voice wavered. "Tell me you don't want to shove your dick into my asshole and make me yours."

A shudder rippled over him as our gazes once more clashed. Lust, hot and thick, grew between us, the kind of evidence that couldn't be denied.

"I don't," he whispered.

"You're a goddamn liar," I shot back, my voice cracking as the pain beneath my breastbone sharpened. "Your eyes, the tension riding your shoulders says otherwise. Tell me you don't feel this." I motioned between us. "This...this energy, this *pull*. It's a damn craving that refuses to relent."

He held my stare but didn't answer.

"You're full of shit." I stood. "A fake ass hypocrite preaching about grace and acceptance." I snorted.

"You need to give yourself some of both. Maybe it'll open your eyes to the truth of who and what you are."

I stormed out of his office, slamming his door shut behind me.

Thank fuck the door to Dad's office was closed. Last thing I needed was even more disappointment for failing to make a "friend."

Mom pulled into the parking lot as I stalked outside, and a lie about feeling sick got me her keys. She could catch a ride with Dad.

I went home, too torn up inside to write music, too angry to do anything but strip, curl up in my bed, and cry. I couldn't even rouse myself to pack a bag and get the hell out of there.

My cell dinged from my nightstand, and I swiped my forearm across my eyes while reaching for it.

Probably Mom checking up on me.

HAFYP: **You're right.**

I huffed a sarcastic laugh and replied to the hot as fuck youth pastor who'd never texted me before: **About wanting me or being a hypocrite?**

HAFYP: **About needing to give myself grace and acceptance. For denying who I am. But I still stand by what I believe, Isaac.**

In the Bible. In God who would damn me and Malachi for what He'd allowed between us. I hoped God wasn't real. Hoped He would prove Himself to be nothing but a pack of lies.

Malachi texted two minutes later while I stewed over the bullshit of a religion based on a God of love.

HAFYP: **I failed you in causing you to fall, and I'm sorry. Please don't take off out of anger.**

How the fuck had he known I'd been thinking about leaving early?

I didn't reply because I had nothing else to say to the man who refused to acknowledge me in the way I needed.

Chapter 19
Malachi

Hypocrite.

Isaac's accurate definition summed me up perfectly.

But he forgot to add liar. Unbeliever. Manipulator. And the list could go on. I was nothing but a filthy sinner. Unworthy of God's love.

I slid off my chair onto the office floor seconds after the door slammed shut behind Isaac and confessed to every single sin I could remember. For giving in to the temptation I'd lied about repenting for. For touching one of God's children—even if he was a man. For enjoying having him in my hands and not truly being sorry for it.

Tears streamed down my cheeks, and my knees ached by the time I finished—but I didn't feel cleansed.

My heart didn't feel new.

I still wanted Isaac with a deep-seated ache that threatened to break me.

Why didn't His promises hold true?

How long would He ask his children to have faith and to believe His plan without some sort of answer or guidance?

It didn't seem right—or fair.

Brian.

A headache spread between my temples as I recognized the tension taking control of my muscles over thoughts of my friend. I wanted to bare my teeth. Plant a fist into my office wall, smashing through drywall. Maybe hitting a stud would cause enough pain to keep me from going down the route that had led me off a path of righteousness five years earlier.

I struggled to breathe normally. Steadily.

Help me, please.

Refusing to let anger dictate my actions, I did what God would have me do. I confessed to Isaac and asked his forgiveness. But I couldn't bear to hear his voice. I took the coward's way out and texted.

Then when he didn't reply, I went on to beg him not to leave—but not just because I didn't want Pastor Bram to blame me for upsetting his son and being the cause of his running off.

I couldn't stand the idea of him going so far away. Admitting that to myself made me feel even more shitty.

Settling in Elkins had been a trial unlike any I'd faced before, and my old sinful nature battled with all I believed to be true.

Isaac never responded, and I hid out in my office like a chickenshit after I could hear the praise and worship team lead the congregation to start the service.

Stretched out on my office floor in a suit and tie, I dialed up Zeke, even though I knew he'd be in church.

"Hey," he surprisingly answered, breathless.

"Hello, Ezekiel," I tried for my usual teasing, but my voice fell flat.

"You okay?" Damn man was intuitive as hell and let my attempts to ruffle his feathers slide.

"No."

"Hold on a second." He muffled his cell, his low voice indistinct as he spoke to someone. A bit of static, like he brushed his cell against cloth, and he came back to me. "What's going on?"

"I fucked up, nothing makes sense, and my mind is seriously fucked up."

"What happened?"

"You got an hour?" I tried to joke again.

"Anything for you."

I quietly spilled the shit of Maine, not leaving anything out, hoping that confessing with my mouth would give me the peace He promised.

It didn't come to flood my soul, and my throat tightened as Zeke remained silent for a few seconds once I finished my agonizing tale.

"Are you drawn to him because he reminds you of Brian?" he finally asked.

"No," I didn't hesitate to answer. "Isaac is different than Brian was. He's...more. Too much." I scratched beneath my tie, the buttons of my shirt snagging my fingernails. "Whatever this is between us, it's ten times more potent than anything I've felt before, Zeke. It's consuming. Inescapable.

"Why would God bring me to a place of temptation when all I've been trying to do is please Him? How could a God of love be so cruel?" Even as I asked the questions, guilt swept in to make my body want to sink through the floor, straight down into hell where I belonged.

Zeke didn't speak.

"Denying Isaac, the connection between us, makes me feel like I can't breathe," I choked out in a mere whisper. "Like I'm drowning. Being around him is life. Oxygen to starved lungs. I don't think I'll be able to stand him leaving—I can't be here when he goes."

"Then don't be."

I pinched the bridge of my nose, wanting to rant and rail on my friend for not offering me Godly counsel. "Give me Bible verses, Zeke. Give me truth. Words to live by."

"I don't have the answers."

I opened my eyes and stared, noticing of a small water leak stain in the textured ceiling. "Isn't the Bible supposed to have all the answers?"

"Supposed to."

That didn't sound like my confident friend. At all.

"What's going on, Zeke?"

He let out a heavy exhale, taking too long to respond. My own issues faded enough from my mind that I grew concerned for him. "It's a story for another time, but suffice to say that pre-marriage counseling young couples is making me question my own faith."

"How so?"

"Like I said—story for another time."

"Fine." I sat back up, one arm resting over my drawn-up knees. "So, forget the Bible and our faith for a minute. What advice have you got for me?"

"We can't just set those things aside," Zeke tried to reason, and I closed my eyes again. "Going with your guts, your heart, will put Isaac beneath you, but it'll also end with you losing your job and the chance to ever influence teenagers in a church setting again."

That last bit of truth hit hard, especially since I thought God had called me to work with teens. I'd wanted to do His will in honor of my parents for their years of sacrifice and love for me.

Was allowing myself to give in to the unholy craving for Isaac worth eternal damnation?

Considering I didn't know exactly what hell consisted of, I wondered.

Would pursuing the feelings inside me, the possibility of...perhaps love, give my soul what it longed for, what God hadn't been able to fill?

That question haunted me for the next half hour after I'd hung up with Zeke, and when Pastor Bram came looking for me after the service, I still didn't have any answers.

He eyed me still sitting on my floor. "Are you okay, Malachi?"

"Yeah." My voice sounded like I'd swallowed a bag full of crushed glass.

"Annabelle said Isaac went home feeling sick."

"He did?" I couldn't bring myself to look at my pastor.

"Did something happen?"

Nothing physical, thank God.

"No," I answered, scrubbing a hand down over my face, knowing I needed to lie for both our sakes. "I've just been on my knees for your son."

The filthy image that flashed through my head made me want to groan.

Pastor Bram let out a sigh. "I guess girding your loins hasn't helped."

Loins. Damnit.

I choked on a cough/laugh, sure I was losing my goddamn mind. "He's a handful."

Shit.

My pastor came fully into my office, offering to help me to my feet. I accepted, my thoughts filled with self-loathing to the point my stomach twisted.

"I know I just started here, but to be honest...I'm feeling overwhelmed," I admitted what I could.

"Do you need a few days off?"

"I hate asking, but it would probably be for the best."

No trace of anger or annoyance lined his forehead when I finally lifted my head. Pastor Bram smiled. "I know just the place, but it won't be available until three weeks from now."

Three weeks. The weekend Isaac turned eighteen and would leave—if he hadn't already.

"That would actually be perfect," I said, forcing a smile.

"You can hang in until then?" Pastor Bram clasped my shoulder, and I nodded. "Good, because the cottage we co-own up on Lake Wallenpaupack isn't rented that weekend. It's a perfect escape and all yours if you want."

"Thank you, and yes," I didn't hesitate to answer.

"It's settled, then." His smile widened. "Now come out and show your face as the congregation leaves. There were lots of wondering glances at your empty chair during service."

"I'm sorry."

"It's okay." He chuckled as I followed him out my office door. "The younger ladies all listened to my sermon for a change. I'm guessing God had something for me to say to one of them that wouldn't have heard were you sitting behind me in full view."

Oh, how easily he accepted the possibilities of God's plan.

Had he known why I'd been absent, he wouldn't have been so understanding.

Chapter 20

Isaac

A week dragged past, raining damn near every day.

I went to the movies with Chris and Tyler without my parents knowledge. Seeing as how the ways of the world were of the devil, Hollywood was a no-no. But when had I ever listened?

Chris brought along a bag of weed, and I smoked my first joint later that night, out in the deep, waterlogged woods.

And fuck, did I feel fine.

Relaxed.

Tyler claimed smoking weed always gave him such clarity, like he could figure out the cares of the world.

I ended up numb and didn't complain, just simply chowed down on fast food fries and a milkshake we snagged from a drive-through on the way back to my house.

The guys dropped me off, even though I still floated high as shit.

Thank fuck my parents went to bed and trusted me with a twelve o'clock curfew.

Neither sat up waiting for me since I'd gone out with kids from the youth group to hang out at Dunks and talk about Jesus over coffee and donuts.

Lies.

I snuck up to my bed, grinning like an idiot.

Stripped bare, I slid between my sheets, thinking I'd never felt such a soft bed.

Instead of lying there and agonizing over Malachi and how my angry thoughts toward him didn't match up with my lustful desires like I'd been doing for what seemed like forever, I passed the fuck out.

The next morning, I called up Chris and talked him into selling me some pot of my own.

He had me covered.

* * *

I cooked up another lie about having an upset stomach to skip church that Sunday. Mom tucked me back into bed before leaving. Dad checked in on me after church, stern and disappointed as always.

But I didn't give a shit. I didn't have to see Malachi.

Wednesday rolled around, and I knew Dad wouldn't let me get away with missing out on two services in a row.

I texted Chris and had him meet me out behind the school for a quick smoke. The nerves I'd felt racing over my skin at seeing the old truck in the parking lot faded more with every hit of the sweet burn filling my lungs.

We ended up giggling like a couple of kids over...well, shit I couldn't even remember.

"My eyes red?" I asked him as we rounded the school for the gymnasium doors.

"Anyone asks, just say it's allergies. Works every time."

"Hey, I'm sorry about the whole Maine thing." I brought up what we hadn't discussed sober.

"I heard your whistle," Chris said with a shrug. "Just didn't feel like taking my hands off of Sara's tits. They're fucking fantastic."

"Have you two…"

"She won't let me fuck her, but we're hanging out. I'll talk her into it eventually."

"What?" I barked a laugh. "You have magic mojo or some shit that gets you into a girl's pants?"

Chris laughed too. "Nah, but that girl gives me heart eyes. She wants me. Lets me have a little more whenever we have a few minutes alone. It's only a matter of time."

"And circumstance," I said, remembering having Malachi all to myself that night in Maine.

"Yeah, that." Chris pulled open the gym's door. "Tough when you've got religious parents breathing down your damn neck."

"Talk about truth," I muttered, following on his heels, keeping my focus on the floor so I wouldn't have to see Malachi. I could feel him, though. Heat sizzled my skin, and I wanted to laugh my ass off for some reason.

Fucking high—felt fucking great.

Grinning, I sprawled into the chair beside Chris, and we whispered a bit until Malachi called our meeting to order. I couldn't focus on what he said, not that I ever truly did, but I caught words here and there.

God's plan.

His leading.

Something about His having our best interest at heart.

I snorted at that one. Finally glancing up, I caught Malachi's glare. I grinned.

He blinked.

Turned away and kept talking.

More Bible verse bullshit, blah, blah, blah.

Chris leaned over my way, starting to rhyme with words Malachi used.

Word. Turd.

Heart. Fart.

Typical guy shit, but they were the funniest rhymes I'd ever heard. I barked out a laugh, fighting to act sober when both Malachi and Miss Jennifer frowned our way.

The second time Chris had me bursting out, Malachi stopped talking altogether and faced us.

"Both of you—out in the hallway. Now."

My blood raced, remembering the last time he'd taken me from the youth circle, but with Chris tagging along, I knew there wouldn't be a visit to the janitor's closet.

We both snickered, stepping into the hallway, Malachi on my ass.

Not on my ass literally...unfortunately.

"Damn," I muttered, imagining that very thing.

Miss Jennifer's voice lifted in song, but the slam of the gym door cut her off.

"I don't appreciate the disruptions tonight, boys."

Chris and I pulled up and turned to face our youth pastor.

Lips in a thin line, eyes hard, he glanced between the two of us. Thank fuck Chris was flying like a kite too or he probably would have felt the energy zapping and tingling across my skin.

I held Malachi's stare.

His gaze narrowed. "Are you high?"

Chris giggled, and I fought to keep my lips from curving. "Nope." I popped the P.

Malachi's shoulders dropped, and his glare morphed into something I was well acquainted with —disappointment.

"I'm outta here." I spun and strode away before he could start spouting off bullshit about making better choices and acting like a child of God since others looked up to me as the pastor's son.

"Isaac!"

I ignored Malachi and pushed open the door, letting myself outside to blow off some steam.

He didn't follow me, and I couldn't decide if I was happy or pissed while sulking on a swing in the play area, waiting for church to end.

Wednesday night service let out ten minutes later, and Dad drove us home. I slouched in the back while he and Mom discussed the message he'd preached.

The second we got to the house, I shut myself in my room, needing a joint, but I didn't have the balls to smoke until Mom and Dad went to bed.

I laid in my bed, fully clothed, hating the feeling of coming back down to reality.

"Isaac?" Dad knocked and opened my door without waiting for me to tell him he could enter. The guy didn't give two shits about privacy when it came to his household.

Thank fuck I hadn't been jerking off.

His brow furrowed as he walked in, Mom on his heels. Concern etched her face, and the wringing hands at her front let me know shit was about to hit the fan.

"I just talked to Malachi," Dad said, his voice stern.

Yeah, I could imagine he had.

"Have you been smoking pot?"

The fucker ratted me out.

"Nope," I lied.

"Sit up."

I did as Dad commanded, holding in my annoyed sigh that would only make shit ten times worse.

"Your eyes are bloodshot."

"Allergies."

"You've never had allergies before."

I shrugged, taking more interest in the torn denim over my knee. "People develop allergies later in life."

"You're no longer allowed to be friends with Chris."

That earned Dad a steady gaze. "What?"

"He's a bad influence."

I glanced at Mom, but she wouldn't meet my eyes.

"He got that girl pregnant two years ago," Dad continued, shoulders back and chin lifted while looking at me, taking his position of authority in the household damn seriously.

"And he repented," I reminded Dad. "Publicly from the pulpit like you and his parents thought best."

"Still." Dad's lips thinned.

"Why would you bring up the past that's been covered by the blood?" I couldn't help but ask, my own brow furrowing to match his. "Who are you to uncover Chris's sins?"

"I'm the father of an impressionable young man who doesn't know how to make right decisions!" His voice shook, his dark eyes growing stormy.

I would have been smarter to shut my damn mouth, but I didn't give a shit that he'd probably try to take the rod to me like the Bible commanded.

"Well, I'm sorry I can't be the Isaac of your precious Word," I half-spat, standing to my feet. "And I'm sorry I can't be the perfect son you hoped and prayed for."

"Isaac—"

"You don't listen to a word I say," I cut Dad off, the bullshit of my circumstances...of Malachi's disappointment in me rousing to an ugly brew of toxicity in my gut. "You couldn't care less about what I think or feel."

"That's not true," Mom started, but I wasn't done.

"Nothing I say is good enough. Holy enough. All you care about is your Bible and the flock God called you to lead."

"Isaac—"

"No!" I hollered at Dad, my hands fisted at my sides. "If you gave me even a quarter of the time you give to your God, your congregation—hell, an eighth of the time you spend readying to preach, you'd—"

"Enough!" Dad barked and started toward me, his hand lifting.

I held my chin high—waiting for him to award me with a reason to escape early.

Mom burst into tears. "Bram!"

Her cry halted Dad's feet, and we glared at one another across the distance.

"I want you out," Dad bit the words.

"No!" Mom sobbed and grabbed hold of his hand. "Bram, please!"

"The day you turn eighteen," he continued, ignoring Mom, "you're on your own. We have offered you everything we could—life, a home..."

I barely stifled my snort when he didn't continue on with the words of unconditional love like a parent should. "Don't worry," I promised, "I'll be gone the second midnight passes."

A muscle jumped in Dad's jaw, and he spun, leaving me and Mom alone.

Tears coursed down her cheeks, and my shoulders slumped.

"I'm sorry—"

"No." She moved in close, grasping my face, her eyes wet. "I love you. Always. No matter what."

What if Dad made her choose between him and I? Telling them my sexual orientation would definitely put her in that position, but I couldn't do that to the one person who'd tried to love me the best she could.

"I'm still going."

Another tear slid down her cheek. "I know."

"There's nothing here for me, Mom," I choked out, hating the thickness wanting to take away my voice. "You've done your best—and I appreciate that—but this isn't my home anymore."

Her lower lip trembled as she nodded. "You need to find your own way." She inhaled a shuddered sigh. "I'll have to trust God to see you through."

I pulled Mom into my arms, wishing I could tell her the truth about who I was to her God and what I thought of Him.

Two weeks.

I could put up with Dad's shit.

For Mom.

Chapter 21
Malachi

Isaac ignored me again.

I did the same with him, and I hurt because of it.

Even more, I hated how he appeared whenever I allowed myself a peek in his direction. He sat slouched at youth group, keeping to himself like he'd done when I'd first arrived.

Pastor Bram informed me about their fallout after I'd told him about Isaac's behavior, one thing I regretted even though his disrespect had pissed me off. Pastor Bram assured me with obvious displeasure in his voice that I only had to deal with his rebellious son for a little while longer.

That Isaac was a disappointment to him reaffirmed strongly in my heart.

Was it any wonder Isaac behaved the way he did? Why didn't he take off early for Nashville like I felt sure he wanted to? And why did I feel the need to talk to him, to make things right between us? I'd have been better off leaving him alone, allowing him his emotions, thoughts, and distance which would separate us for good.

I couldn't.

If nothing else, it was my responsibility to share my story and maybe influence his future decisions.

Perhaps that was why God had led me to Elkins.

Hinging my thoughts on that idea, I went looking for Isaac the day before I planned to head to the Van Dusen's camp on Lake Wallenpaupack. I drove around their neighborhood since he did yard work, both windows down and ears straining for the sounds of a mower.

Isaac labored beneath the hot sun, shirtless and sweating, two blocks from home. Old jean shorts hung low on his hips.

"Shit," I muttered, the ruckus from the small engine of his mower drowning out my curse.

My heart sped as I pulled to the curb in front of the neighbor's house, studying how his legs and backside flexed with every step away from me. Lust kicked in like it always did whenever I filled my eyes with Isaac's lithe body and smooth skin.

I couldn't find repentance in my heart for the curse or the craving that wanted to dictate my actions.

Teeth clenched and unable to pray for strength, I put my dad's old truck into park, shut off the ignition, and sat.

Watching.

Waiting for him to make the turn, to glance up and see me.

Ten agonizing seconds passed before he came into profile, his focus on the grass and the path he intended to take.

Look at me.

As though hearing my thought, Isaac stopped, and his head snapped up, gaze landing on Dad's truck.

I didn't know if he could see me through the windshield, but my breath still caught and time paused for a moment. My mouth salivated for a taste of the sweat on his face. Fingers itched to peel the jean shorts down over his lean hips. Dick throbbed to fill him over and over until we both found release.

"Fuck." I rubbed a hand over my face, and he cut the engine, leaving the air around me silent.

His shoulders rose like he took a fortifying breath, and he walked my way. Steps steady. Chin raised. Like he faced war—and was damn ready for it.

My skin came alive the closer he got, and my pulse raced once I could make out the green in his hazel eyes.

He stood by my rolled down window, and I filled my lungs, dragging in the scent of sweat and soap.

"Can we talk?" I croaked out, realizing I held the steering wheel in a death grip.

Isaac glanced over at the yard he'd been mowing. "Give me a few minutes to finish up."

"Yeah. Okay." I nodded, feeling like a bumbling idiot, and he held my gaze for a few more seconds before heading to work.

His backside drew my focus, and I cursed, sure he put a little extra sway in his step to drive me insane.

Balls and jaw aching, I stared like a pervert while he finished the final three rows of the lawn. He pushed the mower down the sidewalk toward where I waited, his shirt he'd retrieved from the front porch thrown over one shoulder.

Heat waves rose off the blacktop, infiltrating the cab of Dad's truck. Without any moving wind, we would roast talking inside.

I hopped from the cab, knowing that at four in the afternoon he had to be done for the day. "All set?"

"Yeah." He glanced down the road toward home.

"Can I give you a ride?" I offered, rounding the back of the truck.

"Yeah. Sure."

I put down the tailgate, and we lifted the mower together on either side, rolling it into the back.

The second he climbed into the truck, I rubbed my palms against my own shorts, trying to rid them of dampness from sweat and nerves alike.

"Here." I grabbed one of the cold bottles of water I'd brought from home and handed it over.

Starting up the truck, I eyed him in my periphery. He was sucking down the cold liquid, his Adam's apple bobbing. A droplet of salty sweat trailed from his temple down his neck.

I swallowed my groan along with a flood of drool and faced forward before driving away from the curb.

"Thanks," he said, breathless after emptying the water bottle in one chug.

"Hot as hell out there."

"Yeah."

"You're leaving in two days."

Isaac didn't bother responding since I hadn't asked a question.

"I-I hoped to talk to you before you did."

"So talk," he said, his words snipped.

"I'm sorry for ratting you out to your dad."

"Yeah—thanks for that."

"It's my duty as your youth pastor. I want what's best for you—"

"Spare me the bullshit, Malachi."

Lips clamped, I nodded. There would be no making of amends which was probably for the best no matter how much I'd hoped to at least be friends.

The wind whipped through the cab as I drove past his house, but I still sweated inside my T-shirt.

"Where are we going?"

"Someplace quiet."

Tension rose between us at the suggestion we would be alone. Private. Perhaps even in seclusion.

I couldn't allow the temptation.

Two minutes later, I pulled alongside the pines crowding the town park. Kids played on the swings and climbing apparatuses, their laughter and shrieks taking over the silence between us as I shut down the engine.

"Come on." I squeaked the door open and climbed out.

Isaac did the same and tugged his shirt on overhead.

I breathed a bit easier at not having to talk to him with all that skin I wanted to explore on display.

We settled beneath an oak tree a good fifty feet away from the nearest parent watching over the play area.

"I was ten when I realized I liked boys," I started off our conversation without any bullshit. "No women ever caught my attention, and none ever will."

Isaac sat silent, his arms draped over his pulled-up knees.

"I went to Nashville out of rebellion to God," I continued after stating the truth Isaac already knew about my sexuality. "I wanted to prove myself and made all kinds of mistakes that left me feeling empty. The first was being naive enough to believe a big wig in the industry had fallen for me. He promised me a record deal in exchange for my virginity."

My stomach heaved, but I continued before Isaac could interrupt the shit I needed to spew.

"And I gave it to him, only to be laughed at and tossed out his door an hour later. After that, I spent years making bad choices that led to depression and more heartache. The thought of you facing the same thing…" I grimaced as my stomach rolled. Again. "I wish I could keep you from experiencing the hell I did, Isaac. All I can do is beg you to stay in the Word. Pray. Ask God for guidance."

I could feel Isaac's stare on my face but couldn't look at him. Sitting that close, within touching distance, and peering into his eyes would prove my undoing.

"While my mom lay on her deathbed, I decided to rededicate my life to God, thinking of the truth I'd been raised in." I pushed on telling my story in the hopes my ending would encourage him toward the right path. "I lived in the hype, the emotionalism all through college, my best friend Zeke being the one to help me keep my head above water. After graduation and my dad's death last summer, I was faced with life on my own, without guidance from a parent. I decided to change the scenery and start over with a new beginning."

"That's what led you here."

"Yes."

I stared at the little kids running around, seeing but not processing their actions beyond movement.

"It's not sin if you don't act on it," I whispered, hoping like hell Isaac would listen.

"I *want* to act on it."

Hell. I closed my eyes, teeth clenched. He hadn't heard a damn word I'd said.

"More than anything," Isaac said, "I want a taste of the forbidden."

"It's an addictive drug," I choked out, "one that will do nothing but cause harm."

"You know that from experience." Isaac didn't ask a question, but I nodded all the same, needing to voice what I'd lived through—for his sake.

"Yes." I swallowed hard, finally forcing myself to meet Isaac's stare. Goosebumps rose on my skin, the electric current between us zapping with undeniable pulses. "And because of our sins, God took him from me."

Isaac's eyes stated I spewed nonsense, but I drove onward before he could deny what I knew to be truth, what my guilt still held over my head.

"In high school, I fell in love with the new boy in town." My voice wavered, so I tore my focus off of Isaac's face in order to finish. "He was gay too. My first kiss—my first hand job. Blowjob."

I cleared my throat and pulled up my knees like Isaac did to lace my shaking fingers together at the front of my shins. "I instigated, and he followed me like a lamb to the slaughter. We hid our relationship for three years. The day after graduation, he lost control of his car and hit a tree head on. Brian died on impact."

Swallowing hard, I pushed away the hurt that had faded over the years but still stung like a bitch, the feelings of remorse as raw as they'd been at eighteen.

"I'm the one who led Brian into sin, and he's dead because of it."

Isaac snorted, stretched his legs out, and leaned back on his hands, removing himself from my from periphery. "My dad's God is supposed to be love—is that showing love? Taking away life for breaking a book's rule? I'm calling bullshit."

His matter-of-fact statement left me without words. The deepest part of me longed to believe as he did, what I'd told myself all those years in Nashville.

Help me.

The silent prayer rose in my head on its own, and I clung to the image in my mind of the Holy Spirit interceding on my behalf before the throne of God.

"I wanted to think the same," I finally managed to speak, clinging to my faith to keep from floundering. "It's why I went to Nashville. It had been Brian's dream first, and I felt I owed his memory the chance to fulfill what we'd planned to do. We wrote music together. Sang duets in church. It was beautiful. *We* were beautiful."

"You still love him."

I considered Isaac's statement and pondered the ache in my chest I experienced whenever thinking about Brian. "A part of me always will, yes. But he's gone—he's not my future." I turned to catch Isaac's gaze. "I don't want you to hurt like I did, Isaac."

"I have to live my life."

I nodded since my tight throat kept me from speaking.

"It's one thing to hear of mistakes people have made," Isaac went on, "it's another thing to live them yourself. They don't always have to be regrets either.

Sometimes they're the only circumstances that can make a stubborn person stronger."

The kid was too much...

"I have to make my own choices, my own mistakes," he continued giving me his truth. "And in the end, if I see blinding white light after breathing my last, I'll believe."

"At that point, it'll be too late."

"I don't give a shit. If God is the narcissistic prick the Bible makes Him out to be, then I'd rather burn in hell."

A fissure cracked through my heart. There would be no changing his mind, his plans.

"And until it's your time?" I asked quietly, needing something to imagine once he left.

"I'll love and accept others like Dad preaches from his pulpit but doesn't live."

Chapter 22

Isaac

Malachi stood after my declaration on how I planned to move forward, and I followed him back to his perfectly sexy truck. Our silence stretched throughout the ride home.

He helped me unload the lawnmower, and we both stood awkwardly, my hands clutching the old metal handle, his fisted at his sides.

"Your dad offered me use of your camp for the weekend, and I'm leaving in the morning."

I studied Malachi's profile as he glanced over to my parents' house. He'd been unable to hold my gaze for more than five seconds for weeks. "So this is goodbye."

Malachi swallowed and nodded.

Aching pain raced through my chest, but I lifted my chin and shoved my hand toward him even though I'd rather have grabbed him and kissed his mouth.

He eyed my shaking offer and let out a slow exhale before accepting.

Sweaty palms, grasping fingers. Clasping tight to soak in the ripple of want between us.

"Take care of yourself," he whispered, finally lifting his focus to my face.

My eyes stung at the troubled emotion in his, and I nodded, even though I wanted to beg *him* to take care of me. Show me everything I'd dreamed about. Craved. Exactly as his blue orbs suggested he longed for as well.

"I'll be praying for you."

My throat was too tight to tell him not to bother.

Malachi pulled his hand from mine and turned away, his shoulders hitched up. Choosing his God rather than the real, flesh and blood man who would worship at his feet given the chance.

Tension continued to radiate between us until he drove off without looking back, tearing my heart right down its center.

I swiped at my wet eyes the second the old truck disappeared from sight, filled my lungs, and trudged toward the shed out back to put the mower away, every step heavy. Every breath shallow. Every heartbeat painful.

Sleep wouldn't come that night, and my entire last day as a seventeen-year-old was spent the same way as the one before. Sweat covered, driven to make every last dollar before I left for Nashville the next morning.

But rather than focusing on the excitement of escape—freedom—my feet dragged, my stride slow, like slugging through cement. My chest continued to ache, and each time I replayed Malachi driving away from me, my eyes stung.

The day's work lasted longer than the one before, and until I finished, I just wanted to curl up in bed and cry like a pansy. But I had shit to do. It took another hour to finish packing up my things and loading them into the car.

My Camry was gassed up and ready to roll with the sunrise.

One clean outfit and my bathroom bag remained in my room for morning.

We sat down to a late dinner, our final one as a family that from the outside appeared blessed. Godly and whole. Mom barely touched her food, her fork scraping as she pushed it around on her plate.

Dad ate as though unaffected, at ease because he trusted his God.

My knee bounced beneath the table even though my heart sat heavy in my chest.

Freedom meant leaving Malachi behind, and while I wanted the first, I craved the second just as badly.

"I wish you would reconsider and choose God's will for your life."

I glanced up at Dad who'd finished and placed his fork and knife upside down on his cleared plate. He always spoke as if he was privy to God's will for people's lives. But I was done being manipulated and shoved down a path I didn't want.

"I'm heading south in the morning," I told him, my tone firm.

Disappointment—big surprise—flashed in his eyes, only serving to ramp up my resolve. "Nashville can't possibly be the Lord's calling."

I'd had about enough of his bullshit and didn't bother hiding that truth from my eyes as I frowned. "And since when do you know the mind of your God?"

"*My* God?"

"Yes, *yours*," I tossed back, pushing my plate away since I'd had enough. "You stand up on that platform in church like you're some...some God-*sent* prophet, spouting off commandments about love and acceptance, when all I've ever gotten from you is correction and discipline."

"Please, Isaac, it's your last night with us," Mom said, her voice wavering. "Don't do this."

"Do what, Mom? Challenge what's been hammered into my brain since I was a kid, only to never see it in action?"

"That's enough, Isaac," Dad snapped.

I glared at him, his attempts to control me to the last minute raising my hackles. Tension made me stiffen in the chair, my hands fisting on my lap "No, it's not. *I've* had enough—of your hypocrisy and having to live a lie because telling you who I really am would only cause even more disappointment and damnation."

"What are you talking about?" Mom asked quietly while Dad and I held a staring contest.

"I'm. Gay." I bit the words out.

Mom gasped.

Surprise—then disgust—clouded Dad's eyes and furrowed his brow. "Get out," he whispered harshly, with more venom than any snake.

I shoved back my chair, toppling it over in a rush of adrenaline.

"Isaac!"

I ignored Mom and hurried up to my bedroom, her cries and Dad's rantings about me being an abomination, a pervert, reaching me upstairs. My legs shook, and my stomach clenched up tight as I grabbed the last bag, stuffing my bathroom things into it.

My cell sat on the bed stand, and I slid it into my back pocket. Without glancing around my childhood bedroom, I took my bag and strode down the stairs.

Mom still cried in the kitchen.

"No, Annabelle," Dad hissed. "I won't have that—that unholy *creature* in this house a minute longer!"

For the first time, I hoped there really was a hell.

And I hoped Dad burned there for eternity.

The front door slammed shut behind me, and I beelined toward my car, adrenaline rushing, my entire body trembling.

A few hours earlier than I'd planned to leave, but I'd claim my freedom from that awful man all the same.

What father called his son such hurtful, hateful things? What happened to all those teachings about loving the sinner while hating the sin? Dad was only capable of showing hate—toward his own damn son. My chest tightened, but I gritted my teeth over my new truth.

I'm no longer his son.

I hopped in my car without an ounce of regret and tore out of the driveway, the tires squealing. I didn't even spare the house a glance in my rearview mirror.

At the crossroads, I pulled up to the stop sign, my entire body still trembling. The highway leading to Nashville lay straight ahead, the lake house to my left.

My dreams told me to take off toward Tennessee, to live my life and make those choices for myself. However, my heart, my gut turned my gaze east, a desperate longing to prove Malachi was nothing like my dad rushing through me.

Too many unspoken things remained between us. Too much hurt and anger sat in the back of my mind.

Moving on would be difficult without closure, and I couldn't stand the thought of not putting the issue of Malachi Foley to rest before starting my new life.

He might not want to be a part of my future, but I needed to hear those words clearly from his mouth before leaving. I needed to hear for myself that I hadn't been wrong about him, that he wasn't a true hypocrite at heart.

I couldn't go on believing he'd been fashioned from the same cloth as Bram Van Dusen.

I stomped on the gas and yanked the wheel toward my left, fishtailing my car.

My pulse thrummed, beating loudly in my ears. My dick chubbed in the hopes he would have me. My mind raced at the possibility of a new beginning—with him.

Steeling myself for disappointment, I sped up the highway, ready to put my fate in Malachi's hands.

Chapter 23

Malachi

I spent the entire afternoon sitting on the dock down by the lake, simply being. Diving into the cold depths when the sun and heat became too much.

No office phone, no questioning teenagers, and no duties other than trying to figure out my head, my heart, clattered for my attention. Evaluating my emotions wasn't a simple task, but I forced myself to think on them rather than deny. I recognized pain. Disappointment and what seemed like crushing loss.

No joy filled me at having the space, the break I thought I'd needed.

I sipped my third beer while grilling a steak, having repented prior to purchasing the six-pack I'd bought for over the weekend. No guilt rested on my shoulders while I ate my dinner outside. The sun sank, creating a rainbow of color across the sky, but I couldn't find beauty in God's creation. Not even the birds tweeting an early goodnight gave me happiness.

Breathing didn't come as easily as I'd hoped. My chest still ached, the hollowness inside me a constant.

Are You real? I gave up my dream to follow You, trusted You to guide my path. I've held onto my faith, stumbling blindly through the darkness...

A chittering squirrel drew my attention off the inward thoughts, and I watched as two of them scampered up and around a pine tree beside the Van Dusens' cabin.

The small, two-bedroom cottage sat less than fifty yards from the water's edge. Quaint. Quiet.

A good place to rest.

If only I'd been able to find some for my mind.

Letting out a heavy exhale, I gathered up my dinner things and made my way inside.

Minutes later, I stood beneath the shower's hot spray, ridding my skin of the lake's scent. The temptation to take myself in hand and jerk off to thoughts of Isaac battled with the heaviness in my heart.

The loss of him…it hurt like Brian's death had. Hell, it hurt worse, seeming to crush my heart where it lay beating by instinct alone.

A shiver licked over my skin, pebbling my arms, even though heat enveloped me.

I lifted my eyes to the fogged glass.

Someone stood in the bathroom's opened doorway.

Isaac.

I could feel the energy from him feeding my soul, and a rush of adrenaline—excitement and fear combined—made my knees weak. Could he see me through the glass better than I could him? Did he notice how my dick went from lax to interested within seconds?

Shutting off the water, my mind raced over what to do. Why he would be there. What he hoped to accomplish by putting us in a private situation.

It didn't take a single brain cell to guess.

I grabbed the towel I'd slung over the shower wall and wrapped it around my waist before pushing the glass door outward.

It swung, bringing Isaac into sight.

His brow was furrowed, eyes full of anxiety. Shoulders hitched with tension. Hands fisted at his sides.

"Isaac?" I asked, stepping out of the shower and onto the mat, dripping water everywhere.

"I told them."

It took me a second to process his words—and the blood drained from my face, my dick drooping as fast as it'd risen for him. "What?" I rasped out.

"My parents. I told them I'm gay."

My breath left in a rush, and I closed my eyes briefly, thankful he hadn't confessed to our sins.

"Are you going to ask me what they said that hurt more than your rejection or thank me for not getting you fired?"

Shit.

I swallowed hard at his glinting glare. How well he knew me...a seventeen-year-old kid I'd met mere months earlier. "What did he say to you?" I asked, knowing it would have been Bram rather than Annabelle who'd inflicted this emotional pain.

"He ordered me to get out." Isaac lifted his chin.

"What did he say to you, Isaac?" I asked again, taking two steps closer, wanting to offer comfort for the hurt etched in his eyes, the kind of crushing sorrow I couldn't bear the thought of him carrying.

"He c-called me an unholy creature. A p-pervert." His Adam's apple bobbed as he swallowed. "An abomination."

"Asshole," I hissed and swiped my palm down over my face to rid it of dripping water. "Damn him."

"To hell," Isaac stated, his tone finding its sternness again. "For eternity."

Lips in a thin line, I glanced down over him, anger and lust a bitter brew in my guts. He was perfectly trim. Perfectly formed. Perfectly beautiful in his ripped jeans and scuffed black Vans.

"You're leaving."

"The car's packed, but I had to see you first."

"I'm sorry, Isaac."

"Is that your way of telling me to get out?"

I glanced around the bathroom, my emotions tangled, my thoughts and truth at war. "I feel like your final months at home would have been easier if I'd never come to Elkins."

"I wouldn't change a goddamn thing." Isaac stepped in close, an arm's reach away, his hazel eyes peering into mine with intent. Lustful. Hopeful. "I've wanted you from the moment I saw you at the bottom of the stairs. You brought the dead part inside of me alive. Gave me something to cling to rather than the depression always hanging over my head."

His words radiated through me, so damn similar to my own emotions that my throat tightened. "We can't," I whispered rather than admitting I felt the same.

"We actually can."

"It's a sin."

Isaac stepped closer, laying his palm on my chest—damn near burning me and snagging my breath. "If that's what you believe this is, then I want to sin."

"You know I believe it."

"Well, I think you need to start using this—" he grabbed my dick "—instead of your head."

Fuck.

I hissed out an exhale as he squeezed and fondled my length to full life. "Isaac," I croaked, fighting my flesh and its lustful craving by fisting my hands at my sides.

"Hmm?" He studied my lower lip as I tried to lick moisture back to its dry flesh. One squeeze of my balls, and I lost my mind.

"Goddamnit." I grabbed hold of his head and smashed my lips to his, driving him backward until he hit the doorjamb.

"Ung," he groaned, giving me access to the sweet and spicy wetness of his mouth, the warmth inside. Hungry tongues dueled in a primal dance, and I ground my dick against his hand.

He grasped at my towel—it fell to the floor—his hot flesh replacing cotton to rub over my burning skin.

"Oh fuck," I groaned across his lips, panting. Urgency dictated, and I released his head, fumbling with his jeans' button.

"Hurry," Isaac whispered as I pulled back to see what I was doing.

Button.

Zipper.

Shove the jeans down to his ankles.

His gorgeous dick sprang upward into my hands. Hard and leaking—for me.

"Fuck yes." I dropped to my knees to the cool tile without a thought beyond tasting him. Smearing his pre-cum over my lips and licking them clean.

"Shit...fucking hell..."

My mouth closed over his swollen head, his saltiness coating my tongue. "Mmm," I hummed around him, taking him deep.

A thump accompanied his groan, and I glanced up to find his head tipped back against the doorjamb. Lips parted, he panted, and I buried my face into his groin, swallowing around his girth.

"Holy...f-fuck..."

His hips moved with me, giving me what I wanted—his dick shoved down my throat.

Shudders rippled through him, whimpers and gasps filling my ears and making me hard as granite.

I pulled off and shoved my tongue into his slit, searching for more of his salty precum.

"Fuck." He dropped his chin, eyelids fluttering open. Hazel eyes hazed with lust peered down at me.

The youth pastor on his knees, worshiping his cock.

Guilt rose to choke me, but I took him deep again, holding his stare.

Need this.

Need him.

Just this once.

I fondled his tight sack, my fingertip sliding over his perineum.

"Yes—please touch me, Malachi." He licked his lips, his hands finding the sides of my head to hold on tight. "Please. Please…"

He widened his stance, allowing me free access—and I took it, brushing the pad of my fingertip over his asshole.

"Oh God." His head hit the doorjamb again.

I rubbed, sucked, and swallowed around his length, all the while watching the twitches on his expressive face, the throes of passion overtaking him and parting his pouty lips.

Give it to me.

As though hearing my thoughts, Isaac opened his eyes. Met my gaze again—and came without warning, shooting spurts of thickness into my throat.

"Ung…" He groaned, thrust, gulped, and cursed, and my dick leaked precum onto the bathroom floor between my knees. "Holy f-fucking hell, Malachi," he rasped in a spine-tingling tone.

I sucked every last drop from his slit and sat back, my hands falling to my thighs.

Our gazes held, our pants echoing in the small room.

"Another first." A smirk curled the corner of his lips as he sagged against the wall, breathless. He glanced down at my aching dick I refrained from touching. "Want to take more?"

The fuck are you doing?

I closed my eyes, disgust over my weakness rising up like bile to burn the back of my throat. Grabbing my fallen towel, I stood and covered myself. "I'm sorry—"

"Don't you fucking dare." Isaac shoved his dick back into his jeans while I wrapped the towel around my waist with shaking hands.

"You can't—"

"Don't throw me out." His cracking voice made me pause, and I forced myself to look him in the eyes.

Pain filled their depths, the kind that assured me of the hurt Bram had inflicted. My heart ached for him even more than my balls did for release. Sending him away would be beyond cruel, and I couldn't bear to shred his heart more than his dad had already.

I let out a heavy exhale, knowing the temptation I faced in taking pity on the one my entire body longed for. "You can stay in the second bedroom tonight."

His smooth jaw clenched, and he turned without another word.

Once locked in the master bedroom, I leaned against the door and closed my eyes. While regret filled me over my actions, I had zero desire to get on my knees to beg for God's forgiveness. Giving Isaac pleasure and showing him what acceptance and desire could be like pleased me more than him sucking me off would anyway.

Better to give than to receive.

Fuck.

I scrubbed a hand over my face and strained my ears as Isaac went out the front door. Hurrying to the window overlooking the gravel parking area out front, I held my breath.

Hoping he wouldn't leave.

Unable to pray that he would.

He grabbed an overnight bag from the passenger seat, and my exhale rushed out.

Lips in a thin line, he stomped back toward the cottage.

The door slammed once more.

I eyed the wall, tracking his steps down the hallway, the squeak of the other bedroom hinges reassuring me he planned to do as I allowed.

Knowing I couldn't interact with him again that night without taking another of his firsts, I stayed put. Naked except for the towel. Listening as he settled in for the night.

Brushed his teeth.

Flushed the toilet.

But no bedroom door snicked or slammed shut.

He'd left it open on purpose, I didn't doubt. An invitation.

Shit.

I closed my eyes, my ears ringing in the stifling stillness.

A moan reached me.

Another.

Goddamnit. A muscle ticked in my jaw, but I quietly pulled my door open. His bedroom lay diagonal in the hallway, the angle too much for me to watch him jerk off.

I wanted—needed—to see him touch himself while thinking about me.

The craving to fill my eyes ghosted my feet forward, and I moved without introspection. Across the carpeted hallway. Hand on his opened door, I pushed it inward.

Isaac lay on his back, his hooded gaze on me while slowly jacking his length. Ten hot, slick-sounding seconds passed between us in silence before his lips parted. "I know you want me."

I couldn't deny the truth, couldn't stop watching the swollen head of his dick disappear beneath his palm and reappear between his fingers.

He rolled and lifted onto his knees, his ass on offer.

The pinkness of his rosebud made me salivate, and my dick twitched so damn hard it nudged the towel from my waist.

Sucking oxygen through my nose, I strode in, fisting myself. So much hunger for him rushed through my blood that I trembled.

It's not sin if I don't fuck him.

Clinging to that thought, I stood a foot away from his backside, his pale cheeks flexing as he continued to fuck his own hand.

He panted against the quilt.

Needy little brat. I should have swatted his ass red for what he did to me, how he made me feel.

Instead, I fucked my hand hard and fast through a mess of precum, pulling and panting, urging my tingling balls to release.

Isaac whimpered, his hole clenching right in front of my eyes—and I fucking blew like a geyser, spurting up his back.

"Oh fuuuuck," he groaned, his hips jerking in time with mine while I painted his ass cheeks a milky white.

Even emptied, my dick throbbed to fill him. Stuff him full.

Claim and own him.

I backed away, my pulse thrumming, my breath coming in ragged gasps. My body shuddered from having ejaculated harder than I ever had in my life.

Towel, I reminded myself, glancing at where it lay on the floor.

I shut the door with a finality I didn't want to accept.

Closed myself in my own room, locking the door to keep the brat out even though I craved his presence in more than just my bed.

Collapsed on my mattress, my emotions completely spent.

Quiet thoughts.

And an hour later, I still lay in the dark, alone, wondering over the numbness coating my mind and my lack of guilt.

Chapter 24

Isaac

He left me.

On my knees, covered in his cum, my hand smeared with my own release.

Holy fucking hell.

A whispered giggle rushed from my lungs, and I slid my body forward, sprawling on the mess I'd made.

Shit, was that hot.

I giggled again as a shudder rippled through me. I'd never felt so damn sated. Emptied.

Malachi hadn't fucked my ass like I'd hoped he would, hadn't taken me up on that offer of my biggest first, but satisfaction, bone-deep and bright, flooded me.

I closed my eyes, uncaring of the stickiness beneath me, simply wanting to soak in the happiness until it tugged me into dreamless sleep.

Not cleaning up before passing out wasn't the smartest choice, and I regretted it the second I opened my eyes to an early sunrise.

I rolled, the quilt beneath my naked body sticking to my balls long enough to tug at my pubic hairs.

"Fuck." Grimacing, I peeled skin from material and flopped onto my back with an "oomph" escaping my smiling lips at the stretch of his cum dried across my skin.

I hated early mornings, but fuck, did I feel refreshed.

The thought of who laid across the hall pulled me off the bed, and I snagged a pair of shorts I'd put out the night before, tugging them on while trying not to stumble across the carpet.

He'd closed his bedroom door.

I eased the handle.

He'd locked the damn door.

Fucker.

Unable to rouse the energy to scowl, I moved toward the open area, eyeing the lake through the slider doors. Fog drifted above the water, dancing like teasing fingertips over the ripples.

My skin shivered for such a touch.

Grinning, I strode outside and filled my lungs with warm, clean air, scented with flowers and pine.

A gorgeous morning and sunrise.

A new beginning.

Happy fucking birthday to me.

My steps came faster as I strode across the small lawn. Even faster as my foot met the first board of the dock—and I sprinted the remainder of the way, diving at its end.

Cool water swept over my skin, welcoming me into its depths.

Smiling, I kicked and swept my arms back, bringing me to the surface in a gasped rush. Warm air once more kissed my face, and I treaded water, the cells in my body feeling refreshed.

This is what freedom feels like.

I laughed and dove back down, exerting excess energy like I'd done every summer since I could remember. Frolicking and attempting to push water from my path.

A good twenty minutes passed before I felt him.

Rising to the surface, I turned to find what I already knew.

Malachi stood on the porch with a coffee mug in hand. Shirtless, gym shorts hanging low on his hips.

Watching me.

Enough distance separated us that I couldn't tell if he frowned or smiled, but his body appeared relaxed. No tension rode his shoulders, no rigid stance. He simply drank his coffee.

Even more buoyancy lifted my spirits, and I swam toward shore with steady strokes, found my feet, and traipsed through leaf debris and sand until I stepped onto dry land, water streaming down my limbs.

I hadn't thought to bring out a towel.

Malachi's gaze slid down over me, but my balls and dick were too damn chilled to so much as twitch.

I moved closer slowly, even though I wanted to sprint to him, afraid he might startle. "Morning," I greeted him from below the back deck, my head tipped to hold his gaze.

Sleepy blue eyes, sexy as fuck and vulnerable studied my face as he sipped from his mug. "Happy birthday."

My grin split open at his haggard morning voice. There was no stopping my emotions from spilling out. "Best one ever."

"Coffee?" he asked, motioning toward the cabin with his head.

"Sounds good." Other things sounded a hell of a lot better, but I would take him up on his offer since he hadn't come out scowling and telling me to get lost and move on with my life.

I sped up the deck's stairs, my feet barely landing on every other tread.

Malachi eyed my wet body for all of two seconds before turning away, his face unmoved. "Let me get you a towel."

I watched his ass as he walked back the hallway toward the bathroom, and I filled my eyes with every inch of his tanned, tattooed body as he approached again.

His shorts tented with a boner he hadn't sported while out on the deck, but he didn't bother using the towel in his hand to cover the evidence of what I did to him.

Malachi tossed the towel at my face, effectively tearing my focus off his dick.

Time to up my game.

Chapter 25
Malachi

I woke to the first rays of sunshine drifting over my face. As with every morning, I lay still, inhaling and shifting through consciousness. Most mornings, I forced my thoughts on prayer, starting the day right.

But I already felt right. Content. A quiet spirit.

Is this peace from You or because I didn't sin last night? Or is this because of him—Isaac being here—and me not wanting to be anywhere else?

Of course, He didn't answer.

Refusing to further question the serenity and happiness I'd been begging God to bless me with for months, I rolled from bed and tugged on some shorts.

Isaac's door stood open, his bed empty—quilt rumpled.

Had he slept? Left after I'd finally passed out?

My heart beat heavier in my chest, and I hurried toward the front of the house. A grunted exhale escaped me upon seeing his car still parked beside Dad's old truck. "Isaac?" I called, turning to look around the cottage.

He didn't reply.

A quick walk toward the sliders let me know where he'd gotten to.

His pale body cut through lake water like a knife, sure and steady, a haze of fog lingering mere feet above his head.

I realized I smiled while watching him enjoy his freedom. My contentment grew until I released a cleansing sigh. How could life suddenly feel so...damn perfect?

Having his body beneath mine would be even better.

Pushing down my morning wood that'd taken interest in Isaac, I ambled back into the kitchen area and pressed the Keurig's power button. After a quick visit to the bathroom to empty my bladder, my coffee sat ready and waiting. Steaming and fragrant enough to make me smile again.

The warmth of morning greeted me as I slid the door open and stepped out onto the back porch. That first sip of coffee poured down into my stomach, and I let out a silent groan of appreciation in my head.

Isaac still swam, and I enjoyed the sight of him while my taste buds thanked me over every swallow. A murky lake cut by pale, toned arms—I imagined he smiled too.

Eventually, he treaded water, his head swiveling my way.

Did he see me grinning into my mug? Fighting off the outward expression of complete...happiness? Zero guilt rode my shoulders. No regret for my actions the night before. If anything, I regretted not taking the gift that he'd first offered.

And that truth didn't even manage to twinge my conscience. God, the Holy Spirit, sat quiet in my head, same as He'd always done, and for the first time, I didn't care.

I found peace in His silence.

Isaac swam toward shore, holding my stare and all my focus. He walked out of the water, dripping like a pale god of the lake, all lithe muscle and sinew I wanted to lick and bite from head to toe.

A beautiful creature—hardly unholy—one worthy of my affection, and my eyes drank him down as he neared.

"Morning," I managed to croak out, remembering being on my knees for him the night before. Pleasuring him.

Worshiping him.

His grin, the first real one I'd ever seen, stole my breath, and I didn't remember filling my lungs again until I passed from his sight to grab him a towel from the bathroom.

Giddiness lit my insides, and I didn't question my rising desire. I let it free in the tranquility I'd found, allowing my craving for him to swell inside me until my dick throbbed, tenting my shorts.

I tossed the towel in Isaac's face to take his focus off my groin, to hide his calculating gaze and sexy as fuck smirk.

I moved into the kitchen, listening as he dried himself off. "Milk and sugar?" I asked, placing another mug beneath the coffee maker.

"Sure."

"Do you even drink coffee?" I asked without glancing over my shoulder.

"I do now."

Still smiling like a dork, I made the eighteen-year-old's first cup of coffee, and I turned to find him a few feet away—exactly as my tingling skin had recognized. He accepted the mug, our fingers grazing which caused both our lengths to jerk.

Guess the cold lake's effects on him had faded.

I slid onto one of the kitchen chairs and watched him exhale over the mug's top, steam rising toward his nose.

He sipped.

"Well?"

A grimace twitched his lips. "Tastes like burnt water. How can you drink this shit?"

"It's fucking delicious." I slurped another hearty sip myself and made an *Ahhh* noise after swallowing it down.

Isaac's focus stayed on my mouth, and I licked a droplet of coffee clear from my lower lip.

I didn't know what the hell had come over me, where the joy in my heart originated from, but I wasn't going to question it.

How *right* I felt inside.

My mind rested easy. God hadn't answered after years of begging, and I decided to let my emotions lead me since they had somehow found peace without a higher power.

"So, birthday boy," I said with a flirty tone, sitting back in my chair, my mug and hand propped on the table beside me. "What do you want?"

"You," he didn't hesitate to answer.

Isaac set his coffee on the counter, shoved his wet shorts to the floor, and straddled my lap as though I'd invited him to climb aboard. He snuggled in close, pressing his cool skin against my bare chest, soaking in the warmth I wanted to give.

Hell, I wanted him to take more from me. A shit ton, if my racing heart and throbbing dick were any indication.

"Hmm." I released my grip on my coffee mug that wasn't yet empty. I had better things to grasp. Like two plump ass cheeks, also cold to the touch. "You've got a great ass," I murmured, brushing my lips over his.

"It's yours whenever you're ready to claim it." He rocked against my straining length, sending a jolt through my entire body.

Fuck, he felt good on me.

"Hmm," I hummed again and licked along his tongue, waiting on guilt that never hit.

"You taste like coffee," he complained, angling his head away from my hungry mouth.

"You sat on my lap, brat. Deal with it or get off."

Those hazel eyes usually filled with disappointment and hurt smiled again as his lips curled upward. "I'd love to get off—after you give me my birthday present."

"And that would be...me." I didn't bother asking a question.

"Your dick." Isaac kissed my nose. "In my ass."

I pulled my head back to see his face better while sliding my fingers down between his cheeks, fingertips brushing over his hole.

His eyes rolled upward as I stroked with feather-light touches.

"Mmm, yes, please." A gulp sounded, his hazed over gaze capturing mine while he gyrated his hips, grinding against my dick.

My heart thrummed as I stared into his eyes, our souls connected in mutual need. "You're sure?"

"Let me have you," Isaac murmured, rocking again to rub our dicks together as I continued to play with his asshole. "And if your God wants to take me in return, it'll be worth the experience of having your body inside mine."

"It won't," I told him the truth, remnants of sorrow from losing Brian still buried in the deepest parts of my soul.

"It's my life." Isaac clasped my scruffy cheeks in his hands. "And if I want to be struck by lightning for fucking my youth pastor, that's my choice. Show me what it feels like to have a man own me, Malachi." He swallowed hard. "Love me."

Selfishness rose up inside me, an acute sense of determination. Giving Isaac what he craved could only bring me pleasure, and I wanted nothing more than to lavish that affection on him. Undivided attention. Because I could imagine what it would feel like—all the same things I'd always desired and had never found.

Warmth rushed through my body, centering in my groin, every inch of my skin tightening in readiness.

Sure, I damned us to eternal hell, but decision made, I stood, still grasping his ass. He wrapped his legs around my waist, holding tight. "My bed or yours?" I asked, heading toward the hallway with sure steps.

"I don't give a fuck," he stated, his voice husky. He was breathless. Eyes wide and shining. No hint of fear on his face.

I pushed in his bedroom door with my foot, deciding I wasn't about to fuck him on his parents' bed.

Our gazes held, tethered tight, as I crawled onto the mattress before settling my body against his.

"You're so fucking beautiful," I murmured, smoothing his dark, damp hair off his forehead.

Of one mind, our mouths came together, both of us reaching for my shorts. A quick shimmy, lips still fused, and nothing separated us.

Skin on skin.

Heat and hard muscle from mouth to toes.

Two leaking dicks that rubbed with every thrust.

"Fuck, do you feel good," I groaned, holding his hair and relishing the precum slickened length of him sliding along mine.

"My ass will feel better."

I stilled and peered down at him. "I don't have any lube."

Goddamnit to fucking hell...

Isaac scrambled from beneath me, bending over to rifle through his bag.

That ass.

"Damn," I groaned, palming my dick to calm the fuck down.

He hopped back onto the bed, shoving his hand at me.

I glanced down. A packet of lube...and a condom. "Have you done this before?" I asked. The thought he'd been too prepared for a virgin, that someone had gotten to him before me, twisted my stomach up tight.

"No. Just hopeful." Still smiling, he tucked himself in front of me. On his back. Legs spread.

Smooth chest. Tight nipples. Rippling abs and gorgeous, prominent hip bones.

My focus dropped to his drawn-up balls, to the silky soft skin behind and the pink puckered hole beneath. Mouthwatering and beautiful to the point I grew feverish.

Isaac lay spread out like a goddamn buffet, and after having gone without for almost five years, I was ravenous. Setting aside the condom and lube, I leaned in to feast. I licked across his clavicle, tasting the lake and musk of him. All man. Fucking delicious.

He grasped my head as I closed my teeth over a nipple, his curse making my dick twitch against his restless thigh. Nibbling and biting, I made my way southward, exploring every inch of his tautness, nosing and licking. Shadow and light played over his body from the open window beside us as I familiarized myself with every inch of his torso.

Goosebumps rose along the damp trail my tongue left behind, his whimpers and moans like music to my damn ears.

The tip of his dick bumped my chin, and I moved to the side, scraping my scruff down his length.

"Oh fuck." He half sat, our gazes locked while I rubbed my face all over his dick, flicking out my tongue to taste the precum leaking from his tip. "Suck me, Malachi. Please fucking suck me."

"I've got a better idea." I grasped his thighs, spread him wide, and licked over his asshole.

"God," he groaned, falling back to the bed, head tipped, veins popping along his flushed neck. A shudder rippled over him as I licked again. *"Christ...* hell, yes."

My dick throbbed as I twirled my tongue around his hole, tasting and breathing in his musky scent.

He grabbed the back of his knees, spreading to give me better access, and I settled against the bed to eat him until he begged for more. The first probe of my tongue earned me a delicious gasp, and the second had him grabbing hold of his balls and whimpering.

"Feel good?" I asked and slid back in, loving how he tightly contracted around my tongue.

"Mmm." He choked on his moan and swallowed hard. The sight of him, eyes hazed with lust and lips parted to pant while watching me eat his ass, made my dick leak.

With a groan, I dove back in until his tight ring became soft beneath my attention.

"Do you like my tongue in your hole?" I asked, rubbing the pad of my thumb over him.

"Fuck yes." Rasped and thready, his needy voice shot lust straight to my own balls. "M-more...please."

I pushed up to my knees, my saliva leaving his rosebud glistening and gorgeous.

I tore open the lube, not taking my eyes off where I craved to shove my dick. "You ever touch yourself down there?"

"Yeah." No hesitation, no embarrassment. Isaac knew who he was, what he wanted—and I'd never seen anything sexier.

Coating some fingers, I lifted my attention to his face. "Ready for me to stretch you?" I asked, teasing him in slow passes, gentle pressure on his pliant hole.

Pupils swelled, he moaned and pulled his knees back farther, opening himself up to me. "Yes. Fuck yes."

I slid one fingertip past his ring of muscle without resistance into tight heat.

"Fuuuck," he groaned, the tendons in his neck sticking out.

Teeth clenched over the thought of his body sucking my dick in like that, I pressed in little more.

He hissed, his eyes closing, but no discomfort lined his forehead.

A few more tender, shallow strokes, and I rotated my hand while sliding in deep to rub over his prostrate.

"Jesus! Fuck." He arched his back, head pressing hard against the mattress before he grabbed hold of his balls and tugged.

"Mmm." I couldn't help but moan my agreement. It'd been five years since I'd been with a man, but I hadn't lost my touch, thank fuck.

Sliding in a second finger brought on a slight grimace to his face, but he held my gaze, his pouty lips parting again, the pulse in his neck throbbing.

"Okay?" I asked, my voice as strangled as my fingers inside his ass.

"Oh yeah," he whispered, lifting his hips in offering for me to take more.

Sweat beaded on his brow as I worked him open, alternating scissoring to stretch him and rubbing his prostrate. His whimpers and moans made my balls pulse, and I added to the wet sounds of finger fucking by palming myself to smear precum down my length.

"Please, Malachi." He shifted, bobbing his leaking dick over his abs. "I-I'm ready."

Yes.

I pulled my fingers from him, and they shook while sheathing up my dick. A little more lube down over my length and I leaned forward, holding my base.

A pause caught my breath as our gazes locked.

The perfect time for guilt to rise, for my conscience to whisper about the sin I planned to commit.

Nothing rose to mind. No booming voice from the heavens promising fire and brimstone. Not a goddamn thing other than wanting to give pleasure to the young man I felt tethered to the deepest reaches of me.

I released a slow exhale, the responsible part of me needing to give him one last out. "This is what you want?" I placed the head of my dick against his hole and pressed forward enough he'd pay attention to the start of a stretch beyond mere fingers. "To be sodomized? Used for some pervert's pleasure?"

He held my stare, eyes hazed with passion. "I want to be used for *your* pleasure."

No man had ever offered me what Isaac did. Others had taken, gladly received—but they'd never freely given of themselves to me—*for* me.

Heat swelled inside my chest, an ache I'd never felt before—and I needed to share whatever it was with Isaac. I needed to be one with him, deeply imbedded in his soul.

I pushed, breaching his body, and he gasped, teeth clenched over owning the head of my dick.

Insane compression...strangling, perfect heat.

"Fuck are you tight," I groaned through clenched teeth. Glancing down, I watched my dick sink in another inch. Pulling out to the head again made Isaac hiss, but I pushed right back in, gaining ground and damn near swooning over how his ass sucked at my girth, welcoming and wanting. "Goddamn..." I repeated the action, my focus on his face. His furrowed brow. The lower lip caught between his teeth.

I should have felt concern over his obvious discomfort, but I found myself smirking from the bubbling happiness inside me. My quads tensed with the desire to stab into his body, to claim and own.

"Relax, brat," I murmured, grasping his thighs and spreading him wider. "Take the dick you've been begging for."

One last thrust bottomed me out in exquisite heat.

"Oh shit. Oh shit." He lifted his head and grabbed hold of my forearms, panting, his gaze glued to where I'd buried myself in his hot body.

"Holy fuck, Isaac." I fought to keep my focus on his flushed face rather than letting my eyelids fall shut at the perfect sensation of being inside him.

"Fucking hell." Isaac laid back, neck straining, eyes closed as his hole clenched around me. "Fucking *hell,* give me a second. Fuck, fuck, fuck…"

I wanted to devour him, to destroy his ass with years of pent-up lust, but more than that, I wanted him to savor the satisfaction of his birthday gift—needed it—and he had to be present for me to enjoy it. I leaned over him, cradling his face even though he still held tight to my arms. "Hey."

His long lashes fluttered as he opened his eyes.

Like a punch to my gut, a rush of longing, a craving for more than just the physical with Isaac filled me up, making my chest ache.

"Relax, baby. Just look at me—stay with me, okay?" My voice broke.

Baby…I hadn't used any term of endearment since Brian—but calling Isaac that seemed right. Perfect in a way no other name had before.

Isaac's lower lip slid back between his teeth, but he nodded. Moving one hand behind my head, he gripped tight like his ass did around my dick.

"I'll make it good for you, I promise. Just stay with me." I swiped my mouth over his, covering him with my body and kissing him until he went liquid. Lips soft. Hands grasping at my back, my hair. Heels digging into my ass, keeping *me* in the present.

Go time.

Chapter 26
Isaac

Malachi dizzied me with his mouth, distracting me from the thick dick shoved up my ass until I could relax at the invasion. He backed out, dragging his length from my body. One slow, steady push buried him balls deep, and I moaned against his lips, the initial stretch and sting of penetration dissolving into absolute, ridiculous pleasure of being stuffed full.

Two more gentle pull and push movements and I clutched at him, no longer relaxed. Energy raced over my skin, buzzing my cells with enough current to light a bulb. I'd played with my ass before while jerking off, but fingers didn't compare to the girth of Malachi's dick.

He finally filled me up, became one with me beyond connected gazes and mutual longing.

"Oh God, Malachi—so fucking good." I bit at his lips, whimpering. Going out of my fucking mind over being stuffed full of *him.* "So, so good." I continued to chant in my head, lifting my hips to meet his every stroke.

Experiencing the dream of Malachi's dick, every slick glide of him into me—inside my damn head and heart —*that* was fucking heaven. Damn perfection.

He planked and gave me more, thrusting rather than rocking in and out. He held my gaze, his blue eyes hazed with passion, and I clutched at his biceps, my heels tugging him in closer.

So much closer.

I wanted our souls entwined, fucking like our bodies did.

Precum leaked from my bobbing dick, oozing onto my abs that contracted with every push from Malachi. My balls ached, seized up and ready to explode, but I wasn't ready. Needed it to last longer. For an eternity.

His lower lip looked plumper, parted from the thinner upper one. I wanted to bite it. Lick it. Suck it.

"Give me your mouth," I begged, barely recognizing my own voice as ragged as it was.

He shifted his knees for a different angle and drove in while lowering his weight again, rubbing my prostate and trapping my dick between our bodies.

Fucking fireworks exploded behind my eyelids at the delicious friction on my length, and I groaned against his lips.

"Gonna come, baby?" he whispered over my mouth, the nickname bursting bubbles of pure joy inside my belly.

"Yeah." I gasped and clamped down on his lower lip with my teeth, holding on while he slid his abs oh so fucking perfectly over my dripping length.

Oh yeah.

My balls let loose, and wet heat spurted between our bodies, creating a slick mess for him to slide through while stabbing into my spasming ass.

His grunts and groans rushed my blood and made my ears ring.

Heaven buzzed me higher than any joint, and I floated in an ocean of euphoria without a care in the world as Malachi fucked into me over and over, pushing my back along the bed in his attempts to bury deeper.

"Isaac," he whispered my name with a gasp—and shuddered, his dick jerking inside my ass. His deep groan while coming sent a shiver through me that twitched my flagging dick.

I clung to him and licked at his lips as he panted, his head hanging above mine. One last tremor made him go limp in my arms, and he kissed me, his full weight heavy against my chest.

Our hearts raced together, skin and bone separating their life-giving thumps as reality returned.

Slow, languid kisses between us continued long after he pulled out of my sore backside and got rid of the condom. His caressing hands offered affection, giving what I craved until we lay spent. Sweaty and sated. A sticky, perfect mess.

No fucking way were we wrong.

The connection between us only intensified from what I had begged for. I'd never felt so cherished. Accepted.

Whole.

Malachi was all I'd imagined. He was all I could ever want.

"Worth being struck down for?" he asked without a hint of teasing, his eyes unreadable when he finally lifted his head from the crook of my neck where he'd rested for a full on five minutes of peaceful silence.

"Fuck yes—but no one is going to smote me for my supposed sins," I told him, rubbing my hand over his jaw so he would lean into the touch like he'd done a half-dozen times since gifting me the best birthday present ever. "That's your issue. Not mine."

Malachi kissed my palm, the act showing more intimate emotion than the kiss he brushed over my lips a second later.

"I loved how you said my name while coming," I told him, the memory burned into my head for life. Spank bank material and then some.

Our gazes locked, and the contentment, the complete lack of guilt in his eyes resonated with me. "I couldn't think about anything but you in that moment. Couldn't...I just..."

Smiling, I held him tight as he shoved his face back into my neck and breathed deep, his expanded lungs pressing me firmly into the bed. "Yeah," I whispered, closing my eyes, my heart lighter than it'd ever been. "Me too."

The openness between us lingered as we showered together, Malachi offering me full access to his body with his soap. I sudsed him from neck to toes, running my hands over swells and dips, my favorite being the V between his hips.

I jacked his stiffening dick a few times but continued on with my job, loving the coarseness of his leg hair against my palms. I learned his ticklish spots—behind his knees and his ankles of all places—and I learned the areas to touch if I wanted to make him moan. Perineum and balls.

My tongue on both, I sucked at clean skin and the water cascading over his chest and onto my face.

For the first time in my life, I licked up the back of a dick to the salty pre-cum smearing at his slit. Malachi's. My own length leaked at that reality.

"God." He moaned and took hold of my face, allowing me to go at my own pace—learning his flavor, the shape of his swelling head, the silken feel of him over my tongue. "Yes," he hissed, his fingers tightening in my hair. "Just like that."

I moved my mouth over him, holding the weight of his balls in my hands. Kneading. Tugging when they drew up.

"Isaac…"

I took him deep until I gagged, earning me another dick-twitching groan.

"Do you know how many times I fantasized about you choking on my dick?" he rasped, shooting lust straight to my groin.

Fuck.

My dick jerked between my thighs, and I grabbed hold of my balls to keep from shooting off before he came.

He fucked my face a few more thrusts, gagging me each time before pulling me up and into his arms.

He ate at my mouth without restraint, no hesitation or apology for his hunger. And the heat in his eyes when he pulled back showed no reservations. "I want you."

"I'm yours," I told him, breathless as hell.

We both stilled. Staring. Lost in lust—but more than just the need to fuck, for me, at least. I meant what I'd said—this was beyond the physical. It always had been.

Emotion in his eyes rolled over me and filled me the fuck up, leaving no room for depression, doubt, or desire for anything, anyone but him.

If he asked me to not leave, to put aside my dreams for Nashville, I would gladly agree.

Instead, he pulled me from the shower, dragged me into the bedroom without either of us drying off, and shoved me back onto the bed.

I sprawled happily, even though I wasn't so sure my asshole would be that thrilled with what the heat in his eyes promised. Regardless, I wasn't about to say no. Never in a million fucking years.

"Lube?" he asked, grabbing my bag off the floor.

"Side pocket." I laced my fingers behind my head even though my heart thrummed in anticipation. My hole clenched, but I continued to feign confidence over the thought of taking him inside my body again.

My dick was on board. Hard and leaking.

He climbed onto the bed, yanked my legs out straight, and straddled me.

My hands found his thighs.

"I want you," he repeated and tore open the condom.

"Show me how much," I said rather than stating he already had me whenever, however—

He rolled the condom down over my dick.

"Oh shit." I gulped, contracting my abs to raise my head and watch him smear lube down over my length, slowly jacking me, slickening every inch. He was going to put my dick inside his ass. Allow me to own him. "Fucking hell, Malachi."

"Can I?"

"Are you fucking kidding me right now?" I asked, my voice shaking from the adrenaline rushing through my blood.

My fingers clenched his thighs as he lifted and positioned my throbbing dick against his hole. He hadn't prepped.

Our eyes clashed.

"Malachi, shouldn't you—"

He sank down onto me, ripping whatever I'd planned to say from my lungs.

Malachi's body sucked me in without resistance until his ass rested against my groin. Tighter than any fist. Hotter than any hand or mouth. Pure, wicked torture, an overload of sensation...

"Jesus." I gasped, a full-on body tremor moving me beneath him from the absolute *fucking* perfection of being inside his body. "Jesus...fuck."

He planked, his blue eyes holding me captive, his asshole clenching around my girth. "So fucking wrong," he whispered, shifting forward and fucking himself back onto my dick.

"So fucking *right*," I tossed back, grabbing hold of his flexing thighs as he repeated the motion.

I trembled beneath him, the need to move, to fuck like an animal—barely restrained passion—keeping me rigid. Teeth clenched, I watched his face, his slack mouth as he used my body.

"Malachi," I whispered through clenched teeth, my short fingernails digging into his thighs.

"Fuck me."

Christ...

I thrusted to meet him, my breath leaving in a rush over how deeply I buried into his tight hole.

He groaned, head tipping upward, spine arching. "Fuck, you feel good, Isaac. So thick and hard."

My balls seized up against my body at his haggard tone.

"Wish you were bare," he said, as we slid apart and slammed back together again. "Want to feel your cum inside me."

Holy fucking shit.

"Don't talk dirty to me, or I'm gonna blow like the untried brat I am," I stated through clenched teeth, trying to stave off my building orgasm.

"Mmm." He smirked down at me, moving over me like a sex god. The look on his face was so far removed from the stoic Malachi I'd already fallen for that my heart ached along with my balls. "Don't blow yet, baby. Let me ride you."

Baby...

"Fucking hell," I muttered, tearing my focus from his lust-filled eyes to check out where his hot ass swallowed my dick.

Back and forth, slick glides, and clamping heat.

So damn good—I needed to tug down on my balls but couldn't reach them.

Don't blow like a damn kid. Don't blow. Don't blow...

Couldn't see. Goddamnit, I wanted to *see* my dick owning his ass.

"Want to take over?"

"Hell yeah." I shoved at Malachi, desperate to get between his thighs like I'd had wet dreams about, never in a million years thinking I'd experience that side of heaven.

He rolled and raised his legs, hands clasping the backs of his knees. Thick, dripping cock. Blond curls around his tight balls. Lube-slickened hole that looked way too small to take my girth even though it had stretched for me seconds earlier.

My limbs shook as I crowded in close, a little unsure of myself even while my length throbbed to sink deep again.

"Put your dick inside me."

"Holy fuck." I gulped and pressed the tip of my length against his puckered hole.

"Give it to me, Isaac."

Fuck, when he said my name like that…

I squeezed my base and inhaled a shuddering breath to get ahold of myself. One slow push forward and his ass sucked me in like a greedy bitch—all the way in, balls deep. Curses spilled from my clenched teeth as I held still, fighting to not ejaculate at the clear sight of my dick—*mine*—buried inside Malachi Foley's body.

"Fuck. I… Shit." I gulped again, my fingers digging into his thighs.

"Move."

I blinked and found Malachi watching me, brow furrowed, lower lip tempting me to bite.

Backing out damn near made my eyes roll into my head, but I moved forward and grasped his lip between my teeth. He grunted into my mouth with every thrust as my body took over. Fucking without thought. Harder. Deeper—not damn near deep enough.

He didn't complain about my erratic, frantic movements but locked his heels around my ass and pulled me into him forcibly and fast, his hips rising to meet mine.

And it was me who whisper-hollered his name while coming, me who ended up smearing his cum all over our torsos when rubbing my body into his while breathing against his neck.

Absolute. Fucking. Heaven.

Chapter 27

Malachi

We walked through my pastor's cottage in nothing but shorts slung low on our hips. Shoulders brushing, hands groping more than once while gathering supplies to make a late breakfast.

I kissed the back of his neck as he poured batter onto the griddle, and he ground his ass against my groin. The scent of sausage frying on the stovetop filled my nose, making my stomach growl, but I felt more ravenous for the young man in my arms than food.

Holding onto his chest, his back hot and solid against mine, I slid my hand down over his torso, fingertips mapping out every indent between muscle and bone.

"You're perfect," I murmured against his ear, knowing he couldn't be told that fact often enough.

Isaac set aside the batter and turned, grabbing my hips to bring our groins together. Both spent but still wanting.

I kissed him, licking at the fresh cinnamon flavor of his mouth, groaning at how the emptiness in my chest had completely dissipated. He felt good beneath my hands and even better in my heart.

Pulling back, I studied his face. Lips pink and swollen from kissing. Cheeks flushed, eyes free from shadows and...happy.

"I'm not sorry," I told him quietly, smoothing his hair back from his face.

He clutched at my hips, keeping me close. "I was afraid you would be."

So open...when he'd been closed off, cryptic, and hurting before.

"I don't know what it is," I went on, needing to make him understand what I wasn't even sure I did. "I—I've been begging God to fill me, to give me peace and joy, but He never has. All through Bible college, I felt empty, going through the motions in the hope I did right."

He smirked as though he knew where I headed.

"Brat."

Isaac's smile widened, but I kissed it away.

"Pancakes," he whispered against my mouth, and I let him go so he could turn and tend to our breakfast.

I wrapped my arms around his waist and settled my chin on his shoulder while he flipped the golden discs over. "My chest isn't hollow anymore."

"Neither is mine."

A shuddering sigh rippled through me. "I'm happy for the first time in I don't know how long."

"Same."

"They say you can't find joy in others unless you're content with yourself."

Isaac turned again, rubbing his palm along my scruffy jaw. I leaned into his touch, closing my eyes.

"I'm calling bullshit on that one," he stated with absolute assurance.

Chuckling, I kissed his palm. "Why's that?"

"Because you make me feel normal. Accepted. *That* makes me happier than I've ever been—no fucking way is it wrong."

I couldn't argue with his logic. Didn't want to. So I kissed him again before releasing my hold on his luscious body.

"Breakfast." One last peck to his lips and I tore myself away.

Five pancakes and four sausages later, I sat nursing another cup of coffee while he finished eating.

"Do your parents know where you are?"

"No. They probably think I'm halfway to Nashville by now."

The idea of him leaving for Tennessee at the end of... whatever it was we were doing made my stomach churn, and I shifted on my chair.

He glanced up, his gaze questioning. "What's wrong?"

I smiled to ease his obvious tension, hoping to do the same for me. "Nothing. Want to take out the canoe?"

Isaac studied my face for a few seconds, but just when I felt sure he was going to call me out for lying, he nodded. "Sure."

* * *

We spent the afternoon on the lake, swimming when it got too hot, only heading out in the canoe for a half hour before agreeing the seats were too damn hard on our sore asses.

Refreshing laughter infused every conversation, even when he asked about Brian, and I shared it all. Everything he wanted to know. How I'd talked the shy, gay kid into sneaking around with me, even at church, taking advantage of darkened corners and closets for hand and blow jobs.

For the first time, my heart didn't ache at the memories, and I wondered over the reason. The pink skin of the young man who'd been out in the sun too long, the full, smiling lips, the hazel eyes glancing down over my body every so often...Isaac was so much more to me than Brian ever had been.

He understood why I'd struggled to make the "right" choices and the high expectations placed on me by my

God-fearing parents, even though mine had been loving in their leading. We shared the loneliness we'd endured due to the secret parts of us and the craving of affection, of unconditional love from another man.

The need to be ourselves outside of what we'd been force-fed and what I'd dragged my ass back into due to a promise made to my gracious mom.

Or perhaps I'd lived and learned enough to move on from past wounds.

Either way, I gloried in the freedom from sorrow and simply enjoyed the stories I shared with him.

Isaac had no such past to admit to other than fingering himself and jerking off to porn while imagining the only guy he'd craved.

Me. His youth pastor, a man forbidden to him but too tempting to ignore.

"I wanted you to follow me to our bunk room that night up in Maine."

His smirk was contagious, and I filled my eyes with him rather than the small fire we'd built together for s'mores after our grilled chicken dinner. "I knew you were going to be trouble from the start."

"*Just a man*," Isaac repeated what I'd told him all those months ago. He snorted and laced his fingers through mine resting on my thigh. "You're ten times more than most."

"You haven't met that many men," I said, my lips losing their upward tilt.

"Don't get all insecure on my ass."

I raised an eyebrow his way, but he left his lawn chair for my lap, the one beneath me creaking as he settled sideways across my thighs. "This thing might not hold us both."

"Don't give a shit. I've got something to tell you, and I don't want you to see anything but me when I say it."

I gave Isaac my full attention, our arms naturally finding their way around the other.

"I'm young."

Too damn young.

"And my life is only beginning." He studied my face, but I didn't hide. I wanted honesty. Needed it after a lifetime of lies. "But I know who my heart and body craves. This isn't just a bunch of firsts for me like marks on some board of accomplishments, Malachi. I want this. Us. And if that means no Nashville for me, then I'll gladly give it up."

For once, I hadn't needed to pull teeth. Isaac opening up, utter honesty from those lips...I'd never seen or heard such a beautiful thing. But being a selfish bastard at my core, I lusted for more. A tightening of that connection between us, that part inside him that called to me.

"Do you have your guitar with you?" I rasped, my heart near to bursting.

"Yeah."

I brushed my thumb over his lower lip. "Will you sing for me?"

Isaac hopped up without a word and disappeared around the side of the cottage.

The fire popped as I soaked in the meaning of his words—and the ones he'd written and put to song.

Was it possible for an eighteen-year-old kid to know his heart and mind? Was it possible our stolen moments together...could last? A new ache, a sweet one, swept through my chest, and I rubbed at my T-shirt, wondering at the strangeness of it. Not hurt but not joy.

Pleasure/pain, an addictive feeling.

The sun slowly sank beyond the opposite shore of the lake, sending a rainbow of color through the sky overhead. An end to my final day of vacation...

I had no idea what our future held. The thought I wouldn't have a job much longer, that I'd let down my mom settled on my shoulders, weighing me down and stealing some of my happiness—but not entirely. Nothing would stop the ebb of rightness I'd found in my soul.

And another thing I knew for certain—I wasn't about to let Isaac set his dreams aside.

Whistling, he rounded the cottage with his guitar case in hand, and I let out a sigh, my lips tilting upward again.

He settled into his chair and fiddled with the strings until his strumming fingers sounded right in both our ears. With a soft smile on his lips, he started plucking out the tune I recognized from Maine.

He sang to me like he'd done that night when I'd been swamped down by guilt, sharing his heart, his thoughts through music.

Broken.

Bleeding.

His tone rolled over me, his gaze held mine, and the desire sweeping over us stirred my entire body to life, pushing my worries aside for another day.

Wanting to fall. Worship you.

Needing you.

Without words to beg for your touch.

I sat struck dumb, same as the first time, unable to tear my stare off his beautiful face. His fingers manipulated the guitar's strings, gifting my ears with a haunting melody...

Energy buzzed through my veins, my entire body tingling with the urge to take him into my arms again, breathe him in, taste his kiss. Those sexy as fuck lips formed words that struck my heart with understanding.

Love.

The notes faded into the darkness growing around us.

"You wrote that about me."

The duck of his head, the shy smirk affirmed my statement.

"Sing it again."

He did—and the second he reached the chorus I'd caught the melody of, I joined in harmony. Isaac's voice cracked at the first couple of notes of us sensually rising, entwining, but he focused on my mouth like I did his, his tone growing sturdy once more with every word we sang together.

Beautifully.

Over and under, I weaved notes through his, and my pulse thrummed from the thrill, the absolute joy of creating magic with the young man who'd managed to weasel his way into my head and heart.

And later that night as he slept beside me, cramped on his tiny twin bed, I evaluated the fullness inside me. The contentment.

All I'd been searching for in the church, in the Bible... love, excitement, passion—life—I'd found with him. I settled my head onto the pillow we shared, tugging him just a bit closer, even though our skin touched from chest to toes.

What I felt for Isaac went far beyond my relationship with Brian, the one I'd thought had been my love, my partner for life. I'd survived his death, but I knew I wouldn't survive Isaac's.

I couldn't live without him.

I wouldn't.

But as always, I couldn't find the words to beg a God I'd begun to question to let me keep him.

Chapter 28

Isaac

I normally hated Sunday mornings with a passion, but opening my eyes and becoming conscious of why I was hot and sweaty brought a rush of adrenaline, an excitement to start the day.

Malachi.

In my bed, our limbs tangled.

Shifting my head on the pillow we shared, I found his lips slack, parted in sleep.

Hair getting too long on top and curling. Blond scruff lining his jaw and cheeks. Pale lashes lying still beneath his eyes. His slightly crooked nose and freckles darkened from our hours in the sun the day before.

So gorgeous.

I wanted to bite him, lick him awake, but I settled for relaxing there while facing him and just soaking the sight in. Enjoying the chance to study his face. Etching it into my memory forever so one day I could die a happy man.

A humid summer breeze drifted across my skin from the open window behind me, doing little to cool me off as the sweat between our torsos worsened.

The thought of cool water promised relief and twitched my legs with the need to move. I couldn't lay still. And Malachi looked dead to the world. His non-morning ass would need coffee to wake up, and my body already buzzed with readiness for the day.

His heavy breathing didn't hitch as I slid from beneath his arm. Grinning, I took one last, long look over his sprawled body as he settled onto his belly...muscular back, rounded ass. Powerful thighs I'd scratched the hell out of while he'd fucked my sore ass before I passed out the night before.

I tested my backside with a little clench of my ass cheeks, grimacing over the ache left behind from his plundering.

But my dick swelled at the thought of doing it again.

Shaking my head, I forced my feet to carry me away, grabbed my shorts, and headed outside.

No haze of fog hung over the lake, just pure sunshine's rays as it peeked over the trees behind me.

We'd slept in—not surprising, considering how long we'd stayed up "sinning."

Best damn night of my life.

Freedom tasted better than I'd imagined too.

I dove into the water, mentally muttering an *Ah* as the coolness slid over my skin, washing away the sweat and remnants of cum from my belly. My throat decided in that moment to let me know how parched it felt, that I'd never dragged my ass from bed the night before to slake the thirst from fucking for an eternity.

Kicking and gyrating like a mermaid brought me back up to the surface, and I swiped the water from my eyes, checking on the front of the house.

No Malachi yet.

Taking my ass must have worn the old man out.

Snorting a chuckle, I backstroked a few yards, staring up into the sky emptied of clouds. Two birds flitted overhead, one chasing the other.

I thought again of heading to shore for some much-needed water, but I closed my eyes and told myself I'd go back soon. Too many delicious, tumbling thoughts filled my head, demanding my attention.

I'd meant what I'd said about giving up Nashville for him. If he asked me to stay by his side wherever he ended up, I would—because his job as my dad's youth pastor sure as fuck would end the second we returned to Elkins.

Imagining Dad's reaction to seeing us together, hands held, filled me with renewed giddiness as I cut through the water again. Warmth infused my muscles with every steady stroke leading me farther from shore.

A slight cramp grabbed hold of my calf, and I rolled to my back again, hoping to breathe the relentless ache away.

Blue sky. Yellow sun. Cheerful, chirping birds.

Never had I enjoyed a morning more, never had I felt such contentment.

All because of Malachi. His touch, his kisses, his acceptance.

I'd found heaven on earth, and nothing and no one would take it from me.

Chapter 29
Malachi

The scent of Isaac's skin and cum filled my nose, and I buried my face in the pillow, sniffing as wakefulness came over me. I reached for him, needing to know the night before hadn't been a dream.

I lay alone in his bed.

Lifting my head, I blinked with bleary eyes at the sunlight in the window.

The hell time is it?

I sat and rubbed a hand over my face, my stubble starting to itch.

Gotta shave.

But first…

"Isaac?" He didn't answer to my call, and I didn't hear him moving around the cottage. After a quick stop in the bathroom to empty my aching bladder, I shuffled into the kitchen.

No dreamy, pink-sunned skin and pouty lips.

Coffee.

Scratching at the dried remnants of cum around my groin, I flicked on the Keurig.

Awareness tickled along my nape—but not the energy that let me know Isaac entered the room. I turned, my gaze going to the slider and lake beyond. A sense of… something…urged me to go, and my feet moved on instinct.

I slid the door open. "Isaac?" I called, quickly glancing around the back yard, fire pit, and dock. "Isaac?"

"Mal—!"

I whipped toward the edge of the cove, my heart hitching at the cut off holler. A dark head bobbed in the lake along the edge of where placid waters met the current. He sank. Reappeared.

"Isaac!" I screamed and sprinted across the yard, an overwhelming sense of dread choking off my oxygen.

An arm flailed.

The water stilled.

No, no, no! Don't You dare do this to me again!

I dove into the water, still screaming at God in my head, strong strokes taking me toward where I'd seen Isaac last. Adrenaline coursed through me, giving me speed I wouldn't usually have, and I pulled up to the spot, treading water, spinning in circles.

"Isaac!" I shrieked, nausea rolling in my stomach.

Nothing.

I dove, but the murky water proved too hard to see through within a matter of feet beneath the surface.

There was no God in that moment. No guiding light, no silent Holy Spirit prompting me in the right direction.

Just anguish and anger—and the deepest regret that I might not be able to experience a full life with Isaac.

You're no God of love.

I went back under, pain etched in the back of my throat.

Resurfaced and went down again, the sensation of things moving too slowly rippling over me.

Coming up empty, my chest hollowed out with every agonizing second that passed.

I've done everything to please you. Denied myself for years. And for what? Fuck you, and fuck the supposed truth of that book men claimed you wrote.

Isaac had been right. Even if God existed, I'd rather burn in hell than worship the kind of narcissistic tendencies he portrayed.

"Isaac!" I choked out a sob as my legs and arms grew weary, yet still I spun in a circle, searching the water around me and the dark trees on shore, the sun glinting and blinding me.

Isaac... Fuck.

I sobbed, blinking in the bright sunlight, turning my face from its golden rays, and allowing the current to take me southward—toward shore—toward...

A body bobbed feet away from the edge of a neighboring cottage.

Fresh adrenaline burst through me, and I cut across the water with precise movements, no longer tired.

He's okay...he's going to be okay.

Because if he wasn't, I couldn't go on.

Chapter 30
Isaac

Malachi screamed my name, but I couldn't draw breath to reply. I managed the first syllable before water closed over my head, filling my mouth. Choking me.

Should have gone back...

My calf continued to cramp from dehydration, the agony making it impossible to kick, and my arms had long since failed me.

Malachi.

I kicked with all I had left in my good leg, but exhaustion burned through my muscles.

Water crested over my face.

Sunlight.

I lifted a hand toward the warmth, but I sank again.

So tired.

Darkness crowded in, and there was no God. No emotion.

Just silence.

I floated, blinking, no longer choking.

Waiting for blinding light. The pearly gates. Or fire and brimstone.

But there was nothing, just the darkness creeping in, closing over me and offering peaceful, quiet freedom—

Fuck, how my lungs burned.

Hell is real after all.

"Fucking breathe!"

I coughed—and liquid rushed from my stomach. My lungs expanded.

Agony knifed my chest.

I vomited again, heaving and gagging.

"Isaac." Strong hands lifted me the second I sagged. Held me as I fought to inhale through the feeling of jagged glass that cut through my lungs. "Damnit, Isaac." Malachi sobbed, clutching me against him.

It took me a few seconds of shivering to realize we sat on shore.

I blinked at blinding sunlight, pulling blessed oxygen into my aching lungs and becoming conscious enough to take stock of my body. Cold. So cold. Teeth-clattering and body aching.

"You're not dead. Thank fuck you're not dead." Malachi kept muttering. He looked me full in the face, his brow furrowing as he finally came into vivid focus. He smoothed my hair back as water dripped off his and onto my face. "You're okay," he murmured, kissing my forehead. "You're okay. Okay."

We rocked back and forth, and I burrowed against his warm muscle, listening to the steady thump of his heart.

Not dead—but I'd been there.

"Your b-beliefs are sh-shit," I rasped out and coughed, closing my eyes and remembering the darkness as his lips pressed to my forehead. "There's no b-bright light. No p-pearly gates. Only darkness. Accidents."

A tremor wracked through me in Malachi's arms, and he clutched me closer, his arms a vise. "I know."

My first free inhale left in a rush, and I smiled against the softness of his skin I never thought I'd feel again. He'd saved me. The one I worshiped—my Malachi.

Chapter 31
Malachi

Isaac didn't want to go to the hospital, but I wouldn't bend. The twist in my stomach wouldn't rest until I had him checked out even though he swore it'd been nothing but a damn leg cramp due to dehydration that had gotten the best of him.

We weren't in the ER for more than an hour hooked up to an IV for fluids before being given the green light he'd be just fine. I inhaled an unrestricted breath for the first time since seeing him go under the water.

We got back to the cottage, and I took him into the shower with me, holding him close and soaking in the warmth of his skin, the steady pulse of the blood pumping throughout his body.

Alive. Breathing.

The peace, the joy I'd been searching for, had landed in my arms unexpectedly. Contentment and happiness hadn't come from submitting to God's will or from following a dark path he'd refused to light for me.

No. I'd found what my soul longed for in a young man. One who understood my struggles, my mind's workings even when I'd pushed him away in my attempts to stay "pure." He'd given my soul light when I needed it. Flooded my heart with emotion I'd craved for years. I wouldn't ever put distance between us again in any way. Nothing would take him from me—no one.

"Refusing you was slowly killing me," I murmured against his hair, holding his head to my chest. "I had no hope for a fulfilled life because I was missing a piece of myself. *Denying* an important part of myself."

A shudder ripped through me at memories of the emptiness I'd wasted time waiting for faith to fill.

Isaac's arms squeezed around me tighter, keeping us close, without a hint of air between our bodies as warm water cascaded down over us.

"And when you almost drowned today..." I swallowed hard, the truth sending a shudder through my body. "I realized I'd almost lost my heart, the peaceful place I'd been searching for."

Begging God and striving toward, I added in my mind. An empty, useless endeavor that had only gifted me with guilt and heavy heartedness.

But no more. I'd found my truth, the path I would gladly traverse through life.

With Isaac—my light. My salvation.

He looked me full on in the face, his eyes full of emotion I could feel swirling in my chest, tethering us together.

"I survived the sorrow of Brian's death, but I wouldn't survive losing you," I told him, tears welling for at least the tenth time since I'd dragged him from the water and performed CPR. Beat his chest. Demanded he breathe for me. Stay with me.

Isaac laid his head against me again, melting in my arms. His fingertips trailed down my back, offering tender affection. "You saved me," he whispered, his lips ghosting over my skin.

"I'd wanted to save you from *yourself* for the past couple of months," I reminded him, and he pulled back to peer at me, his gaze soft and vulnerable, "but you're perfectly you, Isaac. *Everything* about you is perfect. Don't ever change. Be you. Chase your dreams and be free."

"So you're saying you want me to take off without you."

"Fuck no." I yanked him back against me, the thought of him leaving me behind bring bile up the back of my throat. "I'm just saying that if loving you is a sin, is wrong, then I don't want to be right."

"So cliche."

"Shut up, brat."

He chuckled and bit my nipple.

"Ow!" I jerked away, backing into the hot spray.

"You really ought to get these pierced," he said, squeezing my hard nub, his lips quirking up in a teasing grin.

The time for reflection had come to an end. "Yeah?"

"That'd be sexy as fuck." He climbed up my body and wrapped himself around me, his hazel eyes filling with a look I recognized, one that made me hard within seconds. "The doctor said to take it easy," I told him.

"And the book you believe in—"

"Past tense," I growled.

"—says we'll burn in hell, but I don't give a shit. I want to feel you moving inside me bare with nothing between us, reminding me I'm alive. That we didn't lose what we've just found." His voice broke at the end, betraying a vulnerability I wanted to protect for eternity.

He wound his fingers around my neck, pressing in close, and my hard dick poked at his ass as he ground against me. "Loving you in this lifetime would be worth burning for eternity," I whispered, my focus on his pouty lower lip.

"Love, huh?" His lips curled up, and I leaned in to lick across the seam, water from the shower coating my tongue.

"*Love*." I licked again, and he parted for me, but I wasn't done. "Unconditional." One gentle nibble led to another, and Isaac grabbed hold of the back of my head to keep me still.

"Quit it with the teasing and just kiss me," he demanded, tears in his eyes.

So I did.

Chapter 32

Isaac

Malachi laid me on my bed and tongued my asshole until I begged for his dick. Still, he refused, dragging out my torture by fingering my hole slow and gentle.

Fucking doctor and his suggestions to take it easy.

I needed my man inside me. Deep and fast. Blowing my goddamn mind.

"Malachi," I groaned as he sank a third finger into my body, stretching and twisting to rub against my prostate. "Jesus...fuck."

Pre-cum oozed from my slit, dripping onto my stomach.

"Getting you good and ready for me, baby—" he leaned in to kiss me "—so I can slide my dick straight into your body without having to work for it. Want your tight heat sucking me in, swallowing me whole."

"Fuck." I gulped and clutched at the sheets beside me. "Please, Malachi. I'm ready. Just use extra lube and don't stop once you start."

"Needy little bitch."

Fuck, did I love being called that—almost as much as baby.

"*Your* bitch."

Narrowing his gaze, Malachi sat back, taking his fingers with him and leaving me empty and restless. "You mean that?"

Fuck, the vulnerability in his eyes...

"Fuck yes, now hurry," I demanded, breathless. I grabbed hold of my dick, slowly jacking myself, tugging on my balls to calm the fuck down.

He smeared lube down his length, rubbing in time with me. Three strokes and I had enough of the waiting.

"Give me your dick." I lifted my knees, offering him my hole. And of course, his focus went right there.

Moving in, he shook his head, licking his lower lip. "Damn, you are hot as fuck."

"You love me," I sang to him, smirking as he planked over me. "You think I'm sexy—"

Malachi thrust into my body without warning. Balls. Fucking. Deep. "Damn right I do," he groaned between clenched teeth.

He stole my breath, and the stinging stretch of him… fuck the *feel* of him…bare skin—Malachi—without anything between us…

My thoughts fragmented, curses scattering through my brain.

"Fucking hell," I gasped, grabbing his neck and yanking him down. I could have sobbed at how good he felt inside me. "F-fucking need you," my voice broke.

He took my mouth, ignoring the doctor's orders, fucking me into that mattress like he couldn't get enough of me, my body. Every thrust, every moan reminded me blood still roared through my veins, oxygen still filled my lungs.

He'd saved me.

And there wasn't anything I wouldn't give him.

My body took over, moving with him, seeking release. Chasing fulfillment I wouldn't find anywhere outside of him. Nothing separated us, nothing to dim the pleasure of his slickened skin rubbing inside me, over my prostate, jacking my goddamn heartrate and the need to come sky high.

Mine, mine, mine, my mind chanted with every snap of his hips slapping his balls against my body. "Malachi," I whimpered, holding onto him for dear life.

So much damn *fucking* need...

"Come for me, baby." He grabbed my cock and jacked me off in time to his thrusts, sweat dripping down his cheek as he held my gaze. "Shoot your spunk all over your chest. Coat my hand in it."

Fucking hell, his mouth.

He angled his hips, rubbing me just right.

"Oh fuck." I curled upward onto my elbows and watched him fuck into me, panted for oxygen while my dick disappeared in his hand as he rubbed at my glans. "Fucking hell...right there. Don't stop. Fuck, don't st—"

A burst of cum shot up over my chest, and I gasped, reaching out to grab Malachi behind his neck, bringing our mouths together. Heat burst inside my ass, and I swallowed his groan as he thrust into me, both of us shuddering our release until the very last dribble of cum.

I went limp, falling back to the bed, and Malachi came with me, once more smearing a mess between us, our mouths fused as we attempted to suck oxygen between gasping kisses.

He finally relaxed fully, putting his face into my neck, and I let out a sigh that left me boneless. Depleted and completely spent.

"I'm leaving the ministry."

My breath snagged.

Malachi Foley, the man I'd been after for months, had blessed me with so much more than I'd ever hoped for.

He was giving up his God, his fucking job...to be with me.

Elation swelled in my chest, and warmth radiated throughout my entire body until my eyes burned with unshed tears. I wrapped my arms around him, smoothing my hands down his back, unsure how he would take my congratulations if I verbalized them.

"I never felt the calling some men do," he continued as I struggled to express my feelings. "I only agreed to go because my mom begged me to while on her deathbed."

Malachi brushed his lips over my neck, sending a shiver over my skin. "I tried to force myself into a box in order to please my parents."

"I know how that feels," I muttered, continuing to caress him, making him aware I understood even though he'd told me his parents had adored him until they'd drawn their final breaths.

He lifted his torso away from mine, his face relaxed, his eyes exhausted. "From the first, I felt a connection to you, like our souls..."

"Recognized each other," I finished for him, rubbing my palm along his scruff.

"It's what drew me to you—your pain, your depression over not feeling 'normal.' Wrong."

"We aren't wrong," I assured him even though I figured he had realized and accepted that.

"We're beautiful." He kissed me, a soft brush of lips that curled my toes. "You're beautiful. Wonderfully made."

I snorted a sarcastic laugh against his mouth even as my heart flooded over with happiness. "Let's keep one-liners like that in our past, m'kay?"

Malachi chuckled and backed out of my body.

I hissed at the sting, hating the emptiness he left behind even more.

He drew up onto his knees to spread my thighs wide. Wet heat oozed from my sore hole. "My cum looks good on you."

"Mmm?" Another hiss escaped me as he pushed his cum back into my body. "Caveman."

"*Your* man."

Tears once more threatened. "Promise?"

Malachi slid his finger from my ass, caught my gaze and held it, assurance in his eyes. "For eternity, remember?"

So much damn emotion—I didn't know what to do with it. Couldn't vocalize that I felt the same, wanted the same. For eternity.

"Then that means I'm going to your place with you tonight." I went the teasing route, grinning up at him, my heart as light as a feather on a summer breeze. "I'm staying with you—and you're going to let me."

"Damn right." Malachi knelt over me and planted another firm kiss on my lips. "You're adorable, Isaac Van Dusen. Even when you're a brat. Now let's get cleaned up in the shower and head home."

Home.

My heart pinged as a rush of emotion swelled up inside me. One where I would be accepted unconditionally.

That ping in my chest took on a slight ache, and my throat tightened as Malachi walked out of the bedroom. But going there to stay also meant my dreams of Nashville would end before they began.

Chapter 33
Malachi

I didn't bother with a suit and tie but decided on slacks and a button-down shirt for my last day of walking into Elkins Bible Church. Dad's old truck rumbled out of my driveway, and I pulled up my best friend's number on my cell to give him an update on what had gone down.

"Hey, Zeke."

"No, *Hello, Ezekiel*?" He chuckled.

I turned out onto the main road, heading toward town. "Not in the teasing mood."

"What's going on?"

No point in shooting the shit. I only had a few miles to travel. "Isaac is in my bed."

"Oh fuck." I could imagine him scrubbing his hand down over his face. "My uncle is going to flip."

"He already did—on Isaac for coming out—but he doesn't know about us yet."

"Us, huh?"

"There's no denying it, no stopping it as far as I'm concerned."

"And what does your conscience tell you?"

"That I've found my other half. The light I've been searching for."

"Shit." Zeke kept silent for a few seconds, and I let him absorb all I'd said.

"I'm heading to the church right now to resign."

"You're giving up God's calling on your life for an eighteen-year-old kid?"

"I never *felt* the call, Zeke," I told him, my voice firm. "Never felt God leading me like the Bible promises.

You know I chose that path for my life to make my parents proud, to make up for Brian's death." Even though it *had* been an accident, I quietly reminded myself of what I'd never been able to accept prior to meeting Isaac.

"Is taking a chance with this kid worth eternal damnation?"

I huffed a laugh. "I asked myself the same thing. Countless times. And I've come to the cliche conclusion that being one with him, even for a few moments in time, is worth anything any god might toss my way."

"You've gone so far that you would deny Him?"

I knew the Him Zeke referred to. "I can't believe in a supposed God of love who designs creations with needs and desires that go outside his Word."

"It's because sin entered the world."

"I'm calling bullshit," I stated, sounding like Isaac. "If you had a son, would you allow someone or something to physically alter his makeup? His DNA, the chemicals in his brain, knowing doing so would cause misery?

Would you force him to live a lie in order to be on good terms with you? Tell me that isn't fucked up, Zeke. Explain how that isn't cruel."

"My human mind can't fathom it, but I have to believe that God will make himself known—"

"Spare me your canned words, Zeke," I snapped, my chest tightening.

"I guess we'll agree to disagree." His voice held resignation—not judgement.

Elkins Bible Church came into view as I rounded a bend. "You aren't going to shun me for being evil?"

"Nope. You're like my brother, Malachi. We'll just discuss the stuff we do see eye to eye on."

I let out a heavy exhale while turning into the parking lot. My pulse picked up. "Thank you."

"Good luck with my uncle this morning."

Grimacing, I pulled into a parking spot that didn't have the 'Youth Pastor' sign beside where Pastor Bram's car sat. "Going to need it."

I put Dad's truck into park and hung up, steeling myself for the conversation ahead. Pastor Bram wouldn't be as agreeable as Zeke, and it was only out of my feelings for Isaac that I'd decided a face-to-face with his dad was necessary.

After a quick wipe of my palms down my slacks, I stepped from the truck, pebbles crunching beneath my dress shoes. My legs shook a bit while climbing the stairs, the scent of lemons and purity in the church's foyer causing me to gag.

Rather than shying away from the glass doors and the blue carpet leading to the pulpit, I lifted my chin and faced it, sifting through my feelings. Disappointment came first, but not for failing in what I'd promised my parents. The letdown was from the exact things I'd told Zeke about a supposed God of love allowing hurt on His children.

No loving father would do such a thing, and if he did— like Pastor Bram—that man didn't deserve to be called as such.

I'd given God countless hours—days—to reveal himself to me, but he'd stayed silent. He'd left me drowning in darkness when I'd submitted myself wholly, begging for him to guide my steps. I'd found my way with Isaac's help, and it was finally time to live my truth.

Jaw set, I spun away from the place of worship I would never step foot in again and headed back toward the offices.

Mrs. Howard looked up from her computer when I walked into the shared reception area. "Good morning, Pastor Foley."

I forced a smile, glancing to my left. "Is Pastor Bram in?"

"Yes. I'm sure you heard about his son?"

A shot of adrenaline rushed through me, and I faced her. "Hmm?"

She glanced at the pastor's closed office door. "He ran away."

I wondered what else she knew.

"He's eighteen now," I told her as though that made everything okay.

Her lips pursed, and she patted at the gray hairs she'd tucked into a bun. "He's...*gay*," Mrs. Howard whispered. "Pastor Bram unveiled his son's sin to the congregation yesterday during service and asked us to pray for his soul to choose the right path."

The right choice.

I eyed Pastor Bram's door, ready to let him know exactly where I stood. Without a word to the woman I hadn't realized was such a busybody, I strode over and knocked.

"Come in!" Pastor Bram called.

"Pastor Foley." He smiled and motioned me toward the chair across from him. "Welcome back. Welcome back." The supposed joy of the Lord filled his face, and I wondered if he felt any anguish over losing his son.

I sat, lips flatlined, my gut churning.

"How was your time away? Isn't the lake beautiful? It's so relaxing, so easy to feel the Spirit of God when surrounded by his creation."

"I heard about Isaac."

Pastor Bram's joy morphed into visible hatred, scowl lines forming between his eyebrows, his lips downturned. The hardness in his eyes had me shaking my head.

Without a single word from his mouth, I knew *I* had made the right choice.

"I'm resigning," I said before he could spout off any shit about the man I loved. "As of this moment."

"You can't judge me or this church because of Isaac's evil ways," he stated, his eyes widening as he sat back. "That boy chose a reprehensible life over all things holy. I had no influence in his sins!"

"That *boy*," I said, leaning forward and holding his stare with a hard one of my own, "is an adult now and at my apartment. I left him in my bed. Accepted and thoroughly loved. *Sated*," I added for emphasis because fuck him.

Pastor Bram blinked, and I watched the truth of my words dawn on his face. Rage reddened his cheeks, his lips sputtering. "You—you godless heathen!" He slapped his hand on his desk, but I didn't flinch. "You perverted...manipulating... How dare you?" he seethed, showing his teeth. "Sick pedophile. I'll have you thrown in jail!"

I stood, looking down on a man who didn't deserve his son's pain. "Don't waste your time, Bram. According to Pennsylvania law, he was legal pickings the year before I got here, but even that matter isn't an issue. I love

Isaac. Every part of him, every thought, and every emotion he shares. I felt connected to him the second we met in your foyer, and nothing and no one is going to change that fact."

He climbed to his feet too, hands on his desk and tremors rippling down over him. "You're going to burn in hell for corrupting my son."

"If *loving* your son damns me to such a place, I'll stride through those gates willingly." I turned and walked out, thankful as fuck I'd insisted Isaac stay home.

He'd wanted to face his dad as a couple, wanted to support me in what I had to do. I couldn't imagine how his heart ached and what he'd gone through to hide his truth. At least my parents hadn't been dogmatic, legalistic assholes. They probably would have loved me regardless of my sexual orientation if I'd grown the balls to come out publicly. Too bad I hadn't realized that prior to their passing.

But I was done living in the past, wishing I'd done things differently. The path I'd chosen had led me to Elkins.

To Isaac.

"Homosexuality is an abomination to God!" Bram's shriek accompanied my pulling open his office door.

Mrs. Howard hopped up, her face pale, probably from having heard every word passed between her spiritual leader and one scorned from the flock.

Good fucking riddance.

I strode across the reception area for the other office while Bram spouted off a verse in Romans about committing what is shameful. Recompense—fitting for our ways.

Rather than argue natural law and interpretation with a hypocritical man who didn't know what the word entreatable meant, I set my focus on the future.

I grabbed the lone personal property of mine off my old desk, the last family photo I had from my teenage years. The books I'd studied in seminary sat on a bookshelf against the wall, but I no longer had need or use for those.

"Get out!"

Ignoring the asshole in his office doorway and the quiet, wide-eyed woman watching us, I walked away.

Gladly.

Chapter 34

Isaac

I sat curled on Malachi's second-hand couch, journal and pen in hand, but I stared at the stark-white, empty wall across the small space rather than writing. Full of emotions from the best weekend of my life, I struggled to put them into words.

Malachi had left to give his resignation ten minutes earlier, and my good luck wishes were never more meant than in that moment. Knowing what he faced, I cringed, my heartbeat picking up its pace.

Bram Van Dusen would pour damnation down over Malachi's head and attempt to make him repent. I'd warned him of that sure outcome.

He didn't care. Claimed he didn't fear it. We were consenting adults, free to choose our own way, and to hell with what anyone thought.

How far he'd come in the months since we'd met. Legalistic yet hurting. Dogmatic but broken. Unhappy and struggling.

And now he smiles, his eyes clear. My own smile emerged at the memory of his contented face in my mind.

He'd walked with assurance to his truck while I'd watched from the window, his ass flexing in his slacks and his white button-down stretched over broad shoulders and hiding the tattoos I'd finally gotten to trace with my tongue.

My dad would try to tear him down. Bend him to guilt with words that had been drilled into both my and Malachi's heads since childhood. Having just returned to the "dark side," I wondered over my lover's stubbornness. Would he be easily swayed or manipulated by one of the best into rededicating his life and picking up where he'd left off before giving into the supposed sins of the flesh?

My stomach churned.

"Just stop," I muttered to myself, turning my focus onto the blank page before me. I didn't want to waste one more minute worrying and wondering how his meeting with my dad went—and the possibility of us being over before we'd even really gotten started.

Closing my eyes, I remembered waking in Malachi's arms, memorizing his sleepy blue eyes. Soft skin and hard muscle. How perfectly we fit together when I'd wrapped my legs around his waist.

My dick had no issue figuring out how *he* felt about the whole situation.

I'd been consumed by Malachi...and the inescapable need he satisfied. He drowned me with loving acceptance, and my chest ached from it—for more of it.

Breath exhaling in a rush, I scribbled words illegible to anyone but me, the release of emotion at naming them leaving me as spent as Malachi had earlier that morning. But no tune accompanied my thoughts in black and white chicken scratch. No melody gave meaning and life to mere words.

My cell dinged with an incoming text, and I snatched it off the cushion beside me even though Malachi couldn't have finished with my dad already.

Chris: **Heard you ran away Friday night.**

A heavy, disappointed exhale sagged me back against the couch cushion. **Yeah**, I texted back.

Chris: **Also heard you like dick.**

I pinched my lower lip, not sure how to respond since I couldn't see his face or hear his tone. "Fuck." After another minute of inner debate, I started to type an affirmative response, but the cell rang before I hit send.

"Shit." Swallowing, I swiped to answer Chris's call. "Hey."

"The fuck, man?"

"What?" I asked, my entire body tensing over the anger in his voice.

"You're fucking gay? After all that shit about girls, tits, and ass. Seriously?"

I'd decided to live my truth, so I owned it, knowing I'd already lost his friendship. "Yeah. I like dick. You should try it sometime. It's fucking fantastic—especially shoved down your throat."

"You sick fuck!" Chris cursed, painting a clear picture of what he thought about homosexuality—exactly as I'd expected. "You're a liar of the worst sort."

"*You're* the liar, asshole," I shot back, my brow furrowed and my free hand fisting. "Pretending to be a good Christian boy. You get one girl pregnant, turn your back on her, then try to corrupt Sara all while putting on another face for your parents and the church."

"You piece of sh—"

"Don't go pointing out my *sins* and ignore the fucking plank in your own eye, Chris." I hit end and went straight into his info, blocking his number with shaking fingers.

Fuck him, and fuck everyone who thought like him.

Swallowing hard, I closed my eyes and tipped my head back, waiting for the adrenaline to finish with my body. I counted backwards from ten in a rhythm matching my heart's dancing cadence. I breathed, pausing for a beat. Steadying thumps took back up in my head...

A rhythm rose, the rolling emotions inside me coming to life in a whispered note...another. Slow as a rising sun, complex and yet pulling in the familiar that those with eyes—or in my case—*ears* could relate to.

Innovative and personal, just like all the other music I'd written.

I didn't doubt I belonged in Nashville.

Throat tight, I picked up my guitar and let my gift lead me—as I would have to do regardless of Malachi's time with my dad. But would my heart be willing to go if it came down to choosing between him and my dream?

I closed my eyes and played, pouring my emotion into the words I knew Malachi would understand without me having to explain.

Chapter 35

Malachi

I heard Isaac's voice and guitar from where I stood outside my apartment door—and my hand froze from sliding the key into the lock. A haunting melody, simple chord progressions, but...something *more*.

Out of the ordinary and in some way familiar enough that the notes drew me in.

As quietly as possible, I let myself into my apartment, my focus falling to the back of his dark head bent over his guitar. His raspy voice held a uniqueness I hadn't heard from modern music. Pure, raw emotion. And the way his graceful fingers plucked over the strings? Isaac took listeners along for a ride.

Major labels in the music industry didn't like taking risks, but they no longer mattered as much as they used to—and what Isaac had couldn't be ignored. Advancing technology allowed for production and distribution outside the norm, and my heart raced over the idea of helping him achieve his dreams.

It wouldn't require Nashville.

We could do it together—wherever the fuck we made our bed.

Our bed.

Throat tight, I listened to his clear artistic voice and allowed his emotions to take me along where he went.

Consuming.

Inescapable.

Drowning and aching.

Love...

I lived the words pouring from his lips for another moment, and I stood speechless as the notes faded into silence. He hadn't said it out loud—neither had I, but the sense of more than lust between us had been put to music.

"I know you're there," Isaac said, finally angling to look at me over the back of the couch.

Of course he did, same as I always knew when he entered a room.

Overwhelmed with the hurt in his eyes and my love for him, I strode across the apartment, grasped his face in my hands, and kissed him. Hard and hungry. Wanting to spill the tears building in my eyes.

"What was that?" I whispered against his cinnamon-flavored mouth, both of us breathless.

"My mind's ramblings from the weekend." His eyes held a sheen, same as mine. "My...emotions that I'm not good at communicating."

"I'd say you did a damn good job of telling me how you feel about me," I said, breathless from finally knowing his heart.

"Yeah?"

I grinned and gave him another quick kiss, my stomach fluttering. "Yeah." I rounded the couch and sat beside him since he still held his guitar like a shield. "Want to talk about it?"

"How'd it go with my dad?"

Guess not.

Accepting his boundaries over the ramblings he'd put to music didn't come easily. I swallowed against the disappointment of not exploring what ebbed and flowed between us like a rolling wave, the exact harmony I'd heard in my head as he sang. "Not good."

Isaac snorted, turning away to set his guitar in the case on the coffee table. "Not surprised."

I sat back, giving him space as I shared the shit that had gone down at Elkins Bible Church. Refusing to hide anything from Isaac, I disclosed all his dad had said, even the "Get out" he'd commanded, same as he'd done to his son the Friday before.

"I'm sorry you had to go through that," Isaac muttered, his brow furrowed while he picked at imaginary lint on his gym shorts.

"I'm sorry you had to put up with that kind of legalism your whole life," I told him the God's honest truth.

Fuck that—my truth.

He tried for a grin and looked up at me. "I want to get out of here, Malachi," Isaac said, his voice quiet. "Away from the church's hatred and the backwoods bigots. This society's lies and judgements. Chris and Tyler. I need to experience a different life. I'm only eighteen. I've got plenty of time to make up for all I missed out on."

Yeah, he did. But how long until he realized there was more than Malachi Foley available for the taking? We fit perfectly together in our current headspace and situation, but what about down the road when he changed his present and made a name for himself? When he got a taste of the world outside the sticks of Pennsylvania?

When adoring fans threw themselves at him, offering whatever he desired? Their hearts. Their bodies. Their souls.

He already owned all three of mine, but would he crave more than I could ever give him—even if it was my everything?

I opened my mouth to tell him my feelings but closed it at the thought that I'd be pushing him into choices *I* wanted for him. He'd probably see it as nothing more than an attempt to handle him since that's all he'd ever known from his dad.

Fuck, relationships were hard.

"So now what?" Isaac asked when I didn't respond.

I held out my hand, my chest aching. I needed to feel him against me, his heart beating in time with mine. "We live happily ever after?" I asked with a joking tone so it wouldn't be taken as manipulation.

Isaac crawled onto my lap, his smile unsure enough that the pain in my chest remained.

"We relax for a few weeks," I suggested something other than a fairytale, putting aside my own desires and focusing on the present. "We get to know one another better and decide what we're going to do, where we're going to go."

Rather than argue the togetherness of my suggestion, Isaac released a heavy sigh and snuggled into me. He melted in my arms exactly how I needed in that moment, letting me know I was his home, I was his comfort.

I'm his knight in shining armor—for now.

Focusing on the positives, I held him close. Kissed his hair that smelled like my shampoo and released a heavy sigh of my own.

We would be okay.

We had to be.

Chapter 36

Isaac

We went with the flow, just like Malachi suggested. Singing and writing music together when we weren't job searching. Neither of us wanted to up and move without having direction. And seeing as how I refused to mow lawns in a neighborhood close to my parents, we searched outside of Elkins—in the opposite direction of the church.

All the while, we uploaded our recordings to social media sites that supported music.

Malachi had a digital audio workstation on his computer from years earlier. Add in a monitor and microphone he'd had tucked in a box in the back of his closet and we made our own "recording studio" right there in our living room.

Writing and creating music—gorgeous harmonies—was our passion, one we excelled at.

Together.

My dreams for Nashville morphed into more than fame and fortune with every day I spent with Malachi hunched over our guitars and my journals. I still planned to go, but I wanted him there with me. Creating music together. As partners—and not just in business.

But I couldn't find the words to tell him, and guilt rose whenever he hinted at his feelings toward me and I went the joke route to lighten the seriousness between us.

We uploaded my songs to every platform we could, and within two weeks, without even trying, I had a fanbase of a couple hundred strangers. Those listeners made it easy to find coffee houses and bars with open mic nights close by, slowly widening our reach.

I walked on air, hand in hand with Malachi, heading into the grocery store. We'd had our first gig in

Scranton the night before, a big city compared to Elkins, and the reception we got, the bar's patrons crowding around us once we finished...

They hadn't even cared that we'd kissed right there on stage after the final song.

Fucking perfection. We landed three more gigs because of that performance and were well on our way to growing a solid foundation for our dreams.

My face hurt from smiling—but the grin died when Chris and Tyler exited the grocery store in front of us.

Chris glanced up after pulling his keys from his back pocket, and our gazes connected. His focus went from me to Malachi, to our clasped hands, and back to my face. "Fucking faggots," he muttered loud enough to reach our ears over the distance separating us.

Tyler's gaze jerked toward us, his face paling as his footsteps stuttered. Regret filled his face, tugging his lips downward.

A few other people nearby glanced at us, but I lifted my chin and held on tighter to Malachi's hand. Let the fuckers judge. Let them talk.

Chris turned away, but Tyler hesitated. He opened his mouth. Closed it. And hurried after his friend.

The second we walked into the store's air-conditioned vastness, my shoulders sagged, but the twisting in my stomach over losing my only friends remained.

"You okay?" Malachi murmured, pulling a grocery cart from the line of them just inside the automatic doors.

"Yeah." I'd told him about my conversation with Chris weeks earlier, and he'd been ready to go beat the shithead into the ground. We'd agreed he wasn't worth our time, but I'd felt Malachi's tension at Chris's name calling.

"I want to wrap you up and take you home. Fucking hate that you have to deal with that shit," Malachi muttered.

"I'm not going to let some asshole hurt me enough to be too scared to go into public or stand on stage beside you. Are *you* okay?" I asked, hating the furrow between his eyebrows.

Lips tight, he nodded.

"I'm proud of you," I whispered, leaning against his side, blowing hot air over his ear.

He shivered and turned down the dairy aisle. "Proud of you too. I love how you're unapologetically you."

Love...a word we'd used in passing but not directly. I felt it though, and I knew he did too. For as much as we pushed to get emotions into my journals in prep for music, we should have been whispering that sentiment every other minute of the day.

However, soft touches and the brush of lips not intending to lead to sex but to affirm our appreciation of one another—I'd rather have those things my heart craved than my ears filled with mere words. Hell only knew I'd heard enough of the preaching about love without the practice from Dad.

Feeling lighter, I grabbed the week's flyer from the cart he pushed and flipped to the back for the frozen food sales. "Lasagna!" I said with a grin. "Your favorite brand too."

"Sweet."

Neither of us could cook much, but we put his portable grill to good use. I wished I'd paid more attention to what Mom did in the kitchen and learned from her so I could provide in the ways I knew a woman never would for me.

When it came to "women's work" as Dad had called it, Malachi and I were screwed. But we made do. Shared chores. Attempted to create decent enough tasting food together.

But frozen lasagna?

Delicious and as close to a home cooked meal I feared we'd ever get until we made it big and could afford a full-time chef.

We ambled through the store, shoulders and hips brushing on occasion, every touch intentional as we shopped, causing Chris's bigotry to fade from my mind.

Thinking on the upcoming shows we would perform together, my happiness returned. I even grabbed Malachi's backside when we entered an aisle and found ourselves alone. I couldn't get enough of the man. His hands and mouth on me, the ass he let me own whenever I wanted. Sharing cum and secrets. Cuddles—

Mom appeared at the aisle's end, her cart's forward momentum jerking to a stop as our gazes clashed. "Isaac," she whispered, ragged, her entire body seeming to sag where she stood.

Dad didn't appear beside her, but he never did the wife's responsibilities. I didn't need to fear facing him in that moment.

"Mom." I stepped past Malachi and went to her, noting she'd lost weight when she couldn't afford to.

Tears filled her eyes and slid down her cheeks, and my throat tightened.

Rather than turning away like her husband would have demanded, she came to me. Hugged me. Squeezed me, letting out a quiet sob.

Mom. Smelling like fresh baked bread and flowers. Soft and comforting.

I choked on a sob of my own, knowing our moment couldn't last, so I soaked that shit up. Breathed in her subtle perfume, the dark hair escaping her bun brushing against my nose.

Her arms told me more than any words possibly could. She loved me. No matter what. And when she stepped away, her eyes said the same. "You're still here."

"For now."

She glanced at Malachi behind me, offering him a smile that didn't reek of hypocrisy. "Are you happy?" Mom asked, her focus returning to me.

"More than I thought possible."

Her smile wobbled as more wetness rose to coat her eyes. "Please keep in touch with me," she whispered as though afraid Dad would hear. "Let me know you're alright."

"Maybe we could meet for breakfast someday soon."

She hesitated to answer.

"Or not. I don't want to get you in trouble." I forced a smile and leaned in to kiss her soft cheek. "I'll text. Promise."

Nodding and hands shaking, she retrieved her cart, and we passed in the aisle, going our separate ways, both of us swiping tears from the corners of our eyes.

Malachi laced his fingers through mine, but he didn't speak. I took the time he offered to settle in my heart that Mom and I had closure.

And while I wished she would leave my asshole of a dad and find a better life, a better partner, I knew she never would. For her, love was blind, and I couldn't fault her for that.

I stared at the blond beside me who needed a haircut, but that scruff he'd been lazy about could stay. He looked sexy as fuck, unkempt with his wrinkled T-shirt, and perfect.

Mine.

Even if we never made it to the big time, I knew I would be content.

We unloaded the groceries onto the belt, the magazine rack catching my eye and making me question what I'd thought true seconds earlier.

Rolling Stone's latest cover showed the young girl who'd created a splash in the music industry earlier in the year. At mere fifteen, she'd signed with Columbia thanks to her music videos that had gone viral on social media.

She wasn't exactly unique in voice or song writing, but her reach, her fans, promised the record execs big money. They'd been quick to gobble her up and blast her face and music across the world, reaching listeners her lyrics resonated with.

I craved what she'd accomplished. My heart ached for it.

I wanted to find and connect with people who felt and thought the same as I did. I wanted to stand on stage and take them on an emotional journey. I wanted them to accept and appreciate the gift I knew I had.

Would having a couple hundred followers be enough?

I glanced at Malachi talking to the cashier, his smile easy. Gorgeous. My heart ached even as my dick twitched.

It will *be enough,* I promised myself, even though a seed of doubt remained long after we loaded up his truck with groceries and drove home.

Chapter 37
Malachi

For a week, Isaac seemed broody, escaping back inside himself. While not closed off to me physically, I could feel the distance separating our hearts and minds.

And both of mine sat uneasy.

Discontented in some way, he kept quiet. Knowing his past of utilizing his journal more than his mouth, I let him do what he needed to figure out whatever was bothering him.

But I moved forward with my plans.

I headed out for a few errands, leaving him behind on the couch with his guitar as he struggled with the song we'd been working on together for a few days and wanted to reveal at the gig we had the following night.

Once around the corner from the apartment, I pulled off the road and searched for a number I feared calling.

She answered after three rings.

"Jennifer," I greeted, ready for her to disconnect without a word.

"Malachi! How are you doing? Are you okay?"

I wondered what she'd heard through the grapevine.

"I'm really well."

"I'm so glad to hear it." Her bubbly voice assured me she didn't lie.

"What else have people been saying?" Might as well get the shit out on the table before she asked why I'd called. It would doubtless be a deciding factor.

"That you stole Isaac away and you're living in sin."

Well, she didn't pull any punches. I couldn't help my chuckle. "It's more like Isaac came on to me, I couldn't deny him, and now we're attempting a happily ever after."

She actually laughed lightly, relaxing me back into my driver's seat. "We miss you—the teens miss you."

"They don't think I'm going to burn in hell?"

"They haven't been taught anything different, but your teachings the past couple of months have instilled grace and mercy. A new concept, but more easily accepted by those younger in the church."

"And you?"

"It's not my place to judge, Malachi. You'll stand or fall before God alone when the day comes. But I know your heart and the love you've shown these kids. It's the love of a true Christian whether you consider yourself one anymore or not."

My throat grew tight. "If only more believers thought like you did."

"Yeah, it's a shame how much hatred and hypocrisy are out there these days."

I considered her cousin, our past—the reason for my call.

"I have a favor to ask," I forced myself to say, all for Isaac.

"Anything."

"Is there any chance I could get your cousin's number? The one who lives in Nashville?"

"About that..."

My insides clenched tight.

"...he's left the Christian music industry."

"Should I offer congratulations?"

Jennifer laughed again. "He said he's moving onward and upward in the world. He works for Cadence Records now."

Cadence—the biggest label when it came to unique music. And two of their musicians had topped the charts for three weeks and counting.

Pure luck or an even greater letdown?

"Do you want me to get in touch with him to tell him who you are, that you're going to be calling?" she asked.

I cleared my throat, wanting to keep his and my past exactly that—in our past. "I'd rather just get his number than use you more than I already feel I am."

"It's not using, Malachi. I'd be happy to give you his number."

I obtained Elliot James's cell number after a few more minutes of learning about his life-changing decision and dialed him up, my heart in my throat. Adrenaline running. For years, I'd despised the man for what he'd done, how he'd taken advantage of me and others, but my feelings for Isaac trumped my resentment and need for revenge. Cliché to think that love could conquer all, but for me, it did. Nothing was more important than Isaac.

I'd given up a promise to my mom for him, so what was facing another part of my past if it would make his dreams come true?

Elliot James didn't answer, but I left a detailed message so he would know exactly who I was and why I called. While I'd have preferred cursing him out and punching his teeth in, swallowing my pride meant a chance for Isaac.

And there wasn't anything I wouldn't do for my lover, my light.

Even if it meant I got left behind.

Chapter 38

Isaac

We landed "real" jobs, and Malachi and I slaved together side by side along with a guy named Manuel at Johnson's Orchard. Five days a week, eight-to-ten-hour days depending on what needed done. Apple season had started, the busiest time of the year for them.

And at night, we pursued our shared passion—without the goofy Mexican guy who didn't care that we were as gay as unicorns and proud of it.

Singing together, my writing, and Malachi's recording and producing was what drove us through the long hours until weekend gigs. We shared our music on social media, his excitement over follower numbers keeping me happy, content at our progress in chasing the dream while sweating our asses off during the daytime hours.

Our music followed us through the orchard, and we got caught up singing a cappella, silly ditties about rotten apples and dripping sweat. Late summer's sun gifted us with farmer's tans while we dreamed about being on a bigger stage together.

Shirtless and sweaty, we lounged with Manuel beneath an oak tree at the orchard's edge for lunch on Friday, same as we always did for break.

"Malachi said you got a couple new TikTok followers overnight," Manuel said, crunching into an apple he'd taken from the last bin we'd filled.

"A couple?" I laughed. "Over a thousand. All because of a new video we'd posted of the two of us singing yesterday."

"I saw it," Manuel said, chewing with his mouthful. "Went fucking viral in less than twenty-four hours."

Malachi and I shared a grin.

"You two are fucking awesome," Manuel said. "Like seriously. Damn good music, cool as shit voices, and the way you look at each other when singing… Yeah. Never heard anything like you two. When you make it to the big time, I'm going to cash in on that, you know. I was your first and biggest fan."

"Too bad you can't sing worth a shit," I tossed back, feeling lighter than I had in weeks. "We'd pull you in for backup."

"My back aint getting anywhere near your horny asses," he said, tossing the core at my head.

Malachi's cell rang, cutting into our laughter. He grabbed the phone from his pocket.

"Hold on a sec," he said, still grinning. His smile faded as he looked at the screen. "Be right back." He hopped up while answering with a "Hello," his stride taking him out of earshot.

I glanced at Manuel, and he shrugged. My gaze returned to Malachi's tensed shoulders and wide stance as he stood a few dozen feet away.

"Whoever it was, he didn't look too happy about the call," Manuel said, eyeing me.

"Yeah." I blew out a breath and crumpled up the baggie my sandwich had been inside. "Don't know who the fuck it could be though."

Manuel and I sat silent, but none of Malachi's murmurs could be made out from the distance he'd put between us.

Sitting forward in the grass, knees drawn up, I bit into the apple I'd taken from the bin. Sweet juice burst on my tongue, but my stomach soured over the worries in my mind going rampant.

Malachi shoved the cell back in his pocket. Hands on his hips, he tipped his head back as though in prayer.

My heart stumbled as thoughts scrambled in my head. He had no other family, so it wouldn't be bad news like a death or something. Had Zeke called? I hardly knew my older cousin, but Malachi told me he'd been struggling lately with some personal shit he wouldn't talk about.

Maybe he'd finally caved and unloaded to Malachi, asking for prayer?

Shit.

I gulped a few swallows of tepid water from my jug, my gaze glued to him.

"Any idea what's going on?" Manuel murmured, and I shook my head.

"No fucking clue." My voice came out tight. Strained. Same as my temples.

"Doesn't seem good."

"Thanks, Mr. Positive."

"Sorry. Just sayin'."

"Yeah, I know. Fuck, Malachi, turn around and tell me—"

He turned.

And his smile kicked me in the gut, making me choke down what I'd been saying. I'd never seen him so... thrilled before. Even when balls deep in my ass, spent, and shivering, he didn't appear so damn content.

"Guess it *was* good," Manuel said, but I couldn't tear my gaze off Malachi.

Quick strides brought him back, and he yanked me up off the ground and into his arms.

The half-eaten apple in my hand fell to the ground, forgotten.

Manual made fake gagging noises whenever our PDA got out of control, but I ignored him, gladly taking all Malachi gave, every lash of his tongue causing my heart to race and blood to heat.

"Fuck, you taste damn delicious," he groaned against my mouth before diving in for more. "Like a damn apple pie."

"What was that for?" I asked, breathless when he finally put me back on my feet.

His blue eyes glowed, his grin so damn contagious that my chest fluttered. "I called Elliot James a few weeks ago," he said, the name kicking into my memory within a heartbeat.

"Jennifer's cousin."

"He works for Cadence Records now," Malachi said with a nod. "He checked out your work on social media —and he wants you to come to Nashville."

Holy shit balls.

I laughed. "You're full of it."

"Nope. I gave him your number, and he's going to give you a buzz later tonight to go over some details."

"Holy *fuck*!"

"Right?" Light still filled his face, but the glow inside me dimmed slightly.

My social media, Malachi had said. Elliot wanted *me* to go to Nashville.

"He knows we're a duo, right?" I asked.

His smile faded, and he grasped me behind my neck, holding me close. Eyes on my lips, he let out a heavy exhale.

"Elliot James and I have a past, Isaac."

Nashville.

Malachi's time of rebellion and hitting rock bottom.

He'd told me a record executive had taken advantage of him, lied to him.

Holy shit. Fucking hell...

"Elliot was the one who hurt you," I whispered the thought as it came. He'd actually called the fucker who'd used him...for me. Chest tight as fuck and eyes stinging, I swallowed hard.

He nodded, lifting his focus to my eyes. Trouble filled his, and I grabbed hold of his waist as I felt his instinct to pull away from me. "Why would you trust him with what we've built?"

"Because he came out three months ago, Jennifer told me. He left Christian radio—and I'm willing to take advantage of his connections. I'll do whatever I have to do to make this happen for you."

I chewed on the inside of my lip, studying his face, seeing the decision he'd already come to clearly in his eyes.

Malachi would face bullshit from his past and dig up emotions best left to rest in order to see me succeed.

Fuck. Could I love the man any more than I already did?

I laid my hand on his chest, feeling the steady thump that soothed me whenever I couldn't sleep, the connection between us stronger than ever. "You're going with me." I wouldn't take no for an answer.

He caressed behind my ear with his thumb, the rest of his fingers clasping tight to my neck. "I don't think Elliot and I will ever be the greatest of friends."

"I figured."

"But if you want me beside you through this, I'll face down the fucking devil himself to see you through."

"Good thing you boys don't believe in that red dude with horns," Manual said from behind us, reminding us we weren't alone.

I chuckled. "Yeah," I agreed. "So. *We* are headed to Nashville."

The light returned to Malachi's face, the beauty of his stare filling me up. "If that's what you want."

"I do."

He kissed me, and Manuel let out a whoop.

A few hours later, I pushed Malachi down onto our bed, uncaring that his skin would taste salty as fuck. He shoved off his jeans, and I did the same, desperate to get on him. Show him how much he meant to me, how much I needed him since I still couldn't find the fucking words.

I went for his already hard dick, but he grabbed hold of my head. "You don't want to suck sweaty dick, baby, trust me. Just lube me up and ride me."

I grabbed the bottle off our bedstand, my hands shaking, so much damn joy bubbling inside me that I almost laughed. Flipping the cap, I glanced up to find Malachi's smile gone, hesitation in his eyes when he'd been full of lust seconds earlier.

"What's wrong?" I asked, pausing in my drive to get him slickened up and inside my body.

"I'm afraid the fame will tear us apart—and I don't say that to manipulate you in any way," he hastened to add. "I just never want to be anything but honest with you."

My breath left in a rush.

"No other man, no other dick will ever compare," I said, trying for the most assured tone and look I could offer while dribbling lube over his length that hadn't flagged one bit.

"You've never had another dick." He groaned, watching as I jacked him.

"I don't *want* another dick," I told him the God's honest truth, climbing to hover over him, too impatient to prep. "Give me yours."

"Gladly—fucking always." Malachi grabbed hold of my hips and pulled me down, lifting his torso to take my mouth. I was claimed with one slow, sinking stroke. Filled. Never surer of my thoughts toward him and the emotions I desperately needed to spill from my lips.

Seconds later, I lay on my back, holding Malachi's stare as he glided in and out of my body, every rub over my prostate leaking precum from my slit onto my belly. Our gazes held, nothing between us. Like he knew my mind, he thrust and ground against me exactly how I craved.

Fuck, I could totally lose myself in his light eyes—clear down to his beautiful soul. He never hid his thoughts, his feelings—

"You're so fucking sexy," he said, his tone rasped, sending readiness tingling through my balls.

"I love you." The words came easier than expected, from an abundance of delicious perfection, complete happiness dwelling inside my chest.

His eyes welled, and he sank in deep, lowering his heat over my torso with a heavy sigh as though he'd been waiting to hear those words from me. "I feel like I've loved you forever."

A brush of lips turned into hungry kisses. Caressing hands grasped, and fingertips dug into muscle.

And he whisper-groaned my name while we came together.

As one.

Chapter 39

Malachi - One Year Later...

Isaac lay on the bed completely bare, his pale, beautiful skin still covered with water droplets and his cell phone held to his ear.

I stood in the bathroom doorway, drying off my hair from the shower we'd just taken. A celebratory one after a ball-draining fuck against the hotel's wall an hour earlier.

"Yeah," he said into his cell, his hazel eyes darkening as his gaze slid down over my body. "He's doing well, Mom. We both are."

How far I'd come in a year. From denying myself, stumbling through the darkness, and pleading for fulfillment and light...to finding the home I'd craved.

I tossed aside my towel and climbed onto the bed beside the young man who gave my life purpose, propping up on an elbow and entwining one of my legs between his. He shifted onto his side, bringing us face to face.

My beautiful lover with his still-smooth cheeks, pouty lips...and the small heart he'd gotten tattooed on his left pec. Our initials rested inside, scripted from music notes. Mine lay over my right pec above the piercings he'd suggested I get.

The ones I begged him to tongue whenever he put his mouth on me.

"I'll call you as soon as we're done," he told his mom, smiling at me, the adoration in his eyes making me feel like the richest man on the face of the earth.

Tomorrow it begins...

Our first tour would kick off in Nashville the following evening. We'd been dubbed the cliche dynamic duo, and radio stations and the charts loved us.

From day one, Isaac had declared us a team. Partners no matter what.

Elliot James and I never once spoke of our past, and while I still wanted to smash in his nose on occasion when he got too bossy, I kept my cool. Just told him to let us have things the way we wanted or we'd take our talent elsewhere.

And that talent had landed us the record deal with Cadence I hoped for. Going on tour come morning.

"He's my everything, Mom."

Fuck. I swallowed hard, and our gazes locked, my heart beating heavy in my chest.

"I'm so happy for you, son," I could hear her voice through the cell. "Truly."

"Malachi's the best decision I ever made."

Her murmurs of love came through, and I thanked fate that at least one of his parents had decided to accept and keep in touch with their son.

"Love you too, Mom."

I brushed my thumb over Isaac's lower lip as he hung up and tossed his cell to the side. He snuggled in against me, all damp, warm skin and fresh cinnamon-laced breath.

"Everything okay?" I asked.

"Yeah." He kissed me lightly and relaxed, letting out a sigh. "Dad asks about me on occasion, and he's finally stopped ranting his fire and brimstone bullshit."

One thing I definitely didn't miss about our past—too long sermons about a God of love who didn't deserve worship. Accepting my truth hadn't come easily, and I'd dragged my feet for months, but Isaac had proven too much a temptation, too much of a force of nature.

Looking back, I realized my heart, my soul, hadn't stood a chance of denying us.

"Beautifully Us" was the first track of our album, one already hailed legendary by the LGBT community. Our people. Our family. People who loved without hypocrisy.

"Think he'll ever accept the life you've chosen?" I asked, smoothing his damp hair off his forehead.

"Nope—and I don't care if he doesn't."

Isaac and I had both come far in letting out the thoughts and feelings we'd kept bottled up for years. It took time for personal growth of that magnitude, but having a partner willing to put in the effort, the desire to help the other become a better person, made it easier.

"She said she's proud of me, and that's enough. I don't need Dad's approval when I have hers and yours."

We kissed and snuggled for a few minutes, simply being present and enjoying the quiet before the unknown storm of the next day to come.

Bright lights. Screaming fans.

Singing for the first time in front of a crowd bigger than a few thousand. Isaac owned the stage whenever he stood there with his guitar, face glowing. Voice sure and steady while singing into the mic and drawing in listeners in for the ride of their life.

But he always turned toward me when I joined in the chorus, strumming along on my own guitar in time with his. Our voices weaving without effort, creating beauty like I'd never known. Both of us side by side, same as Johnny and his June.

And our fans loved us. Together, publicly claimed partners, hopelessly in love.

"Ready to make our dreams come true?" Isaac asked, rubbing his palm over my scruffy cheek.

I leaned into his touch but focused on his eyes. "You can start by making *my* most important one come true."

"What's that?"

Threading his fingers through mine, I lifted his hand to my lips, kissing his ring finger. It was time to share the last things in my heart and mind I'd withheld from him. And not out of fear or manipulation to keep him close but because I loved him. Everything about him.

"Marry me," I whispered. "Take my last name. Be mine forever."

Smirking, he turned our hands and bit the back of my thumb. "I already am, but if your insecure ass needs a paper…"

With a growl, I rolled Isaac onto his back, pinning him in place. "Brat."

His gaze narrowed as his lips quirked into a full-on smile. "You love it."

"I love *you*," I told him, grinding my swelling dick against his.

"Show me how much."

"Gladly." I took his mouth and gave him what he wanted, and when the next night came, we walked hand in hand onto stage.

To screaming fans and blinding spotlights.

Isaac's flushed face, the energy radiating off him filled me up with the kind of peace I'd searched for my entire life. I'd found heaven on earth in the arms of a forbidden love.

And I would worship him until we breathed our last.

THE END

About the Author

USA Today Bestselling author Lynn Burke is a CrossFit and coffee addict. Her three spawn and two fur babies dictate how often she can be found hunched over her Mac, typing as fast as her fickle muse cooks up hot stories.

You can find more about Lynn at her website: www.authorlynnburke.com

Risso Family Series

Sandy Ridge Series

Sinful Nature Series

Vicious Vipers MC

Hestie flew up and mounted the white horse behind Poros. To Hermie, she said, "Sorry. No more room."

Prometheus turned to the vampires. "I trust you'll keep an eye on the ship?"

"We will have to do it from below deck." Del pointed to the hint of dawn just beyond the mountains to the east.

Alastair gave an informal salute that ended with a snap of his fingers. "We will reach out to you if we sense anything wrong."

"Thanks." Prometheus tipped his white captain's hat.

"See ya," Hermie said to Del just before he kissed her cheek.

"See ya," she echoed with a smile.

Jinsoo winked at Alastair and then joined Hermie in the air beside Pegasus.

To Jinsoo, Hermie said, "Mount Olympus, here we come."

Hestie wrapped her arms around Poros and leaned against his back as Pegasus soared over the Mediterranean Sea.

"Miss me?" she whispered into Poros's ear as his blond hair tickled her lips.

Poros glanced back at her with a grin, his gray eyes sparkling in the moonlight. "Cute outfit."

She wore very short shorts with a white tank top. But the tank was no ordinary tank. The straps were embellished with layers of gathered fabric making thick, soft ruffles that she found divine. One of the perks of being a goddess unaffected by changing temperatures was that one could continue to wear summer fashions well into fall.

"Thanks. You should see what I bought for you."

She felt him chuckle against her. He wouldn't fight her, like Hermie did, when it came to her fashion choices for him, and she loved him for it.

The sun god, Helios, appeared in his golden cup on the horizon just as they reached Mount Olympus. The gates parted, and the young gods waited near the fountain while Prometheus took Pegasus to the stables. Then, together, they flew up the rainbow steps and into the temple, where the other gods were waiting.

Hestie followed Poros and Prometheus into the middle of the great hall, where the Olympians were already seated on their thrones. Aphrodite and Artemis gave the young gods a smile and a wave as they walked past, as did the three Charities sitting around Aphrodite. Hestie waved back. One of the Charities—Pasithia—dropped her handkerchief at Poros's feet. When he picked it up and handed it back to her, she smiled up at him with a flirtatious gleam in her eyes that Hestie found irritating. What was even more irritating was the blush that crossed Poros's face. Should Hestie be worried?

Across the room, the muses softly hummed a melody behind Apollo. Between Apollo and Hephaestus stood the demigods Gertie and Hector. Hestie gave them each a smile.

Hestie's mom and grandparents, Hades and Persephone, were also there. Her grandparents were seated on the double throne between Artemis and Hestia, where Demeter usually sat. Demeter was probably at her winter cabin with Hecate, since it was late October, the time of year when Persephone lived in the Underworld, and Demeter moped.

Hestie's mother flew over to greet her and her brother. It had only been a few days since they last saw her, but their meetings were usually few and far between.

"You've been shopping," her mother said with a smile and a hug. "You look good."

"Thanks," Hestie said. "Did you cut your hair again?"

The last time Hestie had seen her mother, whose hair was red and curly like hers, it had reached her shoulders. But today, it was cut in a bob just below her ears.

"It kept getting in my way."

"It's cute," Hestie complimented, wondering if she should do the same with her hair.

"I wish Dad could be here, too," Hermie said as he hugged their mom.

"Not while there are mortals," their mother replied. "You know the drill."

Hestie sighed. It wasn't always convenient when your father was the god of death.

Persephone waved at them. "Come stand over here with us."

As Prometheus followed the young gods to linger near the double throne shared by Hades and Persephone, Hestie noticed Athena watching him. But Prometheus seemed to make a point of not returning her gaze. He was still upset with her for the vampire Taavi's death and for putting the rest of his crew in danger.

Poros seemed to notice, too. He squeezed Hestie's hand before leaving her side to say hello to his sister.

"Sit here beside me," Athena said to him, offering him what was once Hera's place on their father's double throne. It was made of gold and was adorned with an eagle and three peacocks.

"I'd rather stand with Hestie," he said. "If you don't mind."

Hestie felt bad for worrying about Pasithia's flirtations. Poros had never given Hestie any reason to doubt his feelings for her. She needed to snap out of it.

Athena, whose long, straight, black hair set off her striking gray eyes—eyes that looked exactly like Poros's—frowned at Hestie. "Not at all."

Ares scoffed as Poros left Athena. What was his problem? At least Hermes had a smile and a wink for her. That put Hestie at ease again. Poseidon, sitting between Hermes and Apollo, made no attempt at eye contact, and Apollo was busy talking to Hephaestus.

Hestie could tell that Gertie was bursting at the seams, anxious to join the ranks of the immortals. She wondered if Gertie would be just as annoying as a goddess, or if she'd settle down, no longer compelled to show off her book knowledge.

Athena stood up and cleared her throat. The muses stopped humming.

The goddess of wisdom began: "Thank you all for coming to this historic moment on Mount Olympus. The young god, Jinsoo, will declare his purpose, and the demigod, Gertie, who has valiantly proven her mettle, will become one of us. These two events will require the consent of our majority. Once these rituals have ended, we will turn our attention to deciding what to do about Sailfish Trading and Shipping."

Hestie glanced at Jinsoo and then across the room at Gertie. They were equally pale and jittery.

"Jinsoo Huang, please come forward," Athena summoned.

Jinsoo left Prometheus's side to stand before Athena in the center of the circle of thrones. To Hestie, he looked small, even as a god, probably because he was only fifteen when he underwent apotheosis.

"Have you found your purpose?" Athena asked him.

"Yes, goddess."

"And?"

Jinsoo swallowed hard and combed his short, black hair from his eyes. "I will be the god of sailors."

Athena turned to the god of the sea. "And this doesn't encroach upon your realm?"

"There may be some overlap," Poseidon grumbled. "But, given my part in recent, tragic events, I'm determined to accept it."

"Poseidon controls the sea, of course," Jinsoo added. "And all the things living in it. He controls the sailing vessels."

"He doesn't control all of the vessels," Hermes interjected. "Shipping crafts are my domain, as are pirates."

"Not entirely," Poseidon argued.

"Brother, uncle, please," Athena said. "This argument has plagued us for centuries, and I doubt it will be settled today. Let us agree that Jinsoo will be the primary caretaker of sailors."

"Hear, hear," Hades cut in.

"All in favor, say aye," Athena said.

The great hall resounded with the gods' assent.

"All opposed?" Athena asked.

The hall was silent.

Jinsoo bowed to the other gods as applause erupted. Then, smiling, he returned to Prometheus's side. Hestie couldn't be happier for him. She only wished Alastair could have been here to see it. Even now, after all the vampires had done to help the gods and humanity, they still weren't welcome on Mount Olympus.

Once the hall had become silent again, Athena called, "Gertrude Morgan, please step forward."

Gertie glanced nervously at Hector before she released his hand and moved to the center of the hall. Hestie supposed that the two demigods were back together. She wondered if Gertie still thought about Taavi, or if she had blotted him from her mind.

Athena smiled at Gertie as she said, "We have asked you here today to join us as the goddess of vampires, who have for too long been underserved by this pantheon. I can admit my own contribution to their mistreatment and neglect. But that is to be no longer."

"I'm so happy to hear you say that," Gertie replied.

"And your father, Dionysus, has no qualms with this decision?" Hermes questioned.

Gertie shook her head. "He's given me his blessing."

"And you have given this proper thought and reflection?" Athena asked her. "Once you accept this yolk, it cannot be thrown off, lest you go insane."

Hestie noticed Gertie's lips were trembling. "Insane? Well, I would never walk away from my responsibilities. I want this. I'm sure of it."

"Well, then," Athena began.

"But I do have one condition," Gertie said earnestly as she looked around the room. "I will only serve this pantheon as the goddess of vampires if Hector, a great warrior and the son of Hephaestus, is allowed to undergo apotheosis, too."

Gasps filled the room, and all eyes turned to Hector, who stood white-faced and gaping. Hestie couldn't believe Gertie was making conditions. Was she crazy?

"I don't appreciate demands, Gertrude," Athena said sharply.

"But Hector would make an amazing god," Gertie insisted. "And we're in love and want to be together."

Hestie sucked in air, wishing Gertie was better at censoring her words.

"How sweet," Aphrodite crooned.

Hector's face turned red and then quickly faded back to a pasty white.

"Your love life is not our concern," Athena said with a scoff. "And I am beginning to doubt your readiness for this transformation."

Aphrodite flew to her feet. "I don't appreciate your attitude toward love, Athena. It may not be our priority today, but it isn't something to scoff at, either."

"My apologies, sister," Athena said in a way that didn't sound sincere.

"What purpose would Hector contribute to the pantheon?" Hades wanted to know.

"Come forward, Hector," Ares demanded. "Did you put her up to this?"

Hector moved to Gertie's side. "I didn't put her up to anything, no. But I do know how I would like to serve, if given the chance."

"Do tell us," Athena snapped with an impatient frown.

"I want to be the god of demigods."

"A trainer of warriors?" Ares asked with his brows lifted. "Like the days of Chiron?"

Hector shook his head. "I can help them train and become strong warriors for you, but I also want to act as an intermediary between the gods and their children."

Hestie noticed uneasiness sweep across the room.

"We don't need a mediator," Poseidon insisted.

"I was just thinking the same thing," Apollo admitted.

"Why do you think we need one?" Hermes asked Hector.

"Because, well, I hate to say it, but…"

"Spit it out," Athena said.

Hector glanced back at his father before returning Athena's gaze. "The gods, for the most part, ignore their children. And their children grow up feeling unloved and neglected. I'd like to remedy this problem by finding ways to involve demigods with their parents."

"Oh, boy," Hades muttered beneath his breath. "This idea is doomed."

Hestie turned to her grandfather and whispered, "Why?"

Ares stood up and answered in Hades's stead. "Because we don't need to be told what to do by another god—especially a new, inexperienced one. We see our kids on our own terms, thank you very much."

Hector glanced back at Hephaestus, who'd remained quiet. "Do you have an opinion on this, Father?"

Hestie had never seen Hephaestus angry, but his red face gave him away when he challenged, "Has it ever occurred to you that gods don't desire to have relationships with their mortal children?"

"It has," Hector said, now growing angry, too. "You've made it fairly obvious, until recently, that is. You showed me your forge."

"I regret that already," Hephaestus growled.

Tears sprang to Hector's eyes.

Hestie's stomach clenched, and her heart ached for Hector. She couldn't stop herself from saying telepathically to Hephaestus, *How can you be so cruel?*

"Then why have them?" Hector wanted to know. "If you don't want relationships with them, why have them?"

"Gods aren't immune to making mistakes," Artemis pointed out.

"So, I'm a mistake," Hector said beneath his breath.

The gods began whispering among themselves.

Ares threw up his hands. "Humankind needs great warriors."

"And great artists," Apollo added.

"And great athletes," Hermes said.

Hector wiped his eyes. "How noble."

Athena shook a fist. "Order. I want order."

The room became silent again.

Then, Athena said, "Gertrude, it's clear to me that your request to include Hector in this pantheon has been denied. And because you foolishly made that a condition of your own transformation, you will not be joining us, either. I think it's time that these mortals left Mount Olympus before they offend us further. We have other business to discuss."

Hestie looked from Gertie to Poros, shocked and upset. Was this really happening? Gertie might lack common sense, but she didn't deserve this.

"Wait," Poros objected. "Shouldn't we put this to a vote?"

Hermes stood up. "I think we should hold off making this decision. Let's give it more time. Right now, our priority should be what to do about STS and its smuggling of humans and dangerous weapons."

"Hear, hear," Poseidon said.

"All in favor of postponing our decision about Gertrude's apotheosis, say aye," Athena said.

The hall resounded with the assent of gods.

"All opposed?" Athena asked.

The hall was silent.

Hestie sighed with relief. Maybe with more time, the minds of the gods could be changed.

"We'll readjourn in a few months' time," Athena said. "Let's move on to more important matters."

CHAPTER TWO

A Fractured Pantheon

Gertie wanted to shrivel up and die.

Instead, she walked on weak knees with Hector to stand on the outskirts of the Olympian temple, near the foyer. She dared not make eye contact with a living soul. She was too mortified to receive their looks of pity.

Hector was also silent and, although he was no longer holding her hand, she could feel him trembling as much as she was.

It had been a disaster, and she just wanted to go home. She wanted to curl up in her cozy bed in her house in Athens, which she now desperately missed. And she wanted Babá to make cake.

She prayed to Morpheus, the god of dreams, to come and get them, to end their misery as soon as possible. They had come to Mount Olympus on a giant white crane—the animal form that Hephaestus took; however, for Hector's sake, that couldn't be their return trip. They needed to find another way. Morpheus had helped her once before. Maybe he would again.

She was relieved when Poseidon stood up and took the attention away from her.

With his sun-bleached hair brushing against his tanned, broad shoulders, the god of the sea said, "We need to cull the corrupt players in Sailfish Trading and Shipping. I recommend that some of us infiltrate the organization disguised as workers. Perhaps we can recruit Prometheus and his band of young gods."

Hermes leapt to his feet. "Are you kidding me? With all due respect, Uncle, STS needs to go. There's no culling the bad from the good."

Gertie thought of her stepfather, James, who was a major shareholder of STS. He would soon go to trial for his part in the human and munitions trafficking, but his hand had been forced, his family threatened. She, too, doubted the possibility of separating the bad from the good. The bad had ways of corrupting the good.

With his turquoise eyes narrowed, Poseidon lifted his hands in protest. "If we wipe them out, we'll open the door to chaos as other smuggling rings try to fill the void. I don't want my sea turned into a battlefield. It would only endanger more lives."

"He's got a point," Hephaestus said.

"I disagree," Ares said. "A monopoly of power gives only an illusion of safety. In truth, it's more dangerous."

"Unchecked power always is," Artemis added.

"Not unchecked," Poseidon argued. "I control STS."

"And look where that got you," Athena pointed out, referring to the way Phorcys, the old man of the sea, had joined with STS to control Poseidon by kidnapping his daughter.

Gertie touched her hands to her cheeks, trying to keep them from turning red. If it hadn't been for her and Prometheus's crew, Poseidon might still be under the control of the crusty old monster known as the old man of the sea.

The old monster, Phorcys, had wanted a temple built in his honor, so that the prayers of mortals might return his old power back to him. Officials in the Syrian government had agreed—in exchange for his help in bringing nuclear arms to their country. The officials smuggled Syrian rebels via STS to be sold into slavery in Russia in exchange for Russian warheads. Fortunately Gertie, along with Prometheus's crew of gods and vampires, had stopped them. But now they needed to be stopped for good.

Poseidon growled beneath his breath. "Ares just wants a war."

"We should destroy their ships and leave them powerless," Hermes insisted.

Prometheus lifted his palms. "What a waste of human design and ingenuity."

"Can't the ships be salvaged?" Hephaestus wondered.

"Not everyone at STS is culpable," Persephone pointed out.

"Exactly," Hades said. "Why should the baby be thrown out with the bath water?"

"Hear, hear!" Poseidon cried with a look of surprise on his face. "For once, we agree, brother."

"With all due respect," Hermes said again, "an organization like STS can't be salvaged. Its disease can't be cut away. If we remove the bad apples, more will rot to take their place."

Poseidon glared at Hermes, his nostrils flaring. "Are you a prophet now, too?"

"Monopolies are the enemy of free trade," Hermes continued. "And the small-time smugglers that attempt to fill the void left behind by STS won't have the manpower or resources to pull off the large-scale evil perpetrated by STS."

Gertie resisted the urge to cry, "Hear, hear!"

"One of them will eventually rise to the top," Poseidon argued, "and we'll be right back where we started. Why not avoid all that danger, death, and chaos and leave STS in control, with me at the reins?"

"Until they capture someone else you care about?" Hermes taunted.

"That wasn't STS!" Poseidon bellowed. "That was Phorcys. With him and his horrid wife, Keto, in the Titan Pit, I'll keep things under control."

If Gertie weren't a lowly demigod, she would have smirked. How quickly Poseidon had forgotten all she and the vampires had done to save his daughter.

For once, Hermie agreed with Poseidon. Why not turn STS into the puppets of the gods and maintain order on the sea rather than wiping them out and opening a void to be filled by other criminals?

"We've heard the arguments on both sides," Athena said. "It's time to put this matter to a vote."

Only the most powerful Olympians had the right to vote, and since Demeter wasn't there, only twelve, including Poros, who had proven to be the most powerful when he overthrew his father, Zeus, would be heard. Hermie held his breath as Athena asked for those in favor of Poseidon's plan to say aye. He was relieved that those opposed were in the minority with Hermes, Artemis, and Ares.

"This is a mistake!" Hermes objected.

Ignoring him, Athena turned to Poseidon. "I'll leave you to come up with the plan and see it through. Please keep me informed."

No sooner had the meeting ended than Hestie rushed across the room to Gertie and Hector. Hermie felt bad for them and wished there was something he could do to change what had happened. Del and the other vampires were going to be heartbroken not to have their goddess, their protector. He and Jinsoo followed his sister to talk to the demigods.

"I'm so sorry," Hestie was saying. "You didn't deserve that."

"I don't want to talk about it," Gertie said.

Red-faced and silent, Hector looked as though he wanted to punch something.

Prometheus and Poros caught up to them, followed by Hermes.

"Let's get back to the ship," Prometheus said.

"I'm headed there now to transport the vampires to my new vessel," Hermes said. "And, fair warning, I don't care what the council decided today. I'm taking down STS."

"To your new vessel?" Hermie asked. "What? Now? Already?"

"Let me help you, Lord Hermes!" Gertie cried desperately.

Hestie gawked at Gertie. "Are you crazy?"

"That's not a good idea," Poros said to Gertie. "Not if you want the other gods to ever agree to make you immortal."

"I don't care anymore," Gertie said, like a petulant child.

"Listen to him, Gertie," Prometheus urged. "Going against the Olympians is a dangerous business." Then to Hermes, he added, "I wish you'd give this more thought. We should work together as allies, not as enemies. What you propose is treason."

Hermie, too, wanted to persuade his namesake to think twice about going behind the backs of the other Olympians, but his efforts were cut short when Poseidon approached.

Poseidon turned to Prometheus. "Can I count on your help in taking over STS?"

"We're happy to serve, aren't we, crew?" the captain said.

Poros grinned. "Count me in."

"We're ready," Hermie said with a sideways glance at Hermes.

Hermes groaned. "Thick skulls, the lot of you."

The messenger god grabbed Gertie and Hector, and the three of them disappeared.

"I don't like the sound of that," Poseidon said.

Hermie didn't either.

Prometheus rubbed his beard. "He's got plans of his own."

"I'll come by tomorrow to discuss ours," Poseidon said.

The captain tipped his hat. "Until then."

Gertie was startled when she landed with Hermes and Hector in the hull of the *Marcella II*. Streamers hung from the rafters. Balloons covered the floor. A big sign overhead read *Congratulations, Gertie*.

"Surprise!" the vampires said together. They stood or hovered near their crates in the very large laundry and utility room, where a table had been set up with grapes, cheese, wine, and a cake with her name on it.

"It didn't happen, my friends," Hermes said. "Once more, the vampires have been snubbed."

"They promised," Alastair said with a look of such disappointment on his face that it crushed Gertie's soul. "What happened?"

"It was my fault," Gertie admitted. She told him about her condition of acceptance as tears poured down her cheeks. "I'm so sorry I let you down. Please, forgive me."

Del flew from the room, sobbing.

"It was my fault," Hector said. "I told her I wanted to be a god, too, and live on Mount Olympus near my father—who hates me. I always suspected, but now I know. I'm just in the way, holding everyone back. Hermes, take me home."

Gertie's eyes widened. Was he going to walk away from her *again*? "We have a part to play in this, Hector. Don't you want to get back at them—at the gods?"

"There's no time for this," Hermes said. "We need to board my ship pronto, before the Olympians try to stop us."

"Stop us from what?" Mahdi asked.

"I'll explain everything later. Just know that Poseidon is against us once again."

Penny reached up and snatched a streamer and ripped it into pieces. Bach kicked the balloons, making half of them pop. Raimo tugged on the sign above him, but it caught on a screw, so he left it.

"Climb in your crates," Hermes said. "I don't want to risk you getting exposed." Then he shouted, "Del, come on!"

The vampires did as they were told. Gertie watched in awe as Hermes, with his mighty strength and speed, quickly disappeared with two crates only to return for another two. In less than a minute, he had transported each of them to his new ship.

Once Poseidon had left the group, Jinsoo said, "Let's hurry, Captain. I want to get back before the vampires leave the ship."

"Surely, they'll wait to say goodbye," Hestie said.

"Did Hermes look patient to you?" Jinsoo argued.

"Let's god-travel," Hermie suggested to Jinsoo, feeling anxious now to see Del. Then, turning to the others, he added, "We'll see you there."

"See you there," Hestie said.

"Take my hand, Hermie," Jinsoo said. "You know I suck at god-travel."

Hermie took Jinsoo's hand and blinked against the pressure as his body left one dimension and appeared in another—the deck of the *Marcella II*.

"Duh, below deck," Jinsoo said pointing to the sun shining brightly overhead. "Why did you bring us up here? Never mind. Come on."

Hermie flew after Jinsoo to the hull, where they found the place deserted, except for streamers and balloons and a sign that read *Congratulations, Gertie* hanging on the ship's rafters by one corner. Even the vampire crates were gone.

"We're too late," Jinsoo said as Chidori flew to his shoulder to greet him.

"What?" Hermie couldn't believe it. "Why didn't they wait to say goodbye?"

"Where'd they go?" Jinsoo asked Chidori.

"The *Black Widow*," Chidori chirped. "Hermes's new boat."

"Did they say where it's docked?" Hermie asked the yellow canary.

Chidori shook her head.

"Did they leave a note?" Jinsoo wondered. He hurried down the hall to his cabin. He returned, deflated. "I got nothing. You?"

Hermie was afraid to look because the hurt would be too much to bear. But he forced himself down the hall to this room. His heart leapt when he found an envelope on his pillow with his name written on it. He pulled out the card and opened it.

Remember that I love you, no matter what.

Hermie's stomach dropped. He and Del hadn't said those words to each other yet. Why would she say them now, in this way? He reached out to her telepathically but heard nothing in return. He prayed to Hermes, his namesake, but the messenger god did not reply.

He tucked the card beneath his pillow and returned to Jinsoo empty-handed.

"Nothing," he said, not wanting Jinsoo to be hurt that Del had left a note and Alastair had not.

"How could they do this to us, Hermie? I've tried to talk to Alastair's mind, but he isn't answering."

"They must be too far away," Hermie said.

"But why leave without saying goodbye?"

Hermie clenched his fist. "I wish I knew."

Hestie gave her mother another hug goodbye before she followed Captain and Poros to the stables. Pegasus was very happy to see them. Together, they flew from the gates and over the Mediterranean, which was now glistening in the bright sunshine.

When they landed on the deck of the *Marcella II*, anchored a mile west of the island of Cyprus, they found Hermie, Jinsoo, and Chidori waiting for them.

"They're gone," Jinsoo said angrily. "They didn't even leave a note."

"I had a feeling that would happen," Prometheus said.

"Have you tried reaching them telepathically?" Hestie asked, "or praying to Hermes?"

Hermie rolled his eyes. "No. We didn't think of that."

"Don't take your anger out on her," Poros said. "She's just trying to help."

Jinsoo sighed. "They must be too far away."

"They'd planned a surprise party for Gertie," Hermie shared. "They had streamers and everything."

"I know," Hestie said. "We bought the supplies in Paris. It was my idea."

Hermie glanced at Jinsoo. "Oh."

Hestie wished there was something she could say that would make her brother and Jinsoo feel better.

"I'm afraid Hermes is planning something," the captain said. "And he's going to use the vampires to make it happen."

"Do you think he took them against their will?" Poros asked.

"No," Hermie said. "They're loyal to him and would do just about anything for him."

Hestie knew this to be true. Hermes had saved them from a miserable life and had given them a purpose. He'd become like a father to them.

"Poseidon is coming tomorrow to discuss a plan of our own," Prometheus relayed. "So, let's get the ship in tip top shape and then enjoy the rest of the evening, because starting tomorrow, we have work to do."

"Yes, Captain," Poros responded automatically.

Hestie led the way below deck to the sad remains of what was to be Gertie's surprise party. The sign had been partly torn from the rafters, and some of the streamers lay in shreds.

"It looks like they took out their disappointment over Gertie on the decorations," she said.

"They felt betrayed," Jinsoo insisted. "Not disappointed. The gods have screwed them over one too many times."

She knew Jinsoo was right. The vampires never asked to be made. They were created by accident centuries ago when Gertie's father, Dionysus, the god of wine, made his first Maenads—women who remained immortal while consuming his wine. The Maenads were vicious and orgiastic, and that night they went home and tore their family members' limbs off. The only thing that could save them was human blood.

Del, Alastair, and their crew had been orphaned by the first vampires. At their orphanage in Athens, they formed a children's choir and sang all over Greece until they, too, were turned when most of them were seventeen. According to Hermie, their lives were miserable as they tried to subsist on human blood. If Hermes hadn't given them their current purpose—patrolling the Mediterranean for stolen goods—who knows what would have become of them. Hestie shuddered to think of it, then sighed as she began to clean up. If it wasn't one thing, it was another. Why couldn't everyone just get along?

After they finished tidying the ship—including tossing all the remnants of Gertie's surprise party, Hestie was about to go to the flybridge with Poros when Hermie and Jinsoo flagged them down.

Telepathically, Hermie said: *Don't tell Captain, but we're going to look for the* Black Widow. *Are you in?*

When? Poros asked, also telepathically, to avoid being overheard by Captain.

Now, Jinsoo said. *Chidori will call for us if Captain comes looking.*

But we have no idea where to start, Hestie objected. *That could take forever.*

We've got to do something, Hermie said. *The vampires need to hear our side of the argument.*

I have a better idea, Hestie said. *Let's go see Hecate in Demeter's winter cabin and ask her to perform a location spell.*

But we'd need something belonging to Hermes or to one of the vampires for that to work, Poros pointed out.

Do either of you have anything? Hestie asked Hermie and Jinsoo. *Maybe Del or Alastair gave you something?*

Hermie's cheeks turned red.

Spill, Hestie said.

Hermie flew to his cabin and returned with an envelope.

It's a card from Del. There's no need to read it. Hecate will know what to do with it.

Great, Jinsoo said. *Let's hurry so maybe we can get back before Captain knows we're gone.*

Together, they god-traveled to Mount Kronos in search of Demeter's winter cabin.

CHAPTER THREE

A Location Spell

So much for Poseidon's promise to support us," the vampire Penny said once they were together in the salon of the *Black Widow*, where the windows had been tinted and the mini blinds had been closed to keep out the sunlight.

Gertie looked up at her through tears. Penny's brown hair was pulled into a high ponytail, exposing the frown lines on her forehead and her chubby cheeks. Sophia, her petite, brunette girlfriend with exceptionally large brown eyes, stood close beside her, trying to calm her down.

"Take a deep breath, Penny," Sophia said.

Gertie wiped away her tears as she sat slumped in a chair.

"It wasn't just Poseidon," Gertie shared. "It was all of them."

"Not all," Hermes pointed out from where he stood hovering over her.

"Gertie, I'm so sorry," Del said—not for the first time. "Not just for you, but for us, too."

Hector, who was pacing in the middle of the vampires, all of whom were standing, ranted, "Even my own father. How could he say that to me?"

"There's something you need to understand," Hermes said to Hector. "It's hard for gods to invest in getting to know children whose lives pass us by in the blink of an eye. For immortals, there isn't enough time.

And the constant pain of losing them, well, it makes you want to keep your distance."

"Forgive me, Lord Hermes," Gertie began, "but that's selfish *and* cruel."

"Watch it, Gertie," the messenger god warned. "I'm the only god on your side right now."

Gertie sucked in her lips. He was right; and she needed him to stay on her side.

"Let's focus on what the plan is," Alastair suggested. "And why we could not wait to say goodbye to our friends."

"Prometheus and his crew are no longer your friends," Hermes dictated.

Gertie looked up at Hector, whose brows had lifted in surprise.

Del's mouth dropped open. "I am afraid that is impossible, my lord."

"Why would you say such a thing?" Alastair asked. "After all we have been through together?"

As upset as Gertie felt over being denied apotheosis—the Titans would have breached the pit if it hadn't been for her in her bull form holding that iron door shut—she was more upset that Prometheus and his crew had chosen to take the opposite side of the STS problem. She had come to think of them as good friends, and now they were to be enemies?

Hermes scratched his dark curly beard. "I'm serious, Del and Alastair—and all of you. You need to know where your loyalties lie. I must be able to trust that you won't give away our secrets."

"But we want the same thing, no?" Raimo asked as he pushed his stringy, dark hair from his eyes. "An end to STS?"

"No," Hermes said. "We don't."

"Really?" Bach folded his long, lean arms across his chest. "I do not understand."

Hermes walked around the room as he spoke: "Prometheus and his crew are working with Poseidon in a futile effort to take down the corrupt leaders and leave the company intact."

"It's true," Gertie confirmed. "They think Poseidon can be the puppet master once the corrupt leaders are gone. They think that without STS, other criminals will fight to fill the void, making the seas more dangerous."

"Could that be true?" Mahdi asked Hermes.

Seeing Mahdi again made Gertie think of Taavi. They looked nothing alike—Taavi's skin had been fair, and Mahdi's was dark; Taavi had been lean and wiry, and Mahdi was thicker built—but they'd shared a similar energy, a happy-go-lucky attitude even in the face of terrible conflict. And, like Taavi, Mahdi wore a smile on his face more often than not.

Hermes wagged a finger in the air. "The only way to end the horrific smuggling of hundreds of Syrians against their will in exchange for Russian warheads is to wipe out the entire STS fleet. Poseidon is deluding himself."

Gertie studied the vampires as they processed Hermes's words. As hard as it was for her to be on the other side from her new friends, she knew it was even harder for the vampires. Del and Hermie were falling in love, as were Alastair and Jinsoo, and all the vampires had grown to love and care for Captain and his crew.

Gertie noticed that Hector was crying again. She reached out to take his hand, but he pulled away. Did he still want Hermes to take him home? Or would he stay with her and fight?

"We need to act fast," Hermes said, "before Poseidon and his lot board the vessels."

"Board the vessels?" Raimo repeated.

"They plan to work undercover," Hector explained as he swatted tears from his face. "To find out who the corrupt leaders are."

"I bet we could just ask my step-dad," Gertie said. "He could name names."

"I'm sure the others will think of that," Hermes pointed out. "But that information doesn't matter for our purposes. We're going after the ships."

"Won't that entail a lot of lost lives?" Del asked.

"Not if everything goes according to plan," the god replied.

Gertie bit her lower lip. As much as she agreed with Hermes about ending STS, she hoped to avoid killing people—even criminals.

Ready? Hermie asked his sister and the others telepathically.

I'm ready, Hestie said. *But I don't think Poros should come. It's hard for him to deceive Captain.*

Poros shrugged. *I'd be worried about you.*

I can take care of myself, Hestie insisted.

We don't have all day, Jinsoo urged them. *Are you coming, or not?*

We're coming, Poros said.

Jinsoo kissed Chidori goodbye and then, together, the young immortals god-traveled to a heavily wooded forest at the base of Mount Kronos, where Demeter's cabin could only be found by those who already knew where it was. After picking their way through thick undergrowth they came upon what, to mortal eyes, would appear to be an abandoned, dilapidated shack—but that was just a glamor. Although simple and built by mortals, Demeter's cabin, with its golden logs, high slanted roof, and large front windows, was a beautiful retreat.

Hestie knocked on the door.

Hecate opened it. "I saw you coming."

"Do you know why we're here?" Hestie asked.

The goddess of magic pushed her long, black-and-white-streaked hair from her shoulders. "Yes, and I hate to disappoint you, but Demi and I are on vacation."

Hermie frowned. "Please? This is important."

"Of course, it is," Hecate said. "That's why you're going to do the location spell."

"Us?" Hestie glanced at her brother.

"You've done it before. You can do it again. Wait here." Hecate closed the door and a moment later returned with her arms full. "Take these." She gave Hestie a stick of dried herbs and Hermie a silver bowl of water. Then, she handed Jinsoo four blue candles and Poros a world map. "Off you go."

Hestie tried to object, but Hecate slammed the door in her face.

As he clutched the silver bowl of water, Hermie watched his sister debating whether to knock again on the door of Demeter's cabin.

"Don't," he said. The last thing he wanted was to have Hecate upset with them.

Her fist hung in the air near her cheek and then dropped to her side.

"I didn't think gods were allowed to go on vacation," she complained.

"I'm pretty sure she, of all the gods, deserves it," Poros said.

Hermie agreed. The other gods relied more on Hecate for help than on any other god. When someone or something was lost, she was their go-to.

"Come on." Hermie led them deeper into the woods.

"Where are we going?" Jinsoo asked as he followed.

About twenty yards in, Hermie found what he was looking for—Demeter's altar.

"Here." Hermie put the silver bowl of water on the altar. "Do you remember how to do it?" he asked his sister.

She pulled her phone from her pocket. "I'm pretty sure I still have Hecate's text with the instructions."

Hermie hoped so. His stomach had begun to ache with worry over Del. Hermes had made her an enemy of the Olympians all over again. This wasn't supposed to happen.

"What do we do with this map?" Jinsoo wanted to know.

"Burn it," Hermie replied. "You'll see. It's pretty cool."

"I can supply the fire," Poros said, bringing out his lightning bolt.

"Uh, that might be overkill, babe," Hestie said. "We don't want the candles to melt."

"Good point," Poros said, putting away the lightning.

"I got this," Hermie said. "God of technology, remember? Fire was one of its earliest forms."

Hermie snapped his fingers and brought a flame into the air. It was one of his favorite gifts.

"Put the candles at each of the cardinal points around the bowl," Hestie said as she studied the text on her phone.

Hermie needed the position of the sun to determine the cardinal directions, but the thick canopy overhead made it difficult to find the sun god. "Where the heck is Helios?"

"It's high noon," Hestie said. "We need a landmark. Hold on."

Hestie flew up past the trees and returned a moment later.

"North is that way," she said, pointing.

Together, they arranged the four candles, and Hermie lit them.

As he was about to light the stick of dried herbs, Hermie heard Chidori's cry coming from miles away, across the Mediterranean Sea.

"Captain's coming!" Poros cried. "Let's get back."

If Prometheus realized they were missing, there'd be hell to pay. He was their captain, and by leaving without his permission, well, it wasn't good.

"Go to my room," Hermie said before he blew out the candles and collected them. Once Jinsoo had the bowl in hand, Hermie god-traveled them through the thick field of pressure into the new dimension that was his cabin on the ship. "Sit there."

Hermie pointed to the chair beside his in front of his computer monitors, where they always sat to play video games. No sooner had they sat in the chairs and Poros and Hestie appeared beside them, than Captain opened the door.

"There you are. I've been calling for you."

"Sorry, Captain," Jinsoo said, panting from his near state of panic. "I'm finally beating Hermie at this game."

"Chidori was really upset," the captain said.

The yellow canary flew into the room and perched on Jinsoo's shoulder.

"We shut her out because we wanted to play *Angry Birds*," Hermie said quickly, knowing Prometheus would have no knowledge of the game.

"Why are you holding that bowl full of water in your lap?" Prometheus asked Jinsoo.

"It's for Chidori." Jinsoo placed the bowl on the desk beside the computer monitor.

Hermie quickly used his gifts to add a layer of protection from the water to the electronics.

Chidori hopped in the bowl and took a bath.

"See?" Jinsoo said. "The perfect birdbath."

Hermie tried not to glance at the four smoking candles in his lap, because if Captain asked about them, he wasn't sure what he'd say.

"Well, I expect everything's in its place and in tip top shape?"

"Yes, Captain," Poros said. Telepathically, he said to Hermie and the others, *I don't like lying to Captain.*

Hermie felt the same way, but what choice did he have?

Once Captain left the room, Jinsoo said telepathically, *That was close.*

Hermie stood up from his chair with the smoking candles. *Let's hurry and do the spell, before Captain comes back again.*

Hestie helped Hermie arrange the candles at the cardinal points around the bowl while Chidori watched from the edge of the desk, where she was drying out her feathers.

Hermie lit the candles and the stick of dried herbs and asked, "What's next?"

Hestie scrolled through her phone, looking for the text from Hecate. Finding it, she said, "The water has to be clear. Better empty this and add fresh water—no offense, Chidori."

Chidori chirped, "None taken."

Poros picked up the bowl. "I'll do it."

"Only three-quarters full," Hestie said.

Poros took the bowl to the head attached to Hermie's room and returned a few moments later with fresh water. Hestie helped him place it in the center of the lit candles.

"Now, we bathe the bowl of water with the smoke from the burning herbs," Hestie said, using her hands to manipulate the air as Hermie held the burning stick over the bowl.

The four young gods watched on as the smoke blanketed the silver bowl. Hestie found the scent of the smoke appetizing, reminding her that she hadn't eaten in a while.

"Now what?" Jinsoo asked.

"Now we need that envelope from Del," Hestie said. "We have to burn it."

"Not the whole thing," Hermie objected as he handed the burning stick of herbs to Jinsoo. He reached into his back pocket and tore a corner of the envelope off and handed it to Hestie. "This should do, shouldn't it?"

"I'm going to need a bigger piece. It has to burn long enough to set the map on fire."

Hermie groaned as he slipped the folded paper from the envelope and stuffed it in his back pocket. Then he handed the empty envelope to Hestie. She wondered what the note said that had her brother apparently tied up in knots over it.

She held the envelope to the flame that was burning on the northernmost candle. It took a moment for the fire to catch hold of it. Once it did, she held the flame on the edge of the folded world map. Gradually, the flames ate at the paper and grew larger and more deeply red.

"Ay, chihuahua," Jinsoo said. "This is super crazy, guys."

When the world map was completely in flames, Hestie dropped both it and the envelope into the bowl of water. She waited for the flames to die before stirring the water with her finger, clockwise, four times. As she completed the fourth revolution, she said, "Please show me the location of Hermes and his vampire crew."

"Is something supposed to happen?" Jinsoo asked.

"Be patient," Hermie said.

Hoping she had done the spell correctly, Hestie watched the water until a scrap of the map floated to the surface. Taking a deep breath, she plucked the scrap from the water and studied it. If the spell hadn't worked, they'd have to come up with another plan for locating the *Black Widow*. She prayed to Hecate that it had worked, because she couldn't bear to disappoint Jinsoo and her brother.

"What does it say?" Hermie asked anxiously.

"They're on the Black Sea near the coast of Bulgaria."

None of them heard the captain's approach until he knocked on the door and opened it.

The four young gods gasped, caught red-handed.

"Captain," Poros said, "let us explain."

"No need. I know what you're up to."

"You do?" Jinsoo cried.

Prometheus chuckled. "You four aren't as sneaky as you might think you are."

"We have to find them," Hermie pleaded. "Help us. They need to hear our side of the argument."

"It won't do any good," Prometheus said. "Hermes has made up his mind and, like you said, they're loyal to him."

"We have to try," Hermie said. "Maybe we can come up with a compromise."

"The Olympians have already made up their minds," the captain said. "There is no compromise."

"Just let us try," Hestie pleaded. "What harm could it do?"

Prometheus sighed and scratched at his beard. "You and Hermie go but be quick. I need Jinsoo and Poros to help me get the ship ready to sail. Poseidon wants to meet in Athens tomorrow afternoon. It sounds like we'll be there a while."

"Athens?" Hestie asked. "Why Athens?"

"Apparently, you're going to question Gertie's stepfather," Prometheus explained. "So, you and your brother need to hurry back. We set sail in one hour."

Hestie could tell that Jinsoo was heartbroken. He was as anxious to see Alastair as Hermie was to see Del.

"Can't Jinsoo go in my place?" she asked. "I can help get the ship ready."

The captain shrugged. "I suppose so. Just hurry up, kids. I want to get this STS business behind us so we can go back to what we do best: helping people."

"Aye, aye, Captain," Jinsoo said.

Hestie watched as Jinsoo and Hermie leapt into the sky and headed north. She hoped they'd find what they were looking for, even if only for the chance to say goodbye.

CHAPTER FOUR

Unexpected Prisoners

For the first time since boarding the *Black Widow*, Gertie paid attention to her surroundings. The salon resembled the lobby of a five-star hotel with its white leather couches and chairs grouped in the center of the long room around two chunky coffee tables. There were blue velvet throw pillows on the couches, along with a graphic chenille throw. Rows of tinted windows were broken up with artwork—a large oil painting on canvas—on each side. There were even lamps on sleek end tables and a wide-screen television mounted in a built-in cabinet console that divided the long salon in half. Ceiling tiles overhead with recessed lighting were framed by a tinted mirror, which eerily reflected everything in the room except for the vampires.

The galley, toward the ship's bow, was even more amazing. A long, mahogany dining table with seating for ten had tapered candles on it with a crystal chandelier hung above it. Past the table was a full kitchen with granite countertops, white shaker-style cabinets, more recessed lighting, and stainless-steel appliances—not miniature appliances like those on the *Marcella II*. These were full-sized. The six-burner gas stove resembled the one in Gertie's parents' mansion in Athens.

There were vases and candle arrangements on bookcases situated beneath the rows of windows on each side. Captain didn't have anything like this on the *Marcella II*. His ship was practical in every way, whereas this one was extravagant. It reminded Gertie of the superyacht her father once owned.

She followed Hermes and Hector past the wide-screen television, past the built-in cabinet console, toward the stern, where the extravagance continued. The second half of the salon contained a built-in heated pool along the center of the room with couches around the perimeter and another wide-screen television on the backside of the built-in cabinet console. Beyond the pool was a gorgeous spiral staircase that led down to the ship's hull, and past that were French doors.

"I know this doesn't make up for all your disappointments," Hermes said to the vampires as they followed him into the pool area, "but I searched long and hard for a ship that would be perfect for light-sensitive beings. You can hang out up here, day or night, and your rooms below are just as nice."

"This ship is incredible," Bach said.

"We'll finish the tour when we get back," Hermes said, as he headed for the spiral stairs, "For now, follow me to your cabins, where you'll find protective gear for daytime missions. The first thing we need to do is move the ship before one of the other gods tries to stop us."

Hermie flew with Jinsoo toward the Black Sea, composing in his mind what he would say to Del when he reached the *Black Widow*. He wanted her to know that he would love her no matter what she decided to do, but only after she could make a more informed choice.

The sun shone brightly in the sky over the Mediterranean Sea as the two young gods flew toward the coast of Bulgaria, over four hundred miles away. They flew as silently and as quickly as they could over Turkey, which took at least half an hour. Hermie knew there was no way they'd make it back to the *Marcella II* in time to set sail. He and Jinsoo would just have to catch up with Captain and the others later.

As they approached Istanbul, located just south of the Black Sea, they observed over a hundred ships, most of them in motion, any one of which could be the *Black Widow*.

"Ay, chihuahua," Jinsoo said. "This sea is busier than the Mediterranean."

"It probably just seems that way because it's smaller," Hermes conceded. "But yeah, I didn't expect it to be this crowded."

"Bulgaria is that way," Jinsoo said, pointing west. "Let's start there."

Even with god vision, it wasn't easy to read the names of each and every vessel they encountered as they flew close to the water's surface, which, while not tumultuous, was by no means calm.

"This is where they should be," Hermes said, deflated, when none of the crafts for miles sported the name they sought.

"Maybe the spell didn't work, Hermie. Maybe they aren't here at all."

"Let's widen our search before we give up, okay?"

"I'm not saying we should give up. If it were up to me, Hermie, we'd keep searching, day and night, until we found them."

Hermie felt the same. As much as he hated disobeying Captain, he had to find Del, to make sure she was okay and that she understood his point of view.

"Does everyone understand the plan?" Hermes asked the vampires and demigods once they had relocated the ship to the Tahanroz'ka Gulf, not far from the southern coast of Russia.

They stood around the mahogany dining table in the galley, where Hermes had just laid out their mission.

Gertie tied her hair at the nape of her neck. "I could be more help to you with the vampire virus pumping through my veins."

Alastair combed his fingers though his short, sandy hair before he covered it with a motorcycle helmet—all the vampires had one to protect them from the sun. "You know that is not a good idea with your susceptibility to addiction."

Gertie licked her lips. It was true. She'd been addicted to Jeno's blood because of the amazing powers the virus instilled in her for the six hours it remained in her body after a vampire fed on her. For those six hours, she had the powers of flight, speed, x-ray vision, invisibility, super strength, and mind control. It was as close to being a god as a mortal could become.

"Then why not turn me into one of you?" she asked with a glance at Hector, who looked horrified at the suggestion. "Turn both of us. If we can't be gods, Hector and I can become vampires."

Hector furrowed his brows. "You know that's not what I want."

"Let's not do anything rash," Hermes said. "The Olympian council may turn you yet."

"You saw Athena," Gertie argued. "I've offended her, and she's really good at holding grudges. I'll never become a goddess now."

"Nor I a god," Hector said. "And I don't want to. I hate them—except for you, Lord Hermes."

The messenger god scoffed.

"You are upset," Del insisted. "You do not hate the gods—especially your father."

"Don't tell me how I feel," Hector said angrily. "I don't even know what I'm doing here. I'm just holding all of you back."

"Don't say that," Gertie replied. "You have super strength and speed. If anyone's holding anyone back, it's me."

"Quit talking nonsense, Gertie," Penny said. "You are bad-ass."

"We have seen your bull form, remember?" Mahdi said with a smile.

And if she could control it, her power to shift might be useful.

"Please also recall that if it were not for your prophetic dreams," Alastair began, "we could not have stopped STS the last time."

Great, Gertie thought. Yet another power she couldn't control.

"We believe in you," Bach said kindly. "Even if you do not believe in yourself."

"And we are counting on you to become our goddess," Del reminded Gertie. "So do not give up on us."

Gertie took a deep breath and clenched her jaw, trying not to cry. Without the powers of flight, strength, or speed, she felt like a liability.

She was also upset with how badly Hector wanted to leave—not just this mission, but her. The fear of being abandoned by those she loved was overwhelming, stifling, and all-consuming. Her parents had left her; her father, Dionysus, had left her; and Jeno, the vampire who'd first introduced her to the underground world of the living dead, had left her. Hector had also left her once before, and he'd promised not to do it again. Was he breaking that promise?

How could she be there for the vampires if no one could be there for her?

"Let's stop wasting time and get on with it," Hermes demanded. "You all know your parts to play?"

"Yes," Del said for the group. "Raimo, Penny, and Mahdi are on lookout."

The three vampires nodded. Penny and Mahdi bumped fists.

"Del and I will be the distraction," Alastair said. "And the rest will be the burglars—or in this case, the smokers."

"Once you pull the lever, these detonate within thirty seconds." Hermes handed Gertie, Hector, Bach, and Sophia smoke bombs. "After they've evacuated the ship, we'll set her ablaze."

"What if they don't evacuate?" Gertie wanted to know.

"They will," Hermes said. "These bombs are suffocating and nasty, which is why you and Hector will be wearing these."

The messenger god gave her and Hector each a gas mask. She slipped hers on, and Hector did the same.

If one of the vamps had bitten her, she wouldn't have to wear it. It was chunky and awkward and uncomfortable, and she could barely see through it—though she supposed the motorcycle helmets were even less comfortable.

"Now, let's get going," Hermes instructed as he led them from the salon and into the air. "Follow me."

Sophia took hold of Gertie's arm and pulled her into the sky after Hermes. Bach did the same with Hector. Gertie shivered a little as the wind chilled her. She pulled her jacket more tightly around her as she clutched the smoke bomb Hermes had given her. Her stomach was grumbling because she hadn't eaten all day, but she didn't dare complain. The gods and vampires often forgot that she and Hector weren't immune to weather and hunger.

As fast as they were flying, it didn't take long to reach the STS vessel. A giant among commercial ships, the bulk carrier stretched three hundred yards long and propelled through the sea toward the Russian port like a great beast. The bulk carrier had five huge grain bins, each about a hundred feet wide and deep, and between the bins stood four enormous cranes. The arms of the cranes were as high as masts and were roped together, probably to prevent them from moving during transport. A flybridge and salon were located on one end, and Gertie knew that's where the sailors would be, above and below deck. It was up to Alastair and Del to distract them long enough for the smokers to set off their bombs.

Penny, Raimo, and Mahdi each hovered in position around the perimeter of the giant vessel while Gertie clung to the side of the ship shivering beside Sophia, Bach, and Hector.

"Are you okay?" Sophia asked her.

"I'd be doing better if you had fed on me," Gertie stated.

Sophia grinned. "If only you knew how badly I want to."

"Do it," Gertie said. "Please?"

"Hermes and the others won't like it. Let's just do what we're told."

While Hermes took control of the flybridge, Del entered the salon and picked a fight with the three sailors there. Alastair went below deck to distract the men in the hull. Sophia, with Gertie on her arm, followed at a distance behind, as did Bach and Hector.

Once they were on solid wood, Gertie followed Sophia, Bach, and Hector through the corridors of the hull to disperse the bombs. It was a bit of a maze. They moved swiftly and stealthily because the vampires leading the way had x-ray vision and could see perfectly well in the dark. It didn't take long for the hull to fill up with smoke and for men to come scrambling for the deck.

"Abandon ship!" the captain called from somewhere above.

Gertie and her team followed the men. She was astonished by how quickly and efficiently they launched their lifeboats and evacuated. Watching now from above the vessel as Hermes dropped the explosives, she felt a sense of triumph at a job well done.

"Oh, no," Alastair, hovering in the air beside her and Sophia, cried.

"What?" Del asked.

"There are still people inside," he gasped. "At least twenty of them." He turned to Bach and Sophia. "How did you miss them?"

"We were not looking for people," Sophia said defensively. "Lord Hermes said they would evacuate."

"They are prisoners," Bach reported. "That is why they did not evacuate."

"They couldn't," Hector surmised.

"More human trafficking by STS," Mahdi growled beneath his breath.

"What do we do?" Gertie wanted to know.

Just then, the ship shuddered as a series of explosions burst like fireworks, throwing planks and metal into air and sea. The vampires and demigods dodged the debris as it flew toward them from every direction.

"We have to do something," Hector cried. "We have to save them."

Gertie agreed. "We aren't murderers, guys! Let's go!"

"Whoa, what's that?" Jinsoo said as he stopped abruptly in the air beside Hermie.

Hermie studied the horizon where he saw something at least six hundred miles north of them. Were those fireworks? No, it was a ship being blown to smithereens.

"Is that the *Black Widow*?" Jinsoo asked with a shaky voice.

Adrenaline, fear, and panic pumped through Hermie as he thought of Del in harm's way. She could be hurt . . . or worse.

"Let's go!" Hermie cried as he shot through the air as quickly as he could. Whether Jinsoo was close on his heels, he couldn't tell and didn't care. He had to get to Del.

After half an hour, he looked back and saw Jinsoo directly behind him. Relieved, he continued toward the fire.

As he grew closer to the blazing ship, he realized it was an STS vessel. The nine-hundred-foot bulk carrier was consumed by flames that licked the night sky like the hungry tongues of snakes. Three lifeboats carried survivors toward a Russian port.

"Wait, Hermie. What's that?" Jinsoo pointed to the splintering vessel. "Are those . . . people?"

Hermie squinted and searched through the debris below. When he spotted the mangled bodies of at least twenty people, his mouth went dry, and he felt nauseous.

Hermie squinted. "Wait a minute. Are they partially desiccated? That means they must be . . ."

"Vampires," Jinsoo finished.

"I'm going to be sick," Hermie said, trying to keep it together.

"Look at them, Hermie," Jinsoo said as tears formed in his eyes. "They tore off their limbs trying to escape from bondage."

Hermie cocked his head to the side. "But vampires have super-strength."

"This makes no sense. Who would do this, Hermie?"

"Those cuffs and chains must be made of adamantine."

"But why? Our friends wouldn't have done this, would they? No way. Right?"

"I don't know what to think. There must be a logical explanation."

Hermie wanted to look away, but his eyes were drawn to the gory sight below as his mind tried to make sense of it.

"Let's find the *Black Widow*, Hermie," Jinsoo said. "Come on."

Hermie left the wreckage with Jinsoo to search for their friends, trying not to imagine the worst.

They hadn't gotten very far when the vampires appeared wearing leather suits, gloves, and motorcycle helmets. They were with Hermes, Hector, and Gertie.

"Thank the gods!" Jinsoo cried. "You found us!"

Relief swept over Hermie when he saw that Del was unharmed, but that relief was short-lived. There was something wrong. The vampires didn't appear happy to see them.

I am sorry, Del said directly into Hermie's head.

Sorry for what? he asked, but no reply was needed, for he'd barely asked the question when the vamps charged him and took him and Jinsoo into their custody. He felt the familiar pressure of god-travel, and when he opened his eyes, he found himself in the hull of an unfamiliar ship beside an all-too-familiar cage—the adamantine cage where he'd been held prisoner when he'd first encountered the crew of vampires.

The wind was picking up, and Captain wanted to hoist the main. Poros had already pulled up the anchor, and Hestie had coiled and stowed the lines. Where were her brother and Jinsoo?

"We'll have to start without them," the captain finally decided.

Hestie and Poros got to work pulling the mainsail up the center mast while Captain sat on the flybridge at the wheel, keeping the ship steady.

"This would be easier with at least one other person," Poros complained. "They should be back by now."

"You finish up here," Hestie said. "I'll start on the stern."

Once all three sails were up, the ship sped through the sea toward the mainland of Greece. Hestie continued to reach out to her brother and Jinsoo telepathically but received nothing in reply.

"What if something happened to them?" she asked Poros, who stood beside her on the front main deck with his face turned up to the sky.

"We should have gone with them."

"But Captain . . ."

"I know. We should have convinced him." Then, taking her hand and pulling her close, he added, "I'm sure they're okay. They're probably on the opposite side of the world on another sea, searching for the *Black Widow*."

Hestie doubted that was true, and she doubted that Poros believed it. But she was grateful for his attempt to make her feel better. She wrapped her arms around his neck and leaned against him, taking comfort in the warmth of his body and the feel of his heart beating with hers.

CHAPTER FIVE

Suspicions

Gertie couldn't bear to face Hermie and Jinsoo as the vampires locked them in the storage room in an adamantine cage near the ship's bow. Adamantine was the strongest metal on earth. Centuries ago, it had arrived in a meteor from another planet. It was so strong that even the gods couldn't bend or break it.

Two months ago, Gertie had dreamed of that very cage and had seen Hermie, Hestie, and Poros captive inside of it. Morpheus, the god of dreams, had witnessed her prophecy and had come to her for help. That's when it had all started, first on the *Marcella II*, where she met Prometheus and his crew and later, on the *Tarantula*, where she met Del and the rest of the vampire pirates.

But they weren't regular pirates. They worked with Hermes to steal artifacts once stolen from oppressed peoples by their oppressors. They then returned the stolen goods to the people who created them.

She had been proud to defend the vampires against Poseidon and the other Olympians when Poseidon was being controlled by Phorcys and STS. And she was proud to stand by them now. But the memory from this afternoon of all those vampires chained in the hull of the STS ship dying horrible deaths haunted her.

She and her friends had tried everything to rescue the prisoners. First, they had tried to end their suffering by allowing them to feed on Gertie and Hector. However, she and her friends soon realized that the cuffs and chains binding them were made of adamantine. The extra strength they garnered from being fed only gave them the strength to rip their limbs to be free of the chains. They immediately bled out and died. Those that hadn't been fed began to desiccate when the sunlight broke through the wreckage. Gertie and her friends had frantically tried to protect them, but they were helpless to stop the horrible deaths.

Now, as Gertie and her friends recounted what had happened to Hermie and Jinsoo, Gertie felt sick. She rushed from the room down the corridor in search of the nearest bathroom. When she found it, she threw up in the toilet. Then she broke into sobs, sat on the floor, and prayed for the souls of the victims.

Hector caught up to her and found her a towel, which she used to clean her mouth.

"Are you okay?" he asked.

"No. How could I possibly be okay? Are you okay?"

Hector shrugged. "It was an accident."

"Hermes shouldn't have been in such a hurry," she said.

"Lower your voice. Better yet, don't speak ill of him at all. He's the only one on our side, remember?"

"Tell me you aren't thinking the same thing."

He helped her off the floor and led her up the spiral stairs to the salon, where they sat together, alone, on one of the leather couches beside the indoor pool.

"Do you really want to go home?" she asked him after a few minutes had passed.

"Not if I can be of help," he said, "but I'm not sure that I can be. My gifts serve me better on land."

"Remember the first time I learned of your powers?" She met his eyes and smiled. "I didn't believe it yet, but that night when you dove off the ferry into the sea, you swam as fast as the dolphins."

"And you, crazy girl, followed me." He touched his finger to the tip of her nose.

"I didn't know what else to do. I tried crying out for help, but no one seemed to notice."

"That was the third time I'd ever seen my father," he said with a sigh. "I was so happy that he came to help us."

"It felt like a dream," she recalled. "He came as a giant white crane and plucked us from the sea."

"That was only two years ago, but it feels like a lot longer."

"So much has happened. So much has changed."

Hector sucked in a deep breath of air and shook his head. "I'm so sorry I got in your way today."

Gertie sat up and squared herself to him. "What are you talking about?"

"You'd be a goddess right now if I'd kept my mouth shut about wanting to be a god, too."

"Stop. It's not your fault. I should have thought things through. Sometimes I'm too much like my father—not James, but Dionysus. I don't always think before I act."

He stroked her ponytail. "You'd be so much better off without me tagging along, Gertie. That's why I think I should go home."

She gnawed on the inside of her lip. How could he still not get it? How could he still be so clueless about her fear of abandonment? Didn't he know her at all?

"If that's how you feel, then go," she finally said.

His eyes widened. "You won't come with me?"

"I'm committed to helping the vampires—even if I can't be their goddess. So, no, I'm not coming with you. But I can't take this anymore, Hector. When things get hard, you want to bail on me." She jumped up from the couch. "If you don't want the same things I want, then let's end this now. My heart can't take this anymore. Let's get this over with."

Hector clambered to his feet. "Are you breaking up with me?"

"Yes." Gertie turned on her heel and fled back down the spiral stairs to her room, where she collapsed on her bed and cried.

"How long do you plan to keep us prisoner?" Jinsoo asked Lord Hermes, after the god and vampires had explained what had happened to the mangled bodies on the STS ship they'd destroyed.

Hermie continued to study Del, hoping that she was reading his thoughts. Although he couldn't hear hers because of the adamantine and the wards marked on the cage, he needed her to understand his point of view. He refused to be her enemy again.

"As long as it takes us to destroy the entire STS fleet," the messenger god replied. "I can't have you getting in the way or reporting on today's mistake—however grave it was."

"What if we swear on the River Styx to say nothing," Hermie offered. "We'll tell Prometheus we never found you, and we'll mention nothing about the STS ship. Would you free us then?"

"Would you really do that?" Alastair asked. "Jinsoo, could you?"

"I've lied to Captain before," Jinsoo said. "You know I just want to be with you. I don't care where. I don't even care what I'm doing. If you come in here with me, I'd be happy to stay in this cage."

"That's so sweet," Penny said.

"Alastair will not be joining you in that cage," Hermes retorted. "But I'll think about Hermie's offer."

As the messenger god was about to leave, Hermie asked, "How did an STS ship get adamantine cuffs and chains? Isn't adamantine supposed to be so rare that even many of the gods don't have any?"

"Maybe they got it from Phorcys back when he was working with them," Raimo said.

"Why would STS be after vampires?" Jinsoo wondered.

Gertie's mind began to spin as ideas fired off, one after another. "What if the Olympians never intended to turn me into your goddess?"

"Athena appeared to be in favor of it," Hermie said.

"If I hadn't insisted on them turning Hector, who would have spoken against it?" Gertie wondered. "Can you think of anyone, Lord Hermes?"

"Do you really believe there's a god out to get vampires?" Jinsoo asked.

Alastair clicked his tongue. "Isn't there always?"

"Maybe this is why Poseidon wants to preserve STS," Lord Hermes said as he waved a finger in the air. "He never liked my pirates patrolling the Mediterranean."

"But we helped rescue his daughter," Penny reminded him.

Gertie stepped further into the room. "You know, I thought it was weird that you weren't invited to Mount Olympus to see my apotheosis. But now it makes sense. They never meant to turn me. They never meant to accept you, either."

Hermie began to pace in the adamantine cage. "I can't believe this— not of all the gods."

"Not all," Gertie agreed. "But some."

"It only takes one," Hermes pointed out.

Hector entered the room. "I just remembered something. My father . . . he was working on an adamantine chain in his forge. I saw it."

Lord Hermes shrugged. "That doesn't mean he had anything to do with the cuffs and chains on that carrier today."

"No, but you said it was rare, right?" Hector asked. "And he had a lot of it."

"A lot?" Hermes questioned.

Hector nodded.

"Maybe Hephaestus is working with Poseidon," Del suggested.

"We should go back," Raimo said. "For the cuffs and chains. Maybe there's a clue as to where they came from."

"I was already planning on that," Hermes revealed. "I have tools we can use to remove the bolts."

"Let us help you," Jinsoo said. "We'll help them, won't we, Hermie?"

"Absolutely," Hermie agreed.

"And how exactly?" the older god wanted to know. "The Olympians will arrest you for treason."

"We could be your spies," Jinsoo said. "And no one needs to know."

Hermie nodded. "We could feed you information."

The messenger god turned to leave. "I'd rather wipe out the fleet as soon as possible."

"Please, just think about it," Hermie called out as the god disappeared. "You don't have to decide today!"

Hermie wished he could hear Del's thoughts as she looked at him with troubled eyes. She did know that he was always on her side, didn't she? And wasn't she still on his?

It wasn't long before he got his answer. Del and Alastair had volunteered to stay behind to guard him and Jinsoo while the others returned to the STS wreckage for the adamantine.

Once they were alone, Jinsoo said, "Let us out of here, Alastair. Do you have the key?"

"Did you mean what you said?" he asked. "Would you really be happy with me anywhere?"

"Of course!" Jinsoo cried. "Don't you already know that?"

"We want to free you," Del said as she rushed to the cage and took Hermie's hand. "And we will, when Hermes permits it."

Hermie's heart sank. "What if he doesn't?"

"He will," Del insisted. "I know he will. So why disobey him now? He gave us the key to test us."

Would her loyalty always be with Lord Hermes? Would she never be loyal to him?

In response, she said, "If I thought he intended to keep you here, I would free you now."

"Then do it," Jinsoo said.

Alastair reached inside the cage to muss Jinsoo's hair. "By waiting, we keep the peace with our lord."

"And our future goddess," Del added. "You understand?"

"He'll only free us if we take an oath on the River Styx," Hermie said. "I'll be forced to lie to my family."

"Your family is against us," Del pointed out.

"No," he insisted. "They don't know about the vampires and the adamantine cuffs. They don't know that someone might be out to get you. If they did, they'd be on your side, too."

"You cannot know that with certainty," Alastair admonished.

"Yes, I can," Hermie insisted again. Then he turned to Del. "If you love me, if you believe in me, trust me in this. Free me now, so I can avoid taking that oath."

"You volunteered to take it," Del said. "What is different now?"

"There's another option I didn't have before," Hermie said. "You can free me."

Tears fell from her eyes as she bowed her head. "I cannot do that, Hermie. I am sorry."

By the time the *Marcella II* reached the port of Piraeus, Greece, it was nearly dawn. Hestie hadn't been able to sleep a wink because she was worried about Jinsoo and her brother, who weren't responding to her telepathically. They had left fifteen hours ago. Where were they?

Poros and the captain had each taken shifts at the helm while the other had slept. While Poros had been at the helm, Hestie had sat with him on the flybridge with her face turned to the sky, hoping to see her brother and Jinsoo catching up to them. While Poros had slept, she'd gone to spend time with Pegasus below deck. Brushing his shimmering white coat had helped her anxiety.

But now, as they approached the harbor and were about to tie on and anchor the ship, her stomach was in knots. Once again, she reached out to Jinsoo and her brother telepathically, and once again, she received no reply.

She was surprised when her father appeared to her just as she'd finished tying on.

"Dad?"

"Have you seen your brother lately?"

She wasn't sure how to answer him. He might be angry with Hermie if he knew he'd gone after the vampires. "Um . . ."

As she tried to think of what to say, she was reminded of how much Hermie resembled their father. Both had bright blue eyes, made brighter by the shock of dark hair that fell across their brow.

"Has he returned from Russia?" her father asked.

"Russia?" Hestie's heart quickened.

Poros came up beside her. "Hermie was in Russia?"

"Near its southern coastline over an STS carrier that had just exploded," her father explained. "I was there gathering the souls of vampires who had died while still chained in the ship. It wasn't pretty, the way they died."

Hestie's mouth and eyes widened. "Oh, my gods, that's terrible."

"I didn't see what happened, but maybe Hermes . . . I don't know."

Prometheus joined them from the flybridge. "I highly doubt Hermes would be responsible for the deaths of vampires."

"I hope you're right," her father said. "This was a massacre. I tried to reach out to Hermie after I saw him hovering over the wreckage, but he never answered. I'm worried."

"I am, too," Prometheus said. "I'll be sure to contact you as soon as he returns."

"We have to go look for him," Hestie insisted.

"I'm already searching," her father assured her. "You have work to do here."

Her father gave her a hug and disappeared.

Thanatos hadn't been gone long when Hermie and Jinsoo appeared on the main deck, looking as if nothing out of the ordinary had happened.

"Where were you?" Hestie cried as she threw her arms around her brother.

"We looked everywhere for them," Jinsoo said. "We couldn't find them."

"We searched the world over," Hermie added. "We're exhausted."

"What about the STS wreckage near Russia?" the captain asked. "Did you see what happened?"

Hermie frowned and glanced at Jinsoo before asking, "What STS wreckage?"

"We don't know what you're talking about," Jinsoo added.

"But Dad said . . ." Hestie began but was cut short by a sharp look from the captain.

"Dad said what?" Hermie asked.

"He's been trying to reach you," Prometheus explained. "Why haven't you answered him? He said he's been trying to reach you for hours."

"I guess I was too focused on our search," Hermie said.

Hestie frowned. Why was her brother lying to them?

CHAPTER SIX

The Furies

Gertie leaned over Hermes where he sat at the long dining room table in the galley of the *Black Widow*. He and most of the vampires were inspecting the adamantine chain and cuffs that they'd recovered from the STS wreckage. She had just joined them after getting a few hours' sleep below deck. Hector was still sleeping in his own cabin. They hadn't spoken since she broke up with him the day before. She wasn't sure why he hadn't left yet, and she was dreading seeing him. It would be so much easier to get over him if he were gone.

"Here's another lightning bolt," Raimo pointed out, holding up the second of two cuffs that he'd found embossed with the symbol.

Hermes reached out and accepted it from Raimo, turning it over in his hands. "This was the set used to chain Prometheus to a rock centuries ago. They originally belonged to Zeus."

"Could someone else have taken them, stolen them, or been given them?" Bach wondered.

"Yes, of course," Hermes said. "But the last time I saw these, Athena had them. I believe she intended to give them to Poros."

"There's no way Poros is behind this," Gertie insisted.

The vampires agreed, speaking over one another.

"No way."

"He would never."

"Poros is a good guy."

"What about Athena?" Gertie speculated. "Could she have taken back the cuffs without Poros's knowledge?"

Del crossed her arms. "She blames vampires for destroying her city. I believe she could be capable of something like this."

"I'm not saying it was Athena," Gertie said. "I'm just thinking out loud."

"Prometheus is taking his crew to question James Morgan," Penny said suddenly. "Hermie says they've just docked in Piraeus."

"No worries," Hermes said, as he continued to study the adamantine. "I already talked to my people. Morgan won't give up any names—that is, if he doesn't want to be known as a rat."

Gertie sucked in her lips. Had Hermes really threatened her stepfather, who was awaiting trial in prison without bail?

"That seems drastic, my lord," Alastair commented. "Was it really necessary?"

"As long as he's quiet, there's no harm done," Mahdi pointed out.

"We have to slow them down every way we can," Hermes said. "Morgan is penitent and wants to help, but he doesn't know what's really going on."

"Nor do we," Del pointed out.

"But we know what our mission is," Hermes declared, climbing to his feet. "I'll store this in a secret place," he said of the adamantine.

Del nodded. "It's interesting to note that the key to that cage unlocks these cuffs as well."

Gertie clicked her tongue. That was interesting, indeed.

"You hold onto it," Hermes said to Del of the key. "We need to get to work. There's another STS vessel scheduled to leave the Russian port this morning. Better gear up."

"The lookout will sweep for prisoners this time," Alastair interjected.

"And nukes," Penny added. "The last thing we want to do is blow up a carrier hiding Russian warheads."

"I'm telling you, the adamantine was warded against me," Hermes said. "I conducted a sweep. I could not see those prisoners."

This was the first Gertie had heard of this. "It was warded specifically so you couldn't see them?"

"That's what I've been saying," Hermes growled.

Gertie's mouth fell open as the pistons fired in her brain. "Then you were clearly the target. Whoever did this was sending you a message."

Hermes narrowed his eyes. "That adamantine may have been warded against all Olympians—not just me."

"The enemy of the vampires wanted you to blow up that carrier," Gertie asserted. "And they wanted you to be responsible for killing those vampires."

Hermes scoffed. "I'm glad you're thinking outside of the box, but your theory has no legs."

Gertie silently disagreed. She couldn't explain how, but she felt strongly about this hunch. One or more gods were less concerned with STS than with ridding the world of vampires, especially Hermes's crew.

As they headed toward the spiral stairs leading to their cabins, Gertie caught up with Del and asked her, "Why did Hermie reach out to Penny and not you? Is everything okay between you?"

Del averted her eyes. "Not really. He is upset that I would not free him while you and the others were gone. He thought he could convince his family to be our allies without lying to them. But I did not wish to take the risk. He thinks I do not trust him."

"Is he right?" Gertie asked.

"I trust him. I do not trust his family."

"But *he* trusts his family," Gertie pointed out. "Which means you don't trust his judgment."

Del stopped and turned abruptly, squaring herself to Gertie. "Are you saying I should have disobeyed Lord Hermes?"

"No. Not at all. I'm just explaining why Hermie is upset."

Del took a deep breath as they continued down the stairs. "I see."

Hermie was appalled as he followed Prometheus, Poros, Hestie, and Jinsoo into the secure prison twenty minutes outside of Athens. He had expected the facility to resemble those portrayed in the movies—sanitary, clean, and orderly with guards in clean uniforms and two prisoners in each cell. He had also expected it to smell of disinfectant, like a hospital. He was wrong on all counts.

An officer—a young, skinny man with dark hair and pale skin—led him and his group down a long corridor that was open to the second floor. There were cells on both levels—tiny cells with two sets of bunks and four prisoners in each. Some had a fifth prisoner who slept on a mattress on the floor. Hermie covered his mouth at the display of inhumane treatment. Animals in a zoo had more room than these prisoners.

Hermie saw two cells with women and over fifty with men. Everyone looked sick. The sound of coughing and sneezing was constant. The prisoners did not jeer at him, as he'd seen them do to visitors in the movies. They glanced at him with expressions of hopelessness, indifference, and resignation. Even when he pinched his nose because he could no longer tolerate the smell of urine, feces, and vomit, no one scoffed or berated him. They couldn't care less that he was there.

They reminded him of the animals his mother used to care for in the shelter—the ones who had been there for a long time. Hermie sensed that these prisoners felt discarded and forgotten, and by the look of things, they were.

The skinny officer led Hermie and his group into a room filled with old furniture: couches, upholstered chairs, bean bags. The furniture was soft and torn and smelled of body odor. A man sat on one of the sofas with another officer standing over him. The officer was broad-shouldered and muscular and wore a menacing expression on his face. The man sitting on the sofa looked posh, even in his gray prison garments. He was James Morgan, and he was Gertie's father.

Poros took the lead. "Hello, Mr. Morgan. We're friends of Gertie's. I'm Poros, and this is Captain, Hestie, Jinsoo, and Hermie. Gertie has been sailing with us for a couple of months and helped us to save a lot of lives."

"I know who you are," James said.

"Then you know we're here to help." Hestie smiled.

James narrowed his eyes. "I was warned to keep my mouth shut."

"Who told you that?" Jinsoo glanced nervously at Hermie. "We just want to stop the bad guys."

"Apparently, you are the bad guys," James retorted.

Prometheus put his hands on his hips. "I'm afraid you've been misinformed. The gods merely disagree over how to handle STS. Hermes wants to destroy the entire fleet."

"We just want to find and arrest the corrupt leaders," Hermie added. "How can that make us the bad guys?"

"One of us has been misinformed," James said with a tilt of his head. "But I doubt it was me. Anyway, I couldn't talk if I wanted to. If I do, I'm dead."

Hermie didn't know why he was surprised to hear that the messenger god had contacts inside these prison walls. But what did surprise him was the threat of life.

"This was a waste of time," Hermie grumbled to Captain. "Let's go."

"Thank you, anyway, Mr. Morgan," Poros said. "I hope you get out of here soon."

"You and me both, kid."

As they turned toward the door, Hades appeared, blocking their exit. He was wearing his black leather jacket and sleek leather trousers with black boots. Even in his mortal form, he looked intimidating.

"Not so fast," the lord of the Underworld ordered. "We need those names."

Both the officers—the one standing behind James Morgan and the one who had ushered Hermie and his group inside—fell to their knees.

Whether they did so of their own volition out of fear, or whether they were brought to their knees by Hades, Hermie didn't know.

"Mr. Morgan will be killed if he helps us," Hestie pointed out.

"This man deserves death, and worse," Hades said. "You saw what he was willing to do—to allow innocent Syrians to be sold into slavery while their political leaders gained nuclear weapons. He was willing to allow hundreds—thousands—to suffer and die."

"To save Gertie," Poros pointed out.

"Her life isn't more valuable than theirs," Hades argued.

"It is to me," James said meekly. "She and her mother are all I have."

"Grandfather, Poseidon is guilty of worse," Hermie pointed out. "Think of all he did to save his daughter. How is that any different? But he's as free as a bird."

The lord of the Underworld turned red, and his eyes grew so wide, that Hermie thought they would pop from his skull. "Careful, Hermie. Don't forget who I am. And don't presume that the gods are held by the same laws as men."

Hermie lowered his head and muttered, "It's not fair."

"Life isn't fair, but death is," Hestie recollected, repeating the mantra their parents had taught them from the time of their birth. They were Hades's favorite words.

"Exactly," their grandfather said. "Now move out of the way so my daughters can do their work."

Hermie flinched when his three aunts—the Furies—appeared in the room with their hair already turned to snakes and their eyes dripping with blood.

Hestie stepped aside to allow room for Meg, Tizzie, and Alecto. They looked fierce and terrifying with their hissing snake hair and bloody eyes. Their familiars were with them. Meg's falcon sat perched on her shoulder. Tizzie's white wolf stood by her side. And Alecto's snake was wrapped around her neck and hissing as ferociously as those on her head.

Meg carried a whip, which she used to strike the floor. Hestie was so startled by how loud a sound it made that she jumped about a foot into the air. Tizzy carried a sharp dagger with a blade that glistened in the light. And Alecto had a metal mace—or bludgeon—with spikes on the end of it.

Hestie shuddered as the Furies surrounded James, who was now trembling with eyes filled with tears.

"They'll kill me if I talk," James stuttered.

"That's not our problem," Meg hissed.

Tizzie stood behind James and touched her blade to his neck. "You're here because of choices you made. Now, you suffer the consequences."

Hestie had never seen her aunts in action—not like this. She held her breath and turned to Poros, whose eyes were as wide as her own.

This isn't right, she said to him.

I know.

How do we stop them? As much as Hestie loved her family, she didn't want to cross them.

Alecto bent over James with her snake hissing only inches from his face. "My baby bites, but my sister's falcon plucks out eyeballs and devours them. Believe me when I say you'd rather deal with me."

"I don't want to die," James said breathlessly as sweat beaded on his forehead. "Please don't make me give up names."

We need to do something, Hestie's brother said to her telepathically.

She glanced his way. *What can we do?*

Prometheus took off his hat, combed his fingers through his dark curly hair, and asked, "Is this really necessary?"

"Everything I do is necessary," Hades replied from where he stood near the exit. Then, to James, he said, "These people threatened your family. Don't you want justice?"

"Can you promise me your protection in here?" James asked through trembling lips.

Hestie flinched when her grandfather growled, "Do not make demands of me!"

"Let's start with one name," Alecto prodded, still leaning over James. "One little name. Come on, James. You can do it."

Hestie's face turned white when she noticed that Gertie's father had wet himself.

"If I name one, I may as well name them all," James, shivering, said. "I'll be dead, either way."

"That's the spirit," Tizzie taunted with the blade still held at his throat.

"Lord Hades," Jinsoo said in a small voice. "Please, stop this."

"Stay out of it," Hades scolded sharply.

Hestie exchanged looks with the other young gods. This felt so wrong. There had to be something they could do to save Gertie's father.

James closed his eyes and seemed to be in prayer. Hestie wondered which god or gods he was praying to. Alecto stepped back, and Meg took her place. The falcon screeched a sharp *kak!*

"Open your eyes, James, darling," Meg said sweetly.

Hestie shuddered again. She closed her eyes, unable to watch.

She flinched again and opened her eyes when Poros, beside her, shouted, "Stop this insanity!"

As he shouted, a bright orb of light encircled his body and emanated from him, filling the room. Alarmed, the Furies turned to their father for guidance.

Hades didn't appear angry. Although the expression he wore was hard to read, Hestie thought he seemed in awe, or bewildered, or both.

"Poros, son of Zeus," the lord of the Underworld began. "Why do you oppose this, when you know that it would help end the suffering and death of hundreds, if not thousands, of innocent lives?"

Hestie studied Poros, anxious for him, but also proud of him, as he responded, "Because every life has value, Lord Hades. Even his. It's not his fault that he's caught in the middle of a conflict between gods. If it weren't for Phorcys, Poseidon, and my sister, he wouldn't be in this mess. The gods put him here, and it's wrong to punish him for it."

Hades chuckled, which surprised Hestie, before saying, "Dear boy, you have a lot to learn about the way the world works, but, given your display of power, I'll respect your point of view for now. Daughters, let us leave this place."

Without another word, the four Underworld gods vanished, leaving Hestie and the others with their jaws hanging open.

CHAPTER SEVEN

Orders

As Lord Hermes and the vampires prepared for that morning's mission, Gertie broached the subject of food. She was starving and thought she would faint if she didn't get something in her stomach soon.

Hermes left the *Black Widow* and returned moments later with a platter of scrambled eggs, sausage, biscuits, and grapes in one hand and a jug of orange juice in the other. Gertie thanked him and grabbed a cup and plate from the cupboard before quickly serving herself.

"We'll need to feed soon, too," Alastair said to the messenger god as Gertie sat down at the dining table. "Tonight, if possible."

Hermes was handing out more smoke bombs. "Of course."

Before Gertie had finished her breakfast, Hector appeared, sleepy-eyed and hot as ever. She avoided eye contact with him as she said, "There's food, if you're hungry."

He grabbed another plate and cup from the cupboard and sat beside her at the table, where he helped himself from the platter. After he'd eaten some of the steaming fresh eggs, he said, "I'm not giving up on us, Gertie."

Heat rushed to her cheeks as she looked up at him. She was surprised by how surprised she felt. Why wouldn't he fight to stay with her?

As he poured himself a cup of juice, he revealed, "I thought about it all night. I'd rather be with you under any circumstances than be without you."

Her throat went dry, almost like there was something caught there. She took a drink of her juice and coughed when some went down her windpipe.

"You okay?" he asked.

She nodded as she coughed again. "Sorry. Wrong pipe."

"I mean it, Gertie," he said. "If you want to be a vampire, I'll become a vampire. If you want to be a god, I'll make the gods accept me as one, too. I'll live whatever kind of life necessary to be with you."

Gertie noticed the vampires were stealing glances at Hector as he professed his love for her. They wore smiles on their faces. Mahdi was even giggling like a little girl.

She knew, however silly they were being, that they were happy for her. She tried hard to keep from crying, but the tears did their own thing and slipped down her cheeks, anyway.

Leaning across the table, she looked him straight in the eyes—a hard, strong, aggressive look. "If you ever say you want to leave me again, that will be it, you understand?"

A smile crept across his face just before he reached over to kiss her. "I understand."

"Are you mortals about ready?" Hermes asked from the other side of the salon.

"We're ready," Hector said. "Let's do this."

Once they were in the air flying over the sparkling Mediterranean Sea—the vampires wearing their helmets and leather gear to protect them from the bright sunlight—Hector, who was held in the air by Bach, said to Gertie, who was held by Sophia, "I thought about something else last night. I think you're right about the vampires. Someone is out to get Hermes's crew. That had to be a message."

"I feel it in my bones, Hector," she declared. "I can't shake the feeling. We must figure out who's behind it."

"I'll do whatever it takes to protect the vampires," he said. "I owe it to Jeno."

More tears sprang to her eyes. She often forgot how close Hector and Jeno had become during the vampire wars. Jeno had been as a good a friend to Hector as Lajos—or anyone, for that matter. She supposed Hector missed Jeno almost as much as she did.

"Thank you," she said. "That means a lot."

After the harrowing experience with his aunts, Hermie was grateful when Captain offered to stop in Piraeus at a burger joint for lunch. Simply Burgers was crowded with locals and sailors, but Hermie didn't mind waiting for a table. A burger was exactly what he needed right now, the best comfort food he could imagine. He still hadn't gotten over the fact that Del hadn't trusted him. How can someone love you and not trust you? And how could someone who didn't trust him be his person? These thoughts had left him feeling gutted and miserable and unsure of himself.

In fact, Hermie had been so hurt that Del hadn't trusted him, that the first chance he had, he had torn up her note and thrown it overboard. Now, as he stood there waiting with the others, he stuck his hand into his trouser pocket where the letter had been and wished it was still there.

Hestie inched closer to him and searched his face. Did she know what was going through his mind?

"Are you okay?" she asked him.

"Yeah. Why?"

"You don't look it."

"I don't know what you mean."

"Why did you lie earlier, when we asked about that STS ship?"

Hermie glanced nervously at Jinsoo. "I mean, we saw a burning ship, but once we realized it wasn't the *Black Widow*, we moved on. How could we know it was an STS ship?"

"Yeah," Jinsoo said. "How could we know?"

Hestie narrowed her eyes. "So, you didn't see the victims trapped inside—the ones Dad says were vampires?"

"No. Absolutely not."

Jinsoo shook his head fervently. "No way."

Prometheus arched a brow.

Hermie was relieved when their conversation was cut short by a hostess flagging them down and beckoning them to a clean table. But his relief was short-lived, for no sooner had they sat down than they were joined by Poseidon.

Hermie kept his eyes on his menu, hoping the god of the sea wasn't there to interrogate him as his sister had.

"I saw what happened at the prison," Poseidon said. Turning to Poros he added, "I can't say I'm not disappointed."

Poros said nothing but seemed unapologetic.

"My brother has gone soft," Poseidon continued. "But no worries. You lot can find the names of the bad apples yourselves."

"What do you have in mind?" Prometheus asked.

A waitress came for their order. Poseidon frowned and gave the girl a threatening glare.

"I'll come back in a few minutes," she offered before scurrying away.

When they were alone again, Poseidon continued, "STS has an office building right here in Piraeus. There's a man I trust—a professor of Maritime Studies at the university. He's arranged for two college students to shadow employees at the STS managerial office."

"Two college students?" Jinsoo asked as he scratched his head.

"I'll let your captain decide which two of you will be those students," Poseidon determined. "Be ready to report to the office at eight o'clock in the morning. Here's the address."

Poseidon gave Prometheus a piece of paper.

"What do you expect to gain from this?" the captain asked.

"The students will be taught every facet of the company, gaining access to the offices," Poseidon said. "They'll be in the perfect position to eavesdrop and snoop. I want a list of suspects by the end of the week. Names *and* locations would be even better."

"What if we aren't able to get what you want?" Hestie asked.

"That's not an option." The god of the sea stood up and left the restaurant.

"Jinsoo and I will do it," Hermie offered, figuring it was the only way he could keep his oath to Hermes. He'd rather snoop around for clues as an undercover agent than be on the ship under the scrutiny of the captain.

"Jinsoo doesn't look old enough to be in college," Hestie objected. "Poros and I should do it."

"I think so, too, Hermie," Jinsoo said. "I'm better off on the ship than in an office building."

"What do you think, Poros?" Prometheus asked.

"Hermie and I should go," Poros prompted. "No offense, Hestie, but Hermie can use his skills to hack into the computer system and see if there's anything to be found in their files."

"That's actually an excellent idea," Hermie agreed.

"Why shouldn't *I* go with Hermie?" Hestie wondered.

"Because I know more about maritime studies than you," Poros said.

The captain rapped on the table with a fist. "Then it's settled. Now let's order and eat, so we can get back to the ship."

Once they were back on the *Marcella II*, Hestie sat beside Poros on his bed, both with their backs leaning against the headboard. She couldn't shake the feeling that Hermie was hiding something from them, and she wasn't sure if she should talk more about it with Poros.

"You aren't upset with me for saying Hermie should go with me, are you?" Poros asked.

"No, of course not. Disappointed maybe, but not upset."

"Okay. Good. You just seem quiet."

"No, it makes perfect sense that Hermie should go, since he's the computer whiz."

"Then, is there something else bothering you?"

Hestie shrugged. "It's just that, well, Hermie isn't a very good liar—not to me anyway. And I'm pretty sure he's lying to me."

"About the burning STS ship with the vampires?"

"Yes."

"Don't you think he's got his reasons?"

Hestie gawked. "You think there could be a good reason to lie to me?"

Poros brushed her red hair from her face. "Maybe. Don't you think it's possible that he found Hermes and the vampires and is protecting them?"

"He knows he can trust me. He wouldn't lie to me. . . unless," the wheels in her head began to spin. "Unless he was forced to."

"He may have had no choice but to swear an oath," Poros pointed out. "It was the only way they'd let him go."

"But Del is in love with him. She wouldn't treat him that way."

"Maybe she had no choice. You know Hermie better than I do, and I trust him completely. Whatever's going on, he's trying to do the right thing."

She smiled at Poros and squeezed his hand. "Sometimes I think you're too good for me."

"Only sometimes?" he asked with a mischievous grin.

Her mouth fell open as she grabbed a pillow and hit him with it.

Hermie and Jinsoo stood on either side of Pegasus brushing his shimmering white fur. As much as Pegasus enjoyed it, the process of brushing was soothing to Hermie, and he wondered if he did it more for himself than for the winged horse.

Chidori was perched on Jinsoo's shoulder occasionally accepting bird seed Jinsoo grabbed from his pocket.

"You stay here and cover for me," Hermie suggested. "They expect a report tonight."

"You stay, and I'll go," Jinsoo countered. "I want to see Alastair. I miss him so much, Hermie. Don't you miss Del?"

"Of course, I do." He didn't add how conflicted he felt.

"You take care of Chidori while I'm gone," Jinsoo said.

"She's *my* bird," Hermie said irritably.

Jinsoo lifted his brows. "Um, Hermie, I think she's her own person. She doesn't *belong* to anyone."

Hermie sighed. "I'm sorry. You're right. I'm sorry, Chidori. Sometimes I get jealous of how close you two are. She used to be closer to me."

Chidori flew to Hermie's finger and kissed his lips. Then she tweeted that she was sorry, but she thought Jinsoo needed her more.

"That was true," Jinsoo said. "Especially after Mina died. But now I have Alastair, too. Still, I couldn't bear to lose Chidori, Hermie. I guess I'm really selfish."

"No, you're right. She's her own person. She can choose who to hang out with."

"Let me go and give the report, Hermie, okay? I have to see Alastair, or I just might die."

"Quit being so melodramatic."

"I don't even know what that means."

"Never mind. Go ahead. But be careful. Remember, you suck at god-travel."

"Don't remind me. I'll be right back. See you, Pegasus. See you, Chidori. See you, Hermie."

"I'll cover for you," Hermie promised.

Jinsoo headed for the stable door and stopped. "Maybe you should go, Hermie. I'm so new at this. What if I mess up?"

"You can do it."

"You go and give Alastair a message for me. Tell him I'm burning to see him."

Hermie laughed. "Okay. If that's what you want."

"I do, Hermie. Go. And hurry. Come here, Chidori."

Chidori kissed Hermie once more before returning to Jinsoo's shoulder.

"Take me with you," Pegasus, who rarely spoke, proposed to Hermie. "I'm bored."

"That can be my cover story," Hermie said. To Jinsoo, he added, "If the captain askes, tell him I took Pegasus out for a ride, so he could stretch his wings."

"Okay, Hermie," Jinsoo said. "Good idea."

Hermie led Pegasus from the stable to the upper deck. Once mounted, together they flew into the evening sky where Helios was just beginning to set in the west. The spectacular colors in the sea below mirrored those in the clouds—streaks of pinks and purples. Hermie's view was breathtaking as he and Pegusus flew away from the sun toward the island of Cyprus, where the *Black Widow* was anchored.

The salon and galley stretched the greater length of the motorized superyacht, so there wasn't much of a deck, and there were no sails. The deck was located toward the stern of the ship and was about five feet wide and ten feet long. As Pegasus landed, Hermie was surprised to find the French doors to the salon wide open to the indoor pool, where the vampires and Gertie and Hector were playing water volleyball. Hermes was nowhere in sight.

"Score!" Bach called after Mahdi spiked the ball at lightning speed.

Hector had gone for a block, and although he had gotten a piece of the ball, it hadn't been enough.

"You were almost stuffed by a mortal," Hector teased Mahdi.

"*Almost* being the operative word," Mahdi said with a grin.

That's when Hermie noticed Del. She looked supremely beautiful in a bikini made with not much more fabric than those Mina used to wear. He supposed she had purchased it in Paris, for he'd never seen her wear it before. He suspected his sister may have encouraged Del to buy it.

"Close your mouth, lover-boy," Penny said to Hermie.

He immediately felt blood heat his cheeks. Del's face paled with embarrassment.

"Where's Jinsoo?" Alastair asked as he climbed from the pool to approach Hermie.

"He wanted to come," Hermie said. "But one of us had to cover for the other. He told me to tell you he's burning for you, or something like that."

Alastair laughed. "It's a private joke."

"Well, let's keep it that way," Hermie said. "Where's Lord Hermes?"

"Gone." Del climbed from the pool and grabbed a towel. "He won't be back until morning. Why?"

"I've come with my report." Hermie shifted his weight nervously from one foot to the other. Perhaps it had been a mistake to come, but he'd been desperate to see her.

CHAPTER EIGHT

Under Attack

As curious as Gertie was to know how her father's interrogation had gone, she was dreading to hear the details. She was relieved when Hermie's report was delayed by the vampires' excitement over seeing Pegasus.

"Come inside, Pegasus!" Alastair called out. "This salon is big enough for you, my friend!"

Seeing the beautiful white, winged horse again affected everyone, including Gertie. There was something about his majestic beauty coupled with his sweet and lovable disposition that made his presence a source of calm in any room. Climbing from the pool, Gertie grabbed a towel and joined the others near the French doors to welcome Pegasus.

The vampires stroked the horse's flanks, back, and muzzle, and he, in turn, seemed to relish it.

"The sun has set," Bach pointed out. Then turning to Hermie, he asked, "Can we take turns riding on his back?"

"Don't you want to hear my report?" Hermie asked.

"It can wait," Mahdi said. "Can't it?"

Hermie shrugged. "I should probably get back soon, or Captain will wonder what I'm up to."

"Can't Pegasus stay with us?" Raimo asked. "There's a lot more room here than on the *Marcella II.*"

Hermie crossed his arms over his chest. "What will Captain think if I return without him?"

Pegasus whinnied and then said, "You could tell him I went home to Mount Olympus."

Hermie gawked. "Are you saying you want to stay?"

"Do you blame him?" Hector asked. "I bet he doesn't get this much attention on Prometheus's ship."

"And now that they have motorcycle gear," Gertie began, "the vampires are no longer restricted to flying at night. Pegasus will never be bored with us."

"Fine," Hermie said. "I'll tell you what I know, and then you can ride Pegasus all you want."

Gertie sensed that Hermie wasn't happy about leaving his friend behind.

"James Morgan refused to talk," Hermie shared. "So, Poseidon is moving on to Plan B. He's got a connection with a professor at the university in Piraeus who set up a week of shadowing for me and Poros at the STS office building there. Poros and I start tomorrow morning. We'll pretend to be college students."

"What are your orders?" Del wanted to know.

"To eavesdrop and snoop around, to find names of key ringleaders. I'm supposed to hack into the computer systems. I'll pretend I can't find anything and stall them for as long as I can. Let Hermes know."

Hermie turned to go. Del followed him to the deck outside. Gertie tried not to listen, but her curiosity got the best of her.

"I'm sorry, Hermie," Del apologized.

Hermie sighed. "I know you were only doing what you thought was right. It just hurt, that's all."

"I wish I could go back and do it differently," Del said.

"Would you?"

"Yes, I would."

Gertie felt sorry for them as Hermie said goodbye. He should have hugged and kissed Del, but he kept his distance. He looked so forlorn when he turned and lifted into the evening sky.

Tears stung Hermie's eyes as he flew from the *Black Widow*, from Del and her supreme beauty and her sweet, sweet heart. He'd forgiven her, of course, but now he was afraid. He was afraid that if he let her get too close to him that she would crush him like a fly—not intentionally, but nevertheless, he'd be crushed. It was hard when Mina was killed, and although he hated himself for thinking it, the loss of Del could ruin him if he allowed himself to get any closer. It might already be too late.

He was also sad that Pegasus had wanted to stay. First Chidori and now Pegasus. Hermie felt like the most unlovable being on the planet.

A loud *pop* in the east drew him from his reverie. He turned around to see the *Black Widow* in flames.

Feeling frozen, bewildered, and helpless, Hermie fell from the sky and dropped into the sea below. He was numb and in a daze.

The coldness of the water brought him to his senses, but he still felt paralyzed with shock.

"Dad!" he cried like a little boy as he sank into the depths of the sea. "Help me!"

Within seconds, his father appeared in the water beside him. Unable to speak, Hermie gestured to the sky.

His father lifted him from the water, where Hermie pointed to the burning ship.

"Let's go," Thanatos said.

Together, they sped toward the fire.

When they reached the ship, Thanatos, one of only two gods to have it, used his power of disintegration to create multiples of himself.

"Stay here," he ordered Hermie.

Then twenty gods of death flew into the burning salon, from which Hermie could hear screams.

Snapping out of his stupor, he could only think of one thing. He had to save Del.

When he flew into the burning salon, he saw his father rescuing Gertie and Hector. The vampires were nowhere to be found. Might they be in their cabins below? The flames blocked his x-ray vision.

With a speed approaching that of light, Hermie flew down the spiral stairs, dodging burning timbers that fell toward him as he maneuvered through the corridor. There wasn't a being in sight. Where had everyone gone?

"Hermie, get out of there!" his father yelled. "The whole ship is about to blow!"

Hermie followed the sound of his father's voice. Just as he emerged from the ship, a loud explosion assaulted his ears, the force of which threw him into the sky. He flailed, disoriented, toward the sea.

"Dad!"

A fist reached out of the water and grabbed him by the arm, but it wasn't his father.

"Poseidon?" Hermie asked.

The god of the sea sprang from the Mediterranean while holding Hermie with one hand and an unconscious and bleeding Pegasus with the other.

"Pegasus!" Hermie cried, deeply disturbed by how listlessly the horse hung in his father's arm.

"What happened?" Poseidon asked. "Who would do this to my Pegasus?"

"Is he still breathing?" Hermie asked.

"I can't tell."

"I don't know what happened," Hermie said. "Did you see the vampires?"

"No. I heard explosions and came right away to find my son sinking to sea floor."

Hermie's father, clutching the half-conscious demigods, flew toward them. "These two didn't see what happened. Let's get to Prometheus's ship and regroup."

Hestie had fallen asleep beside Poros in his cabin when she was awakened by voices speaking in earnest above deck.

"That's my father's voice," she said, as Poros, who'd also been asleep, sat up suddenly.

"Let's go," he said.

They flew to the upper deck, near the flybridge, to find Poseidon kneeling on the floor beside a sprawling Pegasus. One of the horse's wings looked as if it had been put through a shredder. Blood and salt water soaked his fur, and his tongue hung from his mouth.

Hestie covered her mouth and muttered, "Oh, my gods."

Prometheus was offering blankets to Hector and Gertie, who sat coughing on the L-shaped sofa near the flybridge. Hestie's father stood between Hermie and Poseidon, inspecting the winged horse.

"What happened?" Poros asked as he followed Hestie onto the deck.

"We don't know," Poseidon answered.

"The *Black Widow* exploded," Hermie said. "The vampires are gone."

"Gone where?" Jinsoo asked as he rushed to join the group with Chidori flying behind him. "Are they okay?"

Hermie hugged his friend. "It was terrible, and I just froze. I might have helped them if I could have acted faster."

"This is not your fault," Hestie said to her brother.

Chidori landed on Hermie's shoulder and kissed him.

"Thank you, Chidori." Hermie wiped his eyes and said to Jinsoo, "I don't know where they went. Maybe they got away someplace safe."

Jinsoo started to cry. "Oh, my gods. I hope so. I hope so, Hermie. Oh, my gods, is Pegasus dead?"

"No," Thanatos responded. "He's just unconscious. He must have suffered a terrible shock."

"He might be paralyzed," Poseidon said. "If so, let's hope it's not permanent."

Just then, Hestie's mother, Therese, appeared.

"I came as soon as I could." She knelt beside Pegasus and stroked his muzzle. "I'll try my best to help him."

Hestie supposed that her mother, the goddess of animal companions, was their best hope for Pegasus.

"Gertie and Hector, did you see what happened?" Jinsoo asked.

The demigods shook their heads.

"I'll go so as not to affect them," Thanatos said of the mortals before he flew away.

"There was an explosion," Hector said. "Something hit me on the head and knocked me out for a few minutes."

"I couldn't see anything through all the smoke," Gertie said. "I nearly passed out."

Hestie's mother took one of her bows from her quiver and used it to pierce Pegasus's heart.

"What is she doing, Hermie?" Jinsoo cried. "Please, don't kill him!"

"I'm helping him," Therese explained. "My arrows are for animal companions."

"It's not doing anything," Jinsoo said through his tears.

"Just give it a moment," Therese replied as she stroked Pegasus again.

"Thank you," Poseidon said to her.

"Who would do this?" Prometheus asked.

"That's what I want to know," Poseidon ranted. "Was it planned? Accidental? Done by mortals? Gods?"

"Gods," Gertie said, surprising Hestie with her brazenness. "One or more gods are out to get the vampires."

Gertie told Poseidon and Prometheus what had happened with the STS ship after Hermes had destroyed it—that vampires had been found in the hull imprisoned with adamantine cuffs and chains, which had been warded to hide them from Hermes.

"Those vampires didn't make it," Gertie said.

Hestie glanced at Hermie, who bowed his head with shame. So that's what he hadn't been able to tell her.

"I don't think the two attacks are coincidental," Gertie continued. "Lord Poseidon, can you think of anyone who might want to harm Hermes's crew?"

"Athena loathes them," he said, "but she would have seen Pegasus and wouldn't have put him through this."

"Are you sure?" Hector asked. "He is immortal, after all. Maybe his pain was worth it to her."

Prometheus tugged at his beard. "She's capable of a lot of things, but not this."

"I agree," Poros said.

"Then who?" Gertie wanted to know.

"What about my father?" Hector suggested. "I saw him making chain out of adamantine in his forge."

Poseidon frowned. "Of all the gods, he's the least vindictive, I think."

"Except when it came to his mother and his first wife," Prometheus pointed out. "Remember his trick chair? And his stunt with Aphrodite and Ares?"

"That's ancient history," Therese said. "Hephaestus wouldn't do this."

"Who has it in for the vampires?" Gertie said again. "Most of the gods don't really like them."

"Except for Hades," Hector pointed out.

"He uses them," Gertie said. "I'm not sure that's the same thing. But yeah, he wouldn't want to destroy them."

"Hades is fond of them, Gertie," Therese admonished. "You don't give him enough credit."

"Well, I don't think Aphrodite would do this," Prometheus stated. "She knows about the relationships and wouldn't want to break them up."

Hestie glanced at her brother and Jinsoo and wished there was something she could say to make them feel better.

"What about Apollo and Artemis?" Poseidon proposed.

Prometheus lifted his palms. "With what motive? Neither particularly hates vampires any more than the others."

"What motive would any of them have?" Poros pointed out. "That's what we still have to discover."

"What about Ares?" Hermie suggested. "He and Artemis were the only gods that supported Hermes."

Hestie had been about to say the same thing.

"But if Ares supported Hermes, why would he attack him?" Therese asked.

"Maybe his support wasn't sincere," Hestie said.

Poros lifted a finger. "Or maybe he *does* want to destroy the STS fleets but thinks he can destroy the vampires along with them."

"But why?" Prometheus asked again.

"Answering that question should be our focus," Hermie suggested.

"Not your primary focus," Poseidon objected. "I need to get control of STS, so tomorrow morning, I expect two of you to be there to gather as much intelligence as you can."

Hestie glanced at her brother, worried over how helpless he must feel that he couldn't make finding Del his priority.

Don't worry, she said to him telepathically. *We'll do another location spell. We'll find her. We'll find all of them.*

I threw away her letter, he said as he clenched his fists at his side. *I have nothing that belonged to her.*

At that moment, Pegasus opened his eyes and pulled in his tongue and struggled to climb to his feet.

"Not yet, buddy," Poseidon soothed. "Stay down. You have more healing to do."

"Oh, Pegasus!" Jinsoo cried. "I'm so glad you're alive!"

Chidori chirped and flapped her wings with excitement.

"He was always alive," Hermie pointed out.

"I wasn't so sure," Jinsoo admitted.

"At least he's not paralyzed," Poseidon said. "That would have been a hard life for a flying horse."

"What happened?" Pegasus asked. "I feel like I had another night of binging with Dionysus."

"None of us knows," his father admitted. "But we'll find out. I can promise you that."

"Wait a minute," Prometheus said, glancing around. "Where the hell is Hermes?"

CHAPTER NINE

Undercover

After she'd finished brushing him, Gertie pulled a soft blanket over Pegasus, to keep him cozy while he continued to heal. His torn wing had already repaired itself, and the lustrous sheen had returned to his hair. Gertie suspected Pegasus was fully recovered physically, but both the trauma of the experience and the loss of the vampires was likely weighing on him.

Hector returned with a basket of apples, which perked the horse up as he ate them. Hector sat with Gertie on the soft hay beside Pegasus and held her hand as she stroked the horse.

"I wish I wouldn't have talked Hermie into allowing Pegasus to stay on the *Black Widow*." Gertie sighed.

Pegasus gave her a snort, as if to say that it hadn't been her decision to make.

"Don't blame yourself," Hector said. "We all thought it was a good idea."

"I guess."

"I still can't believe anyone would do this."

"Who would?" she wondered for what felt like the millionth time.

"Of all the theories we discussed, I'm leaning toward Ares."

Gertie shrugged. "I'm not convinced that Athena isn't behind it."

"She hasn't always been kind to you."

"No. And she's never been kind to the vampires."

"Maybe she and Hephaestus are in on it together," Hector said.

"Hmm. Could be." Gertie moved closer to Hector and leaned her head on his shoulder. "I wonder if my father might have any insight."

"I had a similar idea." Hector reached into the bottom of the basket and pulled out a bottle of wine. "He sent this to me a few minutes ago."

Gertie sat up. "Sent it? How?"

"I don't know. I was praying to him for ideas, and it just appeared beside me."

She took the bottle. "It's already been opened."

"I opened it above deck. I may have had a cup already." He grinned, and his blue eyes sparkled.

Gertie laughed and then took a sip from the bottle. "I guess my father wants me to use my power of prophecy. The problem is, there's never a guarantee that the wine will work."

"It doesn't hurt to try," Hector encouraged. "And after all we've been through today, we deserve the wine, don't you think?"

"Hells yeah." Gertie took another swallow. "I just wish I knew where the vampires were. Are they in hiding? Or are they being held captive?"

"And what about Lord Hermes?" Hector reminded her. "You don't think it's possible that he had something to do with the bombing and their disappearance, do you?"

"No way. Why would he?"

"I don't know. I'm just trying to explore every possibility to make sure there isn't something we've overlooked."

"Lord Hermes loves the vamps," Gertie insisted.

"What if he wanted to go into hiding by creating a ruse?"

"No way." Gertie drank more wine and then said again, "No way."

Hector put a finger to his lips and said telepathically, *Pegasus is asleep. Let's go up to your room.*

Gertie followed Hector from the stables and down the hall to her cabin, where they got comfy on her bed and took turns drinking from the bottle of wine.

After the buzz lightened her mood, she said, "Thanks for not giving up on us."

"It was never about that. It was about not holding you back."

She squeezed his hand. "Whatever. Let's not get into it again. Kiss me."

As he pressed his mouth against hers, she clutched his hair. If she weren't so worried about the vamps and so bent on using her powers of prophecy to find them, she would have kept on kissing him all night long.

"Mmm," she moaned before taking another sip of the wine. "That was nice."

"Come here."

He took the bottle and set it on the table next to the bed, then wrapped his arms around her, spooning her into him.

"Let's pray to Hypnos to bring us sleep and to Morpheus to bring you a prophetic dream," Hector whispered near her ear.

His warm breath sent a tingle down her spine.

"It's the Fates who send the prophetic dreams," she reminded. "I'll pray to them. But it might be easier if you sing me to sleep."

Hector laughed and pulled her even more closely against him. Then, in a gentle voice, he began to sing:

Before you close your eyes,

After you shut the door and you turn out the lights,

Remember all the days gone to waste.

Let 'em go, your shoulders know sleep's your only break.

And stay a dreamer, every day.

Dream every moment you're awake.

You may feel so far from space,

But someday the stars will remember your name.

Gertie found herself walking alone at night aimlessly along a rocky beach. She heard a scuttling sound from nearby brush. Curious, she picked through the leaves and branches until she came upon the mouth of a hidden cave. Quietly, she neared the cave but was stopped short by the horrible scene before her: Mahdi, Raimo, and Alastair lay injured and partially desiccated on the cavern floor, and beside them, Lord Hermes was imprisoned in an adamantine cage.

Gertie rushed to help but before she broached the mouth of the cave, her eyes opened, and she found herself in her bed beside Hector.

"What is it?" Hector demanded.

Gertie broke into tears. "There's no time to lose. The vampires are dying. We've got to find them, Hector!"

Hermie should have insisted on joining the search party. Instead, he and Poros were wasting valuable time in an office building, learning how to file papers. How had he allowed Captain and Poseidon to cajole him into this nonsense?

He and Poros spent the good part of the day listening to someone talking about protocol. There was a protocol for this and a protocol for that. At one point, he felt like his eyes were beginning to cross. There certainly wasn't an opportunity to hack into a computer system. And all Hermie could think about was Gertie's dream. Was Del even alive? He hoped his father would tell him the truth.

Now, as the workday came to an end, and he and Poros were walking back to the ship, Hermie prayed to his father: *Any sign of her yet?*

No.

Hermie sighed with relief. He wanted her found, but not by his father.

As they reached the docks, Poros interrupted his thoughts. "I know this is a long shot, but did you hear the older man in the office behind us say something like, 'Nike won't be happy'?"

"Nike is a common name in Greece," Hermie pointed out.

"It's a common *surname.*"

"Maybe he's using the surname, like Hermes did when he called Gertie's father Morgan instead of James."

"Maybe."

Hermie studied Poros. "You don't think they were talking about the goddess Nike, do you?"

"I don't know yet."

As soon as they had made their report to Prometheus, Hermie took off. He was determined to search every rocky coast in the world until he found Del. He searched all evening and all night, to no avail. By morning, he was back on the ship so he could shower and change clothes and return to the STS business office again.

The second day was better than the first. Hermie and Poros were left to work independently. Although they were never alone, they were better able to listen in on the many conversations going on around them.

Just before their lunch break, while they were filing reports, Hermie heard a man in the office say, "That's not what Nike asked for."

The other man replied, "Well, that's what she's getting."

So, Nike was a she. Could the men be referring to the goddess of victory?

Over lunch, when most of the employees had left the office building, Hermie found an opportunity to shut himself inside one of the offices and log onto a computer. The system was so easy to hack into that he didn't even need to call upon his powers as the god of technology. He pulled up all the available files and scanned through them, reading several documents per second when *boom*: he found something that would change everything.

Hestie, Jinsoo, Gertie, and Hector returned to the ship after searching for the vampires for twenty straight hours. Jinsoo and Gertie had wanted to keep looking, but Hestie had convinced them to return for water, food, and a short rest.

They went to the salon and sat together at the table. According to Captain, Hermie and Poros had returned from their undercover work only to leave again to continue the search for the vampires.

Hestie had just finished drinking a cold cup of apple juice when her father entered the salon as four multiples. One was carrying Raimo, another Mahdi, a third Alastair, and a fourth—the adamantine cage with Lord Hermes imprisoned inside. The vampires were still in their bathing suits, and their skin had clearly been exposed to fire or light, as they all appeared at least partially desiccated.

"Oh, no!" Jinsoo cried.

The gods and demigods jumped from their seats and gasped at the horrible sight before them. Raimo's body was fatally desiccated. Mahdi had lost a foot, and Alastair was missing an arm.

Jinsoo flew to Alastair's side. "No, no, no, no, no! Oh, Baby! Tell me you're still alive."

"Just barely," Hestie's father said.

"Is Raimo gone?" Gertie asked him.

"I'm afraid so," Thanatos replied. "That's how I was able to find them. Raimo's soul called to me."

Thanatos reintegrated into a single god and said to Hestie, "I better leave before I affect the mortals. I think the other vampires might be saved with human blood."

Thanatos flew away.

"That's what they need," Hermes agreed. "Gertie, Hector, please?"

"Of course," Gertie said.

While Jinsoo cried and prayed over Alastair, Gertie ran to the galley and took a knife from a drawer. Then she cut her hand and allowed her blood to drip into Alastair's mouth. She gave the knife to Hector so he could do the same for Mahdi.

While Gertie was helping the vampires, Hestie asked Lord Hermes if he'd seen anything. Sadly, he shook his head. Frustrated, she flew from the salon and into the night sky, calling for her father. When he returned, she asked, "What do you think happened to the others?"

"I wish I knew," he said. "I'll keep searching. Your Uncle Hip is searching, too."

"When Hermie finds out what happened to Raimo, it's going to crush him, Dad."

"We've got be strong for him—and for Jinsoo. Alastair's not out of the woods yet."

Hermie appeared in the air beside them. "Jinsoo called me back. Dad, please show me where you found them."

"It's not safe," their father argued. "Whoever imprisoned Hermes will return at some point."

"Please," Hermie said.

"I'll come, too," Poros interjected, catching up to them. "I have my lightning bolt."

"Fine," Thanatos said. "Hestie, you stay and help the others."

Hestie watched as her father, brother, and the boy she loved flew straight into danger. She prayed to Selene to watch over them and protect them, if possible.

When she returned to the salon, Alastair and Mahdi had nearly drained Gertie and Hector of blood.

"Are they going to be okay?" she asked Captain and Jinsoo of the vampires and mortals alike.

"They're awake!" Jinsoo exclaimed. "They'll be okay, right, Captain?"

"The mortals will recover," Prometheus confirmed. "And we'll know more about the vampires soon. At least they're conscious. That's a good sign."

"I can feel my arm regenerating," Alastair said breathlessly.

"And my leg," Mahdi spoke up. "It is growing back, thanks to Hector."

Jinsoo smoothed Alastair's sandy hair from his forehead. "Does it hurt to be touched?"

"It feels nice, Jinsoo. Thank you."

"I would have given you my blood, if it would have helped," Jinsoo said to him. "But it's poison to you."

"I know, mi amor."

Hestie stood over the couch, where Gertie and Hector sat slumped together. Their eyes were closed, and they were pale and panting.

"Are you guys okay?" Hestie asked them.

Gertie opened her eyes. They were red and fierce. "I'm so thirsty."

"I'll get you some water," Hestie offered.

"That's not what she wants," Hector related. "We want blood."

Hestie didn't know what to do. They were fresh out of mortals. "Can you make it without it?"

"Yes," Gertie said. "There's a bottle of my father's wine on my nightstand. Would you get it for me?"

Hestie flew down to Gertie's cabin and returned with the half-empty bottle.

"Thanks." Gertie took a swig and handed it over to Hector.

Hector took several gulps.

"Does your father know what happened to the other vampires?" Gertie asked her.

"I'm afraid not," Hestie said. "But he went with Poros and Hermie to search the area where he found the others."

Jinsoo turned to Lord Hermes. "Do you have any idea who could have done this? Did you see anything?"

The messenger god shook his head. "Whoever did this must have been wearing the helm of invisibility."

Hestie gaped. "Oh, my gods! I need to go home and talk to my grandfather immediately."

Hades appeared before she'd completed her sentence.

"So, you were in the presence of the helm?" Hades questioned Hermes. "It's been missing since our meeting on Mount Olympus. Tell me everything you know."

"There's not much to tell," Hermes said. "I heard the explosions and rushed to the ship just in time to walk straight into this trap. Whoever did this was working alone, as only one of us at a time was taken from the burning ship."

"Taken where?" Hades asked.

"A cave near the northeastern tip of Cyprus," Hermes said.

Hestie clicked her tongue. That wasn't far from where the *Black Widow* had been anchored. They'd searched for miles in that area and hadn't seen any sign of Hermes and the vampires.

"Del still has the key to this cage," Hermes added. "She tried to rescue me when we thought we'd been left alone. But whoever was under the helm either returned or had never left. There was a fight. Alastair, Mahdi, and Raimo couldn't move. They'd been injured by the explosions and the flames, to varying degrees. But Del, Penny, Sophia, and Bach had less severe damage and could still fight."

"Where are they?" Prometheus asked.

"I don't know," Hermes shrugged. "The fight escalated and moved from the cave. But if the vampires had won, I think they would have come back."

"Oh, no!" Jinsoo cried. "That doesn't sound good at all."

"No," Hades agreed.

Hestie felt sick to her stomach.

CHAPTER TEN

The Search

Not long after Alastair had fed from her, Gertie began to perk up again as the vampire virus, along with the euphoria, coursed through her. Desperate to do whatever she could to help the vampires, she announced to Captain and Hermes that she was going to search for as long as she had the power of flight and x-ray vision.

"I have to do something," she said. "I can't just sit here, waiting around. I keep thinking about poor Raimo and can't stand the thought of losing another friend."

What was left of Raimo's body still lay on the floor of the salon beneath a blanket.

"My father is showing Hermie and Poros where he found them," Hestie said.

"Lord Hermes," Gertie began, "didn't you say you were in a cave near the northeastern tip of Cyprus? Is that right?"

"Yes," the god replied from his cage.

"If the vampires escaped, they probably didn't go far, since they were injured," Hector speculated.

Gertie stood up. "We should search the surrounding area."

"You should go," Jinsoo said from where he sat near Alastair. "Right, Captain? I want to stay and take care of these two."

Prometheus turned to Gertie. "Give yourself time to come back before the virus wears off, so you don't find yourself stranded somewhere."

"It'll be dawn in less than five hours," Hermes said. "Be back before then."

"I'll go with her," Hector said as he climbed to his feet. "I'll make sure she gets back in time."

"Do you want me to go with you, too?" Hestie offered.

"What do *you* want to do?" Gertie asked.

Hestie lifted her arms and dropped them again. "My father told me to stay and help, but I don't feel like I'm much use here."

"You should stay," Hermes said to Hestie. "Whoever took us will be looking for us, and Prometheus and Jinsoo could use another hand if they have to defend the ship against an attack."

"Okay, then," Hestie said. Turning to Gertie, she added, "But let me know if you need my help, and I'll come as fast as I can."

"Be safe!" Jinsoo called as the two demigods left.

The night was cool, but the vampire virus kept Gertie warm as she and Hector lifted into the air and soared over the Mediterranean Sea from the port of Piraeus toward the island of Cyprus. As anxious as she felt, Gertie relished the feeling of flying independently. The wind in her face and hair and the view of the sparkling sea reflecting the lights below gave her a rush like nothing else. But her exhilaration was tempered by memories of her lost friends. The last time Gertie had flown independently, she'd been with Taavi, and now he was gone. Tears welled in her eyes at his memory. He'd been so happy, even when there was not much to be happy about. He had always found a way to see the bright side of things, a talent she did not possess.

And now Raimo was gone, too. How many more friends would she lose before this conflict in the Mediterranean was over? Would it ever be over?

She used her x-ray vision to search for signs of her friends. There were so many islands along the way, any of which could be hiding the vampires.

"What's that down there?" Hector said, pointing.

There were four robed figures clustered together on the beach of one of the smaller islands.

"Let's get closer, so we can see through their hoods."

"Not too close. I don't know how to make myself invisible. Plus, you always said you've got to be naked for invisibility to work."

"Right. We won't fly too close. Come on."

As they neared the robed figures, Gertie was disappointed to realize that they were a group of monks praying together.

"Let's keep going," she said.

If only the Olympians had made her a goddess, like they'd promised, then maybe she could use her powers to find and protect her friends. Even with the vampire virus, she felt helpless to save them.

An hour passed with no sign of their friends. Gertie was frustrated and anxious and wanted to scream. Then she noticed Selene, the moon goddess, flying slowly over the earth.

"I have an idea," Gertie said to Hector. "Follow me."

Gertie led the way into the clouds that were lingering over the nighttime landscape. Amid them was the glorious silver chariot and its bright and iridescent driver.

"Hello there," Selene greeted as Gertie and Hector approached. "To what do I owe the honor of a visit?"

"We need your help," Gertie said. "Some of my vampire friends are missing. They've been taken."

"I'm always happy to help the creatures of the night," the moon goddess replied, as her long, white hair flowed in the wind behind her, like her long robe, and the long, white manes of her two silver horses.

Gertie caught the goddess up on what she knew.

"I haven't seen them, but I will keep an eye out for you and let you know if I do."

"Thank you, goddess," Gertie said. "Thank you so much."

Hector took Gertie's hand and led her back toward the earth, saying, "I'm sorry, but we'll find them."

"I just hope we find them before we lose someone else."

After a few minutes, Hector confessed, "The thirst is getting to me. I wish we knew a mortal willing to give us a sip."

That gave Gertie another idea. "La Luna Rossa in Syracuse, Italy. That's where they like to feed."

"It's pretty far from here," Hector said. "Do you really think that four injured vampires on the run could travel that distance?"

"What have we got to lose? We haven't found anything—not a sign of them—for miles. Besides, maybe we can get a drink while we're there. We need to replenish our blood in case the others need to feed from us again."

"Lead the way," Hector gestured.

Gertie kissed his cheek, and together they headed for La Luna Rossa.

With Poros beside him, Hermie followed his father to the furthest end of Cyprus, where the land became rocky and narrow and wild. There was little in the way of development on this northeastern tip. Even the trees and shrubs were sparse. But hidden in a small group of shrubs was the mouth to the cave where Hermes and the vampires had been found by Hermie's father. Hermie, along with Poros, followed Thanatos into the cave, anxious for a sign—any sign—that would point him toward Del and the others.

Although the cavern was dark, Hermie's godly vision made every-thing perfectly clear. The chamber wasn't very deep, so it didn't take long to discover that it was empty of life. . . that is, until Hermie thought he heard a whistle.

"What was that?" he whispered.

"I heard it, too," Poros murmured. "A whistle."

The three gods stood quietly and as still as statues, hoping to hear the sound again, but after five minutes, Hermie's father said it must have been the wind.

"Let's search the surrounding coastline," Thanatos suggested.

The longer they searched without finding anything, the more Hermie's belly began to ache. He'd never felt so desperate. He'd cared for Mina and had deeply mourned her loss. He probably even loved her. But he ached for Del in a way that he'd never experienced before. He feared her loss would mean the end of his happiness, and, as his parents had always said, eternity was a long time.

Just thinking about his own happiness made him feel like the most selfish person alive. His own happiness could not be his priority. It could not be what motivated him. He didn't want to be that kind of person. And yet, his heart was aching. It literally pained him. He felt pathetic.

Where are you, Del? he thought, hoping to reach her mind, like he'd been doing ever since she'd gone missing. *Please hear me. Please answer me. I need to find you.*

Hermie?

Del's voice was weak but clear in Hermie's mind. He froze mid-air, his father and Poros having to stop and circle back to him.

"What's wrong?" his father asked.

"I just heard Del's voice in my head." Telepathically he said, *Del, where are you? Tell me where you are, and I'll come and help you.*

He strained his mind, reaching for any thread or fiber of sound that might bring her voice back to him, but there was nothing but the sound of mortal prayers—prayers he heard constantly, like the muttering in a crowded room. He'd become skilled at blocking the complainers whose batteries had died, or whose computers had crashed, or whose phones had merely stopped working, so he could focus on those who really needed him. At this moment, the person he loved was in a life-or-death situation, and she took priority over everyone else.

Del? he said again.

But there was nothing.

"Can you hear her?" his father asked.

Hermie wiped tears from his eyes and shook his head. "Let's keep searching."

After another hour had passed, Hermie heard another voice in his head, but this time, it belonged to Gertie.

I'm at La Luna Rossa in Syracuse. One of Del's regulars, Lorenzo, left on a boat two hours ago. He told the bartender that Del was drawing him to her.

Did the bartender say where Lorenzo was headed?

No. I don't think even Lorenzo knew. But if you can find his boat and follow him, he might lead you to Del and the others. Hector and I are searching now.

Thank you, Gertie!

Hermie told his father and Poros the new plan.

Hestie sat with Jinsoo in his room, where Alastair and Mahdi lay in the two twin beds. Captain had helped move them below deck because the salon would soon become filled with sunlight. He also had taped cardboard over the portal in Jinsoo's cabin to keep out even the indirect light, just to be safe. Once finished, Captain returned above deck to keep watch and to keep Hermes company.

Alastair and Mahdi had healed and were looking better but were still weak and needed more blood. Hestie was anxious for them, and she was anxious for Gertie and Hector who should have returned by now to beat the dawn.

She was also anxious for her brother—not so much for his safety, because he was with Poros and her father, but for his heart. She could almost feel it aching deep inside her own chest.

She heard voices above deck and flew from the room to see what was happening. Poros and Hermie were there in the salon with Gertie and Hector, who were still infected with the vampire virus. All four wore looks of despair and frustration.

"What happened?" she asked.

"We had a lead," Hector said, "but it didn't pan out."

"What lead?" Hestie wanted to know.

"Lorenzo," Poros explained. "One of Del's regular food sources. He'd felt Del calling to him."

"He'd gone out in his boat," Gertie continued. "We searched everywhere for him, hoping he'd lead us to Del and the others."

"Did you find him?" Captain asked.

Hermie nodded. "We found him roaming the Mediterranean in his little, tiny boat, nearly capsized. He'd lost his connection. He couldn't feel Del calling to him anymore, so we helped him home."

Hestie covered her mouth as she processed the sad news. Then she threw her arms around her brother. "We'll find them. You had a lead, and it didn't work, but there will be another."

"I hope so," Gertie said.

"Me, too," Hermie agreed.

They were interrupted by the arrival of Poseidon.

"I saw what happened," he said to the demigods and Hermie and Poros. "I was rooting for you, and I'm sorry it wasn't successful." Then he turned to Hermie and Poros. "But I hope you two are still planning to show up at the STS business office in the morning. We need leads on that front, too."

"As a matter of fact," Hermie shared. "I have everything you need right here."

He pulled a jump drive from his trouser pocket.

"What is that?" Poseidon asked.

"It's a jump drive," Lord Hermes replied from his cage. "It stores digital information."

"And?" Poseidon prompted Hermie.

"STS is laundering money," Hermie revealed. "I've got the financials to prove it. That drive also contains documents that point to three major ringleaders—one in Greece named Tobias Constantine, one in Russia named Matvei Popov, and one in Syria named Abbas Hassan."

"Excellent work," Poseidon said as he took the drive from Hermie.

"Thanks," Hermie said. "Now we can take down the company without destroying the rest of its fleet."

"Like I said," Poseidon said irritably, "I don't want to take down STS. I want to control it."

"Use their fleet and create your own company," Hermie insisted. "Install your own people, hand-picked by you."

"That's an excellent idea," Lord Hermes said.

"I don't have time to start a company," Poseidon complained. "And I wouldn't know the first thing about it."

"I can help you with that," Hermes voiced from his cage. "God of commerce, remember?"

Poseidon turned to Hermes. "Do you really think you can pull it off? How will you take control of the assets? Won't the Greek government freeze or confiscate them? I imagine Interpol will get involved."

"If I ever get out of this cage," Hermes began, "you can leave the details to me."

"We need to find the vampires," Hermie said. "We can sort that out later."

Gertie put her hands on her hips. "These things are connected. I feel it in my bones. The person that trapped those vampires in the adamantine cuffs on the STS ship is the same as the one who blew up the *Black Widow*. We need to find that person."

"We have more information in that regard," Poros revealed. "While we were working undercover, Hermie and I heard two references to Nike."

"The goddess?" Prometheus clarified with his brows lifted.

"We don't know," Poros admitted, "but it's worth looking into."

Hestie folded her arms across her chest and let that new information sink in. Nike was the goddess of victory. Why would she want to involve herself with STS? More importantly, what could she possibly have against the vampires?

"I'll look into it," Poseidon said.

The god was about to dive into the sea when Hermie cried, "Wait!"

Poseidon turned. "You have more information?"

Hermie pointed to the jump drive. "You can't get that wet. It will destroy our evidence."

Poseidon frowned. "I'll deliver it to Athena to keep it safe. Thanks again, all of you, for your hard work on this."

The sea god vanished.

Hestie smiled at her brother and said, "Nice work."

CHAPTER ELEVEN

Another Blast

When Gertie awakened alone in her cabin, she was instantly aware that the vampire virus was no longer coursing through her veins. Her head hurt, her body ached, and she was thirsty—for water. After drinking an entire bottle of water, she took a quick shower and dressed in clean clothes that Hestie had loaned her before going down the hall to Jinsoo's room, where Alastair and Mahdi were still recovering.

Alastair lay with Jinsoo on his bed. Both were awake and talking. Chidori was perched on Jinsoo's finger looking a little jealous. Mahdi was sleeping, or pretending to sleep, on the bed that had once belonged to Mina.

"It's okay," Jinsoo was saying. "I would have fallen for you anyway."

"Am I interrupting anything?" Gertie asked.

"Come in," Jinsoo said. "Alastair was just confessing that he mesmerized me the first time I kissed him."

"That was meant to be private," Alastair said to Jinsoo.

"Oops," Jinsoo said with a bashful smile. "Gertie won't tell anyone."

"Of course not," Gertie promised. To Alastair, she added, "I came to see if you need another drink."

"Do you offer because you want to help, or because you want powers?" Alastair asked with an arched brow.

"Your powers won't do me any good during the daylight," Gertie pointed out. "Not unless we find more motorcycle gear. Yours was destroyed in the blast."

"Do not remind me," Mahdi groaned, sitting up. "All we have is our bathing suits. Even our crates are gone."

Gertie lowered her eyes, wishing she'd kept her mouth shut. Then she offered the canteen that she wore slung over her shoulder. "It's Lorenzo's blood."

Alastair's brows lifted, and a smile crossed his face. "Aren't you a treasure."

He gave the canteen to Mahdi, so he could drink first.

Mahdi took several gulps and then handed it back to Alastair, who finished it off.

"You look better already," Jinsoo said. "Thank you so much, Gertie."

"Yes, thank you," Mahdi replied. "We need more, but this will hold us over until we can feed."

"I think we will feed tonight," Alastair decided. "We are both feeling well enough to go out. Do you agree, Mahdi?"

"Yes. Dear lords, yes. I am bored out of my mind."

"But is it safe?" Gertie asked. "Maybe you should stay here, where others can protect you."

"We want to help with the search," Mahdi said. "We have rested long enough."

"How is Pegasus?" Alastair asked.

"I am going to visit him next," Gertie said. "Want to come?"

Both vampires climbed from their beds. Mahdi held his head, looking dizzy and pale. Alastair stumbled to his feet only to be caught by Jinsoo. Chidori flapped her wings, overhead, chirping her concern.

"Are you sure about this?" Jinsoo asked.

"Yes," Alastair confirmed. "The exercise will do us good."

They reached Pegasus's stable to find the winged horse standing on his feet eating fresh hay.

"Look at you, beautiful," Mahdi praised. "Good as new."

Pegasus leaned his head into Mahdi's chest as the vampire stroked him.

"I'm sorry about Raimo," Pegasus said with tears in his eyes. "He was with me when it happened. I couldn't protect him."

"There, there," Alastair soothed as he stroked Pegasus's muzzle. "You barely survived yourself."

Pegasus hung his head.

"We all miss Raimo," Mahdi said. "I still cannot believe he is gone."

"Nor I," Alastair said. "I hope the others are safe. I hate that we have not heard anything from them."

"Not even a peep," Mahdi added.

Gertie had been about to say that she would find their friends if it was the last thing she did when the entire ship shuddered and leaned hard to one side. The four friends stumbled and grabbed ahold of something to steady themselves.

"Ay, chihuahua," Jinsoo exclaimed. "What was that?"

Chidori flew to Jinsoo's shoulders with an uncharacteristic squawk.

"I think the ship is under attack," Gertie speculated. "Jinsoo and Pegasus, can you take the vampires to the Underworld? You'll need to god-travel. We can't risk them being exposed to sunlight, especially in their condition."

"Good idea," Alastair said as he climbed on the back of Pegasus.

"What about you?" Jinsoo asked Gertie.

The ship shuddered once again and leaned in the opposite direction as Mahdi was mounting the horse. The boards overhead groaned.

"Please, just go," Gertie said. "Okay?"

"Pegasus?" Jinsoo turned to the horse. "Can you do it?"

"Only gods have that power."

Jinsoo frowned. "Oh, no! I suck at it!"

Gertie grabbed him by the shoulders and squared herself to him. "You can do this, Jinsoo. Okay?"

Jinsoo nodded with a look of determination. With Chidori on his shoulder, he threw an arm around Pegasus's neck, and then they vanished, leaving Gertie alone just as the boards overhead burst open and light and flames shot into the hull. Gertie ran down the hall in search of Hector. They found each other at the bottom of the stairs, which were already burning. Without saying a word, they scrambled up the steps and onto the main deck, only to find Hestie and Prometheus unconscious and on fire.

As Gertie ran toward them, she shifted into her bull form and used her horns to scoop each of them, one at a time, into the sea. She and Hector leaped overboard after them, where she shifted back into her human form. Hector used his super-speed to collect the injured and unconscious gods before resurfacing beside her. Gertie and Hector panted and tread in the tumultuous water beside the burning wreckage that was once the *Marcella II* praying to the gods to rescue them.

"Is Hermes still on board?" Hector asked in between coughs from the stifling smoke.

Gertie's eyes widened. The messenger god was trapped in the adamantine cage on a ship that was in flames. If his body burned and his ashes dispersed, he would remain forever in Tartarus.

Hermie and Poros searched every island in the Mediterranean within a ten-mile radius of where they'd found Lorenzo and his tiny boat, but they found no sign of Del, Penny, Sophia, or Bach. At least his father hadn't either, which meant the vampires were alive.

Del, please answer me, Hermie pleaded for the hundredth time, trying to reach her mind. *Tell me where to find you.*

He held a canteen strapped to his chest, close to his heart. The canteen was filled with human blood. When they'd found Lorenzo the night before, the man had begged Gertie to feed from him. He needed his fix.

Gertie had agreed to bite, but she didn't drink his blood. Instead, she filled two canteens and gave one to Hermie to give to the vampires, should he find them.

"What was that?" Poros turned toward the east.

When Hermie followed Poros's line of vision, he saw a ship bursting with flames. A series of earth-shattering *booms* followed.

"The *Marcella II*!" Hermie cried.

Hermie and Poros god-traveled directly above the ship. The decks were abandoned, as was the hull, but still inside the burning salon was Hermes in his cage.

That's when he heard Gertie and Hector's prayers.

"Where are they?" Poros, who must have heard them, too, asked as he searched the sea around the ship.

"There!" Hermie pointed. "Hestie and Prometheus are burned to a crisp."

"You grab Hermes. I'll get the others and meet you in the Underworld."

Hermie flew to the salon and dodged flames and falling debris as he reached for the cage.

Raimo's body was engulfed in flames and Hermes was coughing uncontrollably.

"It's a trap!" Hermes warned between coughs.

Before Hermie could react, a small hand grabbed him from thin air, bringing him beneath the power of the helm, where he saw the face of his enemy.

"So, it is you," he said to Nike.

The small, winged goddess, who, like Iris, was only three feet tall but whose wings were white rather than gold, said nothing as she grabbed the adamantine cage and god-traveled them from the burning ship to a large cavern.

In the center of the cavern was a pool of water and lying beside it were the vampires. They were so still that, at first, Hermie thought they were dead. They lay on their backs with their eyes closed and their arms and legs sprawled haphazardly, as though they'd been dropped.

"Del? Can you hear me?" Hermie cried.

Although Del did not reply, she blinked.

I can't move, she said to him telepathically. *Please help.*

Nike slipped an adamantine cuff onto one of Hermie's wrists. The cuff was on the end of a chain, which the winged goddess then locked to the cage that still held the coughing messenger god. Before he could ask Nike what she intended to do with them, the winged goddess disappeared.

Hermie immediately rushed toward the vampires with his canteen of human blood, but the chain was at least ten feet too short.

"Hold on," he said to Lord Hermes.

Understanding what he intended to do, the messenger god grabbed onto the bars of his cage to steady himself as Hermie dragged the cage across the ground of the cave. The adamantine prevented him from god-travel and telepathy, but it didn't take away his other powers. Once he had enough slack in the chain, he rushed to Del's side, unscrewed the lid of the canteen, and allowed some of the blood to drip onto her lips.

Hestie awakened to the sight of her mother's beautiful face smiling down at her.

"Thank goodness, you're awake," Therese said. "How do you feel?"

Hestie sat up on the bed and looked around. She was in the throne room in the Underworld. Hades and Athena were arguing. Persephone was pacing along the Phlegethon—the river of fire. And Prometheus lay on another bed across from her.

Like her mother, Gertie and Hector were looking at Hestie with concern.

"Where are the others?" Hestie asked.

"Poros went to get them," Gertie explained. "They're at the gate. Cerberus is being difficult."

Just then, Pegasus flew into the throne room with Alastair and Mahdi on his back and Jinsoo, Chidori, and Poros following.

"Where are Hermie and Lord Hermes?" Hestie asked.

"They should have arrived by now," Poros said. "Has anyone heard from them?"

"Great," Athena voiced from across the room. "Add them to the list of missing people."

"Who else is missing?" Hestie asked.

Just then, Prometheus stirred and sat up.

"Captain!" Poros flew to his side. "How do you feel?"

"What happened to my ship?" he questioned.

Hestie was wondering the same thing. Had it been saved? Or was it gone forever?

"We lost her," Poros said. "I'm sorry."

Athena shook her head. "I'm sorry, too, but it's the least of our concerns right now."

"Who else is missing?" Hestie repeated.

"Aether sent a message with Iris this morning," Athena explained. "He hasn't seen my mother in weeks. He thinks something's happened."

Poros gawked. "Our mother's missing?"

He and Hestie exchanged a knowing look. There was only one reason someone would want to kidnap Metis, and it was the thing the Olympians feared the most: someone wanted to free Zeus.

CHAPTER TWELVE

An Emergency Meeting

Gertie held Hector's hand as she stood in the great hall of Mount Olympus beside Hestie. What if the enemy of the vampires was among them? She studied the faces of the gods, who were seated on their thrones waiting for Athena to begin her emergency meeting.

Everyone from the Underworld throne room had come, except for Persephone, who had stayed behind to guard the realm with the Furies. Alastair and Mahdi had even come. Athena wanted them to tell the Olympian court everything they could recall from the attack on the *Black Widow*. Even Pegasus, usually tucked away in the stables with the other horses, was there.

"As many of you already know," Athena began, "my mother is missing. She's been in hiding with Aether to prevent the possibility of my father's return, but Aether hasn't seen her in weeks. Her disappearance leads me to suspect that Zeus's return may be upon us. We need to prepare ourselves."

Murmurs filled the room.

"I've dreaded this day," Aphrodite said.

"It hasn't happened yet," Apollo reminded her.

Athena beckoned to Gertie, causing her heart to race. Just to be sure, Gertie pointed to her chest and mouthed *me?*

"Please come forward, Gertrude," Athena requested. "And tell the others what you told me."

On legs that felt suddenly wobbly, Gertie approached the center of the Olympian court. "It's no coincidence, that's what I think, anyway. An STS ship contained vampire prisoners in adamantine chains. Yes, we blew it up—the crew of Lord Hermes that is—but we were set up. Those chains were warded against Hermes. Whoever tricked us into destroying those vampires is the same person who attacked the *Black Widow* and killed and abducted our, my, friends."

More murmurs filled the room.

"Where's Hermes now?" Poseidon asked.

"He and Hermie are missing," Therese, the goddess of animal companions and mother to Hestie and Hermie, said.

"I was the last to see him," Poros said. "We were searching for the missing vampires when the *Marcella II* was attacked. Hermie went to rescue Hermes while I helped Gertie and Hector. They had Hestie and Prometheus in the sea."

"We were unconscious," Prometheus added. "Knocked out by the blast."

"Their bodies were burning," Gertie continued. "That's why I pushed them into the sea."

"Did you see the explosives that were used to attack your ship?" Ares asked Prometheus.

The captain shook his head. "I was keeping watch but still didn't see what hit me."

"Was it the same with the attack on the *Black Widow*?" Athena asked. "Gertrude, what do you recall?"

"There were explosions," Gertie reported. "Two or three. Maybe four. I was in the pool with Hector and Bach. A beam fell on Hector and knocked him out. A fire started, and I was trapped in a corner, about to pass out from the smoke. Bach tried to help me, but he disappeared before my eyes."

"Can you add anything to that, Hector?" Athena asked.

"No, my lady. I was knocked out before I knew that anything had happened."

"What about the other survivors—you two." Athena pointed to the vampires.

Mahdi and Alastair stepped forward.

"It was dusk," Alastair said. "Some of us were in the indoor pool. Others of us were out on deck, taking turns riding Pegasus."

"Those of us who were outside got the worst of it," Mahdi stated. "Explosives were dropped directly onto us just as Pegasus and Raimo were about to take flight."

Aphrodite covered her mouth. "How horrible."

"We couldn't see them coming," Alastair said. "The bombs dropped out of the sky."

"Did they explode on impact?" Ares asked. "Or did they detonate sometime after?"

"On impact," Mahdi answered. "There was no time to react."

"Are you certain they were bombs?" Hephaestus questioned. "Might they have been lightning bolts?"

More murmurs filled the room. Gertie turned to Poros, whose eyes had widened.

"We hadn't considered that." Alastair admitted. "We don't know what they were."

"A lightning bolt would have paralyzed the gods and destroyed the vampires," Poseidon pointed out.

"Not if it wasn't wielded by a powerful god," Hades interjected.

"And you never saw the perpetrators?" Artemis asked the vampires.

Mahdi and Alastair shook their heads.

"Do we have any clues as to who may have done this?" Ares wondered.

"I'm not sure if this is relevant. . ." Poros cut in.

"What is it?" Athena asked.

"When Hermie and I were working undercover at the STS office, we overheard men talking about someone named Nike. They said she wouldn't be happy. They said she wasn't getting what she wanted. They spoke of her on two separate occasions."

"And you believe this to be the goddess Nike?" Apollo asked.

"I don't know," Poros admitted.

Poseidon stood up. "Poros and Hermie reported this to me last night. I went looking for Nike and was unable to locate her. I find this suspicious."

"Indeed," Apollo agreed.

Poseidon returned to his seat.

"Has anyone seen her lately?" Artemis asked.

The gods glanced at one another, shaking their heads. Gertie wondered if anyone was lying. Then she recalled reading about Apollo's ability to spot a lie. She supposed if someone were lying, he would speak up—unless Apollo was a traitor himself.

"Have you any vision, Apollo?" Athena asked her brother. "Any inkling?"

The god of light shook his head.

"We should form a search party," Hephaestus suggested.

"Our first priority must be to find my mother," Athena insisted. "Which is why I asked Hecate to join us."

As Poros returned to Hestie's side, Hecate stepped forward. "I need something that belonged to your mother."

Athena shrugged. "I don't have anything. Isn't there another way?"

"No, I'm sorry to say, there isn't," Hecate said. "You don't have an article of clothing, a ribbon, a letter, or anything that was once hers?"

Athena blushed. Was she embarrassed?

"My mother didn't give me anything."

"Not even a comb or a mirror?" Aphrodite asked.

"What about a weapon?" Hephaestus suggested. "She made your armor."

"I need something that can burn," Hecate pointed out.

"Surely she gave you a token of her love," Aphrodite said.

Gertie noticed tears welling in Athena's eyes. "There's nothing."

"She gave you life," Gertie blurted out. "*You* belonged to her."

Hecate turned and studied Gertie. "Are you suggesting that I burn our leader?"

"Burn *me*," Poros exclaimed suddenly. "I once belonged to her, too."

The room filled with gasps.

"What?" Hestie muttered beneath her breath. "Poros, what are you doing?"

"We have to do something," Poros said. "If my father returns, we're all toast anyway, right?"

A few of the Olympians chuckled at his choice of words.

Prometheus put a hand on Poros's shoulder. "What you're offering to do is honorable, son, but you don't have to do this. The fate of this pantheon does not rest solely on your shoulders."

Prometheus then gave Athena a harsh look.

Gertie could see that the captain clearly believed that if either of the siblings were to burn for the cause, it should be her. Then, she had an idea.

"Use Athena's hair," Gertie proposed.

Hecate turned and gave Gertie a warm smile. Then the goddess said to Athena, "That could work."

As the blood from Hermie's canteen dripped onto Del's lips, she opened her eyes. It was such a relief to see her. Tears slipped down his cheeks without warning.

"More," she whispered with a faint breath.

Hermie used one hand to lift her head while he put the canteen to her lips. She drank a few sips and then a few gulps. Then she pushed the canteen away.

"Give some to the others," she said weakly.

Hermie was impressed by her willpower when it was obvious that her body craved the blood. He gently laid her head down and went to Penny's side.

Penny seemed less weak as she opened her eyes and said, "About time."

Hermie put the canteen to her mouth. She took a few sips and then a gulp before saying, "Thank you, Hermie."

Hermie did the same for Sophia and Bach, who were even worse off than Del.

When Bach had finished, Hermie returned to Del.

"There's still another few ounces left," he said.

"Give it to whichever of us is the strongest," Del recommended.

"Why not the weakest?" Hermie wanted to know.

"Because the strongest will need to go for help," she said.

Hermie put his hand on her shoulder. It felt comforting to touch her, and he supposed he wanted to make sure she was real. He had begun to fear he might never find her. "It's still daytime and will be for several more hours. Besides, I'm going to call for help myself."

"Give it to the strongest," Del repeated. "For when Nike comes back."

"Do as she says," the messenger god demanded from his cage. "Give it to Penny."

"Do you still have the key?" Hermie asked Del.

"Nike took it," Hermes replied.

"Oh." Hermie returned to Penny, who gulped down the rest of the blood. After she handed back the canteen, she was still weak but able to sit up and look around.

"How do you plan to call for help?" Penny asked Hermie.

Hermie took out his cell phone. No service.

"We're beneath Mount Ida," Lord Hermes explained. "On the island of Crete. Don't expect your cell phone to be of help in here."

"Time for Plan B," Hermie said. Then to Lord Hermes, he added, "Hold on."

"This cage will not fit through that opening," Hermes said. "Don't you think I've already tried?"

"I'm sure of it," Hermie said smugly. Why did no one have any faith in him?

He dragged Hermes and the adamantine cage across the cavern floor toward the mouth of the cave, where, with enough slack, he flew out and into the light. Then, still tethered to the adamantine cage, he took out his cell. Victory! He had service.

He called Hestie.

No answer.

He tried Jinsoo.

No answer.

"Why aren't they answering?" he wondered. He didn't know of any other gods who kept phones on them. Even his mother no longer used one, despite his pleas to the contrary.

From inside, Lord Hermes shouted, "Is there a Plan C?"

Hermie texted Hestie and Jinsoo his location, and then he looked up into the sky at Helios. The sun god was too far away to hear Hermie shout—plus, he didn't want to alert Nike, in case she was close by. So, Hermie used his adamantine cuff and chain to reflect the light back to Helios, creating a signal.

"Come on, Helios," Hermie muttered. "Notice me."

Plan C was cut short when Nike grabbed his arm, revealing herself and another prisoner, Metis, beneath the power of the helm. She hauled Hermie back inside the cave, along with Metis.

Metis was the mother of Athena and Poros and looked like an older version of her daughter. She'd been swallowed by Zeus centuries ago to prevent the prophecy foreseeing his overthrow. The Athena Alliance had set Metis free, and, just last year, Hades had led a rebellion against Zeus who was now, along with Hera, trapped inside the belly of Metis.

There was only one reason why Nike had captured her. She planned to liberate Zeus.

"Why must you keep moving me around?" Metis asked Nike as Nike chained her to the adamantine cage.

"Because I knew that sooner or later Hecate would perform a location spell, and I wasn't ready for them to find you yet," Nike related. "But now, we're almost ready."

"What do you mean *we*?" Lord Hermes asked from his cage.

Nike thrust a hand into the mouth of Metis and pulled her jaw down. Then she thrust in her other hand to stretch the jaw wide open. To Hermie's extreme surprise and trepidation, a hand slipped out and waved.

"Hello, son!" the voice of Zeus called out. "I'll be seeing you soon!"

The hand vanished back inside of Metis, and Nike let go of the goddess's jaw.

"You can't just pull him out of there," Lord Hermes said to Nike. "It's not that easy."

"She forced me to drink a potion," Metis said. "My stomach is in terrible pain, and I've nearly regurgitated him all the way up." Then she added, "But don't worry. I was intentional about giving nothing of mine to Athena. Hecate won't be able to perform her location spell."

Nike shrugged. "I have a feeling Hecate will find a way."

Hermie tried to think. What could he do to prevent Zeus from being freed?

"The other Olympians won't allow you to return to power, Father," Lord Hermes said. "And it won't take long for them to overpower you, especially with Poros on their side."

"Don't underestimate me, Hermes," Zeus shouted, his voice barely audible now.

Hermie sucked in his lips, playing various scenarios out in his mind, trying to determine what would be Zeus's best course of action. What was the deposed god planning?

Hestie watched in awe as Hecate took a pair of shears and cut Athena's hair at the nape of her neck, leaving the goddess of wisdom with a short bob. Hecate then tied each end of the long hair into a knot and set the length of hair on her makeshift altar, which she had conjured in the great hall of the Olympian council.

Beneath a layer of smoke from a stick of burning incense, a silver bowl of water sat in the middle of four blue candles. The candles were lit, and the northernmost flame was used to set the hair on fire. At first, it only produced smoke and a foul stench, but as soon as a flame appeared, Hecate used it to light a world map. Then she dropped the burning map and hair into the water, stirred it with her finger, and said, "Please show me the location of Metis."

The goddess lifted a tiny scrap of paper from the bowl and studied it.

"She's at Mount Ida," Hecate declared, "on the island of Crete."

Hades scratched his beard. "My brother's childhood home."

"Thank you, Hecate," Athena said. Then, to the Olympian council, she insisted, "We need a plan."

Hestie tried reaching out to her brother again but, once again, heard nothing in reply. Her phone had been burned to a crisp during the attack on the *Marcella II*, or she would have tried texting him. She wondered if Jinsoo's phone was working.

"We should send a reconnaissance team to assess the situation," Ares proposed.

"I like the way you think, brother," Athena agreed. "I concur. Who will volunteer to go?"

Hestie was shocked when Gertie was the first to raise her hand.

"I appreciate your willingness, Gertrude," Athena said, "but this is a job for the gods."

"Then make me one," Gertie said boldly. "I want to help the vampires. Please make me their goddess. I've learned my lesson about making conditions. I only wish to serve."

"She deserves it, Athena," Poros, who stood beside Hestie, intervened. "Please consider it."

"Hear, hear," Artemis said.

Poseidon tapped his foot impatiently. "Let's make it quick. The clock is ticking."

Athena looked around the room at her fellow Olympians. "We could use another hand if my father intends to return. All in favor?"

The hall resounded with *aye*.

"All opposed?" Athena asked.

Silence.

Hestie smiled gleefully at their decision, happy for the demigod, who undoubtedly deserved the honor.

Gertie clapped her hands together and shouted, "Thank you! I will not disappoint you!"

CHAPTER THIRTEEN

The Goddess of Vampires

Gertie turned to Hector and gave him a hug, whispering, "I'm sorry."

"Don't be," he chided as he returned the hug. "I'm proud of you."

"But I'm putting the vampires above our relationship," she said quickly.

"I know. That's why I'm proud of you." He looked down at her with a smile, his blue eyes bright.

"What a sweet, young couple," Aphrodite said from where she sat on her throne. "There's power in young love. That is often forgotten."

As much as Gertie loved attention, she didn't like that kind of attention. Her face was hot with embarrassment when Athena beckoned her forward.

"Do you consent to becoming one of us?" the goddess of wisdom asked.

"Yes," Gertie said eagerly. "I do."

Athena took a golden goblet from her Aunt Hestia and handed it to Gertie. "Drink this ambrosia as the power of the Olympians infuses you with immortality."

Gertie took the goblet and put it to her lips. The sweet liquid stung as it entered her mouth and moved down her throat. She felt it continue down her esophagus and into her stomach, where it radiated throughout her body.

A pain deep in her bones made her drop to her knees. Then a tingling sensation took over, making her feel dizzy and light-headed as goosebumps emerged in waves across her skin. She felt her hair stand on end with static electricity. The same electricity lifted her to her feet and into the air. She gasped where she hovered above everyone with her arms spread wide, like a bird's wings. She couldn't move, but she could feel changes taking place.

Her nails grew longer and harder. Her hair was thicker and more lustrous and fell across her shoulders and was at least a foot longer than it had been before. The muscles in her arms and legs hardened and bulked, and her skin took on a lustrous golden hue. Her vision and hearing became more acute, as she could now hear some of the gods whispering.

"She's beautiful," Aphrodite was saying to her Charities.

"She's a huntress like me," Artemis murmured with awe.

Finally able to turn her head, Gertie noticed that a quiver of arrows and a bow appeared strapped to her back. As her body lowered to the floor, and she landed firmly on her feet, she asked, "What are the bow and arrows for?"

"That is for you to discover," Athena explained. "They're gifts from the Fates."

"I received the same when I declared my purpose," Therese said from where she stood near Hestie and Poros. "I soon learned that they worked like the arrows of Cupid, except with humans and their animal companions. Like Cupid's, my arrows, once they strike, are invisible to all except those who share the blood of Eros. Maybe your arrows will work similarly with vampires and their hosts."

Gertie doubted that was the case. Hosts were already willing to be fed on because of the vampire virus, which gave them temporary powers. The arrows would benefit the vampires in some way, but she didn't yet know how.

She turned and glanced at Hector, who stood gaping at her.

"Now we need a plan," Athena changed the subject. "Who else wishes to volunteer?"

As the Olympians discussed their plan, Gertie returned to Hector's side, where he whispered, "You look incredible. How do you feel?"

"Amazing," she whispered back. "I wish my father could have been here to see this."

Hector squeezed her hand. "He'll see you soon enough, I'm sure."

She closed her eyes and prayed to him and was startled when he appeared beside her.

"You came," she said with her mouth hanging open.

"I told you to call me any time," he replied.

Gertie hadn't been sure if he'd meant it.

"Dionysus," Athena said, standing before her throne. "Did you come to offer us your help?"

"I'm happy to be of assistance. What's going on? And why have you cut your hair?"

Hermie sat on the cavern floor beside Del, still tethered to the cage. He squeezed her hand and stroked her hair—anything to reassure her. Metis sat on a boulder not far from him. Having removed the helm from her head, Nike hovered above the pool, smirking.

"Now we wait," Nike said.

"For what?" Lord Hermes asked from his cage.

"Your rescuers," she answered.

"Why are you doing this?" Hermie wanted to know.

"I didn't plan on it, if that's what you think," Nike shared. "At first, I was only after the vampires working for Hermes."

"Why?" Lord Hermes asked as he picked at his beard.

"Because to the victors go the spoils. That's how it has always been. You and your vampires were wrong to interfere with that."

Hermie released Del's hand and climbed to his feet. "Victory over a conquered people does not require the theft of their artifacts."

"That's your opinion," Nike countered. "One of the motives for conquering a people is to take what they have. It's wrong and goes against nature for you to go about stealing things from victors and returning them to the defeated. I won't tolerate it. That's why I took over STS when Phorcys was vanquished. The shipping company had been the victors of the Mediterranean for years and deserved a proper leader."

"What has that to do with my father?" Lord Hermes questioned.

"Nothing," Nike admitted. "Except that I happened upon Metis while she was visiting her sisters on the island of Leto. She, Clymene, and Dione were bathing on the beach and didn't notice me. They were sound asleep. But Zeus noticed me. He had crawled up to peer at me through Metis's nostrils. He said that I was his most loyal subject—which is true. I defended him until the very end, unlike you, Hermes. You turned against your own father."

"I suppose he promised you a position if you helped him," Lord Hermes drawled.

"He didn't have to, but yes, he did, and I'm grateful. And he said he would help me to destroy the vampires if I helped him."

"Where did you get the explosives that you used to attack the ships?" Hermie asked.

"Those were lightning bolts, forged by the Cyclopes," Nike said.

Lord Hermes stood up in his cage. It was only four-feet tall, so he stood hunched over. "What? How did you manage that?"

"Zeus told me a riddle that only he and they knew. It was all the proof they needed. And Zeus offered them an important role in his new regime, to thank them for their loyalty."

Hermie began to pace, worried now that Zeus's plan might work. "Why would you lure the Olympians here before Zeus is free? Aren't you making yourself vulnerable?"

"No doubt they will send a reconnaissance team to gather information before planning an attack. If Zeus were free, you can bet they'd return with their full force. But if they see only me, the rescue party is sure to be smaller in number. And you can bet Poros will be among them, which is precisely what we're counting on."

"Even with Zeus and Hera," Lord Hermes began, "you'll have no chance against him. Poros has become more powerful than my father ever was."

"You don't know everything," Nike scoffed. "Do you think I'd reveal my entire plan to you? You are missing several pieces of the puzzle yet, my old friend."

A murmur came from the belly of Metis, so Nike flew over to the goddess and stretched open her mouth.

"Yes, my lord?" Nike asked as she looked down Metis's throat.

While Nike was thus engaged, Penny flew like a silver bullet across the cavern to slip the key to the cage from Nike's pocket. Penny quickly returned to her original position as Nike was straining to hear her lord.

Nike reached her arm down Metis's throat and pulled. "I can barely hear you. What did you say?"

"I said enough talking. The scouts may overhear you!"

"Yes, my lord," Nike said. "Though, I'm sure I'd sense them if they were nearby."

Hermie covered his mouth to stifle a grin.

"What are you laughing at?" Nike, who noticed, asked.

"Nothing," he lied. "I feel sick. I haven't eaten in days."

As he glanced toward the door of the cave, Hermie had another shock. Gertie was there. He'd only caught a flash of her, and she was gone. But what was shocking was that her eyes weren't red. That meant she did not have the vampire virus in her system. Moreover, the lustrous sheen of her hair and skin resembled that of a god. This meant Gertie had undergone apotheosis after all, and the vampires had their goddess.

Although he couldn't be happier for Gertie and the vampires, he hoped that they and the other gods would be prepared for whatever plan Nike and Zeus had up their sleeves. If Hermie could think of a way to stop Zeus from escaping the belly of Metis, he might circumvent another revolution.

As Athena recruited her reconnaissance team, Hestie flew to Jinsoo to ask about his phone.

"It's dead," Jinsoo said. "Got a charger?"

"Not with me, but I might be able to conjure one, if it can be considered a weapon."

"That won't work," her mother, who'd overheard, said. "Where is it?"

"The one on the ship was destroyed, I guess. But I have one in my room in the Underworld."

"Why don't you and Jinsoo fetch it while the reconnaissance team scouts Mount Ida?" Therese suggested.

"If Hermie isn't answering you telepathically," Poros began, "what makes you think he can answer his phone?"

"If he's trapped in the adamantine cage with Hermes, the phone still works, remember?" she said. "Hermie texted Jinsoo when we were prisoners on the *Tarantula.*"

"That's right," Poros recalled. "It's worth getting the charger, then. I'm going with the team to scout Mount Ida. I'll meet you back here."

Poros kissed her cheek, right in front of her mother, which made Hestie blush. Then she noticed one of the Charities, Pasithea, give her a dirty look. Hestie ignored it and tried to stay focused.

"Okay, Jinsoo," Hestie prompted. "Ready?"

"Can we take Alastair and Mahdi with us? They won't like it here by themselves."

"Can I go, too?" Hector asked.

Chidori chirped from Jinsoo's shoulder, "Me, too?"

"Sure," she said. "Let's go."

Hestie took their hands and led them via god-travel to her room in the Underworld. Persephone appeared within seconds.

"Oh, it's you," Persephone said when she saw them.

"I just need to grab my phone charger," Hestie explained.

Persephone laughed. "Why do you young gods rely on technology when you have superpowers?"

Hestie kissed Persephone's cheek. "Because there are ancient wards that limit godly powers and not technology. If Hermie is in the adamantine cage with Hermes, he can communicate with us with his phone."

"Ahh," Persephone realized. "I see."

"I guess it's a generational thing," Jinsoo said meekly.

Alastair, Mahdi, and Hector laughed.

"Well, I'll leave you to it," Persephone said before she disappeared.

Hestie rummaged through the drawer of her bedside table until she found the charger. Then she plugged it into Jinsoo's phone and into the outlet Hermie had installed.

"This may take a few minutes," she said to the others. "Why don't you make yourselves comfortable?"

Just then, Clifford, Noodle, Cubie, and Galen entered the room and greeted Hestie by licking her knees and hands.

"I'm happy to see you, too, guys." Hestie smiled. "I've missed you."

The others also pet the dogs and the polecat. Chidori flapped her wings ecstatically, showing her joy at being reunited with her friends.

"I didn't realize you had pets in the Underworld," Alastair said.

"Not pets so much as companions," Hestie elaborated. "Cubie and Galen are Hecate's familiars, but ever since Clifford and Noodle moved in, they enjoy staying here even when Hecate is away."

Hestie checked Jinsoo's phone. There was a text from Hermie.

"Guys," Hestie interrupted. "Hermie and Lord Hermes are also at Mount Ida, along with Del, Penny, Sophia, and Bach."

"Thank the gods they're alive," Jinsoo praised.

"I wouldn't thank the gods, necessarily," Hestie said.

"It's good news, either way," Hector said.

Mahdi put his face in his hands. "What a relief. I just hope we can get them back to safety."

Alastair combed his fingers through his sandy hair. "If Nike means to reinstate Zeus, why involve vampires?"

"I don't know," Hestie said. "But this phone may be our way of working with Hermie to come up with an idea to stop her."

"I hope his phone isn't taken from him," Hector said. "Be careful of what you say. If his phone gets into enemy hands, you don't want to give away our plans."

When there was enough of a charge on Jinsoo's phone, Hestie texted: *Hermie? You there?*

CHAPTER FOURTEEN

Reconnaissance

As Gertie flew with the reconnaissance team toward the island of Crete, she took stock of how it felt to be a goddess. It was not what she had expected. She was used to the astute hearing and vision. She also felt accustomed to flying—though it was always at night, and flying beneath the light of Helios added a special dimension to the experience. However, whereas the vampires felt every little tickle on their skin, her skin seemed so impervious as to feel numb to anything it touched.

Even the wind blowing against her body felt different—less harsh but also less exhilarating. She understood now why vampires wore more clothes than the gods. Vampires needed the protection from the elements, while the gods did not.

The voices in her head were also different. As a vampire, she could invade other people's minds and listen to their thoughts. She didn't have that power as a goddess. Yet, she could hear voices. She quickly realized that they were the voices of vampires all over Greece praying for help.

Never before this moment had she understood how much work her duties would require of her. There were vampires in Athens who were hungry and scared. There was a vampire in Piraeus who'd been burned by the sun and was hurting. A vampire in Delphi was lonely and bored. There was a vampire reaper, who worked for Hades, who regretted his decision to go into service to the Underworld. There were other reapers who gave thanks for their sense of purpose.

Among those lifted in prayer was the voice of Del asking for a miracle. She prayed for the lives of her friends, including Raimo, who she didn't know was dead.

Gertie wondered if Del would be able to hear her answer back. *Del, can you hear me?*

She waited for several seconds. Then several more. Del did not reply.

When the island of Crete came into view below, Artemis searched the woods, Poseidon the lakes, Poros the mountaintop, and Ares the coastline for enemies. They already knew where to find the mouth of the cave beneath Mount Ida, so they wanted to first make sure they weren't being watched by enemies waiting to ambush them the moment they drew close to the cave. Gertie's job was to stay above the island to keep watch for incoming forces.

However, Gertie began to recall the last time she had visited the island, when she had gone to see Asterion, also known as the Minotaur, in his labyrinth. As she wished she could visit him again, she suddenly found herself god-traveling without realizing it. A pressure wrapped itself around her and, when she blinked, she found herself inside the very labyrinth she had been imagining.

But it wasn't exactly as she had imagined or remembered, for currently it was filled with angry Cyclopes—at least two dozen of them—and bound in adamantine chains were Asterion and his sister, along with Hypnos and his wife, Jen.

Just as one of the Cyclopes raised what looked like a lightning bolt toward her in a threatening way, Gertie wished she were back on Mount Olympus with Prometheus and Athena and the others who had stayed behind. As she wished it, a pressure wrapped around her and, when she blinked again, she found herself standing in the middle of the great hall. The gods who were there stopped talking among themselves to look at her.

"Why have you returned without the others?" Hades demanded.

"And so soon?" Apollo asked.

"Did something go wrong?" Athena wanted to know.

Gertie felt her cheeks grow warm as embarrassment swept over her. She reminded herself that her mistake had provided her with important intelligence.

She cleared her throat and said, "I had a hunch and went to the Minotaur's labyrinth. You won't believe what I saw."

She described the Cyclopes with their lightning bolts and their prisoners.

"I need to get back to my team but wanted you to know what I saw as soon as possible," she said.

Gertie didn't wait for them to respond. She imagined the island of Crete and found herself back where she had begun in the blink of an eye.

God-travel would take some getting used to, to say the least.

When ten more minutes had passed, Artemis returned.

"Did you see anything unusual?" Gertie asked her.

"No. You?"

Gertie told her about the Cyclopes and their prisoners.

"You left your post?" Artemis asked.

Gertie shrugged, not sure if she should admit that it wasn't intentional.

"You could have compromised the rest of us, but I suppose it worked out in our favor," Artemis said as Ares, Poros, and Poseidon joined them in the sky above Mount Ida.

"What worked out in our favor?" Ares asked.

Artemis relayed what Gertie had seen.

"No wonder we haven't seen Hip or Jen," Poseidon said.

Poros shook his head. "I wonder if Morpheus knows his parents are missing."

"Let's take a closer look at the cave," Poseidon suggested. "Gertie and Poros, keep watch up here. Ares and Artemis follow and watch my back. I'll attempt to get a view of the inside."

As part of her team flew toward the island below, Gertie wished she could go with Poseidon to peek inside the cave. No sooner had she wished it, than she found herself hovering near the cavern door before Poseidon had arrived. Hermie gave her a startled look from inside, and Gertie quickly god-traveled away, back to her post beside Poros in the sky.

"Where did you go?" he asked her.

"I'm still learning how to control my powers," she explained as the blood of humiliation warmed her cheeks.

Gnawing on her bottom lip, she hoped she hadn't ruined the mission.

Hermie wished his adamantine cuff wasn't blocking his ability to speak with the others telepathically. He wanted to know if Penny had a plan for using the key.

"Yes," she whispered, letting him know that, despite the adamantine, she could read his thoughts.

"What was that?" Nike bellowed from where she hovered near the cage.

"He asked if I was thirsty," Penny croaked in a raspy, weak-sounding voice. "And I said yes."

"Too bad we have no mortal blood for you," Nike smirked.

I saw Gertie, Hermie thought, in case the vampires were listening. *She's a goddess now. If you pray to her, she may be able to hear you.*

Just then, Hermie felt his phone buzz. He slipped it from his pocket and saw a text from Jinsoo.

Hermie? You there?

Not wanting to lose his phone to Nike, he returned it to his pocket, determined to wait to use it when it would bring the greatest benefit.

The ringing of a bell made him turn toward the mouth of the cave, where two old nymphs and a goat were entering.

"Uh oh, Ida," one nymph said to the other. "Looks like we've got company."

"I was wondering when you'd show up," Nike said. "You're the nymphs who raised my lord."

"If your lord is Zeus, then you are correct," the one called Ida said.

"He's been anxious for your arrival," Nike elaborated. "He wants you to feed this goddess your goat's milk, so he can have some, too."

A bell hanging from the goat's neck jingled as the beast crossed the cavern.

While Nike was arranging for Zeus to receive his milk, Hermie texted Jinsoo back: *I'm here beneath Mount Ida. Nike plans to free Zeus. She expects Poros to come. I think she will ambush him with lightning bolts made by Cyclopes.*

Then he added: *Keep Poros away from here. This trap is meant for him.*

Hermie quickly returned his phone to his pocket and resumed stroking Del's hair. In his mind, he thought, *I've texted Jinsoo what I know of Nike's plan*—hoping to reassure any vampires who might be listening.

He studied Del's sweet face. She needed more blood. They all did. After Nike's speech, he had wondered why the vampires had been allowed to live at all. Then it dawned on him that the winged goddess had used them as bait, along with Metis and now him and Lord Hermes. Once Nike were to become certain that the gods had taken her bait— that they were indeed planning a rescue mission—there would be nothing to stop her from destroying the vampires.

Del shuddered beneath his fingertips. He studied her face and noticed that despite her dehydration, a tear slipped from the corner of her eye. He clenched a fist, worried that he had caused the tear and her trepidation. He had to stop being reckless with his thoughts.

I will get you and the others out of here, one way or another, he thought intently, hoping she heard. *I promise you.*

Hestie gasped when she received a text back from her brother on Jinsoo's phone.

"What's wrong?" Cubie, the Doberman, asked.

"What did Hermie say?" Jinsoo wanted to know.

"Oh, great," Alastair groaned, having read Hestie's thoughts. "Nike managed to get the Cyclopes to make more lightning bolts, and she plans to lure Poros into a trap."

"That's good to know, Hestie," Hector said. "Excellent work."

"Hermie says to keep Poros away from that cave," Hestie related. "We've got to let the others know. Let's go back, guys. Ready?"

They held hands and god-traveled to Mount Olympus, where the gods were still waiting for the reconnaissance team to return.

Hestie's mother, Therese, updated Hestie and her friends on what Gertie had told them about the labyrinth. When Therese saw Hestie's mouth fall open, she said, "Yes, it's scary, but at least we know about it."

Hestie showed her mother the text from Hermie.

"What is it?" Hades asked.

"Nike has planned a trap for Poros," Therese explained. "Hermie warns to keep Poros away."

The reconnaissance team arrived just as Therese was explaining Hermie's text to the other gods.

"I can't just stay away," Poros said. "My mother is suffering because of my father. This is personal."

"But it's a trap," Athena argued. "You can't just walk right into it."

"I have an idea," Hector said. "What if I go dressed as Poros? We look a lot alike. I could be a decoy."

"They do have the same height, build, and coloring," Aphrodite agreed.

"That's not a bad idea," Hades looked at Hector, "except that it will get you killed."

"Then make him a god," Gertie asserted suddenly. "It will make him more convincing as Poros. Nike won't be expecting there to be two young gods with the same sandy-colored hair and build."

"We can't just keep turning mortals into gods," Athena complained.

"He's not just any mortal," Poros objected. "He fought valiantly when the monsters of the sea breached the gates of Hades and nearly released the Titans from the pit."

"Hear, hear," Dionysus said.

Athena gave him a smirk.

"But their faces look nothing alike," Hephaestus pointed out. "Poros's eyes are gray, like Athena's. Hector's are blue, like mine. The jawline, the profile, they're vastly different."

Telepathically, Hestie said to Hephaestus, *Don't you want your son to live an immortal life with you?*

More than anything, Hephaestus replied telepathically to Hestie. *But what we're talking about is dangerous, even for a god.*

"Hector can wear the armor you made me," Poros said to Hephaestus.

"It won't shield him from godly vision," Apollo pointed out.

"But it might be enough to create a decoy," Artemis said.

"My father has rarely looked at me," Poros said. "And Nike has only seen me once. I doubt they'll know the difference."

Poseidon lifted a finger in the air and began to nod. "If the decoy works, Nike will signal the Cyclopes to surround and infiltrate the cave, which would allow the rest of us to attack from behind."

"Risking the lives of those in the cave," Hades interjected. "If the Cyclopes are armed with lightning bolts, this could mean paralysis for the gods and certain death for the vampires."

"You said yourself that it takes a powerful god wielding the lightning bolt to cause paralysis," Poros said to Hades.

"Yes," Hades admitted. "But if three or more Cyclopes were to throw a bolt at the same god, that could do it, too."

"I'll have to stun the Cyclopes with my trident before they release their bolts," Poseidon said. "It's too bad Hades has lost his helm. It would be useful to us about now."

Hades rolled his eyes. "It was stolen. I seem to recall that happening to your trident and your wife not that long ago. And your daughter, too, just two months ago. And who helped you get them back? Oh, yeah. Me and my family."

"Uncles, please," Athena said.

"What if you attack the Cyclopes while they're still in the labyrinth?" Hector suggested.

"And endanger the lives of Hypnos and Jen?" Hades scoffed.

"Not to mention Asterion and Ariadne," Therese added. "However, it might be safer than waiting for them to surround the cave."

"We'd have the element of surprise," Aphrodite cut in.

"And the Cyclopes would be trapped in the labyrinth," Poros agreed.

"We should go there now with Poseidon and his trident," Artemis said. "Paralyze those one-eyed cannibals before they can do any harm."

"There's no guarantee of success," Apollo said, "but it might be the best plan we've got."

"We'll need four teams," Athena said. "One to accompany Hector, disguised as Poros; another to help Poseidon attack the Cyclopes; a third hidden outside of the cave at Mount Ida to serve as reinforcements against Zeus and against any Cyclopes who survive Poseidon's attack; and a fourth to remain here, to defend Mount Olympus."

"I'll help Poseidon with the Cyclopes," Hades volunteered. "I want to make sure my son and his wife make it out of there unscathed."

"I'll lead the reinforcements," Ares said.

"I can help with that," Hephaestus offered. "I'd like to be there for my boy."

Hestie noticed Gertie exchange looks of surprise with Hector.

"I'll defend our home," Aphrodite stated.

"I want to be in the cave with Hector," Poros said. "I'll hang back disguised as someone else."

"That's not a good idea," Prometheus argued. "The decoy will be compromised if anyone recognizes you."

"I'll go with Hector," Athena said. "I promise to protect him."

"I'll go, too," Dionysus offered. "Zeus is my father, too."

"Make Hector a god," Gertie repeated. "He'll be of greater use to you."

Hestie observed how strong and powerful Gertie appeared as a goddess. The annoying know-it-all had become a goddess imbued with confidence. She wasn't afraid to assert her will on the others.

"We've already created a slippery slope," Athena objected.

Hades raised a hand in the air. "I have a proposition. Let's give Hector temporary immortality so he can serve us in this mission. If we succeed—and that's a big if, considering what we're up against—we can give Hector a series of challenges to prove whether he's worthy to become one of us permanently."

"This sounds familiar," Hestie's mother said.

"I'll do it," Hector declared. "That is, if the Olympian council will agree."

CHAPTER FIFTEEN

Words from the Heart

You don't have to do this, you know," Gertie said quietly to Hector after the Olympians had agreed to make him temporarily immortal. "We can find a way to be together, even if you don't want to have this kind of life. It's dangerous."

"I know . . ."

"From the beginning, you said you wanted a normal life, that you wanted your kids to have a regular childhood with tee-ball and soccer and spelling bees and everything."

"I know, Gertie . . ."

"So, I don't want you to think that the only way I'll be with you is if you do this dangerous thing for a chance to become a god," she continued. "I'll love you no matter what you do and no matter how we live our lives together. We will be together, if that's what you want, no matter what."

"Gertie," Hector cupped her cheek. "I'm not doing this for you. I promise. I'm doing this for me." He licked his lips and sighed. "When I left you last month, it wasn't because I didn't love you. It was because I didn't know who I was. And I needed to find myself. I've been floundering ever since. One day, I'd think I knew. The next day, I'd be at a loss. More recently, when you broke up with me because I said I should leave . . . I said that because I didn't want to hold you back."

"I understand that now."

"Just listen," he implored, pushing a strand of her hair behind her ear.

She sucked in her lips and looked up at him.

"I finally know who I am—or who I want to be. I can feel it deep down in my bones. I'm meant to be a god. I'm meant to advocate for demigods all over the world—to train them to be warriors and to teach them how to connect with their divine parents. I can already see this image of myself teaching the warriors to use song to move the gods, like I've moved them in the past. It's so clear to me, Gertie."

"Oh, Hector, that's amazing," she smiled, hoping he was right, that it wasn't just a dream. "I'll support you no matter what you decide, I just . . ."

He lifted her chin with the tip of his finger and said, "I remember the day you stepped off the bus from Patras. I didn't know at the time that I was already falling in love with you."

Tears filled Gertie's eyes. "Oh, Hector. I love you so much. And when I broke up with you, it wasn't because I didn't want to be with you. It was because I was scared, scared that you wouldn't be there for me." She glanced at Dionysus, who was talking with Athena across the room. "I've got daddy issues."

"I know. I do, too. I understand, Gertie. I really do. And I love you, too—so much. And I promise you that I will succeed in this. I'll become a god, and you and I will be together always."

She closed her eyes and touched her lips to his, relishing the feel of a kiss, not caring who saw it, and hoping with all her heart that he was right. She prayed to all the gods to please help him to succeed.

"Hector?" Athena called from across the room. "Are you ready?"

"Yes, my lady," Hector confirmed.

He squeezed Gertie's hands and gave her one more kiss before he left her side to approach the center of the council.

Gertie watched as Hector accepted the goblet from Hestia and put it to his lips. As he drank the ambrosia, his hair stood on end and became longer, thicker, and more lustrous, and his fair skin took on a golden hue. He rose up into the air, his arms stretched wide, where his muscles, already broad, grew broader. He became taller, his blue eyes brighter. Gertie hadn't believed Hector could be any more beautiful than he already was, but she'd been wrong. He was a masterpiece.

As proud as she felt for his decision to act as a decoy for Poros, Gertie was terrified. How horrible it would be for Hector to gain immortality only to be struck by one of Zeus's lightning bolts and rendered immobile forever.

Hermie sat on the cavern floor beside Del feeling anxious. Jinsoo hadn't texted him any new information, and Nike was watching him too carefully for him to attempt a text again. He wondered how much more time would pass before a rescue party arrived. It could be seconds, hours, days. The anticipation was almost too much to bear—especially because so much could go wrong, the first thing being Nike's destruction of the vampires.

Del shuddered again, and Hermie reminded himself to keep control of his thoughts. He needed Del to know that he had received her letter and had been so happy to read it. He hadn't had the chance to say he loved her back, but he hoped to all the gods that she could hear him now.

I love you, he thought. *I love you more than I've ever loved anyone. The love I feel for you is so different than anything I feel for anyone else. It actually hurts and feels amazing at the same time.*

I still remember the first time I saw you on the Tarantula, he thought. *I felt something even then. I didn't know what it was—a spark maybe. But I knew you were the most beautiful person I'd ever seen, and there was something in your eyes that made me suspect that you were just as beautiful on the inside.*

Del turned her head to gaze into his eyes. He could see that it took her great effort to keep her eyelids open.

It's okay, he thought. *Close your eyes and rest.*

She managed a weak smile before she closed her eyes again.

I will protect you and the others, if it's the last thing I do, he thought.

Metis groaned from her rock beside Lord Hermes's cage. The expression on her face reminded Hermie of Athena. She had the same long, raven hair and startling gray eyes, and—just now—consternated expression.

"Are you okay, love?" Hermes asked her.

"He's nearly to my throat," she said. "He'll be free soon. I'm in so much pain from him being in my esophagus that it's taking all my strength to resist vomiting."

"I'm sorry you're in this position, Metis," Hermes said to her. "I wish there was something I could do to help."

"Stop your whining," Nike rebuked from her post in the cave's center, where she hovered over the pool of water as she held the helm of invisibility.

The nymph who wasn't called Ida smiled and said to Nike, "Thank you for that, mistress. She was grating on my nerves."

"How did you manage to steal the helm?" Hermes asked Nike from his cage.

Nike laughed. "That was fun, let me tell you. Lord Zeus has a special potion that can change a god's appearance. The change will even trick another god."

"He's used that potion before," Hermes growled. "He tricked Persephone with it once."

Hermie knew the story. It was how Melinoe, his aunt and the goddess of ghosts, came into being. It was such a sad story about a selfish father's deception of his daughter and the pinning of the most heinous crime on his brother, Hades.

"It was easy enough for me to find it in his old room on Mount Olympus," Nike continued. "Once I had it, I drank it, and said the words Lord Zeus had instructed me to say. Then I went to the Underworld as Hades and told Megaera to fetch the helm for me. It couldn't have been easier."

Hermie's stomach felt like a knot. Zeus was the biggest a-hole on the planet, and he was about to break free from his prison.

Hermie, I love you, Del's voice said weakly in his head.

He looked down at her only to see her gasping for air. She needed blood, and there was nothing he could do!

Gertie followed Hector into Hephaestus's forge, where his father helped him dress in Poros's body armor.

"I'm proud of you for doing this," Hephaestus admitted to Hector as he was attaching the breast plate.

"I didn't think you cared," Hector said—a little harshly, in Gertie's opinion.

"I owe you an apology, son," the god of the forge said. "I acted selfishly, and I'm sorry."

Hector said nothing as Hephaestus tightened the breast plates.

"You see," the older god continued, "after I divorced Aphrodite and before I married Algaia, I had a relationship with a nymph who had a child that grew to despise me. He resented me for not marrying his mother."

"What has that got to do with me?" Hector retorted, as Hephaestus helped him into more of the armor.

"I suppose I expected you to resent me, too."

"I guess I did. Why did you even get together with my mom if you were already married?"

"Algaia and I had agreed to a separation for many, many years. We get along handsomely now, but we went through a rough patch. It was during that time that I met your mother and fell in love. I knew it was a mistake to give in to my feelings. She was mortal. We couldn't be together. But I was weak."

Gertie felt awkward standing there. She went to look around at the equipment in the forge, to pretend that she wasn't listening.

"The only way I could deal with my emotions was to stay away from her—and you," Hephaestus said. "I'm sorry I wasn't a stronger person for you—and for her. I should have been there. I should have allowed myself to feel the emotions I was trying so hard to smother. Instead, I made things easier for myself and so much harder for the two of you. I regret that, and I'm sorry."

From the corner of her eye, Gertie saw that Hector was trying very hard not to cry.

"That's the past," Hector said. "Let's focus on today."

Hephaestus clapped Hector on the shoulder. "Are you ready?"

"Never more," Hector said resolutely. "This is my destiny. I can feel it."

Hestie found Poros lingering outside of Hephaestus's forge as the other gods were preparing for battle.

"Are you okay?" she asked him.

"Just worried for Hector—for all of us, really. Why does my dad have to be such a jerk?"

"He's much worse than a jerk."

"Don't remind me."

"And you're the opposite of him in every way," she said, as she smoothed his hair from his eyes.

"I hope that's true."

"You know it is."

He leaned down and kissed her, sending shocks of heat and electricity throughout her body.

"If we somehow get separated. . ." he started.

"We won't let that happen."

"But suppose I end up in my father's belly."

"You won't."

"Only the Fates know with certainty what the future brings," he reminded her.

"You sound like my parents."

"Because it's the truth." He caressed her shoulder, slid his fingers down her arm, and took her hand in his. "If we somehow get separated, I'll be sorry, because of all the things I'm looking forward to doing with my life, sharing it with you is the most important."

"Oh, Poros." Hestie wrapped her arms around his waist and pressed her face in his neck. "I love you."

"I love you, too, Hestie. I have for a long time. I'm sorry I don't say it more often."

"You don't need to. I can feel it."

"That's a relief." He circled his arms more tightly around her.

She looked up at him through her lashes. "I remember when I first learned that you were Zeus's son."

"Yeah? What did you think?"

"How unlikely it seemed."

"Thanks a lot," he said sarcastically.

"Only because you didn't possess an ounce of his arrogance or selfishness. The more I got to know you, the more I saw the truth of that. Helping to get medicine to all those mortals without proper access to medical care. That's so amazing."

"I hope after this we can get back to that—if there is an after this."

"I hope so, too. I felt like it was my calling, too, to work alongside you and Captain."

"Speaking of Captain, I want to go and talk to him before we head to Crete."

Hestie followed Poros back into the main hall, where Athena was forming the teams. Hecate and Demeter had arrived to help, as had Ares's sons, Phobos and Deimos. Gertie would accompany Athena and Dionysus to the cave with Hector. Poseidon would lead a team to the labyrinth consisting of Hades, Thanatos, Therese, Artemis, and Apollo.

Ares would lead the group of reinforcements who would lie in wait to help where needed—either in the cave or in the labyrinth. This team was to include Hephaestus, Poros, Prometheus, Hecate, and Ares's sons. Aphrodite and her Charities, Demeter, and Hestia would protect Mount Olympus, with Psyche and Cupid on standby, if needed. Persephone and the Furies would guard the Underworld, with special attention to the Titan Pit. Jinsoo and the vampires would guard the gate with Cerberus. And Amphitrite, Poseidon's wife, along with their crew of Tritons, would protect Poseidon's underwater castle.

Hestie was disturbed to overhear that Morpheus and Iris were missing. She wondered if they'd gone looking for Hypnos and Jen.

Hestie turned to her mother. "What about me? I want to help, too."

"You're still recovering," her father said.

"Please," Hestie insisted. "I've got to go. Please don't leave me behind."

Her parents exchanged glances. Hestie prayed to them to please say yes.

CHAPTER SIXTEEN

The Decoy

Gertie flew beside Hector as Athena and Dionysus led them to the cave beneath Mount Ida. Gertie's heart was racing. Even though she was a goddess with powers, there was so much that could go wrong—and so much at stake, especially the lives of her vampire friends. She couldn't bear to lose another friend.

And even though Hector was temporarily immortal, how long would that protect him? What if he were paralyzed or swallowed and forced to suffer for all eternity? What if they both were?

Her heart skipped a beat, and she gasped for air.

Beside her, Hector asked, "You okay?"

"I'm fine," she said.

Gertie tried to focus on the beauty around her instead of on the danger she and Hector were flying toward. The afternoon sunlight sparkled on the sea below, the waves causing the light to flicker and dance like fireflies. A shimmering rainbow above Mount Ida added magnificent color to the already glorious landscape.

The entrance to the cave was tall and narrow, so the gods entered two at a time, with Hector and Gertie leading.

Gertie immediately spotted Del, Penny, Sophia, and Bach lying on the rocky bank of a pool. Hermie, who had been sitting on the ground beside Del, flew to his feet. He was cuffed and chained to the adamantine cage which still held Lord Hermes prisoner ten feet away. Sitting on a boulder beside the cage was Metis. She was doubled over in pain, looking as though she were about to be sick. Hovering over Metis's head was the winged goddess Nike. She held Hades's helm of invisibility in one hand and a shield in the other.

"They're here, my lord," Nike reported. "Should I signal the troops?"

To Gertie's horror, Zeus emerged to his waist from Metis's mouth, which was stretched impossibly wide.

"I'm nearly out," Zeus said gleefully.

"The troops, Father?" Athena asked. "What troops?"

"Oh, hello, Dionysus," Zeus said, ignoring Athena. "I wasn't expecting you to come."

"Well, I'm here," Gertie's father said. "And I can't say I'm surprised by you. Still looking out for number one, as always."

"Like father like son," Zeus taunted.

"Perhaps," Dionysus said. "Though I've always cared less about power and more about indulging in the pleasures of life. You've always managed to do both."

"Indeed," Zeus agreed. "And I don't intend to stop now." Then, looking down, he shouted, "Hera! Let go of my foot!"

"Should I give the signal, my lord?" Nike asked again.

"Go for it," Zeus said. "But didn't you want to take care of something, first?"

Nike smiled cruelly and pointed her shield toward the mouth of the cave, causing the cavern walls to shake, rocks to fall, and the opening to widen. A beam of sunlight shot into the darkness, directly at the vampires lying helplessly on the bank.

Gertie's friends shrieked with pain as Hermie tried his best to shield them from the sunlight. After trying to lift Sophia and finding herself too weak to do so, Penny flew into the shadows with tears in her eyes.

In that moment, Gertie instinctively loaded her bow and shot off four arrows, one after another, perfectly aimed at the hearts of each of her vampire friends. She felt the arrows infuse their targets with strength and protection from the elements.

Instantly the shrieking ceased. Penny rushed to Sophia, and all four looked at Gertie with surprise.

"Go!" Hermie cried. "Fly away!"

"Not so fast!" Nike made a dash through the air toward the vampires.

Gertie and her father attempted to intervene, but Nike put on the helm of invisibility and vanished.

Gertie took hold of Penny and Sophia. "Grab hands!" she cried to Bach and Del.

Athena rushed toward her mother and drew her sword on her father. "Tell me why I shouldn't kill you now."

"Let them go!" Zeus shouted to the invisible Nike.

Gertie god-traveled with the vampires to the Underworld, to the throne room, where Persephone was keeping guard.

"They need human blood," Gertie cried. "Please protect them. I'll be back."

As Gertie turned to leave, Bach said, "Thank you, goddess!"

Gertie smiled and then god-traveled to La Luna Rossa, where she knew some sailors who needed their fix.

Hermie had never been happier to see Gertie, or to see the back of Del as she flew away from him toward safety.

"Yes, let the vampires go for now," Nike said, as she reappeared with the helm in hand. "I'll find and kill them after my lord is free and his son Poros is trapped in his belly for all eternity."

Hermie glanced from Nike to Poros. So that was the plan? Zeus was going to swallow his own son? Hermie wished Jinsoo had been able to convince the others to heed his warning. Why had Poros come?

Then Hermie noticed two things that shocked him: the first was that the person wearing Poros's armor was not Poros. It was Hector, and he had undergone apotheosis. The second was that Lord Hermes had slightly opened the door of his adamantine cage before closing it again. No one else seemed to have noticed. Penny must have slipped him the key while Hermie wasn't watching.

Athena stood with her sword at her father's throat.

Hermie wished she would just get on with it. What was she waiting for? He supposed it wasn't easy to decapitate one's father, no matter how cruel he was.

"You don't stand a chance, my darling girl," Zeus mocked. "But try, if you must."

"Should I signal the troops, my lord?" Nike repeated.

"Signal away," he ordered.

As Nike disappeared, and Zeus looked down hollering, "I said let go, Hera. I won't leave you in there, my love. I promise. You'll have to trust me," Hermes flew at the speed of light to uncuff Hermie.

Don't let on that you're free, Hermes said before returning to his cage.

"There are no troops coming," Athena stated to her father, her sword still drawn.

Hermie hoped the goddess was right, but a sound near the entrance to the cave, along with the appearance of at least three dozen Cyclopes armed with lightning bolts, proved otherwise.

"Ah," Zeus smiled. "Here they are. Unhand me, or your precious Poros will be the first to feel my wrath."

Nike grabbed Hector from behind while two Cyclopes held his arms and a third pointed a lightning bolt at him.

Dionysus turned to Athena. "How did they escape Poseidon?"

Athena shook her head as Hermes flew as fast as lightning from the cave.

"How did *he* escape?" Nike cried from where she was still holding Hector.

"Don't worry about him," Zeus said. "Bring Poros to me, so I can swallow him once and for all. Then I will be the mightiest god again."

Three Cyclopes grabbed Dionysus while three more took ahold of Athena.

Then more Cyclopes entered with prisoners in tow: Ares and his sons, Phobos and Deimos.

Great, Hermie thought.

But that wasn't the worst of it. Hermie watched in terror as Zeus lifted one of his legs from Metis's mouth, hollering, "I said let go, Hera!"

Paralyzed and numb with fear, Hermie hadn't the slightest clue what to do.

Hestie followed her mother and father across the Mediterranean Sea toward the island of Crete. They'd wanted her to stay behind, because she was still recovering from her burns, but she couldn't. The anxiety over what might happen to everyone she loved had spurred her into action.

Besides, she knew the tunnels of the labyrinth almost as well as she knew the back of her own hand, having played in them with Hermie since she was a baby. Her parents would bring them every summer to visit Ariadne and Asterion.

Poseidon and Hades led the way, followed by Apollo and Artemis. Hestie and her parents took up the rear.

They entered the main tunnel leading to the cavern where Gertie had spotted the Cyclopes. But just as they entered, Hestie saw more Cyclopes armed with lightning bolts come in behind them.

"Mom! Dad!" Hestie cried.

"Scatter!" her father shouted.

Hestie turned into the first tunnel to her left and quickly flew through the web of tunnels she knew so well. She went right, left, and right, and kept going uphill at every turn. The Cyclopes that had begun to follow her had lost her and had turned back. Without night vision, they'd had to rely on the harsh light of their lightning bolts. Also, having only one eye, they lacked peripheral vision and depth perception. Those deficiencies, along with their unusually large bodies and short limbs, made them slow and clumsy. Plus, according to her parents, Cyclopes were not very bright.

The sounds of explosions brought Hestie to a stop. She tried to use her x-ray vision to see through the rocky walls of the tunnels, but Asterion and his sister had long ago warded them, making them impossible to see through.

Another series of explosions shook the cavern floors, causing rocks to loosen and fall to the ground. Hestie hoped that the earth-shattering sounds were caused by Poseidon's trident and not the lightning bolts. Scared but curious, she retraced her path toward the cacophony of sounds.

Before she reached the main tunnel, she stopped suddenly and hid when a stampede of Cyclopes thundered by, exiting the labyrinth. Where was the rest of her team?

After the stampede had passed, Hestie flew toward the largest cavern near the entrance to find the prisoners still bound against the wall in their adamantine chains and Hades, Poseidon, and her parents unconscious on the rocky ground, along with three Cyclopes.

"Hestie, are you okay?" Jen, tethered to the wall with the other prisoners, asked.

"Yes," Hestie said. "What should I do?"

"Listen to me," her uncle Hip spoke up. "The Cyclopes took the trident."

"You have to warn the others," Ariadne said.

"Now," Asterion added.

"Take Poseidon to Mount Olympus with the news and come back for the others once you've delivered it," Jen ordered.

"What happened to Artemis and Apollo?" she asked.

"We haven't seen them," Hip said. "Now hurry."

Hestie did as she was told.

Demeter, Hestia, and Aphrodite came to her aid on Mount Olympus. They laid Poseidon on a couch they had brought into the main hall from Demeter's rooms. While they did so, Hestie told them the news, and then Aphrodite helped her to return for Hades and her parents.

When she and Aphrodite returned to Mount Olympus with the other victims they discovered, to their great surprise, that Hermes had escaped and had news of his own. Although the news was mixed—the vampires had escaped but the Cyclopes had overpowered Athena and her team as Zeus struggled to free himself from Metis—he did have something with him that could change everything: the key to the adamantine cage, which he believed would unlock the cuffs on the other prisoners. Hestie took him to the labyrinth to free Hip, Jen, Ariadne, and Asterion, and, together, they went in search of Ares and his reinforcement team.

Gertie arrived in the throne room of the Underworld with four willing sailors—one for each of the dehydrated vampires who'd been waiting there. Just the very smell of human blood brought her languishing friends from their listless stupors. Like mad animals, they flew to their hosts and fed.

"Remember to stop after one pint," Gertie warned, wondering if she should have brought more people.

Persephone winced and looked away from the sight of the feeding vampires.

"It takes some getting used to," Gertie said to her.

Gertie had barely finished her sentence when Demeter appeared with an unconscious Hades in her arms.

"I thought he might recover more quickly surrounded by people he loves," Demeter said.

"Oh, Mother!" Persephone cried. "Was it a lightning bolt?"

"We think several," Demeter replied. "Thanatos and Therese were hit as well. I'll be right back with them, my dear."

Demeter vanished.

Gertie's heart began to race. "What went wrong? How did the Cyclopes overpower them during a surprise attack?"

"Go find out, Gertie," Persephone said. "And better yet, take one of the Furies with you."

Alecto appeared before Gertie had drawn her next breath.

"Ready?" Alecto asked her.

Gertie had a moment that was utterly surreal. It hadn't been that long ago when she had stood before Alecto with Nikita and Lajos and Hector. Gertie had been trembling in her shoes. And now, here she was a few months later, a goddess herself, going into battle with the terrifying Fury as her ally and comrade.

"Ready," Gertie finally said. "Let's go."

<u>CHAPTER SEVENTEEN</u>

Iris's Rainbow

Gertie and Alecto flew toward Crete in the clear, evening sky as Helios was beginning to descend in his golden cup behind them.

"Doesn't that rainbow look odd to you?" Alecto said of a gloriously large rainbow hovering just over Mount Ida.

Gertie thought it was beautiful but not odd. "What do you mean?"

"There isn't a cloud in the sky," Alecto continued. "Iris moves the rainbow to accommodate her when she refills her pitcher from the sea and adds the water to the clouds."

"Right. To create rain."

"And uphold the natural harmony of the elements," Alecto added. "So why is her rainbow there, at the center of our conflict with Zeus?"

"You don't think it's a coincidence."

"No. Let's check it out."

Gertie followed Alecto to the base of the rainbow near the top of Mount Ida. They took cover in the brush and picked their way through the shrubs. Within seconds, someone grabbed Gertie from behind and cupped her mouth to stifle her scream. The same had been done to Alecto. They exchanged looks of terror only to find that their captors were Artemis and Apollo.

"Quiet," Artemis ordered.

"What's going on?" Alecto demanded as she pushed Apollo away from her.

"Iris's rainbow was hijacked," Apollo said.

"She and Morpheus are prisoners inside," Artemis added.

"Whose prisoners?" Alecto asked.

"The Cyclopes," Artemis said. "There were twenty or thirty of them and only a handful stayed back. The others went to the cave below. They found Ares and his sons and took them prisoner, too. I think they took them to the cave."

"Oh, no," Gertie gasped.

"Nike must have used Iris's rainbow to transport the Cyclopes from their island," Apollo said. "Zeus trapped them there centuries ago because they can't swim or sail and are terrified of the sea."

"And yet they continue to be loyal to him." Artemis sighed.

Gertie glanced around the mountaintop. "What should we do?"

"We need to attack the Cyclopes inside the rainbow and find a way to free Iris and Morpheus," Alecto suggested. "Then we should round up more reinforcements to help us attack the herd of Cyclopes at the cave."

"Those cannibals are carrying lightning bolts," Artemis said. "They may be simple-minded and clumsy, but they can still do some damage."

"Look down there," Gertie said pointing. "Hermes is free, and so are the prisoners from the labyrinth."

"Let's enlist their help," Apollo proposed just before he flew away.

Since the others followed, Gertie did, too.

Hestie hugged Gertie on the top of Mount Ida, relieved to see her friend unscathed.

"I saved the vampires," Gertie said with a smile. "They're with Persephone in the Underworld."

"Thank goodness," Hestie exhaled. "Oh, Gertie, you're such a rockstar."

"This fight is far from over," Artemis said.

Hypnos nodded. "Tell us what to do."

Apollo quickly laid out a plan to infiltrate Iris's rainbow with the archers in the lead.

Hermes scratched his beard. "Let's do this."

Hestie watched in awe from behind as Gertie, Artemis, and Apollo led the attack. Their arrows flew to their targets faster than the Cyclopes could react. Then Hermes flew at the speed of light to confiscate the lightning bolts and to redistribute them to Hip, Jen, Asterion, and Ariadne. To Hestie's great relief, his key worked on the cuffs binding Iris and Morpheus. She hugged them as soon as they were free.

"Nike has the helm of invisibility," Iris, her golden wings trembling, warned.

"That's how she overtook us," Morpheus—his silver eyes wide against his bronze skin—added while his parents took him in their arms.

"We know," Hermes responded. "She's trying to free my father. He may be out by now. Let's hurry. They're in the cave below."

Together, they flew down the mountainside toward the hidden entrance to the cave, where they were faced with a wall of Cyclopes standing shoulder to shoulder, each holding a lightning bolt. Through the wall of bodies, Hestie saw her brother inside the cave still wearing his adamantine cuff and looking terrified. Metis was doubled over beside him with her mouth stretched as wide as a hula hoop. Zeus stood on her tongue with all but one foot showing. The foot seemed to be caught in Metis's throat.

But what was most alarming to Hestie was that Zeus held a lightning bolt in one hand and the trident in another, and hovering over him was his winged servant Nike with the helm. Zeus had the three most powerful gifts from the Fates at his fingertips.

Three Cyclopes held Hector in front of Zeus, who now opened his mouth wide. Zeus must be convinced that Hector was Poros and that by swallowing him, the other gods would submit to him, since he would once again be the most powerful. Hestie glanced around, wondering if Poros was nearby, ready to fight.

Where are you? she asked him.

Close, he revealed.

Unable to locate Poros, she turned her attention back to her brother who, to her surprise and horror, had conjured his sword and, just as Zeus leaned over Hector, cut off the arm of Zeus that was holding the trident. Then Hermie snatched the trident and struck Nike with it. As the winged goddess fell toward the pool of water below, he grabbed the helm from her and disappeared.

Had Hermie really done that?

The rest of the gods charged.

Hestie dodged lightning bolts, swung her sword, and decapitated a Cyclops. Then she saw Poros fly past her toward his father, who was still wielding his lightning bolt and striking toward his enemies from the mouth of Metis.

"Let go of my foot!" he shouted, unable to get free.

Poros flew directly into Zeus's line of fire and grabbed his father by the neck. Impervious to the blasts, Poros lifted his father from the body of Metis with Hera clinging onto Zeus's foot. Then Poros threw both gods into the adamantine cage and locked the door.

Zeus fired his lightning bolt at his son from inside the cage, but the warded adamantine rendered it useless.

"No!!!!" Zeus cried. Turning to Hera, he screamed, "This is your fault!"

"I'd rather be imprisoned with you than see you free and back to your old ways!" Hera shouted back.

The Cyclopes, seeing Nike paralyzed and floating in the pool of water and their lord trapped in a cage, dropped their weapons and scrambled away as fast as their short little legs could carry them.

Hestie followed Artemis, Apollo, and Hermes to herd the cannibals up the mountain toward Iris's rainbow, where they were transported back to their island home. Then Hestie followed her team back to the cave, where the other gods were celebrating with hugs and fist bumps while Zeus and Hera continued shouting at one another.

"I can't believe my own wife undermined me!" Zeus bellowed. "This failure is your fault. You disgust me!"

"I disgust *you*? We wouldn't be in this mess if you hadn't driven our children and siblings away with your selfishness!" Then Hera appealed to the other gods. "I made a mistake wanting to be with this monster. Let me out, and I promise you my support and allegiance."

"Unbelievable!" Zeus cried.

Poros lifted the cage in the air, causing the two gods to stumble and wail. Then he flew with the listless Nike and the adamantine cage into the dark sky. After collecting as many lightning bolts from the cavern floor as they could carry, Hestie and the other gods followed, shouting their victory cries. Hermes carried Metis. Gertie and Hector trailed behind, also laughing and shouting.

But where was Hermie?

Hestie asked, *Hermie? Where are you?*

I went to Mount Olympus to give Poseidon his trident and to the Underworld to give Hades his helm. Now, I'm with Del and Jinsoo and the other vampires. Mom and Dad are awake and here with me as well.

What a relief. You were amazing back there.

It was scary as hell.

And you did it, anyway. You rock, brother! You're the reason we won!

Not entirely, but thanks.

Why did you leave the battle?

Poros told me to. He didn't want the trident and helm falling into the wrong hands.

That makes sense.

When it was obvious Poros wasn't headed for Mount Olympus, Hestie asked, *Where are you going?*

I'm taking my father to the place where he belongs and should have been put in the first place.

The entourage of happy gods followed Poros through the nearest chasm leading to the Underworld, where Persephone and Hades, met by Poseidon and Aphrodite, were waiting. Hades opened the great iron door to the Titan Pit as Poseidon stood guard with his trident, and Poros threw the adamantine cage and the winged goddess inside before the door was shut and bolted again.

The other gods cheered. Hestie felt as though she might burst with pride for Poros.

"Now that my mother is free of my horrible father," Poros announced, "I hope she will live on Mount Olympus where she can be with my sister and where I can visit her as often as possible."

With tears in her eyes, Metis flew from the arms of Hermes to her son and kissed his cheek. Then she took Athena and Poros into her arms and said, "We're free at last."

Hestie was shocked by the transformation in Athena's features. She supposed she'd never seen the goddess truly happy. Athena's genuine smile coupled with the rare display of vulnerability had turned an already beautiful goddess into a stunning display. And Hestie wasn't the only one who had noticed.

By the look on his face, Prometheus had noticed, too.

Hermie borrowed his grandfather's chariot, pulled by the black stallions Swift and Sure, and drove with Jinsoo, Chidori, and the vampires though the night sky toward Syracuse, Italy. Even in the dark, Iris's rainbow was visible ahead, arching over the Ionian Sea where a cluster of clouds had gathered. Del sat between him and Bach on the front bench, where Hermie held the reins. She wore the loveliest smile on her face. He imagined it mirrored his own.

Once Hermie parked the chariot in the sky above La Luna Rossa, they all flew down to the docks and together, they entered the bar.

"Enjoy your meal," Hermie said to Del, as he looked for a place to sit with Jinsoo.

"I won't be long," Del replied before she kissed his cheek and left his side.

Not wanting to watch the love of his life seducing her food at the bar, Hermie scanned the room for a back table and spotted Lorenzo sitting alone in a corner nursing a mug of beer. Hermie beckoned Jinsoo to follow him as he crossed the room.

"Lorenzo, my old friend," Hermie greeted.

Lorenzo looked up and smiled. "Hello, Hermes."

"It's Hermie."

"Whatever, please join me, no?"

"This is Jinsoo," Hermie mentioned as he took a seat.

"And this is Chidori," Jinsoo gestured to the canary on his shoulder.

"A pleasure," Lorenzo said.

"I know it's too soon for you to donate blood again," Hermie noted, "so let me buy you a drink, and we'll commiserate together while Del spends time with someone else."

Lorenzo laughed. "Thank you, my friend."

Hermie raised his hand in the air to draw the attention of a waitress. It was then that he noticed Gertie and Hector entering with smiles and waving at their vampire friends. After the couple had greeted the vampires, they turned and sought Hermie and Jinsoo, who eagerly waved them over to their corner table in the back.

"We came to celebrate," Gertie said cheerfully as she slipped onto a seat beside Hermie.

Hector took an empty chair from a nearby table and sat between Gertie and Lorenzo. "Athena is hosting a party on Mount Olympus tomorrow, but we were eager to party tonight."

"Do I get to drink alcohol too, Hermie?" Jinsoo asked.

"Dude, you're a god," Hermie stated. "You can do as you please."

The others laughed at Jinsoo's comic expression. Chidori bit playfully at his ear.

The waitress arrived, and Hermie asked his friends, "Should we share a pitcher of beer?"

"Sounds awesome!" Jinsoo exclaimed.

"My favorite drink," Lorenzo said with a grin and a nod to his empty mug.

Gertie raised a fist. "Let's do it."

Hermie turned to the waitress. "Better make it two pitchers and five mugs, please."

<u>CHAPTER EIGHTEEN</u>

A Complication

Gertie hadn't realized that gods could get drunk on beer, but after their fifth pitcher of it at La Luna Rossa, she felt wasted. . . and very sleepy. After feeding, the vampires had pulled up a second table and additional chairs and joined them. Gertie hadn't wanted the night to end because she was having so much fun celebrating with her friends—except now she couldn't see straight.

"Do you think I could catch a ride in your chariot?" she asked Hermie. "I don't think I'm sober enough for flight or god-travel."

"I told you to slow down," Alastair grinned.

"I'll carry you home," Hector cut in. "I haven't had as much as you."

"Home?" Gertie asked, not sure where that was anymore.

"Back to my place in Athens," Hector said.

"Ooooh, back to his place," Bach teased.

Hector blushed as he added, "I promise to get us to Mount Olympus in time for Athena's party tomorrow."

"You don't want to miss it," Jinsoo noted to Hector. "I heard they're going to have a memorial for Raimo."

"Thank the gods," Del said with an expression that was bittersweet.

"On Mount Olympus?" Gertie asked, trying to hide how shocked she felt.

"Captain worked it out with Athena," Hermie shared. "Hades told me about it when I asked to borrow the chariot."

"I always liked Raimo," Lorenzo, who was even drunker than Gertie, stated.

"That's wonderful news!" Gertie shouted, and then grabbed her head to stop the spinning.

"Maybe we should get you home," Hector said.

Gertie nodded and turned to the others. "Thanks for letting us party with you."

"Thanks for joining us," Hermie said. "I meant it when I said I owe you everything."

Hermie put an arm around Del to indicate his meaning.

"I'd say we're pretty even," Gertie decided as she attempted to stand, only to fall into Hector's arms.

"I don't know," Penny said. "You were pretty bad-ass."

"She was," Hector agreed, "but Hermie did disarm Zeus and save my life in the process."

"So, we're all bad-ass," Gertie said. "See you tomorrow!"

"See you tomorrow!" Jinsoo called.

The others raised their mugs of beer. "See you tomorrow!"

Gertie allowed Hector to carry her. She closed her eyes and relaxed against him.

The next thing she knew, she was standing inside the Titan Pit. There were two groups of Titans huddled together, apparently having a party. They were laughing with such joy and bouncing around, giddy with glee. Some of them were screaming, too.

Gertie went to the iron door, hoping to sneak out unnoticed, but the door was locked. She was trapped inside with no place to escape.

Why had she been sent to the Titan Pit? Hadn't she helped the Olympians to prevent Zeus's uprising?

After searching her memories for an explanation, she concluded that she must be dreaming.

Less afraid, knowing now that what she was experiencing was *probably* a dream, she made a more conscientious effort to study her surroundings. Because she was unable to see anything but the backs of the celebrating Titans, she flew above them very quietly to get a better view at what they were doing.

Once at the proper vantage point, Gertie covered her mouth with shock. The first group was huddled around Nike, who lay half-conscious on the rocky ground at the feet of the Titans in a pile of white feathers that had once been her wings. Blood spilled from her back where her wings had been torn away. The Titans had also plucked her eyelashes, teeth, and nails and were now using them to cut and poke her skin and eyes.

The second group huddled around the adamantine cage containing Zeus and Hera. The god and goddess stood back-to-back in the center of the cage screaming, as the Titans took turns throwing stones at them and jabbing them with sticks and thin, white, bloody bones. Gertie realized the thin, white bones had been part of Nike's wings. The blood on them was partly Nike's but also partly Zeus and Hera's, for they were covered in scratches and cuts, and Hera was missing an eye. Zeus was also bleeding from his chin where someone must have grabbed his beard and pulled it off.

Gertie shuddered. Although Nike, Zeus, and Hera deserved to be punished for their crimes, they didn't deserve this. She needed to find a way to wake herself up so she could tell the others in case she was experiencing a prophetic dream.

Before she could think of what to do next, the iron door groaned open, and Hector entered. He was dragging Ladon, the one-hundred-headed snake, by a chain through the door. All one-hundred heads had been meticulously wrapped together like the branches of a store-bought Christmas tree to prevent the heads from moving. After the monster was inside the pit, Hector slammed the iron door shut.

"Back!" he shouted to the Titans. "Get back before I unleash this beast on you!"

The Titans scrambled to the recesses of the giant cavern.

As Hector moved across the pit, Ladon broke free of his chains, opened one of his one hundred mouths, and swallowed Hector whole.

Then Gertie opened her eyes and gasped, relieved to find herself in Hector's bed in his room in Athens with Hector snoring soundly beside her.

Hermie parked the chariot in the Underworld stables and the vampires helped him to unbridle Swift and Sure who were enjoying the special attention from Alastair and Bach.

"We'll take it from here," Bach offered.

"Good night, then," Hermie said. Then he turned to Del. "I know Hades and Persephone offered you one of their guest rooms, but how would you feel about spending the night with me?"

With new blood pumping through her veins, Del blushed, and it was supremely beautiful.

"Just to sleep," he clarified. "Or, if you can't sleep, you can lie there beside me while I sleep."

Del shrugged bashfully and then nodded. Relieved, Hermie took her hand and led her from the stables to his room.

When they were alone, he took her into his arms and kissed her like he'd been wanting to kiss her ever since he had first laid eyes on her.

Del kissed him back, but as he grew more passionate and out of control, she lifted her head away from his and said, "So this is sleeping, huh?"

Hermie grinned. "Okay, you got me. I was hoping for a little more."

"Hermie, I'm not that kind of girl."

"No, not that. I just meant a little more than sleep." He leaned in and kissed her again.

To his delight, she kissed him back.

As his emotions became more intense, he said, "Marry me, Del."

Del lifted her face away from his and gaped.

Feeling awkward now, Hermie said, "Please say something. You said you would always love me, no matter what. I feel the same way. Shouldn't we make it official?"

"It is too soon, Hermie," she said.

"But I thought you—"

"Too soon for *you*," she elaborated. "You forget that I'm much older than you. I know what I want." She gripped his shoulders and tilted her face up to his. "I've never met a kinder soul in a more beautiful package."

Hermie grinned. "Then—"

"But you need time to be sure. I have loved before. I have lived as a married woman, so to speak. You need more time to be certain that I am the one for you."

Hermie shook his head. "I don't need any more time."

Del smiled. "Will you take more time for me, because I'm asking you to?"

"Like how much time? A few days, weeks?"

"A year. If you still want to marry me one year from today, I will be more than happy to become your wife."

He supposed he could live with that. He pulled her close against him and asked, "Will you at least make out with me?"

Del laughed. "That we can do, Hermie. That we can—"

He pressed his mouth hard against hers and thought about all the things he looked forward to doing with her once they were a married couple.

Just when he began to question his self-restraint, there was a knock. With his godly vision, he could see through the door—though his wards prevented others from seeing inside—which revealed Hermes standing anxiously outside.

He opened the door. "Your timing literally could not be worse."

"I need your help, Hermie." Hermes glanced inside and noticed Del. "Excuse the intrusion, but this is important."

"Are you sure you don't want to stay the night here with me?" Poros asked Hestie outside of his room on Mount Olympus.

"Of course, I *want* to," she said, "but it wouldn't feel right."

He arched his brow. "It always felt right on the *Marcella II*."

She giggled. "Shhh. It was just Captain there. But here, well, I don't like gossip."

"Who cares what others say?"

"I do."

"It's not like we're sleeping together. We're just sleeping together."

Hestie guffawed. "Poros! Keep your voice down."

"Like that would make a difference."

"Yeah. I guess you're right. Anyway, we know what we are and aren't doing, but the others will speculate. And I can tell Pasithea is looking for any excuse to weasel her way in between us."

He held her more tightly in his arms. "It's been a long time since we've slept apart."

Hestie felt her cheeks burning. "I'll miss you."

"I miss you already."

As soon as he kissed her, she regretted her decision to leave, but she'd already told her parents she would be staying at home in the Underworld.

"Good night," she said.

"Good night."

"I'm so proud of you, Poros. You were amazing today."

He gave her his brilliant smile, his gray eyes sparkling. "Thanks. You weren't so bad yourself."

Hestie god-traveled back to her room in the Underworld, where Clifford, Noodle, Cubie, and Galen were waiting to greet her. They'd prepared a warm bath for her, complete with lit candles, and they waited for her in her room while she soaked.

She'd only been resting her bones in the warm water for a few minutes, however, when she received an urgent telepathic message from Gertie.

I've just had the most frightening dream, and I don't know what to do. I think it was prophetic.

Tell me about it, Hestie requested as she washed herself.

Hestie listened to the details of a horrid dream that took place in the Titan Pit, where the prisoners tortured Nike, Zeus, and Hera, and Hector was swallowed by Ladon.

What if the torture is already happening? Gertie worried.

Don't you think they're getting what they deserve? Hestie asked, having expected that the Titans would be happy to see their old enemies. *Think about what they did to the vampires and what Zeus almost did to Hector.*

Gertie said nothing in reply.

Gertie?

I guess I believe that there should be limits to punitive suffering, Gertie reasoned. *They're already locked in a pit for all eternity. Should they really have to endure physical brutality forever, too?*

Zeus didn't mind doing it to Prometheus.

I don't think we should make our decisions based on what Zeus would or would not do. We need higher standards.

Hestie thought about that for a moment. *Hmm. That's a good point. Why don't we sleep on it, and then tomorrow, you can bring it up to the council at Athena's celebration?*

But what about Hector and Ladon?

Maybe the dream is telling us what not to do.

Okay, Gertie said. *Thanks, Hestie.*

And Gertie?

Yes?

You really rocked it today. The more I get to know you, the more you amaze me. I'm so proud to be your friend.

Thanks, Hestie. That means a lot to me.

Good night.

Good night.

After her bath, Hestie dressed in clean clothes and climbed into her big bed to cuddle with her animals. But she found it hard to fall asleep as she imagined the torment the new prisoners of the Titan Pit were probably enduring. The more she thought about it, the more she came to agree with Gertie.

"You stay here," she said to the animals. "I'll be right back."

Hestie got out of bed and left her room. She flew past the bat cave and Hip and Jen's rooms and across the Phlegethon to the Titan Pit, where she stood outside the thick, iron door to listen.

She didn't have to wait long to hear the screams among the laughter. Hera's wails were especially disturbing.

"Hestie?"

Hestie jumped at the unexpected sound of someone calling her name. It was Hermie. He and Hermes were flying toward her from the Phlegethon.

"What are you two doing here?" she asked when they'd caught up to her.

Hermie turned to the messenger god, who said, "I'm being tormented by my father's desperate cries. I can hear him any time I fly near a chasm leading to the Underworld. I never meant for him to suffer like this. The Titans are relentless in their torture of him. Hermie knows the code to get in. I want to take a look inside."

"Without Hades?" Hestie asked. "That sounds like a bad idea."

"I have to know what's going on in there," Hermes insisted.

"I think I know." Hestie told them about Gertie's dream.

"Ladon?" Hermes repeated. "What a great idea. Ladon was always loyal to Hera when he guarded her golden apple tree in the garden of the Hesperides. We could put Nike in the same cage and have Ladon guard all three of them."

Hestie cocked her head to the side. "Do you really think Ladon would come willingly?"

"Absolutely not," Hermes said.

"Well, we've got to keep Hector away from him," Hestie warned.

But, deep inside, she wondered how much power they had to prevent prophetic dreams from coming true. So far, all of Gertie's dreams had been spot on.

CHAPTER NINETEEN

Remembrance

Gertie had a hard time falling asleep after her troubling dream, but she must have at some point, because the sound of running water awakened her to sunshine pouring in through Hector's upstairs bedroom window.

"Good morning, sleepyhead," Hector greeted from the doorway of his connected bathroom. "I was just about to wake you."

He turned off the tap at the bathroom sink and rejoined her in the bed.

"No fair," she said when he kissed her. "You've brushed your teeth."

"Your old toothbrush is still in there."

"I need a shower, too."

"I'll go make some breakfast," he offered. "I spoke with Lajos this morning, and he invited Nikita over. She'll be so happy to see you."

"Awesome!" Gertie said, perking up.

Her dream had continued to haunt her, and although she wanted to tell Hector about it, she would rather enjoy the morning with their friends and bring it up later.

Once she had showered and dressed, Gertie headed downstairs to the kitchen. Before she reached the bottom floor, she could hear the voices of her friends as though they were standing just beside her, and she could smell the eggs and sausage as though they were right in front of her nose.

"Hey, guys!" she cried when she entered the kitchen.

"Gertie!" Nikita squealed merrily as she skipped across the room for a hug. "Woah! You're buff!"

Gertie gave Nikita a squeeze. "It's so good to see you. I've missed you so much. Are you growing out your hair?"

Usually worn in a pixie cut, Nikita's dark hair nearly reached her shoulders.

Nikita stepped back. "You are seriously buff. And your hair has grown a lot more than mine has."

"You haven't told them?" Gertie questioned Hector.

"Told us what?" Lajos wanted to know, as he combed his fingers through his thick, red hair.

"I thought it was your news to tell," Hector said. "We haven't even discussed who you want to know yet."

"Know what?" Nikita asked with her eyebrows pushed together.

"They're our best friends," Gertie said to Hector. "Of course, I want them to know."

"Then spit it out!" Nikita shouted. "You're killing us!"

"Are you engaged?" Lajos asked.

Blood rushed to Gertie's cheeks, and she avoided Hector's gaze as she shook her head, "No!"

From the corner of her eye, she noticed Hector frown, so she added, "Not that I wouldn't want that—or that I do. I mean, not that being engaged would be a bad thing. What I mean is—"

"Gertie, tell us your news!" Nikita insisted.

"We're gods," Gertie blurted out.

Nikita and Lajos both took several steps back.

"You're what?" Lajos asked.

"Technically, I'm not a god yet," Hector said, as he scooped the steaming, scrambled eggs from the pan onto a platter. "I've still got to prove myself. But we've both undergone apotheosis, and Gertie is a full-blown goddess—the goddess of vampires."

Gertie allowed her goddess form to show a tiny bit—not enough to blind them, just to prove that she wasn't making stuff up.

Nikita fell to her knees and began to tremble.

"I didn't mean to scare you." Gertie rushed over to her friend and helped her up to her feet.

Nikita covered her heart and started hyperventilating.

"Just give us a chance to take it all in," Lajos said, as he rubbed Nikita's back, trying to calm her down.

"I'm sorry," Hector apologized. "We should have broken this to you more gently."

"I don't think there's an easy way to tell your best friend something like that," Lajos said. "That is, if we are still best friends. Aren't we? Or will you live on Mount Olympus now?"

"We're definitely best friends," Hector said. "If I pass my final tests, I don't know where I'll live." He glanced nervously at Gertie. "We haven't discussed that yet."

"I want to live with the vampires," Gertie said. "I'm sure Hermes will get them a new ship."

"And I want to live wherever Gertie lives," Hector continued. "But I'll keep this house, and you can live here for however long you want."

"That's not what I was worried about," Lajos said. "I'm just wondering how often we'll see each other."

"I won't let anything get in the way of our friendship," Hector said.

"Me, too," Gertie said to Nikita. "It will be easy now to go back and forth. I can fly, I can god-travel, I could even borrow a chariot—maybe. Well, probably not. But anyway, isn't it great?"

Nikita continued to frown. "I don't know how to be friends with a goddess. Am I supposed to worship you?"

"I didn't do this to be worshipped," Gertie said. "I did this to serve. I'm the same person, Nikita. I haven't changed."

Nikita took a few steps back toward Gertie. "You *have* changed."

"But I'm the same person inside," Gertie insisted.

"Promise?" Nikita asked.

"Promise. Now let's eat before everything gets cold."

Hermie stood beside Del and his sister in the great hall of Mount Olympus, where ribbons and flowers decorated every pillar, and tables laid with platters of food and drink gave the temple a festive feel. In the center of the circle of thrones stood Prometheus with an unlit torch beside a small, round altar.

Behind Prometheus, Athena towered over all on the dais before her double throne—the seat that once belonged to Zeus and Hera. Her mother, Metis, sat where Hera once sat. Below her, the muses sang a song as the rest of the gods and goddesses were arriving. The major Olympians took their seats at their thrones once they entered, and the other gods stood by them or lingered near the narthex. Hermie and Del and their group of friends, including the vampires, who now wore new motorcycle gear, stood next to Demeter's double throne, where Hades and Persephone sat. Hermie's parents and other members of the Underworld family stood nearby as well. Asterion and Ariadne stood across the hall from them near Hermes.

Athena nodded to the muses, and they quickly ended their song. Then the hall quieted.

Athena lifted her arms and said, "Welcome to our celebration of life and valor. Ironically, we are here today to memorialize Victory—her defeat and our triumph."

Many of those present cheered and clapped.

Athena continued, "The first part of our gathering is a celebration of life, specifically the life of Raimo Baros, who was tragically killed during one of Nike's attacks. Raimo was loved by his friends, who were more like family, and he served his lord, Hermes, faithfully until the end. He will be missed and remembered by all. And, today, he will be honored with the torch of life. Prometheus?"

Prometheus held the unlit torch high into the air. "I call upon Helios to supply our flame."

As Helios appeared in the sky above Mount Olympus and pointed his finger a shot of fire flew from his fingertip and lit the torch.

Prometheus said, "May perpetual light shine upon the soul of Raimo Baros as he joins his family in the Underworld. May he rest in eternal peace."

Although the vampires' faces were covered by their motorcycle helmets, Hermie could hear them weeping quietly behind their masks. Del, who stood close beside him, had begun to tremble. He put his arm around her shoulders to steady her.

"And now, Helios will hide behind the clouds so the vampires may remove their helmets," Athena said. "They would like to honor Raimo's memory with a song."

Helios disappeared. Prometheus left the altar to stand beside Poros and Jinsoo. The vampires removed their helmets. Hermie gave Del an encouraging smile. She smiled back and squeezed his hand.

Then Alastair began in his rich bass voice:

While you live, shine.
Have no grief at all.
Life exists only for a short while,
And Time demands his due.

Then the others joined in, with a lovely harmony:

The rain descends, and from high heaven
A storm is driven:
And on the running water-brooks the cold
Lays icy hold:
Then up! beat down the winter; make the fire
Blaze high and higher;
Mix wine as sweet as honey of the bee
Abundantly;

Then drink with comfortable wool around
Your temples bound.
We must not yield our hearts to woe, or wear
With wasting care;
For grief will profit us no whit, my friend,
Nor nothing mend;
Think not on what we have lost,
But rejoice that we once had.
For grief will profit us no whit,
Nor nothing mend.

As Hermie listened to the incredible voices of his friends, tears formed in his eyes. He and the crew from the *Marcella II*, which had included the vampires for a while at least, had been through so much together in just a few months. Growing up, he and Hestie had been isolated from other kids because of their unusual gifts. Days after they were born, they could talk, and within a few months, they could walk. Except for his online gaming friends, whom he'd never met in person, Hestie was all he ever had. His cousin Morpheus had paid them the occasional visit, and his older cousin Lynn had sometimes been around. But he hadn't seen them daily like most kids saw their friends at school.

Then a year ago, he met Jinsoo, Mina, Poros, and Captain, and he learned what he'd been missing. And now he had more friends than he'd ever imagined possible, and he cared deeply for each one of them. He hoped their destinies would keep them together, so they could continue to enjoy each other's company for many years to come.

"That was lovely," Athena commended the vampires when they had finished. "Thank you. Let's give them a round of applause."

The hall filled with the sounds of laughter and clapping.

"Next," Athena continued, "I want to congratulate everyone here today for the part each played in stopping my father's attempt to return.

Our success depended on contributions from each of you, so you should be proud to have helped restore stability to our pantheon."

More cheers and applause filled the hall.

"Although we all helped stop my father and Nike," Athena recounted, "there are three among us who deserve special recognition. The first is Hermie."

A lump formed in Hermie's throat as he looked up at Athena.

"Thank you for acting so quickly to disarm my father of the trident and Nike of the helm," she said.

The room erupted in applause, and several shouted, "Hear, hear!"

Del beamed at Hermie and patted him on the back. His parents smiled proudly at him.

His sister grinned and said, "Way to go, bro'."

Chidori flew from Jinsoo's shoulder to perch on Hermie's, where she kissed his earlobe.

Hermie laughed and said, "Thank you, everyone."

Athena then pronounced, "Second, I want to thank Hector for the role he played as decoy. It took a lot of guts to put his life on the line, and for that, we will always be grateful."

More applause and cheers erupted for Hector.

Hermie noticed Hephaestus give his son an approving nod.

"And finally," Athena declared, "I'd like to recognize my brother, Poros, the mightiest among us, for his bravery in facing our father head on."

An even louder display of applause and cheers filled the hall. Athena beckoned to her brother to leave Hestie's side to join her and their mother on the dais before the double throne. Poros made his way to stand beside his sister. His mother stood on the other side of him, and the three held hands.

The sight of Poros standing beside his mother and sister looking so happy and relieved filled Hestie with joy. As she clapped for him alongside the other gods and vampires present, tears of pride filled her eyes. He had fought bravely, and he deserved this happiness.

When the applause died down, Athena said, "There is one other god who deserves recognition, and that is Hermes. His quick thinking made everything else possible. For this reason, I ask the council that he be pardoned for his acts of treason against us, when he acted independently to destroy two STS ships. As hurtful as his actions were, he has made it up to us with his bravery against Nike and Zeus."

"Hear, hear!" several of the Olympians cried.

"All in favor?" Athena asked.

The temple resounded with the assent of gods.

"All opposed?" the goddess of wisdom asked.

The temple was silent.

Hestie was glad to see Hermes forgiven and smiling happily on his throne.

"Thank you, Athena," Hermes said. "And thank you, fellow Olympians. Before we end our meeting and begin the eating and the dancing, there is one important concern I'd like to bring before the council."

Hestie bit her lip, worried that Gertie would be mad at her when she learned that Hestie had shared the details of her dream with Hermes, as he now shared them with the entire pantheon.

Gertie glanced at her and gave her a nervous smile, which put Hestie at ease.

"I had the same dream," Apollo announced when Hermes had finished.

Hestie covered her mouth and looked again at Gertie, who was busy explaining herself to Hector. Apparently, she hadn't told her boyfriend about the dream. It must have been hard for him to hear such a terrifying prophecy in front of everyone gathered.

"There are two things that concern me about this dream," Hermes concluded. "One is the perpetual torture my father, along with Hera and Nike, may be enduring in the pit."

"That's the point," Hades said. "It's time they met their just desserts."

"What did Hera do?" Hestia, who rarely spoke up at council meetings, questioned. "The only thing she's guilty of is being devoted to her husband."

"Hear, hear," Aphrodite agreed.

"No one deserves to suffer relentlessly for all eternity," Hestie's mother, Therese, challenged. "That's why we reformed the policies in the Underworld and made it possible for souls to leave Tartarus to spend the rest of their eternal lives in the Elysian Fields, remember?"

"Exactly," Hermes said. "Do my brothers and sisters not hear the desperate cries of our father any time you go near the Underworld? Are you not moved to pity?"

"I heard my sister's cries in my sleep," Hestia admitted.

"I did, too," Demeter said. "I can't bear another night of it. Something must be done."

"I've heard my brother," Poseidon conceded. "And as much as I hate him for what he's done, I don't completely blame him for wanting to regain his power. I do pity him though, and I've always felt grateful for the day he saved us from our father's belly."

"My father and I had some good times," Ares said.

"Likewise," said Hermes. "His list of flaws may be long, but he is not without good in him. He, Hera, and Nike must be protected from this endless torture."

"Can we address the second troubling part of my dream?" Gertie asked, with her hand in the air.

"The idea of bringing the sea monster Ladon into the pit to guard the adamantine cage with all three Olympians inside is a good one," Hermes mused, "however, Hector cannot be the one to do it."

"I disagree," Athena said. "It's the perfect opportunity for him to prove he's worthy to remain one of us."

"She speaks the truth," Apollo confirmed. "Only the Fates know for certain what the future holds. The dream hints at what *may* be, and not necessarily at what *will* be."

"That's not very reassuring," Hephaestus said. "Why must Hector, the least experienced among us, carry this responsibility alone?"

"We wanted a challenge for Hector," Hades said, "and one has fallen into our laps."

"It feels like it was destined," Poseidon shrugged.

"I'll do it," Hector cried. "Please, my lords and ladies, grant me this chance. I won't let you down."

"It's decided, then," Athena said. "Now, shall we eat and be merry?"

CHAPTER TWENTY

Hector's Challenge

Gertie was terrified for Hector. The details of her dream had felt so real. And as much as she wanted Hector to succeed in joining her in the pantheon, she was horrified by the thought of Ladon swallowing him whole. It would mean Hector's death. It would mean the end of the boy she loved. So far, every one of her dreams had come true. This seemed like an impossible pursuit.

She quickly raised her hand and asked the Olympian council, "Can the terms of Hector's challenge be made clear? For example, can he accept help from friends?"

"I propose this," Athena began. "That no physical intervention or aid be allowed. Hector can accept advice and encouragement. He can even take a few friends to cheer him on. But he must carry out the challenge on his own. Any physical intervention from another while he attempts to capture Ladon will immediately revoke his immortality."

"Hear, hear," Hades said. "I like those terms."

"Hear, hear," Hermes echoed.

"Is there a deadline?" Gertie asked. "What if it takes him a week or a month?"

"A month is too long," Ares interjected.

"A week is too long," Hermes said. "A few days and no more."

"Three days," Artemis decided. "That seems fair."

"Three days," Ares agreed.

"Can I use weapons?" Hector asked.

"Absolutely," Hephaestus said. "Any weapon should be at his disposal."

"Any weapon he has access to," Poseidon clarified. "He can't take my trident."

"Nor my helm," Hades added.

"He can take my lightning bolt," Poros offered.

"There are dozens from the Cyclopes locked in the armory," Apollo said. "However, we don't want Ladon paralyzed. That would defeat the purpose of this mission."

"May I borrow your shield?" Hector asked Athena. "The special one with the head of Medusa on it?"

"We don't want Ladon turned to stone either," Athena frowned.

"Not permanently, no," Hector said. "I have an idea." He turned to his father. "And I'll need that adamantine chain you've been working on in your forge."

Gertie met Hector's gaze. There was only one way to undo the effect of Medusa. Did he intend to steal the eye of the Cyclops Polyphemus?

"I volunteer to go with Hector," Poros said.

"Me, too," Hestie offered.

"And me," Gertie said quickly, before someone else took the final spot.

Hector frowned. Telepathically, he said to Gertie, *I don't want you to come. It's going to be dangerous.*

"No, no, no, you don't," Gertie said aloud, wagging a finger at him. "Of course, it's going to be dangerous. While I understand you want to protect me—that's all you've wanted since we met—we're in this together. Being gods is dangerous. We'll protect each other."

"Hear, hear!" Aphrodite shouted.

Hector glanced at Hermie.

"Don't look at *me*," Hermie sputtered at Hector. "I hate the sea and everything in it."

"Not everything," Hestie said. "Not dolphins."

"I stand corrected," Hermie sighed. "I hate *almost* everything in the sea."

Beside him, Del and Jinsoo laughed.

"No offense," Hermie quickly said to Poseidon.

The god of the sea rolled his eyes.

"With that settled, let the party begin!" Athena exclaimed happily.

The gods cheered and made their way to the tables to graze on the food and wine. The muses began to sing, and Aphrodite and Ares danced a slow song together.

Gertie couldn't understand how anyone could be laughing or feeling merry when Hector had just accepted a challenge that might mean his death. How could the party still go on?

Her stomach was in knots. She thought she might be sick.

Hector turned to her and lifted her chin with his finger. "Don't look so sad. Don't you think I can do it?"

She forced a smile. "Yes, I know you can."

"Good. Because I've got this figured out. Trust me."

She nodded. "I do trust you, Hector. I know you've got this."

"Then dance with me?"

She took his hand and allowed him to lead her to the center of the room, where they danced together beside Ares and Aphrodite.

"Isn't young love sweet?" Gertie overheard Aphrodite say to Ares.

"Yes, but old love is better," the god of war replied with a mischievous grin.

Although her stomach hurt and her knees felt weak, Gertie buried her head in Hector's chest and tried to hold herself together.

Hermie wasn't much of a dancer, but he wanted an excuse to hold Del in his arms and a slow dance was just the thing.

"Care to dance?" he asked her.

She followed him to the middle of the great hall and circled her arms around his neck. He pulled her close as he swayed to the music.

"You do not seem worried about Hector," Del remarked.

"No. He has a sound plan."

"What do you know of his plan?"

"He's been talking with me telepathically."

"Oh?" Del arched a brow. "Care to share?"

Hermie chuckled. "Well, you see, everyone assumes he's going to steal the eye of Polyphemus the Cyclops, because it's the only thing that can break Medusa's spell."

"And he isn't?"

"No. He's going to ask to borrow it."

Now it was Del's turn to chuckle. "Why would the Cyclops give up his only eye?"

"He might do it in exchange for a state-of-the-art surround-sound entertainment system from yours truly."

Del cocked her head to the side. "I do not know about this plan, Hermie. From what I have heard, the Cyclopes are primitive cannibals who lead simple lives with their flocks of sheep. What if the Cyclops says no?"

"I hadn't thought that far ahead," Hermie admitted, because he couldn't think of anyone who wouldn't want a state-of-the-art surround-sound entertainment system.

"I hope Hector has a Plan B," she said.

Hestie took the glass of wine that Poros offered. "Thank you."

Pasithea came up from behind Poros and asked, "May I have this dance?"

Hestie forced a smile and tried to hide the fact that she was pissed. She didn't like being the jealous type, but if Poros were to say yes to the forward Charity, Hestie would be even more pissed.

"No, thank you," Poros said. "I'm not interested in dancing with anyone but Hestie, so please don't ask me again."

Pasithea harumphed and raised her chin as she walked away.

Hestie laughed and shook her head. "She won't be the last admirer, you know. You're the mightiest of all the gods. That makes you desirable to every unmarried goddess."

"You're the only admirer I care about." He kissed the tip of her nose.

"So, do you really want to dance with me?" she asked him.

Before he could answer, Hector approached with Gertie and Hermie on his heels.

"There's no time to lose," Hector said. "Do you mind cutting your celebration short?"

"Surely, the clock doesn't start ticking until after the party," Poros pointed out.

Gertie leaned forward. "Poseidon has arranged for a friendly meeting with his son, Polyphemus. He wants us to go with him now."

"If you'd rather stay," Hector began, "I'll understand. Hermie has agreed to come."

"Of course not," Hestie replied. "We said we'd help, and we will. Lead the way."

Hestie followed the others from the great hall, across the plaza, and to the stables, where Poseidon was waiting by his chariot. The sea god quickly finished bridling his three white mares—Seaquake, Riptide, and Crest—and then they all hopped into the chariot and took off for Cyclopes Island in the Ionian Sea.

While they were flying across the Mediterranean, Hestie turned to her brother. "I thought you weren't going to help."

"Hector has asked for a special favor that only I can do," he said. "And I don't mind doing it at all."

"What favor?" she prodded.

"You'll see."

Poseidon parked the chariot in the sky above the hilltop beneath which Polyphemus's cave could be found, not far from the shore.

"Come on, yer dirty mops!" the Cyclops was shouting to his two-dozen sheep as he attempted to corral them back toward his cave. "It's nearly sundown, yer muts. Yer should know when to go in by now."

Poseidon led the way to the sandy bank. "Polyphemus! Over here!"

"Father!" the cannibal said gleefully, as he lumbered across the sand and rocks toward them. "I didn't think yer'd come, too. Yer never come."

"Well, I'm here now," the sea god said. "And we need a favor."

Polyphemus frowned. "Why is it yer only come when yer need somfin?"

"I want to give you something in return," Hector said. "A gift greater than the one I ask of you. How would you like your very own state-of-the-art surround-sound entertainment center?"

"A what-a-what?" Polyphemus asked as he scratched his backside.

Hestie's heart sank. If Hermie had told her the plan, she would have warned him that it wasn't a good one.

Hermie stepped forward. "You'd have access to music, movies, television shows, and video games. You'd never be bored again."

"What is it yer want from me?" the Cyclops demanded.

"Your eye," Hector bargained. "But only for today. I'll bring it back tomorrow—or the day after at the latest."

"My eye? *My* eye? Yer do see I only got one, don yer?"

"That's why I'm offering you such a generous gift in return," Hector explained, looking a bit flushed in the face.

"Son?" Poseidon began. "At least he's asking nicely and not just taking it, as others have done in the past. Can you find it in your heart to work with him?"

"Do I get ter eat him if he loses it?" Polyphemus asked.

"Yes," Hector said. "You have my word."

"Hector!" Gertie scolded. "Why would you agree to that?"

"Swear on the River Styx," Polyphemus demanded.

Hestie tried to dissuade Hector by fervently shaking her head and saying telepathically, *Don't do it.*

"I swear on the River Styx," Hector stated. "If I lose your eye, you can eat me."

"And I want a refrigerator to keep my mutton chops cold," the Cyclops added.

Hector glanced at Hermie, who nodded.

"Done!" Hector said.

"Can I get it in stainless steel?" Polyphemus asked.

"Of course," Hermie confirmed. "With an automatic ice maker built into the freezer side."

The Cyclops smiled. "What about granite countertops?"

"No, sorry," Hermie said.

Polyphemus hung his head. "Alright, alright. Yers can have my eye. But I want the refrigerator first."

"Lead the way to your abode, kind sir," Hermie said.

Hestie followed the others to the cave, which smelled like rotten fish and was stacked with all manner of objects that had likely been brought in by the sea: old shoes without partners, empty cans, fishing rods, an anchor, books with bloated pages, life buoys, cushions, clothes for both men and women, and trunks and chests that may have been filled with treasure—Hestie couldn't tell.

"Where would you like it?" Hermie asked about the refrigerator.

"Here." The Cyclops pointed to a bare spot across from his hearth.

Hermie worked his magic, Polyphemus handed over the eye, and then Poseidon flew away, leaving Hestie and her friends on their own to help Hector to finish his challenge.

As he flew away in his chariot, Poseidon shouted, "Hermes and I are meeting with the authorities to discuss STS. Wish me luck, and I'll do the same for you. Gods know you need it more than I do!"

CHAPTER TWENTY-ONE

Ladon

Standing on the bank of the Ionian Sea not far from Polyphemus's cave, Hestie asked Hector, "So, how does Athena's shield work? I've looked at it before, hanging over Poros's bed, and it didn't turn me into stone."

Gertie had been wondering the same thing.

"You have to push a lever," Poros explained. "The lever removes the cover over Medusa's eyes."

"It's her eyes that turn you," Hector added. "Athena showed me what to do when she loaned it to me. I have the power to conjure it at will."

He held out his hand and demonstrated.

"It's a beautiful shield," Gertie commented. "Let's hope it works."

"Of course, it works," Hector said.

"But how do you know?" Gertie prodded. "I think we should test it."

"You want him to turn some poor, innocent creature to stone?" Hestie asked.

"He's got the eye of Polyphemus," Gertie pointed out. "I just think it would be wise to test the process. Don't you?"

"I agree," Hermie said. "There's a stray sheep up ahead that didn't make it home."

Gertie would have suggested a beetle or a sand crab, but she supposed the sheep would do. She watched expectantly as Hector pointed the shield at the sheep and pushed the lever near the handle.

"Here, sheepie, sheepie, sheepie," Hector cooed to attract the beast's attention.

The animal looked up from where it had been eating grass and instantly turned to stone.

"It works!" Hermie cried.

"Now turn him back," Hestie said.

Hector hesitated. Turning to Gertie he asked, "Do you remember the words?"

Before Gertie could reply, Polyphemus came storming from his cave waving a huge club.

"Why yer good-for-nuttens stole my mutton and made her a rock! Give me back my eye!"

The group of gods fled the island before the poor sheep could be turned back.

From where they hovered in the sky, Hector said, "Let's just go to Phorcys's old castle. At least we know the shield works."

"Lead the way," Poros said.

"This is where I take my leave," Hermie cut in. "Good luck, Hector!"

"Thanks for your help, bro'."

"You're welcome. I know you got this. I'll meet you at the door to the pit."

The two friends bumped fists, and then Hermie disappeared.

As they flew toward the part of the Ionian where Phorcys once lived, Gertie said to Hector, "Don't expect to swim up to Ladon and show him the shield. It's not going to be that easy."

"Where's the trust?" he asked with a grin.

"You might have to fight off his sisters: Chimera, Echidna, and Charybdis. Are you ready for that?"

He conjured his sword and lifted it into the sky.

"Ready as I'll ever be," he confirmed with a wink.

She wished he was taking this more seriously. His over-confidence could do him in.

When they reached the middle of the Ionian, the young gods dived into the water and followed Hector to the bottom where the old, primitive castle rested covered in barnacles.

Gertie had only ever swum in the sea as a vampire, and vampires were unable to hear underwater; however, as a goddess she could hear everything—every swoosh of a sea anemone on the ocean floor, every sting of a jelly fish, and every snap of a turtle. She could also hear the pitter patter of crabs as they scoured the ocean floor for food.

Approaching the old castle, Gertie could hear the monsters inside. She wondered if Hector had a plan.

Do you intend to sneak inside or lure them out? she asked him telepathically, hoping he wasn't making things up as he went along.

Just then, something circled around her from behind and dragged her out, out, out into the sea. Gertie screamed when she realized Echidna's serpent tail had coiled around her, pinning her arms to her side and rendering her helpless.

Echidna swam fast and far before emerging in a cave above the surface. She dragged Gertie from the water to the back of the cave.

Gertie was surprised to see that the others had kept up with them. They joined them in the cave, keeping their distance.

"I'll bite off her head if you come any closer," the half-woman, half-snake warned.

"What do you want?" Hector asked.

"Why have you come to my home?" Echidna snapped.

Hector glanced at Hermie and Poros before turning back to Echidna and saying, "We came to see Ladon. I need a favor."

"I can smell the eye of Polyphemus in your pouch tied at your waist," the sea monster snarled. "Give it to me, and I'll let her go."

"Why do you want it?" Hestie asked.

"I want to eat it," she said. "What's it to you?"

"Don't do it," Gertie warned Hector. "Just go. I'll find a way to fight her off."

"Is there something else I can give you?" Hector asked the snake woman. "Something else you want more than the eye?"

"You," she replied. "I'll forego the eye if you take the girl's place."

"Deal," Hector said without hesitating.

"Hector, no!" Gertie shouted. "What are you doing?"

"Swear," the monster insisted. "Swear on the River Styx that if I let her go, you'll take her place."

"I swear on the River Styx," Hector echoed.

Gertie couldn't believe it. He'd failed his challenge before he'd ever begun, and it was all because of her. It was her fault that he had failed. He'd given everything up to save her.

Hector gave the eye of Polyphemus to Hestie and Athena's shield to Poros. "Finish what I started. The prisoners in the pit still need protection."

Gertie clung to Echidna. "No! I don't concede to the trade!"

Echidna laughed and pushed Gertie away as she coiled her serpent's tail around Hector. "Go away, little girl."

"I'm not a little girl!" Gertie shouted. "I'm a goddess. And—"

Before Gertie had finished her sentence, Echidna's coiled tail slackened, and Hector flew away from her, grabbing the shield from Poros and the eye of Polyphemus from Hestie.

"Come on!" he cried to his friends.

Flabbergasted by his impossible escape, it took a moment for Gertie to snap out of it. What had just happened?

Hestie followed Hector and the others to the depths of the Ionian Sea toward Phorcys's castle wondering who had helped Hector from beneath the helm of invisibility—for someone had. There was no other explanation for his miraculous escape.

As soon as they arrived, Hector kicked in the door, swung his blade at Chimera, and flashed Athena's shield at Ladon, who immediately turned to stone. Hestie held back the urge to defend him as Chimera attacked again, but Hector was quick with his sword and sliced off one of her legs. Then, he quickly wove the adamantine chain around the one-hundred-headed beast and dragged him from the castle.

It was impressive, to say the least.

Hestie could hear Gertie's shouts of glee as she followed her friends into the sky and then down into the nearest chasm to the Underworld.

Hermie met them at the door to the Titan Pit, where he entered the code that unlocked the twelve steel bolts. Hades came to guard the door while Hestie, Poros, and Gertie followed Hector inside.

The scene that unfolded before them was eerily like the details from Gertie's dream. Two groups of Titans were huddled together, bouncing with excitement. Hestie could only imagine what they were doing to their victims. They were so into their torture they hadn't even noticed that anyone had entered the pit, much less a twelve-foot statue of a one-hundred-headed serpent.

But before they had gotten very far inside, Hector stopped, patted his trousers, and cried, "My bag! Where's my bag? It was tied to my belt loop! The Cyclops's eye was inside it!"

Hestie's heart sank.

"Oh, my gods, Hector," Gertie, whose face was as white as the wool on Polyphemus's sheep, said. "You swore an oath not to lose it."

"Um, guys?" Poros muttered quietly.

Hestie turned to Poros, only to notice that the Titans had stopped what they were doing and were staring at her and her friends with hungry, evil looks.

"Let's get out of here," Poros whispered.

Hestie thought to her brother, who was waiting outside the iron door, *Let us out, now!*

The Titans swarmed them as the great iron door opened. Because it was impossible to god-travel in and out of the pit, Hector had to drag Ladon out while fighting off the angry Titans, and there was nothing Hestie and the others could do to help him without compromising his challenge. Fortunately, Hades was there on the outside to prevent any prisoners from escaping. However, the lord of the Underworld hadn't had to lift a finger. Hector managed to get out with Ladon and close the iron door while keeping the Titans back. But Ladon was missing at least four heads. The Titans must have broken them off in the scuffle.

"What happened?" Hades demanded.

Gertie filled him in.

"And what will you do now?" Hades asked Hector.

"I'll be right back," Hector said, and before anyone could stop him, he disappeared.

"I'll go after him," Gertie said, intending to god-travel to Phorcys's castle.

"Best to wait here," Hades countered. "Hector may return just as you leave, and your absence would make him hesitate. You could compromise everything."

Gertie supposed the god of the Underworld had a point.

"Oh, gods, I hope he finds that eye," Hestie muttered, which didn't help matters.

"What possessed him to swear that oath?" Poros wondered.

"What oath?" Hades asked.

Hermie relayed Polyphemus's condition for giving up his eye.

"Hector should have just taken it," Hades said. "Cyclopes are stubborn, difficult creatures."

Gertie thought the same could be said about most gods.

They waited awkwardly for at least half an hour before Hector finally reappeared with his bag in hand.

"Thank goodness!" Gertie cried. "Do you have it? What took so long?"

Hector nodded. "I accidentally went to your kitchen in Athens."

"My kitchen?" Gertie repeated.

"Nikita's parents were there," he continued. "I just left without saying anything and ended up in my living room, where Nikita and Lajos were making out. Again, I just left. Finally, I made it to the castle, but Echidna was there. She screamed at me, fought me. I had no choice but to cut off her head."

Gertie winced.

"Then I found the bag in the entryway of the castle and snagged it just as Chimera charged me."

"Let's get on with it," Hades said impatiently.

Hector took out the eye. "Before I go in there again, can someone tell me the words to say?"

Gertie knew them by heart and was eager to help. "Medusa's eyes did turn you cold and white as snow and hard as rock, but mine will now reverse her curse and what you were will turn you back."

"Can you say that again?" Hector asked. "But slowly this time?"

"Um, guys?" Poros interrupted, his eyes wide.

Gertie followed his sightline to see the huge statue of Ladon reanimating.

What had she done?

"Better do something," Hades warned.

Acting quickly, Hector flew with the end of the adamantine chain and wrapped it around all hundred heads four or five times. He pulled the chain taut, drawing the necks up and straight like the branches of a store-bought Christmas tree tied in rope.

Gertie's knees weakened. Ladon looked exactly as he had in her dream.

"Open the door," Hector said with his sword drawn.

Hermie entered the code that turned the twelve bolts. Hector led the way, dragging the growling Ladon behind. Gertie followed with Poros and Hestie at her heels. A feeling of déjà vu overcame her, and she struggled not to faint.

The fact that Hector had entered first had already changed things, she reminded herself.

But just as he'd done in the dream, Hector shouted to the Titans, "Back! Get back before I unleash this beast on you!"

And just as they had done in the dream, the Titans fled to the dark recesses of the cavern.

But unlike in her dream, Hector jerked the end of the adamantine chain hard as he flew around the cage holding its exhausted and sobbing prisoners. As he pulled, Ladon spun like a top. By the time Ladon had finished spinning, Hector had secured the beast flush against the adamantine cage.

Now that the one hundred heads were no longer chained together, Ladon shrieked and struck out as far as he could reach.

As impressed as Gertie was by Hector's accomplishment, she wondered how he planned to get Nike into the cage now that Ladon was strapped to it. The goddess of victory lay unconscious on the cavern floor on a pile of white feathers. Hector flew toward her just as one of Ladon's mouths opened wide to swallow her. It took every ounce of self-control for Gertie not to intervene, especially because it appeared as though her dream were coming true in real time. Ladon looked as if he were about to swallow Hector whole.

But at the last moment, Hector lifted Nike into the beast's nearing mouth and flew out of the monster's reach.

What had Hector done? Feeding Nike to Ladon wasn't supposed to be part of the plan. Had he just ruined everything?

CHAPTER TWENTY-TWO

Judgment

Gertie sat beside Hector in a recliner in Hector's basement with a bowl of warm, buttery popcorn between them. They were watching Netflix with the vampires, Hermie, Jinsoo, Lajos, and Nikita. It was the season finale of a series they'd all been hooked on for weeks. Everyone was sprawled out on the three sofas, recliners, and gaming chairs before the 72-inch, widescreen television.

It had been two months since Hector had secured Ladon in the Titan Pit before returning the eye to Polyphemus, and Gertie was beginning to worry that the Olympian council had decided to let Hector's immortality revert. That's what happened three months after apotheosis if no purpose was declared. Hector knew his purpose, but he hadn't been allowed to declare it yet. The Olympians had shifted their focus entirely to Sailfish Trading and Shipping. Charges had been brought against the company, and Poseidon had managed to expedite the trial date. An international tribunal had decided to try Gertie's father along with Tobias Constantine, Matvei Popov, Abbas Hassan, and STS's chief executive officer and primary share holder, Antonio Barcelona, together. Hermie and Poros had been called in to testify. The prosecution had made its case. The court was now hearing from the defense.

Meanwhile, Prometheus and Hermes still hadn't managed to find new ships to replace the *Marcella II* and the *Black Widow*. Consequently, Gertie and the vampires had been staying with Hector. They'd been offered rooms in the Underworld, but the vampires had become restless there. And although Gertie's house was significantly larger than Hector's, Mamá and Babá would not have been comfortable with the arrangement. Plus, Hector's basement was perfect. There was plenty of room for everyone. Even Jinsoo, Chidori, and Hermie had come to stay.

Gertie's thoughts were interrupted by the prayers of a vampire in distress.

"Duty calls," she stated, climbing out of the chair.

"You want us to pause it for you?" Hermie asked.

"No, that's okay. I don't want to make you wait."

"I'm hungry, anyway," Alastair said. "Why don't we go feed and come back. Then we can watch the end together?"

"There's a computer server in the Ukraine that I could help get back online," Hermie admitted.

Jinsoo jumped to his feet. "There are two sailors struggling in a storm. I was going to ignore them, but I guess I can go help them now."

Hector paused the show. "I'll be here when you get back."

"We're not going anywhere," Lajos said of him and Nikita. "We'll keep you company."

Gertie kissed Hector's cheek and flew to Larissa, where a vampire who had been taking the subway had been seriously injured.

When Gertie arrived in the near-empty passenger car, she found a small child who appeared to be six or seven years of age, but Gertie could sense that she'd been around for a few decades.

"A group of boys figured out what I was and attacked me," the girl explained. "I was weak—I hadn't fed in so long."

"I'm here to help." Gertie shot one of her arrows into the vampire's heart. "This arrow will reinvigorate you."

"I feel it," the girl said as color returned to her cheeks.

"Do you have a safe place to feed?" Gertie asked.

"Yes. Thank you, goddess," the girl said sweetly.

Then both the vampire and the goddess flew away.

Gertie arrived back to Hector's basement before the vampires and other gods had returned.

"You ate all the popcorn?" she asked Hector.

"I can make more," he said.

Gertie frowned. "No, that's okay." She climbed into the chair beside him. "I'd rather you sit here with me."

"This kind of feels like the old days," Nikita recalled. "I'm so glad that we got to spend the winter break together."

"Yeah, it's been nice," Lajos said. "It's hard to believe another year is behind us."

"Can you believe I'm already halfway done with my first year of college?" Nikita asked.

"I can definitely believe it," Gertie said. "I knew you'd do well."

"And Lajos graduates from the Police Academy in May," Nikita added.

"Everyone has a plan but me," Hector mumbled.

"You have a plan." Gertie combed her fingers through his hair. "We just have to pray that the gods see it, too."

Hestie hovered in the air beside Poros over The Hague, Netherlands—a city on the southern coast of the North Sea. They were there with a handful of other gods—Hermes, Poseidon, Athena, and Apollo— watching the international tribunal hold its trial for key players in the Sailfish Trading and Shipping smuggling ring. Gertie's stepfather was among those being tried.

"I wonder why Gertie isn't interested in watching this," Hestie whispered to Poros.

"I don't blame her," he said. "Who wants to witness their own father being slammed?"

His comment made her realize how hard it must have been for Poros to be responsible for his father's imprisonment. The other gods had been so proud and so forthcoming with their praise. They'd celebrated with more than one party on Mount Olympus. But no one, not even Hestie, had considered the emotional turmoil Poros was likely undergoing.

She had been the one to convince Poros to watch the trial. Now, she wondered if their time might be better spent doing something else. Prometheus would know what to do.

"Plus, it's boring," Hestie said. "Let's go look for Captain."

"Sounds good to me," Poros agreed.

"Do you know where he is?"

"This morning he told me he was looking at a ship in Malta."

"Let's go!"

Together, they flew across Europe, past Italy to the island of Malta, and scoured the boat dealers along the coast in search of their captain.

"There he is," Poros pointed to BJ Marine. "I wonder why he's just standing there on the dock."

"Come on."

Hestie led the way to an empty vessel docked nearby, where they could take on their mortal forms so as not to draw attention to themselves. Then they walked along the wooden planks to their captain.

"A penny for your thoughts," Hestie offered.

Prometheus turned and grinned. "Well, hello, Hestie and Poros. What are you two doing here?"

"Looking for you, obviously," Poros said. "Any luck finding our next ship?"

"None, I'm afraid." He pointed to the double-masted beauty in front of him. "I thought this one might do, but she's out of my price range. Even with the Persian darics we sold at the end of the summer, there's not enough to purchase her. And, you know, she's not exactly what I'm looking for."

"What are you looking for?" Hestie wondered.

"I'll know it when I see it," Prometheus stated.

Hestie laughed. "That's the same thing I say about good fashion."

Telepathically, Hestie said to Captain, *I'm worried about Poros. Defeating his father may have been harder on him than we realized. Could you talk to him?*

"Are you kids hungry?" Prometheus asked suddenly. "I wouldn't mind grabbing a bite to eat."

"Nachos sound really good," Poros said. Turning to Hestie, he asked, "Care to share a platter?"

"Do you even have to ask?" she grinned.

On the day the Olympian council was to meet in the wake of the STS trial, Hermie was feeling on top of the world. He had convinced Del to leave Athens with him early, so they could take Pegasus for a spin before the others arrived. She sat behind him in her motorcycle gear with her arms around his waist as they soared through the bright blue sky over the shimmering Mediterranean.

"Isn't this the life?" he asked.

"It is a wonderful life, Hermie," Del replied. "But I am anxious to get back on the sea."

"Seriously? I thought you hated the sea."

"Yes, but I love my job. I like making a difference."

Hermie supposed he understood. He liked making a difference, too. But he wasn't sure of his place anymore. Would he continue to serve Prometheus in their mission to get medicine and modern technology to people in need? Or would he ask Lord Hermes if he could join his crew, so he could be close to Del?

"What will you do, Hermie?" Del asked, as though she had read his mind.

He sighed. "I don't know. I know I want to be with you, but I don't think thieving, even for a good cause, is my purpose."

Del pressed her helmet against his back and said, "I understand."

After some time, they returned Pegasus to his stable on Mount Olympus and joined the other gods in the great hall.

Athena had already begun addressing the council. Hermie and Del lingered in the back by the narthex, so as to not interrupt.

"And as you may have heard," Athena was saying, "the international tribunal found the men guilty of money laundering, human trafficking, and smuggling weapons of mass destruction. They were sentenced to twenty years without the possibility of parole—that is, except for James Morgan, stepfather to Gertrude Morgan. He was given a lighter sentence of five years, thanks to some finagling by our very own Hermes."

"It wasn't finagling, really," Hermes explained. "I just helped the defense team prove that Morgan was not willfully complicit."

"Nevertheless, it's good news all around," Athena said.

Hermie squeezed Del's hand and whispered, "I couldn't have hoped for a better outcome."

"Yes, but I am still nervous to hear the council's judgment of Hector," Del whispered back.

"And we have more good news related to that matter," Poseidon announced as he stood before his throne. "Hermes and I were able to purchase the remaining ships in the STS fleet at a bargain price. We plan to rebuild a new company of our own that will dominate the seas and keep them safe."

"Indeed," Hermes said, also standing. "And one of the ships we acquired is a superyacht with features similar to those on the *Black Widow*."

Del gasped beside Hermie and glanced across the hall at their friends. The other vampires had lifted their brows and dropped their jaws in anticipation of what the gods were going to say next.

"This superyacht has one major difference, however," Poseidon said. "It runs on both engine power and sail power, having two masts—one on each side of its long salon."

Hermes nodded. "Which leads us to our proposition. We would like to offer the *Guardian*—that's the name of the ship—to Prometheus and his crew on the condition that he work with my V Team in addition to carrying out his own mission of helping vulnerable communities."

"There's even a room large enough for Pegasus, should he wish to join you," Poseidon added.

"And we'll sweeten the deal by providing you with medical supplies for your work," Hermes said.

Hermie wished he could see Captain's face, but the Titan was facing away from him. Hermie had no clue whether Prometheus would be willing to take on both crews and a dual purpose. But he hoped and prayed to the captain that he would. It would mean that he wouldn't have to choose between being with the person he loved and fulfilling his duties. He could do both.

"I can see by the look on your face that you need time to think about it," Poseidon said to Prometheus. "Take all the time you need."

"But not too much time," Hermes suggested. "The sooner we can all get back to our missions, the better for everyone—for us and for those we serve."

"Thank you," Prometheus said. "I will give this some thought and have an answer for you within two days."

I hope he says yes, Jinsoo said telepathically to Hermie. *I can't leave Captain. But I want to be with Alastair.*

I know what you mean, Hermie replied. *I'm in the same boat—pun intended.*

As much as Gertie hoped and prayed that Prometheus would accept the proposition given to him by Poseidon and Hermes, she was anxiously awaiting to hear the council's decision about Hector's challenge.

Athena must have heard her prayers, for she lifted her arms and said, "And now it's time for us to discuss what happened two months ago in the Titan Pit. Before the council can reach a decision about whether to give Hector a permanent role in our pantheon, we must address the outcome of his challenge. While Hector succeeded in capturing Ladon and securing the beast to the adamantine cage, offering protection to Zeus and Hera, Hector did not give Nike the same protection. In fact, some might say he made her torment worse by feeding her to Ladon. It is up to us to decide whether this failure on his part constitutes a failure of the overall mission."

Beads of sweat began to form on Gertie's forehead. She wished she had a chair because her legs felt too weak to hold her up. She lifted an inch from the ground to relieve them of her weight and nervously shook out her hands.

If Hector were denied a position as a god on the pantheon, it wouldn't be the end of the world, she reminded herself. They would still be together for as long as he lived. They would have years and years together, Fates willing. It would be okay, wouldn't it?

And yet, the prospect of living with him eternally as gods and servants with the power to make a difference in the world was so appealing, so alluring, so desirable, that anything less would be nothing but a sore disappointment—worse than that. It would be an agonizing defeat. She hoped the council would agree that Hector hadn't failed. He may not have completely succeeded, but he hadn't failed.

She prayed to each of the gods there today: *He may not have completely succeeded, but he didn't fail.*

Poros interrupted Gertie's thoughts by raising his hand and stepping forward. "I have a question for Hector. Do you mind?"

"Please," Athena said.

Poros turned to Hector. "When Ladon was about to swallow you, why didn't you scoop up Nike and fly out of his reach? Why did you hand her over?"

Hector's face was pale, and his lips were trembling ever so slightly when he admitted, "Because she begged me to do it."

Gasps filled the hall.

"Nike begged you?" Poros asked.

"From the moment I entered the room," Hector elaborated. "First, she asked if I would swallow her, and I said I couldn't because if I were to lose my immortality, she would be freed. That's when she asked me to give her to Ladon. She wanted relief from the Titans, and being swallowed by an immortal was the only guarantee she believed in."

Gertie's mouth fell open and she prayed to Hector: *Why didn't you tell me that?*

I don't know, he replied. *I suppose I was ashamed that I'd failed the challenge and didn't want to talk about it.*

But you didn't fail, don't you see? Aloud, Gertie said, "This means he didn't fail, technically, doesn't it? His actions show mercy and good judgment in the heat of the moment!"

"Hear, hear!" Hermes shouted.

"Hear, hear," a few other gods said together.

Gertie's heart began to race.

Athena lifted her arms in the air for silence. "All in favor of making Hector a permanent member of our pantheon, say *aye.*"

The great hall resounded with the glorious assent of the gods.

"All opposed?" Athena asked.

The hall was silent.

Gertie jumped up and down and threw her arms around Hector's neck, crying with joy against his warm skin. The gods, goddesses, and vampires applauded and cheered. Gertie couldn't recall ever feeling happier than she was in this moment.

"I love you Gertie," Hector murmured close to her ear.

"I love you, too, Hector!"

CHAPTER TWENTY-THREE

Guardians of the Sea

The night that Hector's immortality was made permanent, Hestie decided to stay over with Poros in his room on Mount Olympus. Who cared what the others thought or speculated? She and Poros knew their truth, and that was all that mattered. So what if they shocked the other gods on Mount Olympus?

She'd just showered and changed into fresh clothes when she overheard Prometheus speaking with Poros in the adjacent room.

"I've been doing this for a long time," Prometheus was saying. "But in the past ten or so years, it's become more and more about you, Poros."

"What's become more about me?" Poros asked.

"My life. My purpose. You're like a son to me, and I want you to be happy."

Hestie looked at her reflection in the mirror over the bathroom sink as tears welled in her eyes. She was so happy for Poros—so happy that he had someone like Prometheus in his life.

"I *am* happy," Poros said. "I don't think I've ever been happier."

"That can't have been easy, what you did."

"No."

"And you might feel conflicted about it. But you did the right thing. You know that, right? Deep down in your gut, you know that?"

"I think so," Poros said.

"Good. If you ever need to talk about it . . ."

"Thanks."

Then the captain said, "I'm telling you this to explain why this decision about the *Guardian* isn't mine alone. What do you want, Poros?"

Hestie held her breath, wondering what Poros might say. She'd already shared her hope that the captain would say yes, but Poros hadn't shared what he wanted.

"I think we should do it," Poros deliberated. "We can all help each other and be even better at what we do."

"You don't think the vampires will be a distraction to Hermie and Jinsoo?"

"Not as much as they'd be if they were on a separate ship," Poros said. "In fact, I'm not sure you'd have much of a crew if you were to turn down the proposition."

"I wondered that, too."

"We could always recruit more," Poros pointed out. "But it wouldn't be the same."

"No, it wouldn't."

"Then we've made our decision?" Poros asked. "Am I looking at the new captain of the *Guardian*?"

"Indeed, you are. And I'm looking at its first mate."

Hestie's tears slipped down her cheeks as she smiled gleefully at her reflection. She couldn't wait to board the *Guardian* and to make it her new home. Even more, she couldn't wait to tell Hermie, Jinsoo, Gertie, and the vampires. As much as she wanted to tell them telepathically, she forced herself to wait. The honor belonged to the captain.

The urge to tell became even harder to resist when she and Poros were invited to a party at Hector's celebrating his victory. She wanted to tell them so badly! But the night was about Hector, and she didn't want to take anything away from that. Dionysus had come with several bottles of wine and a few satyrs, who played rowdy music on pipes. Lord Hermes had also come, and he accompanied the satyrs by playing on a pipe of his own. The dancing and the drinking went on for hours. In the end, she and Poros had crashed in one of Hector's upstairs bedrooms.

So much for shocking everyone on Mount Olympus she thought, as her head hit the pillow and she crashed hard for the night.

A week after Prometheus had accepted the position as captain aboard the *Guardian*, the young gods and vampires, along with their guests Lajos and Nikita, met one evening at the port in Piraeus with Captain, Hermes, and Pegasus to board the ship for the first time. Hermie was in awe of its size, for it was even bigger than the *Black Widow* had been, with longer decks at the bow and stern—an upper one at the bow and a lower one at the stern and each with a mast. There was also a flybridge near the ship's bow with a helm that reminded Hermie of the one on the *Marcella II*.

The galley and salon were set up the same way as the *Black Widow*, with a full kitchen, long dining table, and posh seating before a widescreen television closer to the bow, and a long indoor pool surrounded by couches nearer to the stern. Even the spiral staircase leading below deck was the same; however, in place of French doors to the stern deck, the *Guardian* had something resembling a garage door that rolled all the way up, exposing the pool to more sunlight. Although that wasn't a desirable feature for the vampires during the day, Hermie imagined it would be quite nice for swimming and stargazing at night.

Below deck were a dozen cabins, in addition to a captain's suite, and a sizeable storage facility that made a perfect stable for Pegasus. As soon as they'd reached the corridor, everyone made a dash to claim their room. Hermie didn't care which was his, as long as there was room for multiple computer monitors.

Lord Hermes had a special surprise for the vampires.

"I know you've become accustomed over the past few months to sleeping without your crates," Hermes said, "but I had new ones built for you in case you ever need to retreat into it. I already put them in the cabins, so feel free to move them if you want a different room. You'll know which crate is yours because I had your names engraved on them. You will also find a gift inside."

Hermie and the other gods followed the vamps around, curious to see their gifts. Penny and Bach got a collection of books. Sophia got yarn and knitting needles. Mahdi got a phone with earbuds with a library of music already loaded on it. Alastair got a paint set and a few small, blank canvases. And Del got a journal and ballpoint pen.

Everyone seemed really pleased with their gifts. Del was so happy that she cried.

After the tour everyone changed into bathing suits and broke into teams for a water volleyball tournament—except for Nikita and Lajos. Even though the pool was heated, it was still too cold for the mortals. Instead, they refereed. Hermie had never enjoyed playing a physical game as much as he did that day with his friends.

But their game was soon interrupted by the arrival of Poseidon, who flew into the pool area with a look of urgency on his face.

"I need your help," he said. "Echidna, Chimera, and Charybdis are out for revenge. They've already attacked one of the ships in my new fleet and are holding its captain hostage. They want Ladon."

"Ay, chihuahua," Jinsoo said. "I was going to go help the sailor after the game."

"Thank the gods you've got your priorities straight," Alastair teased.

"Ladon seems content where he is," Poros pointed out to Poseidon. "Hera strokes him all day long like a lap dog."

"They can't be reasoned with," Poseidon said of the sea monsters.

"Tell us what to do," Prometheus replied. "We're here to help."

Everyone changed from their wet suits and geared up to go. Lajos said he and Nikita would stay with the ship until their return.

As they flew across the evening sky toward the Messina Strait, Hermie glanced at Del in the air beside him and gave her a smile. As long as they were together, he would be happy. Even rushing into danger wasn't so bad with her by his side.

"I feel the same way, Hermie," she said.

As Gertie flew beside Hector toward the Messina Strait, she said to Poseidon, who was just ahead of them, "We should offer something to the sea monsters in place of Ladon."

"What did you have in mind?" he asked.

"One of the STS ships," she said.

Beside her, Hector blurted, "Are you crazy? Why would sea monsters want a ship?"

"Their home is falling apart," she said. "And now that Phorcys and Keto no longer live there, the siblings may feel lost. A new home—a ship of their own—might make them grateful enough to leave us alone."

"That's not a bad idea," Alastair said from behind her.

Hermes, who had flown way ahead of them, must have heard her, because he circled back and asked Poseidon, "What do you think?"

"I think there's logic in what she says."

"I think so, too," Hermie, behind her, agreed. "And I could fit the ship out with cool technology that will make their lives more enjoyable."

"Seems unfair that Ladon is stuck in the pit while his sisters sail the seven seas on a luxurious ship," Penny pointed out.

"You would think so," Poros said. "But I swear, the last I checked, Ladon was purring like a cat. Hera has thrown all the affection she once felt for Zeus onto her new pet, and Ladon seems to love it."

Gertie was pleased when Poseidon negotiated the deal without anyone having to go into battle. It was probably the easiest mission the new guardians of the sea would ever face together.

After the captain of Poseidon's barge had been released, Gertie and the rest of Prometheus's crew returned to their ship to continue their celebration. Gertie enjoyed telling Lajos and Nikita how they had avoided a fight by using her idea.

Later that night, as Gertie and Hector flew Nikita and Lajos back to Hector's house in Athens, Nikita, who was holding Gertie's hand, said, "I've been trying to tell you something all night, and it never seemed like the right time."

"Is this the right time?" Gertie asked.

"It's as good as any," Lajos said.

"We're engaged," Nikita shared. "Lajos and I are getting married after he graduates from the Police Academy."

"That's awesome!" Hector said. "Congrats, guys!"

Gertie hugged her friend. "I'm so happy for you."

"I want you to be my maid of honor," Nikita said.

"And I want you as my best man," Lajos said to Hector.

"Of course," Gertie accepted.

"You got it."

"I can't wait," Gertie said. "We can have your bridal shower on the *Guardian*!"

"Why not the wedding, too?" Hector said.

"What a great idea!" Nikita exclaimed. "Your mom wants us to have it at your mansion, but the *Guardian* would be way cooler."

"We'll have to ask Captain, of course," Gertie noted, "but I'm sure he'll say yes."

When they reached Hector's house, Gertie and Hector visited with their friends for a little while before returning to the ship. As they flew home—what they now considered home—Hector said, "It's amazing how fast time goes by. It seems like yesterday that I was starting my senior year in high school and meeting you for the first time."

Gertie flashed him a smile. "How impossible it would have seemed then if someone would have told us that, in two years' time, we'd be gods *and* guardians of the sea with a crew of other gods and vampires."

Hector circled his arm around her waist, kissed her cheek, and flew close beside her the rest of the way home.

THE END

Thank you for reading my story. If you enjoyed it, please consider leaving a review. Reviews help other readers to find my books, which helps me.

Vampires and Gods is a crossover series with characters from *The Underworld Saga* and *The Vampires of Athens Series*. If you haven't yet read one or both of those series, visit my website to learn more: https://www.evapohler.com/books.

Dionysus, a prequel to *The Vampires of Athens Series*, will release on May 10th. This prequel tells the story of Gertie's father, the son of Zeus, who, after being banished from Mount Olympus by his cruel stepmother, Hera, goes to the island of Naxos, where he grows the vineyards that produce his mystical wine. It is on that island that he falls in love with Ariadne. But their marriage is doomed from the beginning and, broken-hearted, he creates a group of companions known as the Maenads and begins his tradition of drinking and dancing on Mount Kithairon. Desperate to fill the ache in his broken heart, Dionysus searches for love again, but his second love story ends even more brutally than the first, leaving him gutted.

Then, centuries later, he learns that Philomena's child—their child—did not die with her, and although he's slow to allow himself to have hope, everything changes.

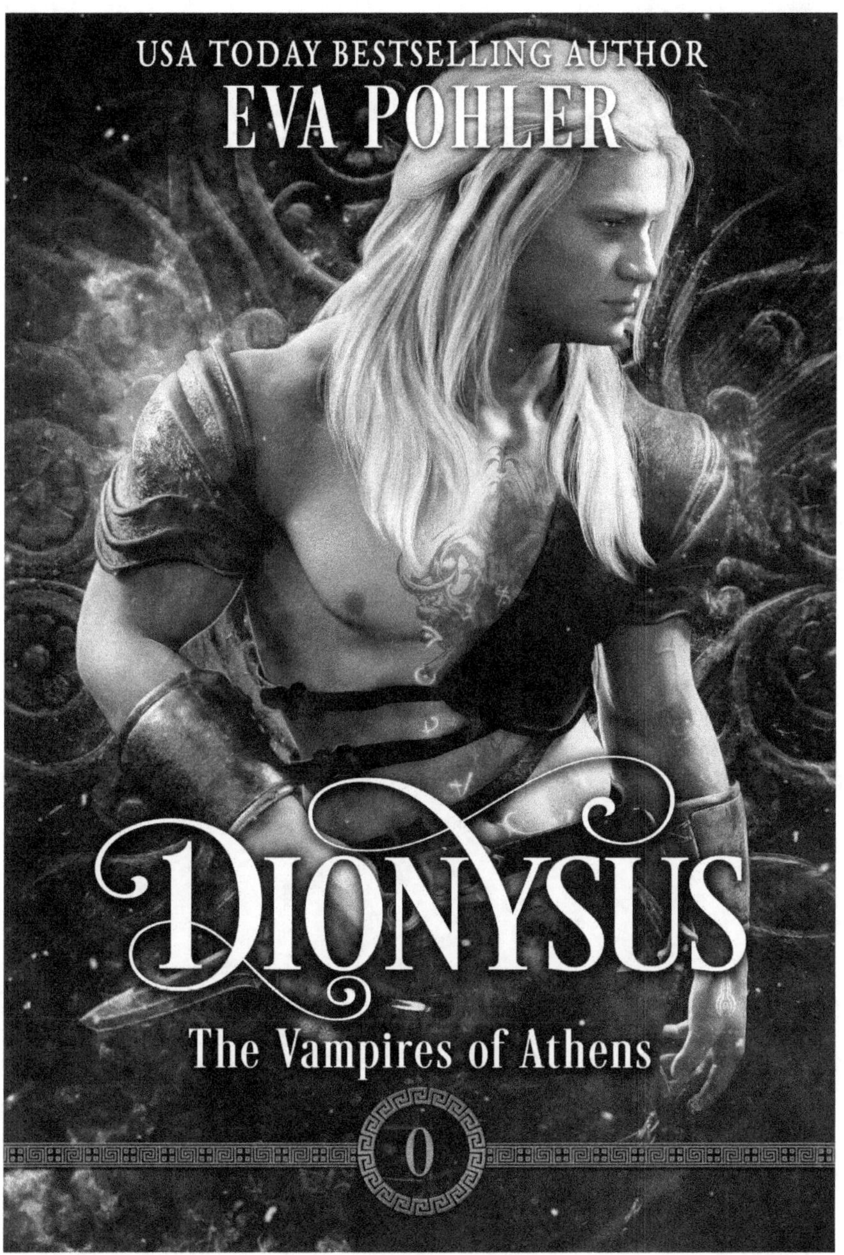

To preorder your copy of *Dionysus*, please visit my website at https://www.evapohler.com/the-vampires-of-athens-series.

Meanwhile, please enjoy the first few chapters of *Persephone*, a prequel to *The Underworld Saga*. Like *Dionysus*, this prequel can be read before or after the other books in the series.

CHAPTER ONE

The Meeting in the Asphodel

Hades sat on his throne alone in his underground palace. What did it matter that he had more subjects in his kingdom than either of his brothers? What did it matter that he had the world's most precious and beautiful jewels displayed on shelves in his chambers? His life couldn't be more boring. He stood up and kicked a golden turtle that was a part of the altar leading to his throne. The golden image flew through the air until it crashed against the wall opposite him. Even tormenting the evildoers of the world no longer brought him any satisfaction. He hated his life. He might as well still be a prisoner in his father's belly.

It still hurt him to think about how his mother hadn't tried to save him. She'd saved her youngest son, but she'd allowed her husband—Hades's father, Kronos—to swallow the rest of them. And once her children had finally been set free, they fought their father and his supporters for ten years. During that time, Hades's mother, Rhea, had disappeared. He'd never had a chance to know her love. Had she cared about him at all? Had she wondered about the person he'd become? If not, was there a person anywhere in this whole world who loved him?

He flew from his realm to spy on the people in the upperworld. As he hovered in the sky above them, he hoped for entertainment, but since he didn't care about any of the players below him, he found no joy in their pleasure or sorrow in their pain. He felt numb to everything around him and went home.

Weeks, months, and years went by. The only break he had from this growing despair were the few minutes each day when he wrestled with Cerberus. The three-headed guard dog was his only friend, but the beast could never leave his post at the gate. As it was, Hades took a huge risk in distracting him for even a few minutes.

Was there no way a god could end his existence?

Hades decided to pray to the Fates. He prayed to them every day. His request?

Bring me change. Anything is better than this.

"Enter," Hades said in the language of the ancient Greeks when, months later, he sensed the Fates outside his door.

He wondered if their arrival had something to do with his prayer. He could only hope.

Clotho, the oldest of the three and the spinner, lifted a bony finger and said, "We already know you will agree."

Hades narrowed his eyes. "I thought you couldn't see your own futures."

"No," Lachesis, the measurer, said. "But we can see yours."

"And you agree," Atropos's hoarse voice snapped, like the shears she used to cut the thread of life. "So, here's the deal."

Hades hung back in the shadows at the edge of the clearing watching his future bride. Although she was alone in a field of flowers with nothing but blue sky above her, she walked with a sense of purpose, as if she were looking for something.

He'd seen Demeter's daughter many times when he had dealings on Mount Olympus, but he'd never looked at her with the knowledge he possessed today. The Fates were never wrong. In exchange for refuge in his kingdom, they had told him to choose wisely, and when he had given them a blank look, they had pointed him in the direction of Persephone. This was the woman who would spend eternity married to him.

So why was he hiding from her? He'd had no problems attracting women into his arms, but as soon as he'd invited them home to the dreary depths of his underground palace, the delight in their eyes dimmed as quickly as the souls ferried through the gates by his boatman, Charon. Yet this beautiful, shining young goddess, as bright as spring-time, was destined to be his. Why should he hide?

This was the change he'd been longing for.

He removed his helm of invisibility and stepped into the light. The goddess, Persephone, noticed him at once.

She had no smile for him. Lifting a delicate wrist into the air, she used a golden bracelet to deflect the sun's rays into his eyes. He blinked against the reflection of Helios, the sun god, and when Hades looked once more for Persephone, the goddess was gone.

<u>CHAPTER TWO</u>

Persephone's Request

Since their meeting in the asphodel, Hades sought every opportunity to see Persephone again. So what if the Fates were right (and they always were)? It could be centuries before Persephone ever noticed him, and he was beginning to feel impatient.

He saw her at court on Mount Olympus when Zeus laid out a plan to prevent a Titan uprising. Persephone sat stiffly and quietly on the double throne beside her mother. Hades stared at her, willing her to look at him, but she ignored him. Suspecting that Demeter had blocked others from communicating with her daughter, he left Mount Olympus that day feeling frustrated.

Hades saw Persephone again at court when the gods banded together to think of ways that they could help Perseus defeat the Gorgons. Persephone sat beside Demeter again, but this time seemed restless. Hades sensed that she wanted to be anywhere else but among the gods at court. But no matter how often he looked her way, she never returned his gaze. How long was he supposed to wait before his future bride became aware of his existence?

He saw her a third time on Mount Olympus during the discussion of the impending war between the Greeks and the Trojans, after Eris's apple was awarded by Paris to Aphrodite—not because she was necessarily the more beautiful, but because she had the best bribe.

Again, he tried to get Persephone's attention, and again she ignored him.

So Hades resigned himself to the Fates. He would stop trying. He would stop allowing himself to get so worked up in her presence. He would be patient if not indifferent. Their meeting was bound to happen one day—the Fates were never wrong.

One day, he was walking among the asphodel in the same location he had first seen Persephone—after the Fates had revealed her as his future wife. He found it interesting that she, too, often walked near the chasm with the flowers at her feet and the sound of the rushing falls behind her. This was one of his favorite spots in the world, for it was near one of the entries to the Underworld; but it was also bright, fresh, and full of sweet songbirds and scent. He came here to refresh his mind before returning to his duties and to the dead.

This time, he didn't try to speak with her. He didn't want a repeat of their first encounter. Instead, he turned his back to her and continued his walk. If the Fates were right—and they always were—then there was no need for him to force a union.

Today he had come directly from an argument with Poseidon about the Hydra's sinkhole. Hades was frustrated and needed to breathe in the song and the scent before descending back down, down into the loneliness of his chambers. He was taken by surprise with her approach.

"Why do you come here?" she asked, half hidden behind an evergreen.

Although he was startled, he didn't turn to look at her, afraid he would scare her off. "For the same reason as you, I suppose." He tried to keep the desperation from his voice. He'd been longing for this chance, and he didn't want to screw it up.

"I doubt that," came her frank reply.

Hades grinned, but she wouldn't have seen it, since he continued to keep his back to her. "Then why do you come?"

"You must swear an oath on the River Styx to tell no one."

This time he turned and met her steady gaze. If he had ever believed she was frightened of him, her wry smile and cool demeanor proved him wrong. He himself was trembling, and she was as firm as rock. "An oath? This must be serious."

"Do you swear?"

"Yes."

She moved closer to him. "I come here to hide."

"From what?"

"My mother."

He bent his brows, wondering why such a beautiful goddess would have a need to hide from an equally beautiful mother. She shared Persephone's corn-colored hair and golden-brown eyes. Perhaps Demeter was harsh, or demanding, or belittling. Hades had no relationship with his own mother, and, since becoming adults, his sisters had always been distant—he ruled what they considered to be the most repugnant realm on earth. Consequently, he knew very little about women. He'd gone from living the first part of his life in his father's belly to the second part in the depths of the Underworld. "Does she mistreat you?"

Persephone shook her head. "Never. It's nothing like that. In fact, it's the opposite. She smothers me."

"I don't understand." He picked at his curly black beard—an old habit that was hard to break. While he'd been inside the belly of his father, touching his beard had been Hades's way of figuring out how old he was.

Persephone stepped from the edge of the woods into the clearing and sat on a stump at his feet, sending a rush of excitement up his limbs and to his chest. "I love my mother. I truly do. But sometimes I can't breathe around her. Honestly, I just want some time to myself."

Hades frowned, worried he had infringed upon her solitude. He shifted his weight, ready to leave her company, when she grabbed his boot.

"Wait," she said. She gave him a nervous laugh as she let go of his boot. "I meant I want time away from her, in the company of others."

"I see," he said, hiding his relief.

She climbed to her feet and looked up at him. "I want to go on an adventure. Can you take me someplace different?"

He narrowed his eyes, unsure if he could trust what was happening. Was this the same goddess who'd ignored him for so many months? "You do know who I am?"

"Of course, Lord Hades." Her face turned bright red, and she took a step back. "I'm sorry. Am I bothering you?"

"Not at all. I just wonder what kind of adventure you hope to have with the lord of darkness."

At that moment, Hades sensed Demeter calling out to Persephone from the sky above them.

"It's my mother!" Persephone said, rushing into Hades's arms. "Hide me!"

He conjured up his helm and slipped it on, and, as long as she was in his arms, she remained invisible to all but him.

Don't speak, he warned her telepathically. *The helm offers invisibility, but we can still be heard.*

She looked into his eyes with a mischievous grin, and he was at once exhilarated.

Take me for a ride in your chariot, she pleaded. *I want to see the Underworld.*

CHAPTER THREE

Persephone's First Descent

Hades was relieved that Persephone seemed happy beside him as he took her in his chariot across the evening sky, above clouds of pink and purple. Just because she was fated to be his bride didn't mean she would be happy. He was really hoping for happiness, though.

"Are you sure my mother won't see us?" Persephone twisted her beautiful mouth into a playful grin.

"So long as I wear the helm, everything I touch is undetectable, even to the gods."

"Is that true for anyone who wears it?" she asked.

"Yes, but none but I do."

"Won't you let me try it on?" Her golden-brown eyes gazed at him expectantly, and for a moment, he almost said yes.

What power was this? She was capable of spellbinding him with a look? Maybe he needed to be more guarded around her. "Would Zeus let you hold his lightning bolt, or Poseidon his trident?"

She frowned and turned her head to gaze at the pink clouds below.

He wanted to please her, but his helm was off limits. It was one of the three most powerful objects in existence. Surely she would understand. "It was a gift from the Fates, meant for me alone."

"I thought it came from the Cyclopes, after the war with the Titans."

"Yes, but the Fates decreed it."

"Oh."

He changed the subject. "Would you like to see my palace?"

She turned her lovely face to him once more. Her corn-colored hair streamed like a wedding veil in the wind behind her. He wanted to reach out and touch it. "If it's not an imposition."

"Not at all, if you're sure you want to go."

"Why wouldn't I be?" She frowned.

"You must not be familiar with the general attitude of the Olympians toward my domain."

"I'm familiar. I just find that attitude a bit obtuse."

He suppressed a grin as he guided his black stallions—Swift and Sure—down into the nearest chasm leading to the Underworld.

He gave a subtle wave to his boatman, Charon, and then to his guard dog, Cerberus, as he flew the chariot over the Acheron River where it met the Styx. His heart skipped a beat as the gates closed behind them. This was his very first willing guest to come with him this far into his domain in all the years he'd been lord of it, and he was especially delighted that she would one day live with him here forever.

She just didn't know it yet.

He parked the chariot in the garage and left the horses bridled for their return trip. He doubted she would want to remain with him in the Underworld for long.

When she stepped from his chariot, she cried, "Where have you gone?"

He removed the helm. "If I wear this, you can only see me when we're touching, and even then, only if I tell it to."

"You *speak* to it?"

"As a matter of fact, I do. It does get lonely down here." He laughed, to make sure she knew he was joking.

She laughed, too. "I can imagine. What do you do down here?"

"The dead keep me busy." After saying so, he realized he needed to be less morbid if he was to woo her. Why did this have to be so difficult?

He led her from the garage and into his enormous chambers, which were full of brilliant stones—one of the advantages of being the lord of the Underworld.

"You have every precious stone imaginable," she said, gazing around at his collection.

"Take anything you like," he said.

"You can't be serious!"

"I'm rarely anything else."

She laughed. "Well, that's no fun. Maybe you need someone to help you be less so."

He watched as she picked up an emerald here, a diamond there, studying them before putting them back.

"These are exquisite." She looked up at him. "But I just want to admire them, not keep any of them for myself."

He was hurt.

She seemed to notice his frown, because she quickly added, "Except maybe this one."

She chose a small opal he had polished to a radiant sheen. It was his favorite of the specimens, and he was glad that she would keep it.

"To remember you by," she added.

"Will we never meet again?" He sounded more arrogant than he had intended. He couldn't help but appreciate the irony, considering what he knew.

"I don't know," she said, coyly. "Will we?"

She was a crafty one, turning it around on him. He liked it.

"I believe we will," he said.

She smiled. "Can you show me more of your kingdom?"

He wasn't sure how much to show her—he didn't want to bore her—but he decided to start at the beginning. He took her hand and led her to the chamber of judgment, which a soul entered as soon as it passed Cerberus.

Hades told her about the three places to which the souls were sent by his judges—The Fields of Elysium for the good, Tartarus for the wicked, and Erebus for those who needed more time to forget their pain. He also showed her the five rivers that flowed through his realm and told of their purpose. She was already familiar with the Styx, on which the gods swore their oaths, but she had not seen the beautiful river of fire, known as the Phlegethon.

"I love the way it reflects on the cavern walls," she said, much to his pleasure. "Sometimes a crystal catches the light just right."

"I put the crystals in the walls for that purpose," he said, pleased that she had noticed it.

"It's breathtaking."

He took her hand. It was a soft and dainty thing, but he knew it was also powerful, and he shouldn't forget that.

He led her along the Phlegethon and showed her the various realms. He first took her to the Elysian Fields, which were cast in the purple glow of embers washed up on its shore. Elysium was an island surrounded by the Lethe, with streams marbled all through it.

"The Lethe is the river of forgetfulness," he explained. "It helps the souls forget so they can spend eternity in bliss."

The island stretched further than any eye could see, and it was populated with thousands—hundreds of thousands—millions—of souls frolicking in the fields, lounging beneath trees, and playing in the streams.

"They do look happy," she said.

He then showed her Erebus, where the pained souls lay at the bottom of a pit full of the Lethe waters.

"Those souls need more time," he explained. "They're not yet ready for the fields. Some of them are victims of terrible crimes."

"You're more compassionate than I expected," she said.

"Not compassionate," he corrected. "*Just*. Life isn't fair, but *death* is."

"I like that," she said.

Then he took her to Tartarus and showed her the three main areas—the main hall of torture, the seers' pit, and the Titan pit, which was the deepest of all.

"That's where we keep the Titan prisoners, the ones we fought during Zeus's uprising," he explained.

Her eyes widened. "How exciting! Do you ever worry they might escape?"

"Never. That iron door is impenetrable."

He showed her the fields of poppies and asphodel near the dream world. Then he led her back to his rooms.

"Where do you sleep?" she asked.

He found it curious that a maiden would wish to see his bed chamber. He was more amused than offended.

"Right this way," he said.

He walked through the main room of the palace to the corridor which led to his bed, explaining the reason for the inlaid Mother of Pearl in the door—the shell was the best at maintaining the most powerful wards. When he turned back to her to get her reaction, she wasn't there.

He flew back to the main hall of the palace. She wasn't in sight.

He balled his fists as he looked over to where he had carelessly laid his helm.

It was gone.

CHAPTER FOUR

Hide and Seek

Persephone lifted the helm and placed it on her head. She'd only planned to wear it for a moment before putting it back, but the lord of the Underworld noticed her absence immediately.

Within an instant, he was standing right in front of her. She froze, terrified, expecting him to scold her, to threaten her, to throw her out, but he pounded his fist on the table from where she had taken the helm and roared. He couldn't sense her. Tremendous relief swept over her. She covered her mouth to stifle a giggle.

This could be fun.

For many minutes he just stood there, thinking, and this gave her the chance to study him. Now that she could freely stare without his knowing, she was able to more fully appreciate his beauty. Dark curly hair and a dark curly beard starkly contrasted his deep blue eyes and pale skin. His nose and forehead were classically prominent, his neck thick, his lips full and moist. She leaned in and took in his musky scent. His massive chest rose and fell quickly with his agitation. The muscles in his jaw flexed.

Then he god-traveled out of the room, and she was left alone.

She wandered down a winding cavern toward the garage, where she heard his voice.

"On my orders only, boys. On my orders only." He was talking to his black horses.

He thought she would dare to take his chariot?

Suddenly he turned and glanced in her direction. She froze and held her breath. He stared her way for several minutes, sniffing the air. She broke into a sweat.

Then he walked right past her down the winding tunnel. She followed him, realizing now that she should have given back the helm as soon as he had noticed it missing. She could have apologized, and he might have accepted it. Now, she'd gone too far.

She hadn't meant for him to notice! She was going to slip it right back off. She'd just wanted to see what it was like to wear it for only a moment, but his senses were too sharp for that. She should have known!

Now what was she going to do? He might eat her alive and she'd be stuck in his belly forever. Her mother had told her stories of angry gods swallowing their enemies. Demeter had spent countless years, along with Hades, in the belly of their father. Later, Zeus, now lord of them all, had swallowed Athena's mother, Metis. As far as anyone knew, Metis was still in his belly.

Persephone wondered if she should run away and hide.

Hades passed his chambers and continued along the Phlegethon.

It occurred to her that he knew she was there and that he wanted her to follow. Why else would he walk rather than god travel?

They walked for what seemed like miles before the lord of darkness stopped and pounded on a wooden door. The door opened and he went inside. She barely made it in behind him before the door slammed closed.

In the center of the room was a table, and around it sat the Fates.

Lachesis, the measurer and the plumpest of the three, said, "We see you."

"I came to ask about our deal," Hades said.

Clotho, the spinner, looked directly at Persephone.

Please don't tell, Persephone prayed to them.

"What about it?" Atropos, the cutter asked.

Lachesis rolled a set of clay dice. Then she cried, "Double six! The throw of Aphrodite! I win!"

"We knew it would happen," Clotho said. "The minute we saw Hades, we knew it was time."

"I have been waiting for this moment!" Lachesis said. "I already know what I will make the two of you do." She said this to her sisters.

Hades took a step closer to the table. "When I agreed to provide you a safe haven here in my kingdom, in exchange for the name of the goddess I was destined to marry, was that name based on my own choice?"

"You will choose," Clotho said. "We just know the choice ahead of time."

Hades put a fist on his hip and shifted his weight. "So it is possible for me to choose differently?"

The three Fates glanced at Persephone. Surely they weren't discussing *her.*

"Why would you wish to choose differently?" Atropos asked. "Demeter's daughter is lovely, is she not?"

Persephone flinched. They *were* discussing her!

"She's a thief," Hades said angrily.

"What makes you say that?" Lachesis asked, glancing from Hades to Persephone.

Please stop looking at me, Persephone prayed to them. *You'll give me away!*

"She's taken the helm," he replied. "She could be anywhere."

"Indeed," Clotho sang. "Now roll the dice, Atropos. It's your turn."

"Can you at least tell me how long I must wait before the helm is returned?" he asked.

"That wasn't part of the deal," Atropos complained as she shook the dice in her cupped hand.

"But I will tell you this," Clotho said. "One of your descendants will have a set of twins who will one day restore faith in the gods and in humanity after both have been all but lost."

"Clotho!" Atropos chastised. "Why can't you contain yourself?"

"You knew I was going to say it," Clotho said dismissively.

"Nothing good ever comes from knowing the future," Lachesis insisted.

"Don't worry about the helm," Clotho said. "You know it comes back. Just wait for it."

"It might not be as far away as you think," Lachesis added.

The other two Fates chuckled, and Persephone knew her goose was cooked, but she was still reeling with the knowledge that one day, she was to be the Gatekeeper's bride.

Hades stomped out, and Persephone followed, flying rather than walking to keep up with his fast pace, so as to make no noise. As they entered his chambers, she nearly gasped when he removed his shirt and tossed it on the table. His muscular back rippled with his movements. When he turned, his hard stomach drew her eyes. He kicked off his boots, leaving them in the middle of the floor. Before she could look away, he'd pulled down his trousers and stepped out of them, adding them to the pile on the table.

He stood before her completely bare.

CHAPTER FIVE

A Spy Is Shocked

Persephone turned away from the bare god standing before her, but then, remembering that she was invisible, she slowly turned back around to stare. She observed every muscle on his body as he stepped into a pair of lounging pants. Without thinking, she gasped. Then she covered her mouth and hoped he hadn't heard. If he had, he didn't show it.

She followed the shirtless, bare-footed god from his bed chamber into a pantry, where he loaded a bag with apples, pomegranates, and cake. He slung the bag over his shoulder and strolled, on foot and without god-travel, along the Phlegethon toward the River Styx, turning left at the Acheron, past the room of Judgment, to the main gate.

Hanging back some distance, she watched the god set down his bag and give the cake to his three-headed guard dog. As she studied Hades, she thought on what she had overheard him say to the Fates. Was she really to be his bride?

She was delighted when, after the cake was eaten, Hades took a stick and played a game of fetch with Cerberus. The two of them made an adorable picture, until things seemed to get out of hand, and she thought for sure one of them would get hurt. She almost intervened when the game ended with Hades pinned to the ground. All three heads bared their teeth and growled. Persephone took a step toward them, on the brink of giving herself up. One of Cerberus's three heads turned in her direction. She held her breath.

Hades seemed unconcerned and only laughed. "Okay, Cerberus. As you wish."

The god and beast wrestled, flailing and rolling all over the rocky embankment of the river. At one point, Hades slammed Cerberus against the iron bars of the gate, and then Hades was flung into the river. Cerberus panted on the shore as Hades flew from the water, soaked. Persephone had expected him to be angry, but he wore a playful smile.

At the sight of him, she began to feel rather warm beneath the helm.

"Well, done, boy. You've earned yourself another treat."

Hades reached for his bag and tossed three apples up into the air, and each was aptly caught by a different head. Then Hades did something she did not expect. He carefully approached the beast and wrapped his arms around the center neck.

"You're a good boy," Hades said.

The beast licked its master with, not one, but three, tongues.

Persephone giggled, and then cupped her hand to her mouth.

"I had a feeling you were there," Hades said. "Remove my helm and give it back."

Her face burned with mortification as she lifted the helm from her head. "I'm sorry, I…"

He took his helm and glared at her. "Never do that again."

"I swear. I only meant to try it on, but then you noticed right away, and…"

He stepped closer, the rise and fall of his chest nearly touching hers. "Swear on the River Styx that what you say is true."

She looked up at him, frightened and breathless. His black curly hair and beard glistened with moisture, and beads of water dripped down his bare skin. Even his lips were wet. "I swear on the River Styx."

Then he circled an arm around her waist, pressed her against him, and kissed her.

***

If you enjoyed this sample, please visit evapohler.com to order your copy of *Persephone*. While you're there, sign up to receive two free ebooks.

EVA POHLER

Eva Pohler is a *USA Today* bestselling author of over thirty novels in multiple genres, including mysteries, thrillers, and young adult paranormal romance based on Greek mythology. Her books have been described as "addictive" and "sure to thrill"—*Kirkus Reviews*.

To learn more about Eva and her books, and to sign up to hear about new releases and sales, please visit her website at https://www.evapohler.com.

EVA POHLER'S BOOKS

Young Adult Fantasy

The Underworld Saga

Persephone: A Prequel (You could also read this after the other books in the series)
Thanatos
Challenge of Hades
A New Goddess
The House of Hades
The Athena Alliance
Hades's Promise
Hypnos
Hunting Prometheus
Storming Olympus

The Vampires of Athens Series

Vampire Addiction
Vampire Affliction
Vampire Ascension
Dionysus: A Prequel

Vampires and Gods

The Marcella II
Pirate Academy
Guardians of the Sea

Mysteries and Thrillers

The Mystery House Series

Secrets of the Greek Revival
The Case of the Abandoned Warehouse
French Quarter Clues
The Hidden Tunnel
The Haunting of Hoover Dam
The Ghost of Blackfeet Nation
The Shade of Santa Fe
A Holiday Haunting at the Biltmore
The Enchanted Bungalow

The Nightmare Collection

The Mystery Box

The Mystery Tomb
The Mystery Man

The Purgatorium Series

The Purgatorium
Gray's Domain
The Calibans